PROMPT

GENERATION 1

AUTUMN

BLUE FORGE PRESS
Port Orchard ✹ Washington

Prompt Generation 1 Autumn
Copyright © 2020
by Blue Forge Press

First eBook Edition March 2021
Second eBook Edition January 2025
First Print Edition March 2021
Second Print Edition January 2025

ISBN 979-8-89439-038-3

Cover and interior design by Brianne DiMarco

For information about film, reprint or other subsidiary rights, contact: blueforgegroup@gmail.com

Blue Forge Press is the print division of the volunteer-run, federal 501(c)3 nonprofit, Blue Legacy (EIN 83-4307421), founded in 1989 and dedicated to supporting artisans marginalized due to race, age, disability, economics or other factors. We strive to empower storytellers from all walks of life with our four divisions: Blue Forge Press, Blue Forge Films, Blue Forge Gaming, and Blue Forge Sound. Find out more at www.BlueForgeGroup.org

Blue Forge Press
7419 Ebbert Drive Southeast
Port Orchard, Washington 98367
blueforgepress@gmail.com
360-550-2071 ph.txt

*to everyone who has ever found
gender or gender roles
to be ridiculously confining*

TABLE OF CONTENTS

PROMPT

GENERATION 1

AUTUMN

SEPTEMBER

THE PROMPT

STATEMENT ISLAND
BY JENNIFER DiMARCO

I love holding you. That's when I feel your strength. And feeling how strong you are? I grow stronger myself."

Charre first said that to me when we were halfway through a bottle of Underground wine, watching the monthly migration of flying puffers from the whalebone fire escape our slumlord had installed to meet code. Any other time and Charre was so steely she was almost made of metal—sharpened and polished by this new world so she reflected whatever she saw; she's a Mimic after all and that's what they do.

I always thought she meant it symbolically. Some Sapphic-laced geek-speak for: "Together we're unstoppable."

So I bought her a necklace from a gentrified Tinman down at the Harbor. His matte orange bowtie clashed with his shiny plates and rivets but his selection of jewelry was unparalleled to any of the indie shops on the island, all transported from his own shop down on Reuse Alley in the city proper. He certainly didn't bring over any of his off-world gemstones or asteroid-mined exotic metals, and he wares were trinkets compared to what you'd find in the galactic market on Pandora, but all the pieces were one-of-a-kind, reworked and renewed from old world cast offs recovered and deradiated from the molten ruins of Earth cities.

I swiped him two coins and a fifty bit tip for the convenience of not having to take a Crosser (I can't abide the way leviathans smell) for a slender stainless tag with the corners cut off in a fine Adama cut (forty-five degrees) and embossed with a classic Underwood typeface: Unstoppable.

I had no idea Charre was serious. Literally serious. Literally: As my skillz grew, so did hers.

If you're a timeslip noob or a millennial boomer, you're probably lost already unless you're a cosmic groupie; in which case: Hi! How are ya?

Let me try to catch you up:

This was all back in '52. The era of cuff-rolled green jeans and Jeffree Dean with his come-hither third eye. An era when PepsiUp still contained illicit spice; spirulina mini burgers had sesame seed buns, and bombshells came in two varieties. It was also the Golden Age of comix so every other immigrant landing on Elon Island for processing was quick to write in the Hero archetype to fast-track citizenship— even though only one in a thousand kept the classification after their first week's work.

We'd arrived at Earth on the ISS Hawking, folding time to make a 'slip every hour on the hour and using the snap-back to accelerate to the next fold point. (The ship was named after Steven Universe Hawking, the first AI to prove self-sentience, if you're into ships and trivia... a pretty common Ven diagram if you frequent the coastal boroughs.)

Traveling by 'slip was slow going compared to other modes but beggars can't be choosers and both Charre and I were from (different) planets that had fallen to bacterial attacks. We had to be quarantined for a year anyway so touring the Sol system seemed a good idea at the time. I think we always knew we'd settle on Earth... but let's be honest: With a global population of barely over two hundred million (only 25% native), it was one of the only planets still accepting refugees.

We'd even had choices: There'd been forty-three city-states with vacancies on the Northern continent alone when we docked in orbit, fourteen months after we'd first left our home worlds. Huddled together over a tourism tablet, Charre and I had ooed and awed at the sights, all along pretending we hadn't always known where we wanted to be. By the time we boarded a shuttle for touchdown, we were past pretense and talking openly about the lawless, contumacious, limitless possibilities of Faregrounds.

Then we switched to an immigration tablet and reality set in: In Faregrounds, we could afford a sixth floor cardboard box on First Avenue, just inside the exhaust zone of the daily shuttle. It would be a box with a private toilet and kitchenette, sure, but did we really want to asphyxiate on fumes without any of the fun side effects? And so the decision was made as the Unbuckle Your Seatbelts sign came on and an ICE officer materialized to fill the entire galley of the shuttle and block all egress. She was blue like me but thick—a Tank for sure— with black stripes iridescent like oil slicks and Charre elbowed me for staring. But I still think we got preferential treatment. Blue solidarity and all that.

We took a short-term lifetime lease on a fourth-floor walk up with solar, running water (hot and cold), a private crapper and a pretty big shower. The kitchen was smaller than the one we'd have gotten with the cardboard box but air quality was well within tolerance ranges for both our species. But we weren't in Faregrounds. Our new home was a twenty-five minute leviathan ride southwest.

Statement Island.

You wouldn't know it now in 2162—a decade after our arrival—but back then the whole island was positively suburban. Nothing over ten storeys, no fast mate franchises, lots of green belt factories scrubbing the air and quite a few swampy patches to wade through and remember home fondly. This was all before the Grosse War when the Ohmu and the Kraken Elite rearranged the face of the island, draining the swamps into the Atlantis Sea through deep impact runnels and splintering the single land mass into an uninhabitable archipelago of two dozen skerries.

Well, almost uninhabitable.

But I'm losing focus. Let's bring this back around. Back to the beginning in 2152:

Par for the course with any immigration protocol, Charre and I agreed to occupations, paid for various permits (PDA, Necessary Nudity, Houseplants), forewent others (Reproduction, Private Transport, Religious Fervor), and walked off the shuttle with a week's advance on our salaries and a lease signed in blue and purple blood. We swallowed our skillz pills and headed off with a complimentary ICE tablet that we could bake at 350 for thirty minutes after it led us to our apartment. (It tasted like chicken which neither of us had eaten before and neither of us wound up liking.)

I spent that first crossing vomiting green and yellow bile into the Narrows, overcome by the flatulent stank of the leviathan we rode on top of and wondering why the hell the Crosser couldn't chew a few alpha-galactosidase enzyme caplets and spare my (albeit sensitive) olfactory organs. In a world saved from oblivion by bioengineering, you'd think a little thing like a farting ferry boat would be easy to fix.

"Kohn? Look at the sky."

I'd been walking through the apartment, pleased even though

it was still empty and considerably colder than I was used to. I went to the largest window that Charre had climbed out of ten minutes prior and frowned. "Is that safe?"

Charre just smiled, flashing all four rows of pearly sharps. "It's fused bone." She shoved the curved railing to show it didn't budge. "Some massive animal's skeleton stuck to the side of the building for emergency exodus. Recycle reuse is Earth's motto."

Once we found out it was a salvaged sperm whale ribcage we felt a little differently (the captain of the Hawking had been a Baird's beaked) but that first night we found everything about our new home endearing, quirky and charming.

I stepped out onto the bone balcony and looked up where Charre pointed a tentacle. "Oh...." Words failed me.

The canopy of night, devoid of visible stars, ruled by a single fractured moon, seemed to shimmer in waves of luminous spheres. Each one was the size of my head or a summer melon and enrobed entirely in pale pink with white spikes. From among the spikes sprouted two chitin wings, each barely extending beyond the round body of a puffer so its flight appeared comically improbable. But fly it did—they all did! There were at least a hundred of them—quite swarmy really—moving from here to there under the light bouncing off a cracked Selene.

"I love it here," Charre whispered and I looked at her. She was enraptured, enchanted.

Now it was my turn to smile. I slipped under her tentacle and she wrapped her arms around my waist, holding me from behind and resting her chin on my shoulder. "I knew you'd like it here."

"Earth is home...." She was testing out the sound and feel of it. Her body thrummed with pleasure that seeped into me through the sensory patches along my spine. "We are Earthlings."

"We are indeed." I remember feeling so content, so hopeful,

so universally exactly where we were meant to be. Plus we were together. After a long distance relationship across light years, a failed marriage-and-murder on my part, and an expensively expunged criminal record on Charre's, we were finally together and ready to begin anew. Clean slate. Fresh start. All that jazz.

I didn't know then that a Mimic and a Hero would be magnets for everything seedy, everything underhanded and illegal... basically event horizons for the entire population of Faregrounds.

Less than six months into our lives as Earthlings, I sat at our table made of a petrified mangrove trunk and a giant sand dollar and listened to the feed from our new social box—a gizmo that pulsed soft colors while it gave you all the news of the day in your own native tongue. Night had fallen and my shift was over; I was a daylight Hero because that's what was needed on Statement Island at the time so Charre and I worked opposite shifts (an easy mistake for a newcomer couple). Charre was getting ready for her night at the Orchid Mantis (a Faregrounds club) and I would have gone to her but the last time I tried to surprise her with a little *amour* in the shower we'd gotten tangled in the curtain beads and had to call a rescue team. Whoever invented "string" should be arrested and tied in knots. Just saying.

That night in particular we were the perfect example of two people who had turned their lives around. I was proud of us.

"Do you think we should get a pod?" Charre walked out of the bathroom naked and glowing a pale lavender. She smelled like salted caramel and sweet chocolate which had nothing to do with her body wash.

"Private transport? We haven't even been here a year!" Not only had we passed on getting a permit for that but even a one-seater pod would cost—

Charre flipped her backpack onto the table and winked at me

with both her inner and outer lids. Her deep purple lashes were ridiculous. I especially loved feeling them flutter against my thigh.

I opened the hook and loop band on her flower-shaped backpack and then stopped moving entirely. Charre had to smack me on the back to get me to breathe again. "Where did you get that much money?" I finally managed as I sucked in air like a newborn jellydog emerging from the sea.

Charre sank down into the only other chair at the table. It molded to her unique body and curled forward to cradle her tentacles so she could still motion freely with her arms and hands; Charre had started talking with her hands in the Earthling fashion that was so popular. She held them palm up and out to the side in a pose called No Big Deal. "Tips have been really good."

I just looked at her for a long quiet moment. I mean... as quiet as Statement Island ever was. We'd learned that first night half a year ago that the din from Faregrounds traveled easily across the Narrows. Cacophonous wasn't a strong enough word. It was more a discordant, asperous dissonance that waxed and waned without warning or apparent pattern and so was always present, never quite predictable white noise to be ignored. I'd wanted to buy noise canceling ear caps but with six ears the price was prohibitive. Looking again at the twenty pounds of coins in Charre's backpack, I didn't think anything would ever be cost prohibitive again!

"I had no idea flare-tending was so lucrative...." I pointedly let my words trail off as I held her gaze. To my knowledge, Charre had never lied to me before; in her home system, lying was punishable by death but we were a very, very long way from Chapprieal and the few worlds that still hosted her people.

"With two arms *and* two tentacles?" Charre lifted her thick purple eyebrows as lush as her lashes. "I can do some pretty amazing things."

I relaxed into the suggestive heat of her gaze. Tell me something I don't know about Chappriealans, right? Mixing fancy drinks and catching them on fire was child's play. Her customers should see what she could do with two arms, two tentacles, and three sets of genitals! (Or not. We had always been exclusive and monogamous. My failed marriage and successful murder had revolved around polygamy and I was definitely not hardwired for it.)

I touched her face, puffing my chest out like a proud something that had a chest and puffed it out when it was, you know, proud. Like a salamander, maybe. "Anything that means you won't smell like a Crosser every morning."

Charre laughed so uproariously we almost missed the coyote boys warning us of the stranger.

Are you lost again? I'm trying really hard to keep the storyline linear and straightforward but you've probably already noticed that there wasn't much straight about me and Charre. We were arguably as crooked as creatures come in terms of twisty and turning our bodies and minds into whatever we needed them to be to survive.

As a Hero, I was the face of aid and justice for ten hours every day, drifting silently through my assigned neighborhood, five square miles of personal terrain where it was up to me to maintain order for every living thing. Sometimes I called in salvage crews to remove ancient warheads from the shoreline. Other times I floated up into the highest boughs of willow trees to retrieve pet hamsters. And still more times, I was snapping the neck of an abusive spouse or a rapid arachniorse. When on shift, Heroes were connected to the Authority Intelligence (what AI had become) so I was officer, jury, and executioner. On shift, I could think in 120 FPS while the AI judge (which was really a global network) could instruct me in nanoseconds so there was no lag.

When I was on shift. Only on shift. Off the clock, I processed information like any other Hunte and I certainly couldn't drift or float or neutralize a fueled up junkie or cracked attacker. I'm mentioning all this because I need you to know that, legally, I wasn't a Hero when it all happened. Charre's skillz pill had put thousands of drink routines in her mind and muscles and she had memorized dozens of them on her own so she could whip us up a pair of Flaming Flamingos or Birthday Cake Martinis but my skillz were not accessible to me after work hours.

Someone collapsed hard against our front door. Which was also our only door. Someone... or something.

I don't want to lie and say we both jumped up and ran to investigate. Or that my Hero skillz kicked in or activated after hours somehow and I was driven to help. The truth is: We just sat there for another moment or three. We looked at each other and spoke soundlessly in that way that certain couples have. Neither of our species are telepathic but Charre and I have an emotional shorthand of glances and expressions, a silent language of our bodies that speaks volumes along the channel of our private connection.

We went toward the sound together.

When the curvy human woman with her moonlight skin and platinum blonde coif tumbled unconscious over our threshold, we realized our door had been the only thing holding her up. We also realized our lives would change forever. Again.

We'd been Earthlings for less than a year but even we knew of the meteoric climb to fame, activism, and sex appeal of media star Marilyn Molone.

Charre took a "sick day." A old hold over from when the planet was majority populated with humans and their shitty immune systems that were further compromised by deadly cocktails of genetic errors—specifically the double shot of competitive and hierarchal behavior often called the Octavia Principle after the scholar who wrote the thesis.

It was more likely that Charre or I would sprout puffer wings and fly across the sky on the night of the full moon than we'd be unable to work due to some microbial germ. It was an unexpected and high-toll benefit of coming from worlds conquered by the Brine. Survivors received free treatment from the Intergalactic Alliance of Systems that made us immune to all common bacteria and viruses alike. But a survivor's toll wasn't just emotional; the treatment was expensive—we'd be paying the Alliance a tithe until the day we died. The Alliance didn't want their greatest enemy to spread through the universe and their pacifist policies didn't allow them to euthanize exposed survivors. Between me and Charre, millions of Brine had probably been killed during our antiviral treatment. But the Alliance didn't see Brine as alive. Long story short: Charre could stay home without penalty and neither of us were afraid when Marilyn finally awoke and announced, "The Brine are trying to kill me."

At that point I had several instantaneous questions: Where is your security detail? Why did you come to us of all people? Have you been exposed already? Have you contacted the Alliance for treatment? Does anyone else know the Brine are on Earth?!

But Charre spoke first: "How do you know their motives?"

Leave it to Charre to cut through the emotional baggage and cultural niceties to the nitty, gritty, bloody blue heart of the matter.

Marilyn sat up slowly. She wasn't very tall and looked especially fragile curled up in the corner of our inflatable couch. I felt bad because we'd had relatively ruckus sex on that couch just yesterday night and I hadn't gotten around to cleaning it yet. We'd slipped off her high heels so as not to risk puncturing our furniture and her nylon-covered feet stuck to the upholstery a little. Oops.

She drew her cream-colored, long-haired jacket more tightly around her. I think it was made of gold skultula silk or maybe dyed borzoi but when we'd moved her to the couch the jacket had felt softer than anything I'd ever worn, that's for sure.

"I'm a biological physicist," Marilyn told us carefully. "My life's work is trying to establish communication with the Brine. My name is—"

"—Marilyn Molone." I finished her sentence for her and looked from her wary, exhausted face to Charre. Charre's eyes were narrowed and she was staring at the woman with what looked like intense scrutiny.

"You know me?" The desperate hope on Marilyn's face was almost too much.

"You're..." Charre began slowly. "...a media star and activist for human rights."

The smallest bit of color that had crept into Marilyn's fair cheeks drained away. She bowed her head, curling into her jacket as if searching for comfort that we obviously weren't providing.

"You don't know me," she whispered, more to herself, I think, than to us.

Charre blinked all her lids and looked at me. I let my confusion show on my face and felt a cold chill even though it was only early autumn and the windows were closed against the distant din of Faregrounds.

"You... *look* like you," I offered lamely. What did I know of comforting human women? Even as a Hero, I rescued, retrieved, and rehabilitated all numbers of species but it was all accomplished with a certain level of detachment. Plus, I'll say it again: I wasn't on duty so my skillz slumbered.

Marilyn plucked at the soft spider silk or fur of her jacket that most likely cost more than the entire brownstone we lived in. I felt pretty certain I'd seen photos on the feed of her wearing that very same gold-and-cream wrap.

"When I came to this morning..." She was whispering again. "...I was nude."

Then she looked up at us. She looked truly at us as if for the first time.

"Where I come from," her voice was very strong for someone who had apparently been unconscious more than once today. "Aliens don't exist."

And that's how we knew that the Marilyn Molone who sat on our sticky couch, in our working class walk-up on Statement Island was not the Marilyn Molone who lived in the Venus Penthouse, made movies in Sky City, and advocated for human-only spaces. No, this bombshell (and she was very beautiful, seemingly identical in every physical way) was from a world, timeline, dimension, alternate reality where it was still okay to call someone an alien to their face.

Infinite variations. It's a misleading phrase. Or maybe just an ignorant one. Though it seems pretty judgmental to call something ignorant just because it's archaic. If "infinite variations" was the best they knew, who are we to disparage them?

I can imagine Charre's toothy smile even now. There would be love and tenderness on her face as she flashed her array of sharps. She'd learned early in our relationship that I had a fascination with parallel worlds and she'd known pretty much from that first night that I had a soft spot for Marilyn in particular. I honestly don't know whether it was her wide deep blue eyes spaced far apart in her face, or her white-blonde waves of collar-length hair, or even the little mark of beauty to the side of her full lips, but whatever it was, I wanted to protect her. I wanted to believe her. I didn't want to be an alien... I wanted to be an ally.

So we learned that the dimensional possibilities only extended as far as was probable for a single entity—one world for every shade of gray. And those were planes above our own. Whereas the manifestations that were opposite and opposing, lay in under-planes below our own. And every entity on every plane influenced the possibilities above and below.

I think it's most accurate to say: Parallel worlds exist as beautiful gradients each bleeding into one another with influence but without mutual awareness.

Now that I stop and think about it, I suppose that seems pretty close to infinite but it's a gradual infinity; the most disparate shades were so far apart they might as well not exist in one another's timeline of reality.

Do I sound like a biological physicist yet? In our world, we had known Marilyn Molone no more than as a talented, passionate actor who wanted to carve out safe havens for her dying people. But in her world—"her" meaning the Marilyn that collapsed against our door that night—we were Charlotte and John Rubicon, childhood friends who had supported her rise in the emerging study of microbial life forms.

Flash forward ten years and our Marilyn (who wasn't *ours* at all) would be dead and *their* Marilyn (who we'd grown to love) had returned to her world with a mind so full of cosmic truths she would hold the highest office of her nation for not one but four terms.

We'd come to Earth and everything had changed. The trajectory of our shared destiny—what Charre and I were meant to be and do. Charre was a Mimic now. She knew how to blend in and make people feel comfortable around her, want to be with her. And I was a Hero. Skillz on or off, I was meant to help.

Our apartment became a lighthouse. A beacon across the

broken island after the war and a haven long before that across dimensions. Marilyn was the first but far from the last and our lives grew fuller, more complicated, more dangerous and mysterious and wondrous with each new traveler we encountered.

What did you do today?

THE DARKEST DISCOVERY
BY LAUREN PATZER

The wide open expanse of the hilly tundra soothed Alan Jeffries' soul. The crisp blue skies brought cleansing thoughts to his mind. The loneliness of living so far from civilization was a small price to pay for the safety of the world at large. This was where his darkest impulses could find no purchase—alone at the end of the earth. So it was with no small amount of displeasure that Alan greeted his first visitor in ten years.

Doctor Brenda Higgins walked the two and a half miles from the air strip through the sparse tundra. Her long, curly brunette hair writhed in the wind like an angry pit of vipers. Alan scowled at the approaching figure, knowing instinctively it was likely his old physician friend on a misguided mission of mercy, then disappeared into his cabin and locked the door.

Inside the cabin, Alan ran his hand through the pale strands of blonde hair hanging like a mop on his head, got on his knees and frantically dug through the plastic bin he stored beneath his bed. Under the bundles of additional winter clothing, he located the prescription bottle of tranquilizers that would put him out in under twenty minutes. It was empty. He threw it across the room with such force, the plastic cracked and the lid flew off.

His head snapped toward the door with a snarl as Brenda rapped on it insistently.

"Alan, it's Doctor Higgins," her muffled voice announced.

"I came here for solitude! Your company is not welcome!"

"I can't stay out here through the night, "she replied. "I'll die from exposure."

"You'll die of something worse if you come in!" Alan shouted as he backed away from the door, a mixture of fear and anger contorting his face. "Why don't you go back to the hangar?"

Alan knew the hangar wasn't heated, so it wasn't really a viable option. The temperatures would drop below freezing at night and the only insulated thing in the building was an underground tank full of fuel for the planes.

"I've got tranquilizers," Brenda shouted through the thick wooden door.

Alan's face calmed a bit. His eyes darted around the room nervously. He glanced at the hallway leading to the other rooms in the small cabin. With a quick mental calculation, he realized none of the doors would hold against his onslaught if he wasn't sedated. Even at the hangar, she might not be safe from him if he succumbed to the beast inside. He'd designed the inside of the cabin to contain him if the need arose. But it had never really been tested. The beast hadn't really been fed in years, so he wasn't sure it would survive the brunt of insane hunger that would manifest. He walked to the door and opened the cover on the small window.

"Open the pane and pass the tranquilizers inside. If I'm awake enough in twenty minutes, I'll let you in," Alan said, not looking through the window into her eyes. He knew he'd behave foolishly if he got lost in her eyes again.

Without a word, Brenda pushed the full pill bottle through the opening. The bottle clattered to the floor and Alan snapped the small door shut quickly. He snatched the bottle off the floor and went to the faucet to draw some water from his insulated tank. He popped a pill into his mouth and drank down two cups of water with it. The tranquilizers always left him feeling dehydrated afterwards. He thought back to the last time he'd used them before he'd left and felt a stern hollowness occupy his mind.

The compound in Tanzania had been large and practically impenetrable, but the vultures who wanted his blood hadn't let that stop them. It was only when they faced his full wrath that their insane hunt came to an end. Flashes of the slaughter at his clawed hands made him catch his breath. He hadn't thought about that day in so long, he was hoping the details would completely disappear, but the visions of severed limbs, fountains of blood and the copper taste of his victims flesh made his pulse quicken. His fingertips began to pulse and he feared he'd transform before the tranquilizers took effect. He slowed down his breathing concentrated on the strands of grass growing out on the tundra, blowing in the nearly ever present wind, twisting and shuddering under the omnipresent air currents.

He sat on the floor and assumed a Zen position, breathing and concentrating on the calm wind outside. To her credit, Brenda didn't knock or disturb him for the full twenty minutes. When she did, he knew the pill was taking effect as he felt a bit groggy standing up and walking to the door. Even though he knew he was well under control, he still paused at the door, remembering her scent and the soft touch of her skin against his. He almost didn't open the door.

He flipped the locks open and the steel reinforced Australian buloke barrier swung open easily. As it revealed her to his eyes, he cast them downward to avoid her gaze. He didn't need the recriminations, but worse would be the forgiveness. He couldn't let her into his heart again even if he let her into the building.

Brenda stepped through the opening and gently closed the door behind her.

"Alan, you're looking…lonely," she said.

Alan grunted and walked to the bed. He sat down on it and waved to the lone chair sitting in front of the widescreen television.

"Thank you for the refills, although I rarely need them way out here," Alan said as he slid back across the bed and rested against the wall. His eyelids felt droopy and his limbs heavy, but even thus sedated, he was a danger to others—just not likely to her, at least for the moment.

"I've brought some stronger things along, the strongest ones you've heard of and some new, even heavier experimental sedation if needed," Brenda said.

"Why are you here?" he asked simply. He didn't care how she'd found him. He'd used a good deal of subterfuge to hide his trail, but even he needed supplies every once in a while. He guessed Melanie, his executive assistant, had told her how to find him, so there must be good reason for it besides a desire to reconnect. He was less concerned about the military, industrialists or rogue governments trying to get to him. Those he could handle with the swipe of a claw and a considerable gnashing of teeth.

"I believe we've found a cure," Brenda said. Alan risked a glance up at her face and saw that she was serious. He shuddered as he met her deep blue eyes and quickly looked away. He chuckled.

"We've been through this before," Alan said. "The virus is deeply imbedded in the tissues. I would literally need to die before this virus leaves my body. Even then, it might not."

Brenda nodded and sighed.

"We had to adjust our approach," Brenda said.

"You think you can sneak up on it?" Alan said mockingly. "It's in my brain, the deepest parts of my adrenal medulla. It knows when it's being attacked and defends itself by transforming the host. I assume you remember how this works.”

His tone belied the years of research and her doctorates in multiple disciplines. Of course she knew how his sickness worked. It had been her life study, the reason for their meeting in the first place and the reason they'd gotten so close. Too close.

“We think we can apply a patch to allow you to control it, real time, with no ill effects,” Brenda said.

“Control it?” Alan laughed bitterly. “Seven hundred and fifty-three, Brenda. Does that number sound familiar?”

“Alan,” Brenda replied quietly.

“Trained mercenaries, all at once, sent to subdue me so they could harvest this virus from my organs for their own ignorant and evil uses. Dead in less than an hour according to some estimates. The only ones who escaped never landed on the ground and were over two hundred feet up. I slaughtered everything else. You can't control chaos.”

Alan closed his eyes and took a deep breath.

“A reprogrammable drug pump we can resupply through an access port is a permanent solution if it works,” Brenda said.

“You're wasting your time,” Alan said.

Brenda stood up.

“I was afraid but not surprised you'd say that,” she said as she walked toward him.

He frowned and attempted to move, but the drugs were taking effect. He saw her raise her arm and a small dart gun puffed a bit of smoke as the first projectile hit him in the chest. He could feel himself going under and saw her reload the gun, a second dart hitting him in the leg seconds later. Even as he went under, he felt the beast trying to rise from the depths of his psyche. Two more pinches in his limbs and everything went dark.

When the darkness cleared, Alan's head was pounding with the worst headache he'd ever experienced. He rolled onto his side on a cold floor and retched. When the dry heaving finally subsided, his headache had faded to a dull thrum. He took a deep breath and examined his surroundings beyond the splashes of vomit and gray concrete he'd seen so far.

He blinked his eyes as he took in a cavernous, enclosed square hundreds of feet across and just as tall. Far up on one side, there was a glimmer of glass which he assumed was an observation window. The ceiling sported several skylights; they were far enough up that he wasn't sure even he could reach them when the beast took him over. He searched for an opening but only managed a faint outline in one wall he assumed was a reinforced vault-like door likely stronger than the walls themselves which were probably made of reinforced concrete several meters thick. But apart from what looked like an inescapable prison for him, the most intriguing part of the room was Brenda Higgins sitting in an easy chair on the far side of the room reading a book. She looked up from the book and then set it down.

"There are bottles of water behind you to rehydrate," she said.

Alan grunted and grabbed one of the bottles. He opened it and drank the lukewarm water in just a few seconds. A second one disappeared just as quickly. He raised his hand to his forehead and noticed it had no strands of hair hanging down. Feeling around his skull, he noticed faint stubble and a scar on the back of his skull with a small metallic circle imbedded there.

"What have you done to me?" he growled.

"What you wouldn't allow," Brenda said simply.

"You had no right," Alan grumbled. He pulled off the hospital tunic he wore; it was stained with vomit.

"I had no choice," Brenda said.

"You could have left me alone," Alan sneered. He stood up and tested his balance. Squeezing his eyes shut, he re-centered himself and took a deep breath. He walked toward Brenda.

"Seven hundred and fifty-one," Brenda replied as she watched him approach her. She didn't seem concerned even though Alan could go off the deep end and rip her to shreds. Seeing him shirtless brought back a longing for the relationship they'd shared so long ago, reminding her it was out of reach, possibly forever.

They both knew he wouldn't hurt her voluntarily, but alone in an enclosed space with no tranquilizers in sight, Alan felt it was a dangerous chance to take. He wanted to know why she'd taken it.

"Seven hundred and fifty-three," he replied testily.

"No," Brenda replied. "You only severely wounded two of them. They were buried and unconscious beneath their compatriots when the Chinese military recovered them."

"Shit," Alan replied.

"They got what they were after," Brenda said evenly. "But they had no way to control it once they had it. The two infected mercenaries slaughtered all the personnel at the secret base and got out, eliminating three small towns in rural China before they were subdued. Recognizing they were well beyond their understanding, they contacted the only expert on the subject."

"You helped them weaponize it?" Alan was dumbfounded. He'd nearly reached where she was sitting.

"It's difficult to weaponize that kind of chaos. They called me in to cure it. The two mercenaries were sloppy in beast mode. They failed to kill several people and the Chinese found they had an epidemic they didn't understand and couldn't control," Brenda huffed. "They wanted to keep it secret, of course, but I-"

Brenda's words faltered a bit as the emotions took over. She squeezed her eyes shut.

Alan's heart hurt to see her in pain. He felt a bit of anger and the beast knocked on his medulla, but he was surprisingly able to push it back down with ease.

"I thought surely the international community would be able to step in and humanely resolve the crisis. I released the information about what was happening to the world governments. When the Chinese found out…"As Brenda looked into Alan's eyes, tears brimmed her own. "They just slaughtered the infected and called it a hoax."

"I'm sorry," Alan said.

"Three camps, 75,000 or so people. They set off small nuclear devices and called it weapons testing," her voice trailed off and she stared into her memories for a moment, the horror of the consequences of her actions playing over again and again in her mind.

"You can't control the actions of a government like that, Brenda. You did everything you could."

"I let the world know your secret, Alan," Brenda said. "Once it was out of the bag, it was only a matter of time. You're international public enemy number one now."

Alan looked around the room with a new sense of dread. The walls were evidently the least of his worries. Brenda stood up and grasped his arms.

"Alan, if the cure works, they won't kill you," Brenda said, hope shining in her words and her eyes.

"You said you couldn't cure it," Alan said flatly. His face showed despair and defeat instead of anger.

"If you can control it, it can't be unleashed again unless it's intentional. That's as good as curing it."

"You should leave, if I can't control it, you'll be killed," Alan said.

"I don't want to live without you, Alan," Brenda said. Her eyes searched his. "I've felt the same way for twelve years. That's not going to change."

Alan placed his hand on her cheek and smiled for what seemed the first time in years. Time seemed to melt away in that instant; he remembered every glance, every touch and every smile they'd shared.

"Then let's get started. What do I do?"

"Well, for starters, go to that far corner. They're going to try to get the beast to come out and I don't want to be collateral damage to their attempts," Brenda squeezed his arm. "Do whatever you can to keep it bottled up. I've given you every tool I know how to. The rest is up to you."

She stood up on her tiptoes and kissed him. He grabbed her around the waist and held her tight for a longer kiss than she was expecting, but she didn't pull away. Reluctantly, he broke the connection and she rested flat on her feet again.

"Stay safe," he said as he turned and walked to the corner. Brenda let him walk away from her grasp and took a deep breath. She sat back down in the chair and swiveled it to watch. A clear, thick glass wall rose around Brenda along with a thick steel ceiling sliding out from the concrete wall.

"Brenda?" Alan shouted with concern.

"It's OK, Alan. It's for my safety," Brenda sat still, unconcerned.

"All right," Alan said looking up to where the control booth window shielded the other observers from his possible wrath. "Let's get this over with!"

"Commencing," a voice announced over a hidden speaker.

Alan looked around and didn't notice anything. Brenda was looking around as well and didn't see any obvious tests. She stood up and her feet splashed in the accumulating water around her feet. She ran forward and pounded on the glass.

"This wasn't what we agreed to!" She shouted.

"What's wrong?" Alan shouted. Then he noticed the water rising at her feet at an increasing rate.

He ran forward to the glass and hit it with all his might. The thick barrier resisted his attempts.

"You bastards! I'm not going to play your game!" Alan screamed and willed the beast to come forward. That's when he felt a shift in his head as it was flooded with the chemicals from the implant. He raged as a normal man, pounding at the glass as the water rose. Brenda treaded water and grasped at the top edge of the transparent wall, water seeping out from the edge and trickling down the outside. The despair in Alan took over everything as he watched the light go out in Brenda's eyes, her lungs filled with fluid. He fell to his knees, his hands sliding down the slick surface. When he needed the beast, it wouldn't come. Why?

"Now that we know you can be controlled, we can begin your training," a man's voice announced over the speakers. Three uniformed men walked into the room, the two in the lead armed with tranquilizer guns. The officer behind them smiled as he entered.

With reckless intent, Alan leapt to his feet and rushed them. The two men fired and the tranquilizer darts hit their mark. Alan fell to his knees again and continued crawling until his body stopped responding to his mental commands.

"She was innocent! You didn't have to kill her…" he gasped.

"Well, Mister Jeffries, someone had to pay the price for your crimes. Why not lose something you cared about when so many others have lost what they cared for?" The officer smiled as Alan continued to struggle against the tranquilizers. "Your resistance is impressive, even when you're not in combat mode."

"I'll never fight for you," Alan mumbled.

"Pain is an amazing incentivizer for troops and others. That device in your head can reward and punish just as easily as it can control your combat effectiveness. It had additional functions your hapless doctor friend was unaware of," the officer said as he glanced up casually at the floating form in the water. "She truly was innocent to the last."

Alan reached for the officer with a surprising swiftness that caught the others off guard. He nearly reached him before taking two more darts and they jumped on him, finally bringing him down. He fell into the depths of darkness a second time.

Again unsure of how much time had passed, Alan woke up in his bed in his mansion in New York. He felt his head and there was a bare growth of stubble there along with the bump of the port in his skull. He took his time sitting up. A note addressed to him sat on the nightstand next to his bed. He reached for it with slightly trembling fingers and flipped it open.

"You're under constant surveillance, Mister Jeffries. Any missteps and we'll activate the pain protocol of your implant, turning it off only at our leisure. You'll receive orders soon. Keep your strength up. You'll need it."

Alan dropped the note on the floor, got up and walked to the front room of his mansion. He looked around and could see the changes made, the small surveillance cameras added to his domicile. His senses picked them up and noted each location. He calmly made himself some breakfast and consumed it rapidly, fighting back the nausea he felt having consumed solid food for the first time in what he felt may be days or possibly weeks.

He finished his meal, put the dishes in the dishwasher and walked back into the bedroom. He bent down to pick up the note, set it back on the nightstand and grabbed the lamp, quickly pulling the cord from the back of it. He shoved the live wire into the port in the back of his skull. He held it there until the pain made him pass out.

Knowing his healing abilities hadn't been affected by the implant, he knew he'd only be out a matter of seconds, maybe as long as a minute or two. Not long enough for them to mount a physical offensive.

He awoke to the smell of burnt flesh and a dull, throbbing ache deep inside his skull. He got up and winced, noting the pain was already lessening and would be completely gone within minutes. He looked directly into one of the cameras in his room.

"You're first mistake was assuming you could control chaos," Alan growled into the camera. "You're second mistake was killing the only reason I controlled my darkest impulses. You want to see the beast? I'll make sure he spreads to every corner of the world."

With a roar, Alan's body transformed. His arms lengthened, sharp claws protruding from his fingertips. He grew another six inches in height as his legs increased in girth two-fold. His feet became clawed paws. Hair pushed up through every pore. His head lengthened, his mouth protruding into a wolfish snout. He looked at the camera one last time with large yellow eyes and grinned, saliva dripping from his canine teeth. Throwing his head back, Alan howled, then leaped out of his bedroom window to the grounds one floor below and disappeared into the woods surrounding his estate.

THE INCIDENT AT MASON RIDGE VALLEY
BY HIROMI COTA

No shit, there I was: knee-deep in bullet casings and hand grenade pins. Haw! Naw, I'm just funnin' you. It was ankle-deep, at best.

Anyways, I had a bit of a situation out at Mason Ridge Valley, which is the dumbest damn name for a valley. Listen, you know what a ridge is, right? High part of the ground? Usually in a line? So, there are two sides that go down from there. But, with a valley, two parts go up. There's usually a ridge on each side of a valley is what I'm sayin'. So, why would you name a valley after something that's off on the side of it instead of the river or stream that's probably in the middle? I'd have called it Whisker Stream Valley, but no one asked me. Anyways, Mason Ridge Valley.

Back then, it wasn't part of the city; it was unincorporated, although I'm not rightly sure why corporations got a say in the matter. Eh? Ehhh? Fine. Your mama hated my puns, too. It was unincorporated territory, so it wasn't strictly speaking my job as deputy to go out and do anything out there. Out of my jurisdiction, you see. That didn't mean that I didn't go out there and see what I could do to help. Most of the people out that way weren't bad folks; they just didn't want to be part of the city or were just on their way somewhere else.

These days, the canyon's a techy commercial park, but back then it was basically a hobo camp, or a "homeless encampment", I guess you'd say these days. Travelers from all over, you know? Canyons aren't great to live in during the rainy months, but foraging's easy, especially back then. They were mostly Romani, what ignorant folks call "Gypsies," 'cept that word means Egyptian, which doesn't have nothin' to do with the Roma. Historically, the word "gypsy" got used to talk a whole mess of shit about the Romani, gettin' them into trouble with some evil folks, who didn't take kindly to—the hell was I saying?

Oh, yeah. So, the folks over in the camp were a mix of folks, like they usually are. Mostly Roma, but also some folks actin' like good ole boys from back East, 'cept their accents weren't quite right and they sure didn't look like they were equipped for farmsteadin'. I figured they must've been run outta town somewhere and were lookin' for a fresh start. Can't fault 'em for that, whatever their crimes in the past were.

Officially, the whole damn camp was trespassing on Old Man Ford's land, but we couldn't legally roust them and I didn't give a shit about stoppin' 'em, so Ford just had to accept the fact that there were fifty to a hundred folks livin' off his land at any given time. But, honestly, who cares? Old Man Ford had a couple hundred acres. He could ride for days without seein' anyone aside from his ranch hands, so it's not like he didn't have plenty of other land.

'Course, that didn't stop him from wanting more. He'd paid a whole dollar and twenty five cents for that parcel of land, so he was willing to hire a few gunmen to scare people off their technically unlawful homes. Worse, he didn't care if those guns killed people. For a whole dollar twenty-five cents worth o' land. I'm not joshin' you. That's how cheap land was and how awful rich folks is. He didn't even have any plans for it; he just didn't want anyone else on the land.

How'd I know about the gunmen? Well, 'cause Ford asked me if I wanted in. He asked Sheriff Ke-etch, too, but Bill just laughed in Ford's face. I reckon that made Ford mad as hell, but it's not like he didn't have it coming. An old, white, rich man asking an Indian, excuse me, Indigenous man for help in taking land away from some nomads? You can bet I laughed, too.

I didn't know who else he asked, but I figured it'd be someone with more guns than sense. You know the type: proud of things they didn't do, protective of things they don't have, angry at things that don't affect them a whit. After Sheriff Ke-etch and I got done laughin' and lookin' after things around town, we figured we'd ride out to the Valley and make sure that things were OK out there.

What we saw there when we arrived was just—well, shit. I guess I'll just start with how it felt. We were crossin' the Mason Ridge into the valley a smidge after sundown. We figured if anything was going to happen, it'd be around then, so we'd be right there to put a stop to it in case the hired guns wanted to try their hand at a massacre. It was dark as hell. There was a full moon out, but the clouds weren't helpin' matters a whit. The clouds were patchy, but the sky was more clouds than patch. Besides it being darker than it ought to be, it was damn quiet. Usually, I'd hear some fiddlin' or drums or singin' or something before I even set eyes on the camp. Some kinda music to let us know where we were. But, nope. Not so much as a jingly bell. No fires or nothin', neither. Just this wall of quiet darkness.

I was about to ask Bill if we were in the right place when I heard someone holler out, screamin' like the Devil was after them, watchin' them race up the opposite ridge on the other side of the valley and fall ass over teakettle off the other side. Then, it was quiet again. Bill sucked his teeth and unslung his rifle. I did likewise. Well, the rifle bit. I didn't suck my teeth so much as mutter "What the hell" and say a little prayer.

Even though it didn't make the best tactical sense, I let Sheriff Ke-etch go on ahead. He was a better rider and was far better at seein' in the dark than I was. Some ignorant townies had claimed that because he was Indigenous, he had magic powers that gave him the eyes of a cat, but he just plain spent a lot of time outside. Nothin' magic about that; it's just hard work. Those same damn fools would probably say that it was Swedish magic that gave me big arms instead of a life growing up workin' the land. Anyways, it wasn't a great idea for us to go down one by one, in case we needed to shoot. I wouldn't be able to fire over his head safely. But, again, he could see and ride better than I could, so it's what we did.

We started makin' our way down to the valley floor, horses amblin' down the grassy slope, when his rifle snapped up into his shoulder and he said something in his native tongue. I don't rightly know what it means, but I'd worked with him long enough that I knew it meant something like "Stop moving and pay attention." So, that's what I did. I pulled my rifle up to my shoulder, too, just in case. I didn't figure I'd have anything to shoot, certainly not anything I could safely shoot at, but—well, when your boss gets ready to shoot something, it seems like a bad idea to not be ready yourself.

I still couldn't hear nothin'. Not even a bird or a 'squito. Just the sound of my horse Cassie's breathing: heavier than it ought to be given how slow we'd been moving down the ridge. Maybe she was a mite tense. I sure was. Sheriff Ke-etch had only used that phrase a few times before and it never came before anything nice.

A twig or something snapped, and the Sheriff hollered out for someone to, "Hold it right there!" I couldn't exactly see who was there, but I didn't need to see clearly for me to point my rifle in the right direction and make his threat twice as big. Fortunately, it was off to the side; I wouldn't need to worry about accidentally hitting Bill.

"Just take it easy. We can all get home OK tonight," I added, hoping that a less stern voice might hedge our bets. Bill's tough approach gets most folks to surrender, but every now and then, there's some damn fool who gets his hackles up when challenged or someone who's scared as hell and ready to do somethin' stupid. That's where I come in with my reminder that life isn't just right now; it's also tomorrow, so let's not do something rash.

Either a patch of clear sky popped up or my eyes finally started workin' in the night and I could pick out the outline of the man we were pointing our guns at. It was one of the kids from town, undoubtedly out here to earn a few dollars hurtin' folks. He didn't look like that enterprise was goin' so great.

"You gotta help me, Sheriff!" he wailed.

"Where's the rest of you? Where are the folks who live here?" Bill asked, gettin' straight to the point.

"I don't know. I don't know! Those things are out here! They got Cris and R.B., and I don't know who else, but we gotta get out of here before they come back!" the kid ranted.

None o' this made a whole lot of sense to me, but if the old man's gunslingin' kids got roughed up by the campers, I wasn't gonna cry a whole lot. But, there wasn't no sense in lettin' this kid get beat any more; he'd clearly had enough.

"Y'mind if—" I started to ask Bill.

"Yuh," he responded before I'd even finished.

"All right. Come on up here, tenderfoot." I holstered my rifle and gave Cassie a little nudge with my knees to get her over to the kid. I held my hand out to him while she brought us closer. He hustled towards us, barely not tripping over grasses, roots, and other thick vegetation of the valley. His fingers brushed against mine before he barreled away like he was shot out of a cannon. Some kind of animal snarl shot past me in the same direction, and the little patch of clear sky closed back up.

We were in the moonless dark again. With that animal. Based on the voiceless trashing in the brush, the kid wasn't with us no more.

"We go now, " Bill ordered. He didn't need to tell me, but I'm glad we were on the same page. I drew my pistol. Better for things that were close and fast. Not that I wanted to take a shot while it was so damn dark. I heard a bit of steel on leather that told me the Sheriff had come to the same conclusion. Then, I heard somethin' else. A baritone growl, bass notes stepping down like a hangman comin' off the gallows, lookin' for his next customer.

Then, I heard another.

And another.

"Are we —" I asked just to ask. I already knew the answer.

"Yuh." We were surrounded by those things.

"Cougars?"

"Don't know."

"What'd'you mean you don't know? You know everything in Oregon."

"I know everything *natural* in Oregon."

My horse bucked as she kicked out at something behind us. By the time I'd swung my head and gun to see what it was, it had vanished back into the night. Another baritone wave of a growl creaked to life right behind me as soon as I was facing to the rear. It had to have been right between Sheriff Ke-etch and myself. And then it was somewhere else before my eyes could even point in the right direction. I was going to die out here. My horse knew it, too. Whether it was pure luck or love that she hadn't thrown me off and ran for her life, I'd never know, but Cassie stayed put.

Every time I'd been out here had been a pleasant trip until now. The campers were always kind and polite, sharin' food if they had it, songs if they hadn't. I'd do the same back to 'em. The campers might not have technically belonged here, but they'd made their home along the Whisper. Now, they were probably dead, either from the kids or from whatever these animals were. As terrible as my own imminent death was, I couldn't help but think back to the times I'd checked in on the folks out this way. The music, the meals, the feeling that you could be from anywhere, but if you were in the Valley, you were home.

"Whatever you're whistling, keep it up." I blinked at Bill, realizing that I *was* whistling. One of the songs I used to whistle when the campers asked me if I had something to share. While I whistled, the gallows creak growls were silent. You might be thinking as I do these days, "were those animals actually the campers?" Damned if I know. I'm certainly not one for putting out any rumors of the supernatural that might get someone lynched. I didn't remember the Romani having any stories like this, but they weren't the only campers. I'm not sayin' the allegedly 'good ole boys from back East' were responsible for this mess, but I'm not *not* sayin' it, you understand me? Whatever those things were, they knew me from my song and it made them want to eat me less. I whistled it as long as I could as Bill and I made our way out of there. When my lips gave out, I sang it. I didn't know the words, but I knew the tune well enough. I sang it until my throat cracked and I couldn't no more. By then, Sheriff Ke-etch knew how it went and he took over. The rest of the way home. At least an hour of singin' for each of us.

I don't know when the animals left us, but when we were lit by the yellow gas lights of town, we were alone. The song? Well, I don't know the name back then, just the tune, taught to me by my Swedish

Mormor. I'm sure she tried to teach me the words, too, but I've never have much of a head for languages. Yeah, yeah. The song's name. I'm gettin' to that.

Varulven.

The Werewolves.

I don't think those things were cougars. At least, not full-time cougars.

THE MAGIC WITHIN

BY AMBER RAINEY

The landscape ahead looked like nothing more than the furtherance of desert sand and looming mesas she had seen for days. The dry air caused ripples of heatwaves to weave across the horizon, mocking her thirst. The sun beat down upon her in its relentless pursuit of her demise. Yet, Poppy continued to put one foot in front of the other, determined to find her destination despite the odds. She could hear her mother's voice in her head, *You'll never find it. This is a fool's errand. You are not worthy.* Poppy's back straightened ever so slightly and she chided herself on letting her mother's words affect her, even so far from home. She had to complete this mission. His life depended on it.

Days Earlier

Poppy watched the drumming and dancing with a heady sense of burden upon her shoulders. This wasn't a celebration. The dancers were asking the gods for rain to heal the broken land and drive away the disease haunting their tribe. The droughts were nothing new to them, it was weathered every year and the celebrations when the first rain droplets fell lasted for days. However, this year had been different. A new sickness had infected the herds and, in turn, the people of her tribe. The healer had done everything in his power but even he fell victim to the dreaded disease. Now, a quarter of her tribe had gone to the great hunting grounds in the sky and another quarter were lying in their beds awaiting the same fate. There were murmurs among her people—the gods were angry and this would be their end.

Poppy refused to believe the rumors. Her tribe was not ready to die off. She was not ready to go. She had only recently come into the age of pairing and she had already given her heart to Green Meadows. She wanted to pair with him for the rest of her life. She wanted to bear him children and grow old with him. She wanted to be with him until her hair was long and white and braided by the skilled hands of her granddaughters. She did not want to die of the disease decimating her tribe.

Poppy watched the dancers. Green Meadows led the dance, his steps graceful, his solemn cries piercing the night. The song rolled over her, her eyes closing, her mind repeating them in silent please to the gods. She dare not speak them aloud for fear the gods would be angered by her untrained pleas.

Oh gods, the wisest of the wise.
We beseech thee.
Our tribe honors thy wisdom.
We gladly accept your judgment.
Forgive us oh gods.
Deliver us from this pestilence.
We shall forever honor thy mercy.
Oh gods, we beseech thee.

Green Meadows gave one last, long wail and the drumming stopped. The air was still. Her entire tribe held their breath, waiting for an answer from the gods. A lone coyote howled balefully and the tribe exhaled as one. Poppy watched Green Meadows. His shoulder tensed and he shook his head sadly -- almost imperceptibly. Poppy bowed her head. The tribe may have been fooled by the coyote but Green Meadows had not. It was not the sign they had hoped for.

"Did they not accept our prayers?" Poppy asked as she caught up with Green Meadows near his home.

He stopped with his back turned towards her. He squared his shoulders and she heard him exhale a deep breath. Then he turned and regarded her a moment without speaking. It was slightly unnerving to Poppy and after a few moments of meeting his gaze, she lowered her eyes and tried not to wring her hands. He could reduce her to a puddle with his gaze and she was loathed to admit he had that power over her, even to herself. Green Meadows stepped towards her and grabbed one of her hands, bringing it to his lips and placing a kiss on her knuckles. Poppy resisted the urge to wrap her arms around him. It would not be proper of her until they were officially paired by the chief.

"They will. Just not now."

"But, why not?"

Green Meadows chuckled, "Always curious. You never settle, do you?"

Poppy bristled and pulled back her hand. Green Meadows gave her a regretful look.

"I did not mean to offend. It is a trait I admire in you."

She resisted the urge to smile at his compliment. Truthfully, she might never have taken offense in the first place if her mother had not reprimanded her earlier that evening for being too curious for her own good. She warred inside herself with wanting to be herself and being a good daughter. Her mother was not well suited for a daughter and reminded Poppy on a daily basis that she wished she'd been born a male.

"Poppy?"

Poppy startled and looked up. It was the first time Green Meadows had ever called her that. He had generally been very formal with her, always calling her by her full name, Red Hair Like Poppy. She looked deep into his eyes and warmed at the love she saw in them. He took her hand again.

"We must trust in the will of the gods. Our people will survive this long summer."

"How do you know?"

He shrugged, "The gods have a plan. A protector will arise and vanquish the death. Only then will the rains return."

Poppy's eyes widened. It sounded as if Green Meadows were speaking in prophecy, only something the healer would have done. Only, the healer was no more and her tribe was left to persist on their own with what he had been able to teach them before his death. Green Meadows met her eyes and stared into them.

"Do you understand?" he asked hopefully.

Poppy thought a moment, then nodded her head.

Green Meadows looked around, then seeing they were alone, quickly placed a kiss on her lips. Poppy immediately felt a jolt of electric heat go through her body. She barely had time to register the pleasing warmth before Green Meadows dropped her hand and disappeared into his home. Poppy stood in the moonlight and tenderly touched her lips. She smiled and skipped back to her home, the weight of the evening's revelations no match for the power of his kiss.

"Poppy... Poppy... you must awaken now."

Nonnie's pleading tone broke into Poppy's dreams. She sat up with bleary eyes, rubbing them and looking around. There was no light, only Nonnie's darkened figure hunched beside her.

"Nonnie? What…"

Poppy was cut off by her grandmother's hand on her mouth. She narrowed her eyes, trying to get a better look at Nonnie's face but it was still too dark. Nonnie thrust something into her hands and she realized it was her winter cloak. She was about to argue when Nonnie shushed her again and pulled her towards the outside of her home. Nonnie exited and waited for Poppy to stand, then she grabbed Poppy's hands and started pulling her away.

"No words, child, just follow," Nonnie whispered.

Poppy shook her head but Nonnie didn't wait to see if she had agreed. Poppy tried to get her bearings and then walked more easily next to her grandmother without having to be pulled. Realization about their destination dawned on her when Nonnie stopped. Ahead of them, Poppy could see Green Meadows home. There were elders standing around the tent. Poppy's heart dropped to her stomach.

"No. Not him."

Poppy clung to her grandmother, willing her to say the disease had not infected Green Meadows.

"Hush now. There is work to be done. Come with me," Nonnie said as she stepped towards the elders.

"Nonnie, I can't!"

"We shall see," she replied.

They walked up to the elders, all in deep conversation. One of the elders acknowledged Nonnie with a tilt of his head. The chief emerged from the tent and all grew quiet. The chief bowed his head and Green Meadows father let out a huff—the only sound he would permit himself to make. The chief put his hand on the father and squeezed. He noticed Nonnie and Poppy standing at the edge of the circle of men.

"Grandmother, what is it you do here?"

Nonnie bowed her head, "Oh great chieftain, Red Hair Like Poppy has brought her best winter cloak to aid in Green Meadows healing."

Poppy looked at the cloak in her hands and realized it was her ceremonial winter cloak. It was only used for the long winter's night celebration. The rest of the winter, it served as insulation on the wall of their home. It was a very fine garment. Her mother would be none too pleased to realize Nonnie was offering it to a sickened one. A lump caught in her throat. The sickened one was Green Meadows. No one had yet survived the disease. She fought back the tears at what it meant for her. She was brought back to reality by a none too subtle jab of her grandmother's elbow to her ribcage. She looked at Nonnie and then to the chief.

"As I was saying, this is highly irregular for one not paired," the chief intoned.

Poppy nodded and bowed her head. The chief placed a hand on her hair. Poppy resisted the urge to run back to her home and cry. It felt as if she stood in front of the chief for hours before he lifted his hand and sighed.

"I will allow it, grandmother."

Nonnie pulled on her arm and Poppy walked inside Green Meadows' home. She waited as Nonnie spoke with his father. His father stared at her for a moment, then nodded his head and walked out. Nonnie placed herself in front of the doorway, her back turned to Poppy. Poppy looked across the room to where Green Meadows lay in his bed. She arranged the cloak across his legs and then knelt beside him.

"Green Meadows?" she spoke quietly.

He opened his eyes and smiled. He reached out a hand and Poppy took it. He squeezed it but his normal strength failed him and Poppy could tell it took a great deal of effort. She covered his hand with both of hers and squeezed back. A tear escaped down her cheek and he frowned.

"Do not be afraid," he said.

Poppy shook her head, "How can I not?"

"I am not afraid. I have seen a protector."

"Who is this person? Why have they not come forward?"

Green Meadows closed his eyes and smiled. Poppy cocked her head to the side, wondering if the delirium had come on. It was too soon but then, she had seen him earlier that night and he had seemed hale. Perhaps she had less time than she thought. It could be hours instead of days before he ascended to the great hunting grounds. Poppy sobbed aloud at the thought and he opened his eyes again.

"Poppy, Nonnie has the answers you seek. Trust in her guidance. Trust in me."

Poppy looked to her grandmother then back at Green Meadows. She reached out a hand and swiped a sweaty piece of hair off his forehead. She met his eyes. She expected to see madness in them but they were clear. She saw the strength he always bore. She saw his love. Most of all, she saw a shining trust in her, the likes of which no one had ever shown her. She hesitated and then nodded. He weakly squeezed her hand again and then smiled. She squeezed back and started to rise but he pulled her towards him. She hovered over him and he lifted himself up to whisper in her ear.

"I will hold on for you," he said and kissed her gently on the cheek.

Poppy pulled back to question him but his eyes were already closed again and his arm went limp. Poppy stared at him a moment longer, waiting to see if he would regain consciousness. Light poured into the home as his father entered. Poppy rejoined her grandmother, giving her a questioning look. The look she got in return had her hold her questions and follow Nonnie out into the dawn.

"This is madness!" her mother shouted.

"Quiet," Nonnie chided.

Poppy's mother looked at Nonnie as if she were ready to skin her alive. The rage pouring out of her mother was enough to fill their entire home with heat. Poppy would have laughed if she weren't so preoccupied with everything that had transpired since Nonnie had woken her that morning. Now, she sat in front of Nonnie as her grandmother braided her hair, placing poppies into the braids and powdering them with special herbs, the recipe known only to her grandmother. One day, that recipe would be hers, as long as Nonnie were the teacher. Her mother would never think to teach her the old ways as it would be wasted on a daughter. Nonnie hummed as she braided and Poppy's mother stormed out of the house. Nonnie chuckled and Poppy turned to ask why but Nonnie yanked her head back in place. Poppy waited for the braids to be finished. Then Nonnie patted her head and Poppy knew it was permission to move.

"Nonnie, how do you know it exists?" Poppy asked warily.

"My dear child, I was there."

Poppy's eyes grew wide.

"When?"

"Many, many moons before your mother was born. We faced this same predicament. I am the only one left who remembers. Now, the chief and the elders believe it to be myth. An old woman's story. I know the truth."

"Green Meadows believes you. That is good enough for me," Poppy said as she smiled at her grandmother.

Nonnie nodded, "It is love alone that will be your companion for the journey. Are you ready for that challenge, child?"

Poppy nodded. She would do anything to please the gods and save Green Meadows. Her mother might think Nonnie mad but Poppy had never seen anything but wisdom in the old woman's eyes. No one knew how many summers Nonnie had weathered. All respected her, even the chief. Poppy knew respect was earned in her tribe and Nonnie had clearly earned the respect of every last man, woman, and child. She chose to follow the directions and have a chance of saving everyone. A protector, just as Green Meadows had predicted.

"It is time to begin," Nonnie instructed.

Poppy rose and followed her grandmother out of the home. Nonnie chanted a few words while Poppy stared off in the direction of Green Meadows home. Nonnie finished and handed Poppy a long eagle feather. Poppy grinned up at her Nonnie, who winked. She recognized the eagle feather from the home of Green Meadows, it's quill wrapped with beads to represent his family. Poppy stashed it inside her dress. Nonnie kissed her on each cheek and then led her to the edge of the camp.

"You must continue walking until you feel you cannot walk anymore. Then walk some more. You must have faith in your task. You must follow your heart and help those in need, great or small. Finally, you must love. Love conquers all. Do you understand, child?"

Poppy nodded hesitantly.

"But... where is it?" she asked.

Nonnie chuckled and placed a hand on her chest.

"The directions are within. Trust and you will find it. No more questions, you must go."

Nonnie gave her a little push. Poppy turned back to say something but Nonnie just held her arm out, her finger pointing towards the setting sun. Poppy smiled and waved then turned towards her destination with a purpose. Her hands started shaking, belying her nerves, but she ignored them and just put one foot in front of another, walking towards her destiny.

oppy sat down gingerly in the shade afforded by a large mesa. It had taken hours to reach the relative shelter from the heat. She was exhausted, her muscles tired and her feet throbbing. She started crying and screaming, yelling for all the world to hear her frustration. She pulled her knees up and sobbed into them. Green Meadows was not going to survive and her plans for her future were dying, along with her body, in the desert. Nonnie had misremembered. There could be no other explanation. She cried until there were no more tears and then sniffled. Once her noises had died down, she heard a small voice. It startled her and she looked around, trying to discern the origin.

"Who... who's there?" she hiccuped.

"Down here," the voice replied.

Poppy looked at the ground on either side of herself and then pulled back slightly. She saw a small weed, newly wet from her crying. She chuckled at herself. Plants did not speak. She made sure the plant was not crushed because of her carelessness and then went back to feeling sorry for herself.

"Why do you cry?" the voice spoke again.

Poppy shook her head, "Plants do not talk. It's all in my head."

It was the voice's turn to laugh, "Certainly not. This plant is my food."

Poppy's head whipped back to the plant. She looked closer and then saw a fat caterpillar on the leaf. It had a piece of the leaf in its hands and periodically bit off a piece and chewed it while Poppy's mouth fell open. The caterpillar finished the leaf and then stood on its hind legs.

"I thank you for providing my food with a bit of rejuvenation, but I ask, why do you cry?"

Poppy shook her head and took in a deep breath. She closed her eyes tightly and willed the hallucination out of it. Surely, animals did not speak. She must be suffering from heatstroke. She felt a slight tickle on her hand and looked down to see the caterpillar sitting there.

"You are quite strange. Your hair is not like the others," the caterpillar said conversationally.

Poppy snorted, "I am strange? You are talking!"

The caterpillar shrugged, "I can go back to ignoring your plight if it is what you wish."

The caterpillar started to crawl off her hand. Poppy warred with herself. She had not spoken to anyone in days. Clearly, she had gone mad, but the caterpillar did seem like good company. She turned her hand, effectively keeping the caterpillar in place.

"Wait, it's just that I am not used to such things," she explained.

The caterpillar stopped walking.

"It is understandable. We don't stop to chat very often."

"We?"

"My kind. We have a greater purpose. I can sense that you do as well."

Poppy shrugged and her shoulders deflated.

"I thought I did but I have failed."

"Failure is only an option if you give up trying."

Poppy shrugged again, "I can't go on much longer."

"You can't go back, either."

Poppy thought for a moment. No, she couldn't go back unless she went back successful. She would take her dying breath in order to save him. Nonnie believed in her. She had to believe in herself and be worthy of their faith.

"Ah, see. I knew I was right about you."

"How so?" Poppy asked.

"You have what it takes, just as your grandmother did," the caterpillar said wisely.

Poppy shook her head, "You can't possibly have known her."

"That much is true but we have stories, the same as you."

Poppy raised the caterpillar closer.

"Do your stories include what I seek?"

The caterpillar nodded and pointed to the horizon. Poppy looked hopefully, trying to see more than the desert before her. She squinted really hard until her eyes started watering. The caterpillar chuckled again and Poppy looked at it forlornly. It patted her finger and inched closer to her face.

"Did your Nonnie not give you any instruction?"

"How did... oh, never mind. Yes."

"And?"

"She told me to look into my heart and what I seek will be found," Poppy grumbled.

"Your heart is not here," the caterpillar said, pointing to its head."

"But..."

The caterpillar began to inch its way down her arm.

"I have faith in you, girl."

"Wait... what do I do once I do find it?"

The caterpillar stopped and regarded her for a moment. It listened to the wind and watched as the sun sank. Then it nodded and turned back to her, as if an unseen force instructed it.

"You will find what you seek. Take in the water to restore your body and your resolve. Then take as much as you can with you, back to your tribe. Along the way, water every plant like the one you watered today. Only this time, instead of your tears, use the water you find. Then wait. Your heart will do the rest. It is time for me to go, girl."

Poppy gaped at the caterpillar as it inched its way back onto the plant. She played its words over and over in her head, wondering if she had truly gone mad. She watched as it began munching on a leaf again. She made up her mind and sent a silent prayer up to the gods. As she did, she could feel a sense of peace surrounding her. She looked back down at the caterpillar.

"It's Poppy," she blurted out.

"What is?" the caterpillar asked with a perplexed tone.

"My name... it's Poppy. Technically, Red Hair like Poppy but Nonnie called me Poppy since I was born," she explained.

"Nymphalidae," the caterpillar responded.

"Thank you," Poppy said with a smile.

"My pleasure," the caterpillar responded.

Poppy awoke with a start, the sun was already high in the sky. She looked around her impromptu bed. She yawned, wondering what had become of her friend, finding no caterpillars on the plant. The only odd thing was a small pod hanging off one stem of the plant. It was a delicate-looking thing of green with tiny gold dots. Poppy laughed out loud, surely the heat had gotten to her if she believed her dream to have been real. Nevertheless, she had a renewed sense of purpose and for that she was grateful. She looked off into the horizon and wiped her eyes at what she was seeing. In the distance, there appeared to be a circle of mesas, a misty fog seeping out of the gap between the two protrusions.

Poppy leaped to her feet. She gathered her things and began walking with a renewed purpose. She knew the mist meant water. The caterpillar, or her dream, had been right. She only needed to believe in herself again and rediscover her purpose. She had almost let the heat and the misery of the desert divert her from her path. She walked with determination, ignoring the part of her brain telling her she wasn't getting any closer. With each step, she thought only of returning to Green Meadows. As she walked, her heart felt as if it was getting fuller and fuller. A warmth spread throughout her body that had nothing to do with the heat of the sun.

Finally, after many hours of walking, which felt like a trial of her resolve, she came to the opening between the two mesas. The mist swirled around her feet and the sight before her caught her breath. As impossible as it seemed in the desert landscape, a shimmering blue lake sprawled before her, it's banks covered in bright green foliage. Butterflies flitted around the plants landing a moment before taking off again. She could see a caterpillar on a plant near her feet. She stooped to talk to it but it seemed none too interested in anything but chewing on the leaf in its mouth. She chuckled at herself. Of course, caterpillars didn't speak.

Poppy hesitated only momentarily before she dropped her things, removed her dress, and dove into the water. It felt as if the weight of the world lifted from her shoulders as the dirt dislodged from her skin. She spent a long while just soaking in the pool and staring up at the sky. The sun was now covered by a pleasant, puffy, white cloud. The sky was a vibrant blue, no other clouds in sight. It was as if the magic of the place protected her from the harshness of the outside world. Poppy sighed in contentment. She relaxed and floated on the surface of the pool.

After many hours, Poppy finally returned her mind to her present problems. She resolved to follow the instructions of her friend—real or imagined. She got to work washing out her long red hair. She rebraided it as best she could, mourning the loss of her namesake flower decorations but enjoying the feel of clean hair. The powders Nonnie had put in her hair were also gone and she had no replenishment. She shrugged, assuming the gods would understand and grant her leniency on rituals. She washed out her dress as best she could and then set it on a rock to dry. It was as if it took no time at all before the garment was warm and dry. Poppy gathered her skins and filled them all with the water from the pool. She left the pool and walked to the edge of the clearing, taking one last look around. Then, she turned towards home, stealing herself for the long journey ahead.

She hadn't been walking for very long when she turned around to get one last glimpse of the magical pool. To her astonishment, it was no longer visible. Poppy turned in several circles, thinking she had the direction wrong, but everywhere she looked, she was met with the usual desert landscape. Poppy shook her head in disbelief. It was as if the pool had vanished just as the caterpillar had done. She felt a nagging feeling in the back of her mind as if something were silently pulling her towards home. Shrugging, she continued on her journey. Along the way, Poppy watered each plant she saw with some of the water from the pool.

After several days of walking, Poppy finally saw the outskirts of her tribe's camp. She nearly wept for joy. However, the camp was eerily quiet as she walked past the first homes. Then, she heard wailing and followed the sound to the center of her camp. Her mother lay at the foot of a makeshift bed, wailing her heart out. Her father lay in the center of the bed, deathly pale. Yet Poppy could see his chest rise with breath and she let out the one she was holding. Nonnie stood at his head, praying, her face lifted to the gods. As if poked by an invisible finger, Nonnie straightened and met Poppy's eyes.

"The protector has returned," she said solemnly.

The whole tribe turned towards Poppy. Poppy flushed red as her hair and tried to stand tall. She was uncomfortable with the scrutiny. A hand gently pushed her from behind and Nonnie held her arms aloft. Poppy walked into her grandmother's arms and Nonnie hugged her tightly.

"You know what to do?" Nonnie asked hopefully.

Poppy nodded. She noticed the plant at the top of her father's head. She used the last drop of water from the pool to water the plant. Nothing happened and a murmur went through the assembled tribe.

"Worthless girl," her mother sneered.

Nonnie held out her hand and Poppy's mother stopped speaking with an air of defiance in the way she crossed her arms. Nonnie looked at each tribe member, meeting their eyes. Each one nodded silently. Poppy looked at her grandmother expectantly.

"Red Hair Like Poppy has returned. She is now the protector. We must wait now."

Another murmur ran through the tribe. Poppy was exhausted. She leaned on her grandmother, willing the old woman to give her strength. Nonnie smoothed the braids around Poppy's face and kissed each cheek. Poppy stared into her grandmother's eyes.

"He lives yet," Nonnie said quietly.

The relief Poppy felt was palpable. Her knees nearly buckled at the answer to her unspoken question.

"Go to him. Wait," Nonnie instructed and pushed Poppy towards Green Meadows' home.

Poppy entered the home, nodding a hello to Green Meadows' father. His father whispered something into his ear and he responded in a raspy whisper of his own. His father nodded and put a hand on Poppy's shoulder, squeezing it just before he left the home. Poppy went over to Green Meadows and sat next to him. A tear fell down her cheek. He was so pale, his eyes sunken into his skull and his lips tinged blue. He reached up and weekly wiped the tear away. Poppy laid her head on his chest and he stroked her hair with his thumb.

Poppy sat vigil by Green Meadows bedside for many days. He did not get any worse but he wasn't getting any better. Her own father had passed and her mother had railed at her during one of the only moments she had allowed herself to leave Green Meadows side. Her mother spat on her and forbade her ever come near her home again. Poppy cared not. Her home and her fate now rested in the survival of Green Meadows. She was dozing when she heard a great commotion outside. She checked on him, satisfying herself that he was comfortable as he could be, then went outside to investigate. Nonnie stood outside the home.

"Nonnie, what is happening?" Poppy asked as she shielded her eyes from the light.

"Look."

Poppy looked in the direction Nonnie was pointing. She frowned, wondering what she was seeing. The sky was darkened by what appeared to be a moving black and gold cloud. As it got nearer, Poppy realized it was full of the butterflies she had seen at the magical pool. They landed on the plants around her tribe's camp and the one that had sat at her father's head. They were a silent army, flitting from plant to plant.

"What does it mean?" Poppy asked in wonder.

"Your wait is almost over," Nonnie responded cryptically.

The butterflies stayed for several days and then disappeared as fast as the had come. Poppy watched in wonder when the tiny eggs they laid hatched into caterpillars, each one devouring a plant around the camp. At first, the people of her tribe complained bitterly, pointing fingers at her and blaming her for the curse. However, as the plants were decimated, the disease stopped killing first the animals they hunted, then the tribe members who depended on the animals for sustenance. Deaths no longer occurred. Those who had been afflicted started getting better. All but one.

Poppy swiped angrily at the tears on her cheeks, plopping down to one of the last caterpillars still eating. All of the others had turned into the odd chrysalis. She stared at the caterpillar, watching it eat and wishing it would just stop like the others before it.

"She promised me," she accused the caterpillar.

It stopped munching on its leaf and looked up at her. It peered at her as if it was a loss for words. Then, to her surprise, it wiggled in a gesture that seemed to tell her to get closer. She rolled her eyes but did as it bade.

"What is it that bothers you so?" the caterpillar asked.

Poppy huffed, "She promised me he would get better."

The caterpillar nodded.

"He will."

"But how!" Poppy cried out.

"With your magic."

Poppy scoffed. She leaned back, staring out into the sunset and willing the tears in her eyes to stop. She couldn't go on much longer. She couldn't bear the suffering in Green Meadows' eyes. He tried to hide it from her but she saw it all the same. Everyone was better but him. Perhaps she had taken too long to return and it was her fault.

"It isn't," the caterpillar said.

"What?" Poppy asked incredulously.

"It isn't your fault. You are the protector. You have prevailed."

Poppy sneered, "Have I?"

The caterpillar sat on the leaf, silently staring at her. Poppy turned away, letting the tears flow freely down her cheeks. For all her trials, the one thing she had wanted most was slipping from her grasp. She wished, not for the first time, that she had not been "chosen" in the first place. Her Nonnie was wrong, things would not work out for her.

"If you think that way, you are right."

"What do you know of my thoughts?"

"I know you think of giving up. If my kind gave up, we would have died out long ago. Yet look around you," it said as it gestured to the plants around it.

Everywhere she looked, Poppy saw a chrysalis. She didn't know what to make of them. They seemed like odd little protrusions from the plants the caterpillars had eaten. Nonnie had warned the tribe not to eat them, they would cause more death. Therefore, many had stayed away from the plants entirely.

"I don't understand," Poppy shook her head in defeat.

"Bring the one you love here tomorrow morning. Wait for the sun to rise high into the sky. Trust, once more. Now, I must be going. I tarried too long waiting to speak with you and now my fate is sealed. Yet my ancestors would be proud of me."

Poppy watched as the caterpillar slowly crawled off the plant, towards the small stream. She watched it walk into the stream and float away on a leaf it found near the edges of the bank. She was more confused than ever. She stood up, hanging her head in misery, and went back to her vigil by Green Meadows' side.

"Poppy... you must awake," Nonnie said.

Poppy startled awake, wondering if she were dreaming, yet again. Nonnie stood over her as before, many moons ago. This time, her grandmother did not carry her cloak, but held onto a makeshift crutch. Poppy looked towards Green Meadows who regarded her with amusement tinged with pain. He shrugged and smiled.

"Nonnie, what's this about?" Poppy asked grumpily.

"You must take him to the plants by the stream. Hurry."

Nonnie was already by Green Meadows side, helping him

stand. For an old grandmother, Poppy was surprised at her hidden strength. Green Meadows leaned heavily on the crutch and Poppy rushed to his other side, holding him up and willing him not to fall. She tried to ignore the rush of warmth she felt at his closeness. She looked over at Nonnie with a small measure of annoyance and Nonnie just beamed back at her. Poppy shook her head but led Green Meadows out of his home and to the stream.

Poppy fussed over him as she helped him sit on the ground. The air held a weigh to it, as if holding its own breath. Poppy suppressed the shiver that ran down her spine. She smoothed out Green Meadows' hair, rebraiding it deftly. As the sun rose, the plants around them came to life. A butterfly crawled out of each chrysalis and sat, slowly flapping its wings. Green Meadows was intrigued and Poppy could merely stare at the wonder in his eyes. His body glistened with sweat and she could see a green tinge to his skin.

"We should return you to your bed, Green Meadows," Poppy implored.

He shook his head.

"Please, you'll catch your death."

Green Meadows looked at her. He took her face in his hands and gently kissed her forehead. He rested his head on her forehead and linked his fingers with hers.

"I will not die, you have frightened death. It will not take me for a long time," he said with certainty.

"How can you say that?"

"Look around you."

Poppy closed her eyes, not wanting to listen to him. She didn't want to see the horrid plants that had sickened the man she loved. She didn't want to deal with the strange animals that tore their bodies apart just to be reborn. She didn't want to face losing her world.

"Poppy, my love, look at me," Green Meadows whispered.

Poppy opened her eyes. A tear slid down her cheek. He had never been so intimate with her, even in all the days they had spent together since she returned. He wiped the tear off her cheek and then smiled.

"Look around you," he repeated.

Poppy looked around him and gasped at what she saw. The air was full of black and gold butterflies fluttering around them. They acted as if they waited for a sign. Poppy shook her head. She didn't know what they waited for. A butterfly landed on her outstretched hand.

"Red Hair Like Poppy, may we help you?" the butterfly asked.

Poppy looked at Green Meadows. He nodded at her in encouragement. Poppy thought about what she wanted in her head and it was as if the butterfly could read her thoughts. The moving cloud descended upon Green Meadows, who sat patiently still while they landed on him. He chuckled once or twice as Poppy watched in amazement. As each butterfly landed, sat for a moment, then flew off, the color of his skin returned to normal. A butterfly landed on each eye and when it was gone, the pain was gone from Green Meadows' eyes. The last butterfly left and it was as if Green Meadows was a new man. There was no trace of the illness.

The butterfly landed on Poppy's shoulder and whispered something into it. Poppy laughed and the butterfly flew away. She looked towards Green Meadows and throwing caution to the wind, she threw herself into his lap, kissing him as long as she dared. Then she reigned kisses on his face, everywhere she could touch -- his eyes, his nose, his lips again, each cheek. Finally, he fell backward and she fell on top of his chest. She made to move off of him but he tightened his arms around her. She raised up so that she could look him in the eyes. She studied them, looking for any trace of hesitation and found none. Poppy kissed Green Meadows with all the love she felt and he kissed her in return.

Many, many moons later

Grandmother Poppy, you cannot be serious," Nymphalidae scoffed.

Poppy pulled the girl's head back around to finish braiding her hair. She ignored the little whimper her granddaughter gave her. She learned well from her own Nonnie. The child would learn in time.

"I am as serious as the sun rises and sets."

"It's just an old legend," the girl whined.

Green Meadows walked into their home and across the room. Poppy followed his movements. He was getting slower in his old age, but still as handsome as she remembered. He stopped and turned around, waiting for Poppy to continue speaking.

"So then the butterfly whispered into my ear and flew off," Poppy continued.

"Grandmother, that is just not true," Nymphalidae said, petulantly yanking her braid away from her grandmother's fingers.

"Tell her grandfather. Tell her it isn't true. She actually believes butterflies cured you of the great illness."

Green Meadows shrugged, "I like her stories, granddaughter."

Green Meadows winked at Poppy, causing her to chuckle. Nymphalidae jumped up, stomping towards the door.

"You two are impossible," she huffed and went out the door.

Green Meadows sat next to his mate, putting an arm around her and kissing her hair.

"Must you antagonize her so?" he asked cheerfully.

Poppy shrugged, "I am merely preparing her for the inevitable.

"Ah, is that all?"

"Well, I do like the way her cheeks blush any time I mention Eagle Feather and her destined pairing."

"There it is, you are hopeless, my love," Green Meadows chuckled.

"Quite the contrary, as you well know," she intoned.

Green Meadows smiled and kissed her. She sighed contentedly when he pulled back and wrapped her in his arms. They sat in blissful silence a long while before Green Meadows squeezed her and turned her to face him. She could see he wanted to ask something but he did not speak.

"What is it?"

"What did that butterfly say to you?" he asked.

Poppy laughed.

"All this time and you have never asked," she wondered.

He shrugged, "It does not mean I never pondered."

Poppy smiled. Green Meadows waited expectantly. She took her time, building up the suspense until she could see he was about to burst with curiosity. Then she leaned forward until she was a hair's breadth from his ear.

"She said, *My ancestors were right, you are quite strange.*"

Green Meadows guffawed and Poppy laughed along with him. She rested her head on his chest, reveling in the strong beat she heard within. She sent a silent prayer up to the gods for helping her protect and save him. She also prayed that the gods watched over her friends on their long journeys, wherever it led them.

ELSEWHEN
BY MARSHALL MILLER

The man trudged ever closer to his once distant goal. It had not been an easy trek. The man had started in a low and hot desert; progressed to a more refreshing high desert environment, and now was nearing a green patch of foothills attached to an unknown mountain range. At least the name of the mountains was unknown to the traveler. The one fact that Jack Hays knew was that the green he could see bespoke of vegetation. And vegetation needed water to keep that beautiful green color.

Jack had been surviving on hit and miss supplies of water since he had woke up in this strange land. The Day Sun he saw during the first minutes of consciousness looked like Earth's Sol. With the sunset in the evening and the bright object, the traveler called the Night Sun, and two moons appeared, Jack knew he was no longer in Kansas. More importantly, Jack had no magic ruby slippers for a return home.

There was some luck in this new world as a thunderstorm soaked Jack the first day. Still confused, unable to remember his own name and fearing a suffered stroke, the chilly rain did revive him enough that he checked his clothing for usable items. A 12-ounce plastic drink bottle and a sandwich bag gave him the ability to save some of the rainwater before it sank into the sandy soil. Again, whatever gods or goddesses of Luck existed on the world he had christened Elsewhen provided him with only a day in full low and hot Arizona type desert before Jack traveled to a slight incline and into a high desert motif. By then, the man's wits began to return, and he could read the contents of his wallet. However, his memory was still very sketchy.

Jack found some papers in his wallet that said he was retired at age thirty-five from a law enforcement position, and he had memories of wearing a military uniform. But his brain held no specifics. Some survival training came to his forebrain, and he soon began to organize what was on his person.

Jack remembered having a firearm and a vest or jacket, but he had neither when he awoke. He had a money clip with one hundred dollars in bills plus a small folding blade and nail file. Jack recovered a ring of keys with an extended handcuff key and a P-38 military style can opener attached. His footwear was sneakers, which soon became hot in the sand, less so as the ground became less sand and more soil. A long-sleeved shirt, slacks, and underwear, that was it. The first night was cold, with no fire. Jack was never a smoker, so no lighter nor matches. His cellular phone still turned on but had no signal once his brain remembered why it was in his pocket. A nice lady named Jane left him a message asking when he would be home and said she loved him. The voicemail and a gold wedding band on his hand informed Jack he was married.

But he had no memory of marriage nor children.

Despite his confusion, Jack's luck held as he stumbled upon the remains of a body and a smashed up AK-47 rifle. The discovery the second day told him that he was not the only human to fall through the rabbit hole. Previous training enabled him to insert the one bent round into the weapon and achieved a functional chambering. Now he at least had some protection, if he even needed it.

Two days of more walking towards what looked like mountains on the horizon, and he found the remains of another body. A small rain shower wetted Jack but still no signs of anything edible. He had some belly fat so the man would not starve to death anytime soon. The remains led to the discovery of a source of calories.

Jack discovered what he named as crab scorpions. Large and with a round body about a foot across, they looked like land crabs but had a short scorpion tail, stinger and all. The creatures were feeding off the remains of the corpse when Jack saw them. Jack found a good-sized rock and used it to smash a couple of them while dodging the others. He cracked open the large claws and sucked the raw meat out. Jack knew he needed to find a source for fire or risk being sick from raw meat parasites. At least the protein makeup on this world was digestible, a subject seldom addressed in most science fiction stories.

Using other stones and kicking with his feet, Jack finally cleared them from the remains. A quick search of the corpse revealed a thin leather belt and a broken flint blade knife. Jack used the sharp flint to cut loose a small skin pouch, and then he scrambles back from the body as the crab scorpions came back to contest him for the desiccated corpse.

"Have it, assholes. I don't eat human flesh."

Using another large rock, Jack smashed a smaller eight-limbed late comer. The man then continued his trek. An hour later, Jack found a local equivalent of a tumbleweed and decided it was time to try out his fire-making abilities. The remains of the flint blade and the steel nail file from his money clip enabled him to create sparks when the file struck the flint. The tumbleweed was so dry it was soon aflame. Within minutes, he was roasting the crab creature.

The crab thing provided a too small meal, but it was better

than nothing. Jack sucked a bit of moisture from his prey and then took a small sip of his dwindling water supply. The late thirties former resident of the Americas looked up at his goal. The green area higher up on what appeared to be high foothills of a broader mountain range seemed closer, but not enough. If there were no more rain showers or other sources of water, Jack would be in serious trouble.

Jack surveyed the area until he saw a clump of low brush and short trees near some boulders. Those would provide some shade until nightfall. Jack needed to conserve his strength and reduce fluid loss. He had not reached the point of drinking his own urine, but that was next. Some distant past survival training told him it was possible.

Jack soon made himself a rough sleeping spot in some soft dirt under the low pine and mesquite like trees. After checking the area for creepy crawlies, the man was soon asleep. He awoke with the rising of the Night Sun and the two moons. Jack had named the moons Tiny and Squirt, with Tiny being the bigger of the two. They reminded the former Earthman of the moons of Mars, at least of pictures he had seen. He grunted and spoke to himself.

"Too bad this is not Barsoom, and Dejah Thoris is not around. That good looking woman would help me, even if I am not John Carter."

Jack took a small sip of water and was startled by a flash of lightning and a crash of thunder. Some small animal scurried past him towards a hidden burrow. The man looked towards the sky and saw a rapidly advancing mass of dark clouds. Jack moved away from the trees, lightning magnets, and huddled next to a couple of nearby boulders. Sure enough, a bolt of lightning split a small pine tree and lit it afire. Moments later, the rain came.

The rainfall was heavy and stinging, but Jack stood and suffered the storms furry. He was soon soaked and shivering but was well hydrated for once. He dug a hole and used his sandwich bag to line it so the rainwater would pool. Rivulets coming off the boulders enabled him to fill his plastic bottle and drink some more. Then the thunderstorm was gone.

Jack looked around and saw the pine tree was still smoldering. He looked inside the destroyed trunk and saw there was a tiny flame. Jack retrieved a business card from his useless billfold and held it to the fire. It lit, and Jack added a couple of saved pieces of tumbleweed. He soon had another small flame in the interior of the lightning-struck tree. Now the traveler needed something to roast.

Jack recovered a long splinter from the tree and began to look for any creatures disturbed by the storm. He soon found a good-sized snake exiting its flooded burrow. Jack quickly smashed it with a rock before the animal realized there was an apex predator around. Using the pieces of the flint knife, Jack cut its head off being mindful of the fangs. He skinned it as if he had done this in the field before although he had no specific memory. Using the long tree splinter as a spit, he was soon roasting the snake.

An hour later, Jack felt full with two small pieces of snake meat remaining. The night air was cold, so Jack began walking once again. Less heat meant he sweat less and using less water. As he walked, the American (that was what he remembered as his home) tried to piece together his memory and his reality.

His billfold documents and cellphone said he was an American from someplace named Tacoma, Washington. The name had a vague image attached to it, just out of reach of his conscious memory. The name Jane had an image from the cellphone attached (once he remembered how to view the saved pictures) but not sharp recollections. If this Jane loved him, she would be worried sick. Yet, he had no such attached feelings towards her. Hell, he could not remember anything about her past than the saved cellphone picture.

Then there was this place he called Elsewhen. One set of

recollections his brain provided was some science fiction stories about wormholes and alternate universes. Jack smiled to himself.

"Well, I just proved String Theory and attached universes," he said out loud as his mind provided him the concepts. Now it was a matter of learning the rules of the world to survive. For one thing, the humanoid bodies told him there must be other peoples on Elsewhen. The fact there were corpses bespoke a violent environment. Some of the violence could have come from other humans. Jack would have to be careful of anyone he met.

His stride began to eat up the distance, and it looked like the first patches of green in what could only be foothills of a mountain range seemed within his grasp. Jack then found the next body.

Some buzzard type birds alerted the man to the death ahead. The birds were actually the size of what he remembered from school as ancient condors. Birds that size could be dangerous, and Jake had a weapon with just one round in it. He scanned the area and found a couple of good-sized stones for throwing. Predators and scavengers tried to avoid unnecessary injury, so thrown rocks may chase them off of their prey. At least, long enough so Jake could examine what looked like a dead human.

There were four of the giant condors pecking and squabbling when Jake threw the first rock and hit one in the neck more by chance than skill. It let out a screech and stumbled/hopped back. Jake screamed like a Banshee and threw the next rock, waving his arms like a madman. The four birds apparently thought discretion was the better part of valor as they all hopped and then flapped their hung wings to struggle to get airborne. A breeze coming from the mountains helped in their endeavor. Jake hot-footed it towards the body as the condors landed some fifty yards away.

The corpse was female, its long bronze hair braided in an intricate pattern. The dead female wore a light chain mail shirt over a colorful blouse. A flint headed arrow completely pierced the feminine throat. Next to the body was a large bolt action rifle. Jack grabbed the gun and worked its massive bolt action which looked like an enlarged version of a German Mauser.

"Where did that bit of knowledge come from?" Jake mumbled. He realized that he seemed to have a treasure trove of martial and survival knowledge from a previous life buried in his memory. A quick pat-down of the body revealed three live .50 caliber shells which reminded him of the Old West Sharps rifle rounds favored by Buffalo Hunters. The rifle contained a spent shell which Jack saved and replaced with a live one.

"Now we are cooking with gas," he said in a loud voice. Jack had a weapon with a hefty punch which he raised above his head as he yelled at the condors.

"Want to try me now, assholes?"

As he continued his search of the recently dead body (less than a day), Jack realized he had a long history with death and dead bodies. They did not phase him. He assumed it was not because he was a funeral director. Further searching resulted in the find of an over-under two barreled massive pistol. In historical India on Earth, it would have been called a Howdah pistol, carried as a back-up on big game hunts. In the pistol pouch was some six spare rounds of a type of long .50 caliber shell, but shorter than the rifle's cartridges. He looked at the dead woman warrior and thought she must have been a powerful woman to handle the weapons she carried. Jack knew men who would have had difficulty shooting such firearms.

Jack recovered a small water flask, and a matching one containing wine as one of the Condors suddenly landed some ten yards away. With his off-hand, he tossed a rock at the condor, and it cawed as it hopped backward. The big birds were becoming impatient as their hunger persisted. Eventually, they would rush him. With that thought, Jack hurried the scavenge of the body.

A minute later and Jack had taken off a long cloak, a belt with a copper knife and a bag containing some pieces of jerked meat. The belt also had a small concealed money purse sewn in. The other condors were beginning to approach, so Jack snapped the flint head of the arrow shaft off as a final move and then backpedaled from the corpse. He decided the mail would not fit him and would just be extra weight in a hot climate. Jack looked at the ground and saw the equine hoofprints he expected. The horse was gone, possibly taken by the woman's killer. But he or she did not strip the body of weapons and valuables. The spent shell in the rifle told a tale that may be the attacker was shot. Jack began to follow the hoofprints up the incline of the foothills, ever watchful for the Amazon's attacker.

Jack decided the woman was an Amazon and would understand why he did not hold a funeral service for her. He murmured a short prayer for a quick trip of the Warriors spirit to whatever afterlife they owned. Another group of people who had fallen down the rabbit hole to Elsewhen.

An hour later, Jack found the remains of the Amazon's attacker. He whistled as he saw the body. Despite some scavenging by the local wildlife, it looked similar to photographs he had seen of Commanche warriors. Plains Indian Tribes on this two mooned world? Was there a rhyme or reason to who was transported to Elsewhen?

"Is this Purgatory maybe?" he asked out loud. Jack then scanned the body and the area. His supposition about a bullet strick was correct. There was an impact wound on the Comanche's left floating rib. The man had bled out and fallen from his captured mount. The warrior had an excellent steel Bowie knife and a quiver with two flint arrows. Jack found no bow and assumed scavengers had taken it to chew on. Comanches also carry lances, but Jack saw none. He did strip the moccasins of the Comanche's feet.

Again Jack mumbled apologetic prayers to whatever Gods ruled this world for no burial. The Comanche had no food nor water, so Jack was still faced with those shortages. Once again, Jack began his trek towards the green.

As he walked, Jack noticed hoofprints in the same direction as his plotted course. His mind finally reminded him that horses had sensitive noses and could smell water miles away. He smiled at the remembered knowledge.

"I'll just follow you, Horsey," said Jack. "You're better at finding water than I am."

Jack adjusted his newfound booty on his body and continued his trek. The fact a horse was headed towards a water source made Jack quicken his pace. The Day Sun rose in the sky until it was at the equivalent of Noon, Local Time. This made Jack realize he did not know for sure if the Everwhen day was twenty-four hours. It seemed the same to his internal clock, but he could not be sure. Another mystery to be ferreted out.

Day Sun was past its zenith in the hot afternoon sky when Jack noticed his goal was within reach. Some mile ahead, a green batch of something reflected the sunlight. The slope seemed to flatten out onto a possible plateau with the actual high mountains still miles further. Jack found the wind to start a jog.

A slight breeze brought the familiar feel of the water as Jack tried to run faster. He concentrated on insuring he did not trip and fall on the trail the horse was following up the incline. As Jack worked his way up a small rise, he saw what appeared to be watery mist setting low over the top of the increase.

"Water," he said out loud. Then Jack saw it. Bubbling up from the ground was clearly water sufficient to provide a small babbling brook. As Jack reached the source of the critical moisture, he looked beyond the rise and stopped in his tracks. For the bubbling water did form a babbling brook which worked its way down the reverse slope and ended in a lake. A lovely, clear water lake.

Just beyond the mile-long lake was a smaller pond. And beyond the second body of water was another pond. All three bodies of water sat on a small plateau which interrupted the slope of the foothills of the more distant mountain range. Jack knew he would not be thirsty any time soon.

As Jack slowly surveyed the tableau, he saw the missing horse carefully making its way to the lake's edge. The horse took a quick drink, then moved back. It was a good-sized brown colored mount with a saddle and bags still on its back. The horse also seemed wary of the lake or something in it as it repeated the short drink then retreat action some three times more as Jack watched.

"What's up, horse?" Jack said out loud as he slowly descended down the slope towards the lake, He unslung the beat-up AK-47 with its single live shell as he had a good idea of the ballistics of the assault rifle. That is if the weapon fired.

The horse made one more approach, began to drink then dashed away from the water's edge as something brook the surface of the lake. As the creature scrambled up into the shallows, Jack first thought it was a species of 'gator or Croc. But as Jack examined the beast more, it looked more like a very oversized Iguana. A memory of Darwin's discovery of ocean-going iguana in the Galapagos Islands confirmed the observation that the thing was another animal whose ancestor had come through the Looking Glass.

The horse beat a hasty retreat as the monster scrambled up onto dry land. It moved fast but not as quickly as the horse. Jack brought the AK-47 up to his shoulder and hoped the sights were somewhere near accurate. The lizard was meat and also a threat to the human using the lake. Thus, it was an easy decision for Jack to decide to expend a rifle round on it.

"Here goes nothing," he mumbled moments before he fired.

The range was close to two hundred meters, under normal circumstances not a far distance for the AK. But this was not normal. Once again, the Gods of Luck were with Jack as the jacketed thirty caliber bullet struck the monster iguana broadsides. It penetrated the hide, and the creature began to thrash about as it attempted to find the invisible enemy who had just hit it. Jack dropped the empty AK and unslung the massive bolt action. Jack knew the mass of the bullet for the late Amazon's long gun more than made up for the lack of jacketed ammunition.

There was no need for a follow-up shot as the lizard thrashed, then collapsed into a heap. Jack supposed his bullet had struck a vital organ. The horse watched as Jack made his way down the slope to the body. Jack poked the monster iguana several times with the rifle barrel before he set to slaughtering it with the dead Comanches Bowie. Jack tossed the guts aside and saved what looked like the liver and a shot heart. He also cut off a large chunk from the tail as Jack remembered 'gator tail was a delicacy to some. He sliced strips of meat from the haunches and ribcage area before his growling stomach told him it was time to cook a meal.

Jack found another tumbleweed and began to build a fire just up from the sand and rock lake beach. The horse slowly made its way to the human, and Jack was able to grab its bridle. He could ride but was not a prominent horseman. However, the horse allowed him to remove the saddle and saddlebags, then trotted away in search of forage. In the saddlebags, the Earthman found some balls of rice, stale bread chunks, spices, and dried apples. Jack began to hum to himself as the thought of a flavorful meal brought a smile to his face.

Jack used a small tin plate from the Amazon's saddlebags to warm the rice balls as he dripped blood from the raw meat pieces as a flavor enhancer. He placed pieces of meat on flat stones he moved to the edge of his campfire as he threw more wood fuel on the flames. Within a half an hour, Jack was chowing down on the first decent meal in over a week. Jack used the Bowie to slice some slips of wood for use as chopsticks and pokers. After additional slices of meat scorched by the campfire. Jake finally felt full. He walked over to the babbling brook which fed the lake and refilled his plastic water bottle. Jack washed the small tin plate and then scooped about an ounce of water into it. A quick return to the campfire and Jack sat down, leaning against a solid rock. He drank the water from the tin pan and took a swig of wine from the scavenged flask. Jack belched.

"I feel almost human," Jack said. He sat and contemplated his status. Jack had about twenty pounds of butchered meat left, some slow cooking near the campfire. There were a few pieces of jerked beef in the Amazon's bags as well as the stale bread. Jack had finished off the rice balls. With a water source, the only things limiting Jack's stay at this oasis was food and shelter. There was still meat and ribs to be recovered from the monster iguana. Hopefully, the water source would attract other animals which Jack could hunt. Shelter might be obtained from salvaged wood and digging around the larger rocks to create a small den. Mammals had survived the extinction of the dinosaurs by being able to burrow into the ground and build dens. What was good enough for them was good enough for Jack.

With that thought, Jack grabbed the Bowie and walked back to the dead lizard. As the man neared the head of the oversized iguana, something came boiling out of the lake. Jack backpedaled as he pulled the large Howdah pistol from his belt. The creature from the lake was a smaller version of the iguana. The lizard ignored Jack, grabbed the remains of the dead specimen, and drug it back into the lake. It soon disappeared under the lake waters.

"Shit," cursed Jack. He could have tried to shoot it, but his ammunition was limited. He shrugged and made his way back to his campfire. Jack had a full stomach and some saved meat, so he was far from starving. He would have to plan a means to deal with the lake denizens if he were going to remain here until humans arrived. Jack recognized this area as a true oasis to be used just before the descent into the hot and dry desert. The American was lucky he had arrived in Elsewhen this close to the water source.

Jack spent the rest of the afternoon using the tin pan and the Amazon's copper blade to dig around the base of nearby boulders. The horse did not return until the Day Sun was setting and the two moons began to rise, to be followed by the Night Sun. Jack escorted the horse over to the brook and made sure it understood this was where safe water flowed. He collected some short grasses and fed the horse, used some to wiped the horse down and then returned to his den. He also picked up the smashed AK-47 as he figured the metal parts may be of some use. Jack covered the entrance with chopped brush and lay down with the saddlebags as his pillows. With the rifle and large pistol close at hand, he was soon asleep.

Some growls and horse whinnying plus a bray woke Jack. He was up with the pistol in one hand and the copper blade in the other. He pushed the concealing brush back form the entranceway of his den. What he saw stopped him in his tracks.

What looked like crosses between coyotes and wild dogs were arguing over the gut remains of the iguana. Jack had left them some fifty yards from his makeshift den, hoping they may attract a condor or two he could kill. A couple of the canines were taking an interest in the horse and were circling it. Jack had a sudden memory of a pet dog sometime in his life, so dogmeat had not on the menu. Jack stepped forward and bellowed.

"What in the Hell do you think you are doing?"

Six pairs of canine eyes snapped in his direction. The coydogs or whatever they were seemed to be cognizant of the human voice as they all stared at him as their noses worked. Then one slowly padded towards Jack. A dirty brown looking dog, maybe a shepherd mix, looked to Jack as a specimen which could have been someone's pet on Earth. This made the man think that maybe dogs and other pets fell through the looking glass into Elsewhen.

The two canines following the horse suddenly took an interest in Jack and began to circle towards him.

Bursting from the lake was the same smaller iguana lizard as yesterday. It lunged and snapped at one of the two circling dogs, narrowly missing a stable bite. The canine yipped and darted away just as Jack strode forward, aimed, and shot the Iguana in its snout. The lake lizard hissed and let out a barking noise before it began clawing at its snout. Blood began to spout from the nose area of the lizard just as the rest of the canine pack started an instinctive coordinated attack.

They snapped at the rear legs as if to hamstring the beast, then caught at its blooding snout when it tried to bite one of them. The substantial tail of the iguana bowled one canine over as the creature attempted to paw at its facial wound. It turned towards the water, and Jack lunged forward to slash at the tail with the copper blade. The iguana paused for a moment to turn towards the new threat. As it did, two dog animals both latched onto the bloody snout and began to pull it across the lakeshore. The lake monster slashed at the attackers with its front claws, and they danced backward, just as two other canines bit its tail.

Jack stuck the pistol and copper knife under his belt and glanced around for a large stone. He found a football-sized rock, pulled it from the sandy soil with both hands, and lifted it above his head. The monster iguana lashed its tail around as the canines danced about, barking and growling. With the creature concentrating on the dogs/coyotes, Jack was able to scramble forward and slammed the large rock between the lizard's eyes near the bullet hole. Blood spurt from the bullet hole as an artery had been sliced. The iguana, stunned by the blow to its skull, staggered about as the canines bit at its extremities. The arterial blood spurted more as the lizard had trouble coordinating its limbs in an escape bid towards the lake. A final stagger and the iguana collapsed. The lizard shuddered, then lay still as blood kept spurting from around the bullet wound.

Jack watched as the canines feinted and snapped at the lake beast. When it did not respond, each of the four-legged predators began to look for a body part to chew on. The apparent Alpha male claimed the tongue and soon ripped it from the lizard's mouth. As the pack chowed down on the new massive source of meat, Jack jogged back to his den under the boulders and recovered both the rifle and the Bowie. When he reapproached the carcass, the Alpha showed its teeth and snapped at him. Jack jabbed the gun's heavy barrel into the sensitive canine nose which elicited a yelp and a retreat.

"Get this straight, dog," Jack yelled, "I am the apex predator, not you. So, I *will* eat from this prey. Got It?" The man then circled to the rear of the Iguana and began slicing steaks off the tail. As he did, he sensed a body near him. He looked up at the dirty brown canine which had seemed unafraid of him. Jack saw it was a 'she' and as he looked closer, had a pet collar around her neck.

"So you came from Earth, also. What some steak?" Jack cut a chunk from the tail as he asked and tossed it to the bitch. She caught it, chewed on it, then swallowed. Jack laughed.

"Take the dog out of the home, can't take the home out of the dog."

Jack soon had as many bloody hunks as he could carry. He made his way to his den, put the meat on some flat stones he had collected. Jack soon used some harvested dried grass and another business card from his useless billfold to get a flame from the still-warm campfire coals. Jack feed some more pieces of wood he carved off a small stunted tree branch typical of high desert vegetation. In moments, he had a friendly fire going.

As Jack prepared the older meat for cooking and stashed the new steaks in the saddlebags towards the back of his den, he noticed the brown dog approach. This creature was no coyote mix, but an actual dog. The man smiled and dug out the few remaining pieces of jerked meat. He tossed them from where he sat one by one by one, ever closer. The female dog slowly approached, then began a slow wag of the tail. Jack chuckled, a sound the dog recognized as she wagged her tail more. The Earthman slowly presented his left hand, backside up, for the dog to sniff. The she-dog sniffed, then licked drying blood off it.

"Can I scratch your ears?" Jack asked. Then he slowly moved his hand and scratched under her muzzle. With that, the dog stepped forward and sat on his lap as if it were the most natural thing to do. The man laughed as he scratched canine ears. He looked closely at the collar. There were no tags, but the name 'Sheba' could be made out in the leather.

"Hmm. Sheba, is that your name?" Jack asked. The dog answered with a quick lick to the face. Jack scratched some more ear, then gently pushed Sheba off his lap. He recovered the tin pan and poured some water from the Amazon's small flask for Sheba to drink. She quickly lapped it down.

"Well, I guess I need to figure out a water dish for you," said Jack. He scrounged some more flat rocks, lined a small dug hole and stretched his tattered plastic bag over them as a seal. Next were several trips to the lakeside, ever mindful of the other canine and possible further denizens of the water. Using his plastic bottle and the small flask, he soon had the water hole filled. If it leaked, it was slow.

Jack also stripped some thick hide off of the giant iguana. He took it back to the campfire and laid the hide bloody side down on some hot rocks. Jack vaguely remembered some tanning techniques, thought he could keep the hide from going bad. Jack shrugged. He had a canine helper who protected the den, as she snarled when a couple of the other pack members tried to approach. Everything else from here on out was a plus.

The rest of the day Jack spent cooking the meat, hung some in a crude attempt to smoke it after he used pieces of the short trees near the lake and two ponds to build a crude meat rack. Sheba stayed near his side other than to leave to do her business away from the den. Jack surmised the dog had not been in Elsewhen that long, but long enough that she instinctually attached herself to a pack. He wondered if she was 'fixed' or could still have pups. The man knew he would soon find out if even one her former pack were gravid.

Former pack. The words had a unique ring to them and seemed accurate based on Sheba's attitudes since he allowed her into his new world. Sheba had been someone's loyal companion on Earth. She made the decision to transfer that loyalty to him.

The canine pack Alpha tore a huge leg bone with meat attached from the iguana and began to carry and drag it off. Jack thought there were either pups nearby in a den or the Alpha was going to bury and cache the meat for lean times. Two other of the wild dogs or coyote mixes followed suit with small amounts. The predators had been stuffing themselves with the newfound bounty all day, and would now leave to sleep it off. That told Jack they knew the lake contained remembered historical threats. Only the strong and smart survived in Elsewhen.

One canine hung back. It was a young-looking male who slowly made his way towards the campfire. As he neared, Jack saw he was not a coyote, and might just be an unkempt stray like Sheba. The female stood and growled a warning, and the young male stopped. Jack stood and petted his new friend.

"Let me try something, Sheba. I'll let you have the final say."

Jack took a hunk of partially cooked meat and used the copper blade to slice pieces off of it. He walked towards the young male. Tossing small pieces of meat to the canine, he approached. The dog ate all that was given, then lay down. Finally, he rolled over, showing he had young dog testicles. Jack bent over and gently scratched his muzzle as Sheba came up at the show of submission. She sniffed the male all over, looked at Jack, then walked back to the campfire. Jack knelt next to the male dog and saw a problem. Wrapped around its throat was a choke chain which was rapidly becoming too small. It was already tangled in fur and seemed to become embedded in the skin.

"Well, boy," Jack whispered. "We found each other just at the right time. That is about to choke you-permanently."

Over the next hour, Jack used a piece of flint to cut the tangled fur around the choke chain, His partial memory finally told him to look in the butt of the trashed AK for a cleaning kit. Using the screwdriver-like piece and the cleaning brush, Jack managed to find a weak link in the chain and work at bending next breaking it. The dog laid quietly as Sheba watched. Finally, Jack turned a weak link enough to break it. The chain came loose as the dog whimpered a bit from losing some skin and hair. Jack poured some wine from the Amazon flask mixed with hot water to clean the wound as best he could. He tossed the choke chain out towards the lake. Jack would let some vermin insects clean it.

The dog licked Jack's hand then allowed Sheba to lock his wounded neck. The man smiled.

"One minute alone, the next minute instant family," Jack mumbled. He looked at the male dog.

"In the power vested in me, I name you Solomon, Sol for short, as we already have a Sheba." At the sound of Jack's voice, the young male wagged his tail.

Over the next weeks, Jack expanded the den and searched the three bodies of water for useful items and material. He found a couple of rusty cans that assured his thoughts about this being a traveled pathway to and from the desert areas. Jack also found a larger tree some one mile away, which provided wood for an atlatl and a staff for a spear. The atlatl he tested with the two arrows and found he could launch them with sufficient force for small game hunting. Jack made a spear using the copper blade as the pointy end.

The canine pack came back once more to the iguana remains, and Jack let them. The survivor used some recovered skin and sinew to make rawhide chords he used in a small bola. Jack found it mysterious that he remembered all these survival skills but only knew his name from the papers in his old billfold. He looked at the photos saved in his cellphone before shutting it down and removing the battery. Maybe later, the Earthman would figure out a way to recharge it. Right then, the photographs were of someone else's life on Earth.

Jack used hot water and the limited cleaning supplies from the saddlebags to clean the Howdah pistol and the large rifle. Again, some arcane knowledge in his brain told him how to keep black powder and the priming material in the rimfire cartridges from corroding the two weapons. The man figured he must have been a weapon aficionado during his previous life, whatever that was on Earth.

The spear he made came in handy when a lizard snake (snake lizard?), something six feet long with a snake's sinewy body but short legs tried to attack the horse. The creature moved fast for being so low to the ground, but the horse dodged it as Jack pinned its head to the ground. It took a couple of minutes to die, then Jack cut the head off completely and tossed it aside. It looked to have fangs, and Jack did not want to screw with any toxins just then. The snake thing provided some tasty meat and skin for a belt.

Jack used the horse, which stuck around the water supply and human companionship, to drag the remains of the monster iguana to the other end of the lake. About that time, the giant condors showed up, and Jack wrapped the bola around one's neck. Stunned, Jack used the spear to finish it off. It took a bunch of feather plucking and gutting to prepare the giant turkey for roasting The carrion-eating bird did not smell good but once cleaned and cooked, it tasted just fine. The condor provided some twenty-five pounds of meat enjoyed by both Jack and the dogs. He kept the bones from Sheba and Solomon as he would chicken bones. The dogs already had a couple of iguana limb bones to chew for entertainment.

The smaller of the two ponds provided some Earthlike cattails which Jack roasted and also used some when they softened for cleaning himself. He had no toilet paper, and there were no corncobs around. Jack spent a day scrounging up some more flat stones, then dug a man-sized hole using the two rusty cans and a wooden spade he had fashioned from the short trees located on the slopes above. The Earthman pounded and pressed the flat stones into the makeshift bathtub, then used some sticky clay mud to seal the cracks between the rocks. A day later and Jack was rewarded with a downpour from a thunderstorm. The dogs huddled in the den as Jack used the stinging rain as a shower. He had created a separate rivulet to feed into his tub, which was soon filled. After the storm passed, Jack heated some flat stones in an enlarged campfire, then dumped them into the bathtub. Jack then slid into the water and soaked in his limited clothing. Jack knew he would need furs and hides or some clothes from live humans, not dead ones. Eventually, the two dogs stepped in and allowed Jack to perform a cursory washing on them using sand as a scrub before they exited and shook.

"You two do not know how nice this feels," Jack told the two dogs as he lay back to soak some more. Jack was lying in his tub, half dozing when he heard and felt a large object falling through the air near him. Jack jerked up in time to see what appeared to be a helicopter slam into the lake. The massive piece of metal sank quickly, but Jack saw what he identified as the tail rotor of a Viet Nam era Huey. Jack scrambled out of the tub, put his ragged shoes on. The two dogs were slowly making their way to the lake, noses working a mile a minute. He grabbed the rifle and the pistol, then strode towards the lake. The impact had sloshed water several feet up on the shore, and Jack looked for any lake denizens that may have been thrown from their home. He saw two fish that he scooped up and threw further up on the shore.

Some flotsam and jetsam bobbed to the surface, and Jack saw the body. He splashed into the lake, figuring any predators would be stunned by the impact of the flying machine. Jack drug the unresponsive figure to the shore, then rolled it onto it's back. It was a man in fatigues.

"Hey, buddy—" Jack stopped speaking when he saw a piece of the skull was missing. "Shit," he swore. One of these days, Jack hoped to actually talk to a live human in Elsewhen. A partial memory bubbled up, and Jack knew he had seen many bodies like this. Death was a part of his past life on Earth. In a businesslike manner, Jack stripped the uniform and boots from the soldier. He saw the rank and insignia denoted a Sergeant. The fatigues had the oversized pockets of the Jungle variety, and Jack found some treasure in them. There was an old .38 caliber Smith and Wesson revolver, probably circa World War Two, that someone had bobbed the barrel back to two inches. It was fully loaded with six tracer rounds, perhaps for signaling. But tracer bullets still killed people.

From the man's belt, he removed a survival knife with a serrated top edge. In another pocket were a Zippo lighter and a sodden packet of cigarettes. Jack did not smoke, but the Zippo worked so he could give his flint shards a rest. In another pocket, he found a flask full with scotch whiskey. A package of chewing gum and a soaked sandwich rounded out the finds.

Jack split the sandwich between the dogs and set the rest of the booty in the sun to dry. He dragged the dead body, now just in its OD underwear, some fifty yards down to a patch of soft and sandy soil. Recovering his wooden spade, Jack began to dig.

An hour later, Jack laid Sergeant Reed to rest. The dog tags gave Jack a name, and he wrapped them around a crude cross he made with two sticks and some dried sinew.

"Wished you had lived, Sergeant," Jack said. "The dogs are great but are not conversationalists."

Jack put several small boulders on the grave to ward off scavengers and then walked back to the lake. The Earthman cautiously fished out a plastic map case and a couple small pieces of light metal. Examination of the map told hin the helicopter had come from 1970 and Viet Nam. So as Jack had surmised, Elsewhen received people and things from all times and places.

Jack went back to the den with the dogs and wiped the recovered items down as best he could. He now had a 'belly' gun with six rounds to add to the Howdah with seven and the rifle with three remaining shells. Not enough to start a war, but something more to fight with should the need arise.

Jack checked his foodstuffs and decided that even with the recovered fish, he would need to go hunting in the next day or two. Jack gutted the fish and then began to slow roast them over the campfire as Sheba and Solomon intently watched. Jack had ground up various seeds, and some cattail remains to make a flatbread. He used the tin pan to fry up the poor man's tortillas, then divided a fish and a tortilla between the dogs. Jack ate the rest of the food and soon had a comfortable full stomach. Sheba and Solomon curled up for a late afternoon nap as Jack looked over the somewhat dried map. It looked like the 'copter was headed to the Vietnam/Cambodian border, so it may have been involved in the Cambodian Invasion if Jack's memory on this was correct. He grunted. Funny how he could remember arcane facts bit little about his own life.

The man cleaned up the 'dishes' then walked back down to the lake. Jack snared a dead fish that bobbed to the surface. It looked to Jack that there was no other monster iguana's in the lake, nor any sign of any other predator. If the signs remained the same, Jack might risk a swim and a dive to the wreck. The tail rotor looked to be just a foot or two under the surface.

Jack went back to the den and cooked up the recovered trout. He shared it with the dogs as he watched Day Sun set and Night Sun rise with the two moons. Things could be worse, he thought. The survivor had a full stomach and two canine companions to share some newfound booty. Jack called it an early evening and went to sleep.

Jack was up at dawn and relieved himself as Sheba began to growl. Somebody or something was approaching from the mountain range side of the oasis. He zipped up and grabbed the rifle. The recovered, 38 revolver was in a pants pocket as were the two spare shells to the large gun. Jack walked towards the nearer of the ponds and crouched beside a bush. He heard a horse snort as the two dogs lay next to him.

Weaving their way down a small game trail which passed the two ponds were four horsemen. As they neared the lake, one noticed Jack's den and called out, pointing. The Earthman saw they wore copper-colored helmets and chest plates, and a form of jodhpur pants. One rider carried a lance with a little flag attached. Jack surmised they must be a small military unit by their uniform appearance. He stood up, holding the rifle at ready and called out.

"How about stopping right there, guys."

The horseman reined in their mounts and one called out in what sounded like Chinese. The second rider spoke with an air of one who was in command, and the lead horseman slowly spurred his horse towards Jack, some twenty-five yards away. Jack could now make out their Asian countenances as the lead soldier approached. The man reined in his horse some fifteen yards from Jack and spoke.

"England?". The man asked.

"American," Jack replied. "But I speak English, as do you."

The rider nodded his head affirmatively and seemed to be organizing his words in his head. He then saw Sheba and Soloman as they separated and approached the horse patrol from different sides, crouching some distance away.

"Dogs, You have dogs," the Asian said.

"They're family," answered Jack. "Now, how about you tell me why you are passing through."

The second Chinese man who must be the officer in charge barked out orders at the English speaker. The subordinate nodded, then spoke once again.

"You-see machine-fall from sky, Yes?"

"Yes, I did. It sank in the middle of the lake."

"Any-people on it?"

"One dead man. I buried him over yonder."

The English speaker conveyed Jack's answer to the officer in Chinese. The officer barked out more orders as he spurred his horse and approached. Sheba growled, as the English speaker spoke to Jack.

"You must come with us."

"Why and where? And tell your boss not to draw that pistol."

The officer seemed to be cursing as he looked at the growling Sheba. The man pulled a revolver from a holster as he glared at the dogs. Jack shouldered his rifle as he yelled: "Don't!"

A shot rang out from behind Jack and higher up on the slopes above. The officer's horse screamed, bucked, jerked, and toppled over into the lake shallows. The Chinese officer was pinned beneath his mount as the English speaker tried to draw a similar pistol from his belt. On automatic, Jack shot the man from his horse, the large bullet punching a hole through the chest plate with ease. Sheba and Solomon charged the other two riders as the lancer tried to impale them and the fourth soldier drew a carbine from a scabbard.

An arrow missed the fourth soldier's face by a hairs breath as what Jack would describe as an Indian warcry echoed around the oasis. The lancer's horse reared as the dogs snapped at its front legs and then bucked as the canines switched to the hindquarters. Jack yanked the revolver from his pocket and aimed it at the rider with the carbine. A second arrow flew and hit home this time. The rider dropped his carbine as an arrow impaled his throat. The Chinese soldier grabbed at his neck and fell from the saddle. The lancer tried to control his mount and turn it around to flee. Another shot was fired, and Jack saw the lance carrying rider jerk and fall from his horse.

A stereotypical buckskin wearing frontiersman rode up on a large mount and lept to the ground. He was closely followed by a muscular plains Indian in buckskin breeches.

"Howdy, Pilgrim," the frontiersman bellowed. "Friends, so don't shoot us."

Jack looked at the dying horse in the shallows and saw the officer free himself from his mount. Screaming and cursing, the officer pulled a short copper-colored blade from his belt. Jack shot him in the chest. The Chinese man fell back into the lake and lay still. The full metal jacket bullet had penetrated the copper cuirass.

"That pistol of yarn has a bite," the frontiersman said. "I'm Mountain John. This here Comanche is called Big Wolf." Mountain John's massive frame and dark beard told Jack how he got his name.

Jack looked at the Native American while still holding the .38 revolver.

"I'm Jack Hays. I thought Comanches did not like white men."

John laughed.

"We have an understanding. Wolf don't kill me, I don't kill him."

Big Wolf dismounted and made his way to the dead horse in the shallows. He pulled a large Bowie from a sheath and began to slaughter the beast.

"We'll eat right tonight. If Dirty Mike don't find any more Chinee sneaking around. Sometimes they send out scouts first."

"Your friend is out looking for more people?" asked Jack.

"Chinee claim this oasis. Their traders come through here a couple times a year. They barter with people in the Central Mountains, people out past the North Desert. They are riled when we come up here from Freetown."

"Freetown?" Said Jack.

"Yessiree. We chased the Chinee bastards out, Well, not all of them. Just the Emperor's boys."

"There is a Chinese Emperor in Elsewhen," stated Jack.

"You call it Elsewhen?" asked Mountain John. "I call it Last Place. For this is the damn Last Place, I want to be!" John's laughter was loud and long. Sheba and Solomon padded up to each side of Jack and eyed the strange men.

"That's a damn fine bitch. If you can breed her, the pups will be worth a fortune."

Jack looked at Sheba and scratched her ears. Solomon had tried to hump her once, but she had rebuffed him with a snarl. Jack thought he had seen some menstrual blood recently but was no veterinarian.

"We'll see what happens. Right now, I'm just trying to figure things out. "

John paused for a moment, then spoke.

"You don't remember everything, do you?'

"No, I don't."

"Well, Jack. Some people come and remember the past, others don't. Some people can't handle it and kill themselves. We have people from all times and places. God only knows why. Hell, Mike and I were aheadin' to the Alamo when ZAP! We're here."

Jack looked at Big Wolf, slaughtering the horse.

"How about Big Wolf?" Jack asked.

"Near as I can figure, he was from about 1850 or so," replied Mountain John.

"How long have you all been here?"

"Five, six years is my guess. Time seems funny around here."

The Comanche warrior drug the body of dead Chinese officer from the lake as fresh steaks, the heart, and liver bled from atop the equine ribcage. The Indian pointed to the bullet hole in the cuirass and grunted.

"Is that just copper plate?" Jack asked John.

"Yessir. There is tons of copper around. The Chinee control most of the iron ore, coal and such, make steel. These copper chest plates are more for a show, though they will sometimes deflect a bullet or a blade."

John walked over to the man Jack had killed with the rifle.

"Here, have a look." John tossed a pistol taken from the dead Chinese at Jack. He caught it and turned it over in his hands.

"Looks like a Colt Navy, but with Chinese writing on it," said Jack.

"Them Colts came after Mike and me," John answered. "But a bunch of others at Freetown say the same. Chinee are good at copying things."

"This one was made for rimfire ammunition, John."

John chuckled.

"Yep. After Mike and me again. Hell, caps and ball were the newest things when we were heading to the Alamo."

Jack started to toss it back when John waved him off.

"Keep it. You killed the Chinee, you get the spoils."

The three men spent the next half hour collecting the spoils from the dead as the two dogs looked on. A few pieces of jerked meat were tossed their way by Mountain John, who belly-laughed as every bit was caught. All the copper armor was piled together, and the weapons divided based on who killed who. Jack wound up with a rimfire pistol and a lever-action carbine that was the spitting image of a Volcanic from the 1850s. It had been modified to take the same rimfire .38 caliber ammunition as the Colt pistol clone. The bodies of the riders were dragged some fifty yards away and piled high with the dry brush the men could scavenge. The corpse would be cremated in the morning, along with the remains of the horse. As Big Wolf took the horse steaks over to Jack's campfire, a third man rode up. Dirty Mike looked like a smaller and lither version of John.

"Hey, Mike. Meet Jack here. From the old U.S.A. also."

"Pleased to meetcha," greeted Mike as he shook Jack's hand.

"Dirty Mike gets his moniker from fighting dirty, not from not bathing," John said with a grin.

"Hey, I like a good bath every month or so," Mike replied

Jack passed around the flask of whiskey from the dead Viet Nam veteran to the great enjoyment of the men, even Big Wolf.

"Wolf here can drink with the best of us," said Dirty Mike. "He ain't like some of those drunk Injuns you see hanging around trading posts."

Dirty Mike looked at the former Amazon rifle.

"You got that off'n a big woman, warrior type?"

"Her dead body, yes," answered Jack. He then saw Wolf looking at the two arrows next to the atlatl.

"I took those off of a dead Comanche," stated Jack."He and the Amazon had an argument and both lost." Jack walked over, picked the arrows up, and handed them to Big Wolf.

"Here. You can use these arrows better than me."

"Thank You," replied the Comanche. The Indian placed the arrows into his quiver, then continued preparing the horse steaks for roasting. The three 'white men' stood watching the warrior as he used copper rods from his saddle pack for roasting spits, arranging them around Jack's campfire. Sheba and Solomon watched with keen eyes, drool forming around their muzzles.

Mountain John laughed.

"Those two will be well fed tonight, and they know it."

"Well, they deserve it," said Jack. "They help keep me alive."

"What next, then?" asked Mike. "You wanna stay here, try and scavenge from that flying machine in the lake?"

Jack paused for a moment as he formed an answer. He had been living day to day with the dogs. Maybe his sketchy memory slowed his planning ability as he had not given the future much thought past where to find the next week's meals. Finally, Jack answered.

"I'd like to keep whatever was in the helicopter out of the hands of people who may misuse it. It was a war machine, more advanced than what you and the Chinese have from what I have seen."

The three other men laughed.

"Jack, you have to come to Freetown," said John. "We have people there with flying machines, motorcars, better guns. That's why we fought off the Emperor from New Bejing."

"Can you get some of them up here?" Jack asked.

"That's our job. We scout, then report back about stuff like that machine in the lake. The city-state council will send a team up here to get it."

Jack thought for a moment, then replied.

"How about I stay here, and you guys go get this help. I have those two Chinese guns and some fifty rounds of rimfire for them. I can hold off another small patrol if need be."

"Whoa, Hoss," said Mountain John. "Next time, once one of the horses that ran away make it back to their stable at New Bejing, the Chinee will send a dozen or more horsemen. You can't hold them off."

"I'll stay here with him," interjected Dirty Mike. "You and Wolf here high tail it to Freetown. You hurry, you can make it in four days."

'If we don't run into Dragons," replied John.

"Dragons? You mean these lake iguanas?"

"Two-legged lizards," Big Wolf stated as he produced four small steaks on the metal spits for the men. "We can kill them, but they are tough. They are as tall as a man."

Jack stared at the three scouts. Elsewhen was becoming weirder by the moment.

"Okay," said John. "Mike stays here and plays cards with you. Big Wolf and I leave at sunrise, and haul ass."

Everyone grunted acknowledgment and then began eating their steaks. Jack started to feed Sheba and Solomon some of his meat until Wolf brought two large steaks for them. Jack laughed when he saw they were more substantial than the men's pieces of meat.

"We must keep these wolf cousins strong, happy," said the Comanche. "Their kind warned us many times of danger."

"Ain't that the truth," added Jack.

There were new steaks, and Mike produced two-quart bottles of beer from his saddlebags. The men passed the beer around as they talked, two very full canines now laying near Jack snoozing away.

"Watch this one at cards, Jack," John said as he pointed at Mike. "He cheats."

"Just 'cause I win, don't mean I cheat."

"I just had a memory," said Jack. "I played some cutthroat Texas Holdem' at a place called Las Vegas. I think I can handle one man."

"Well, if it's a fun game from Texas, I'll play it," stated Mike. "But I have a question, Jack."

"Go ahead, Mike."

"Some of the newer people talk about-moving pictures. They said these were stories about people like us three, Mountain Men and Injuns. Did you see them? Were the people in the stories like us?"

Jack looked at his three new friends in Elsewhen, thought of the dead Chinese soldiers awaiting a cremation bonfire in the morning. He grinned.

"They can't hold a candle to you three. Not a single candle."

The Day Sun set and the Night Sun rose. The ancient waters of the oasis reflected the lights of another passing day. The men may come and go. The lakes and ponds remained.

CALL ME KITTEN
BY ELIZA LOEB

He hadn't been sure how long they had been riding. All he knew was that it would get them further away from where they began, and for what reason? He had just barged into her room late in the night and offered his hand with a choice. He didn't pause to explain the blood or dirt on his clothes. He didn't bother telling her what he did to her brother, though the bastard deserved it.

Instead, he shut down his business, cashed out what funds he'd accumulated over his long life and destroyed what evidence of his existence that had once been.

"Where are we?" Lucrezia Markova asked as she pulled her helmet off. He had slowed for a pit stop at the nearest gas station, intent on filling the tank of the black 2004 Kawasaki and speeding off as soon as they were able. He had to estimate that they were somewhere between Alexandria and Richmond, given the density of the trees. Definitely a good distance away from Seattle.

"We're at a seven-eleven," he finally responded.

"Stowe…" she grumbled back and he rolled his eyes.

"What Lu?"

Stowe had forgotten how long ago the sun had set and turned to face his shorter companion. She had been narrowing her eyes with her arms folded over her chest. Her face twisted into a displeased scowl as her lips formed into a soft pout.

In all honesty, it was moments like these that caused Stowe to take a step back and steel his breath. He was never sure how to react to her when she was like this, without wanting to take her somewhere dark and secluded. He could feel his insides flutter as the thought of her bare and pinned beneath him emerged from the deep crevices of his mind. He reveled in the idea of her chest rising and falling as sweat trickled down her curves while she writhed beneath his ministrations. These sorts of things nearly drove him to the edge, yet were better left for a more reasonable time.

"You haven't spoken to me in over a month."

Had it been that long?

"Ah."

"Have I done something?"

"No."

"Then what?"

Lucrezia's violet eyes glowed up at him, unrelenting as they bore in to his own. What was he to say? What was he to do? He tried to turn his head to look away, yet she reached up to coax him back. He wondered how she saw him in that moment. He wondered what it was about him that kept her by his side, and why was she so trusting?

"Why do you question so little of me?"

Stowes eyes filled with a pained curiosity in that instant. And the smaller of the two hadn't been confident as to how she should answer him. Lu had little to no reason to question him as he had been nothing other than forthright to her. He never lied and never hid the truth without good reason, but other than that, they did question why they trusted so much. Could it be that he was real? Lu was never quite so superficial as to stay with someone for their good looks, such things would be a matter of ill judgement. Was it because he liked keeping her around and she liked being wanted for something other than someone elses incestuous desires or needs? She caught her reflection in the security mirror of the gas station and gave a low sigh. The person looking back at her was a waspy little thing with short black hair and skin pale enough for her to seem ill. Her brother said it came close to a mix between ivory and alabaster, and yet she saw it more as a curse. A reason to be touched by unwanted hands as he had proven to do. She began to ruminate over the last time she had been with him...the things he whispered and the way she felt. In many ways she despised herself for not leaving when she was able. But after she met Stowe....

"You make me feel safe," she finally answered. "I don't feel judged around you and you never take advantage of what vulnerability I allow myself around you."

She moved to brush a stray lock of strawberry blond hair from his face. Watching his grey eyes as they bore into her, as though he were a lover asking for reassurance that she wants him for him. She immediately pulled the breaks in her mind. Stowe was not her lover, and thinking that he was was a dangerous path to follow. And in that moment, she broke her gaze and looked down, nursing the self inflicted wound she had caused herself.

"That is to say I trust you."

Stowe wanted so desperately to sweep her up into his arms right then. He wanted to hold her close and kiss her in a way that said how much she meant to him. Yet he did his best to refrain from taking the situation for granted for his own selfish reasons or motives. He ached for her to make the first move and would remain content with what he had with his companion if she decided against it. She was a silly little thing that he had grown to endear, despite knowing how a younger version of him would never have dreamed of developing romantic interest, yet here he was. And he already had, despite himself. Needless to say, it hadn't been as though he hadn't tried to avoid the bloody endeavor. It wasn't his decision to be caught mid transformation as the sun set. It wasn't as though he were forcing Lucrezia to stay. And looking at it, he could easily have chosen any one of the models or Hollywood actresses in his reservoir and any one of them would have been at his feet as either a man *or* a woman. Yet it was this too polite little mouse with her too cute little button nose and her damn stubborn and bookish behavior, always questioning the reality of things or trying to make an iota of sense of whatever situation or person she came across. And he had been around her for so long that he hadn't been sure as to whether or not it delighted or infuriated him.

He forced himself to sneer at her, wrinkling his nose as though the vampire had placed a raw piece of durian root beneath it.

"A little misplaced, don't you think?"

"I think you give yourself less credit than you're due."

A long pause followed before Stowe attempted to retort. Nothing could be said. No wise cracks or snide rebuttles. Nothing about Lucrezia's character.

Given the situation, it was being made pertinently clear that his companion was growing more and more frustrated with him by the second. And usually, the two would break into an argument. He would try to make his points and she would turn it around with her own oppositions. Needless to say, Lu had been surprised that it hadn't gotten to that situation as of yet.

"What if I don't deserve it?"

A smile stretched across Lucrezia's lips as she for the very first time pulled the Nephilim into a tight embrace. She nuzzled her face into his chest and took in his scent, finding comfort in knowing that she was with her master. Her heart leaped with joy the moment she felt his strong arms wrap around her waist. She thanked the stars that the two had stopped for her to hunt some time back, as she had no desire to lose herself to her thirst. She didn't want to hurt him as the world had already done.

"Well, isn't this sweet?" came a voice.

It was unfamiliar to Lucrezia, despite being sweet with a venomous edge.

Stowe looked up from the embrace and pulled his companion tighter against him, doing his best to protect her, as a pair of piercing blue eyes gleamed from the dense brush of the forest across the street. And before he knew it, a woman with bronze skin and fiery red hair, clad in black leathers emerged from the darkened path. Her boot heels clicked against the pavement as the gas station lights further illuminated her features. Upon recognizing her, Stowe nearly lost his composure, releasing Lucrezia and dropping to his knees in apology. The vampire of the two looked up to study the woman, taking note of her gold tipped ears and manicured claw tipped fingernails. And from what Lucrezia could tell, there was no sign of ill intention, despite the displeased expression on the other woman's face. And as she pulled to a stop, Lu could only raise her brow at the air of disappointment that the stranger had been giving off. The woman glanced down at her and folded her arms before scowling back at Stowe.

"It would have been much sweeter if you had announced you and yours upon entering my territory, but I digress."

Stowe bowed his head respectfully, placing his right hand over his heart and refraining from looking up. From what Lu had been seeing, the woman he had been kneeling before had been his regent. And usually, he never kneeled—let alone bowed—to anyone.

"My lady Ariane, I—"

"Don't kiss ass in front of your Girlfriend, little boy," the Sheriff chided. "It's demeaning."

Stowe sputtered and Lu could feel her cheeks heat up. Lucrezia never once assumed that Stowe saw her as anything more than a supernatural ward. And even then, he treated her more as a comrade or confident than anything else. She took a breath and slowly released as the red haired woman began to pace back and forth, occasionally eyeing Lucrezia with a raised brow. Lucrezia however, looked her in the eyes with each time she passed her. Stowe, on the other hand, kept watching over the two like some sort of hawk. Unfortunately, Ariane took swift notice.

"Ease up, boy," she barked. "You're making my ex-husband look like a damn lion with how much I see you shaking in your boots."

Ariane turned her attention back to Lucrezia, waving what objections Stowe had been attempting to make in those moments before turning back to her silent conversation. Lucrezia could see Stowe watching her from the corner of her eye, waiting for something to go wrong or a moment where he would likely need to step in. Yet the moment never came.

"Tell me, little one…" Ariane directs to Lu. "Do the two of you have a destination in mind?"

Come to think of it, Stowe never said anything about where they would be settling. If anything, it was nondescript and left undiscussed.

"I suppose my master and I would have found a place that we found the most comfortable or familiar and wound up settling there."

"So if your *master* led you off of a cliff, would you follow him?"

"To be fair, ma'am, if my master led me off of a cliff, I would be saving his ass."

"LUCREZIA ATHENA MARKOVA!"

Lucrezia and Ariane turned and shot Stowe a dangerous look, forcing the man to freeze in his tracks. He had never seen Lucrezia throw such daggers in the way she had, yet proceeded to remain as still as he could be. In his mind he had hoped that no one else would stop by, or that the two women before him wouldn't look down. In general, he hadn't been quite so sure how to process the situation. He reeled back, containing his shock at the little vampire girl for speaking so...well speaking so outwardly to a damn fae queen.

Ariane, on the other hand, smiled warmly as she slowly bowed to Lu in earnest.

"A pleasure, Miss Markova. Please do keep the stupid boy in line during your stay." She whipped around and glared at Stowe. "As for you, Alexandru..." She continued. "Your new post is going to be along the East Coast where I can keep a bloody eye on you. I'll make sure you have a place to stay for the night, but for your sake, you are to take what is offered and stay where I want you."

Stowe, to his dismay, could not say no.

As the months passed and seasons changed, many things changed. Lucrezia and Stowe's identities remained the same and one challenge after another had been met in stride. The house that they shared, had been assigned to both of them by request. Lu would make meals for Stowe and then go hunting around night fall. They both shared equal responsibility around their new home and took on arrest both together and separately. It was, if anything, almost similar to the life they had when living apart in Seattle. But neither complained. For Stowe, it was nice to come home to someone who would smile up at him and ask about his day. For Lucrezia, it was nice to have someone who respected her boundaries and genuinely cared about whether or not she had felt safe.

However....

Things seemed to change when they had hit their year mark. The two were sent to patrol the docks of Brooklyn out of suspicion that there may be some breach of treaty between the local solitary groups. And while the two waited, they began to play a game. The game had started off innocent at first, and as time went on things began to grow more and more intense. Before they knew it, Stowe had Lucrezia pinned beneath him, giggling softly as he grinned triumphantly at his victory. His eyes then went to her lips as the giggling slowed to a halt and he found that she had been gazing up at him. Daring him to make a move. Her fingers trickled along his arm and paused at his shoulder as she bit her lower lip. She leaned up and brushed her lips against his, testing the waters and pulling back to see if her master would reciprocate. He paused, thinking for a moment as he moved forward and caught her chin between his thumb and forefinger, pressing his lips to hers as the smell of earth and peonies filled his senses. He could feel her fingers clutch at the front of his shirt as he pressed forward and struggled to discard his jacket. Her legs intertwined with his as she whimpered with need and he reached for the lever at the side of the passenger seat to press her back further. They both remained unsure of whether or not this was a passing fantasy, yet neither truly cared at that moment. But the moment Stowe felt the jingling of his belt, everything skid to a halt. He tore himself back and found himself panting and gasping for air. She was looking up at him with surprise and wondering what she had done.

Did he not want her? She wondered.

Stowe could see her processing the situation and nodding, almost in acceptance as hurt and disappointment slowly built a wall between the two. And he mentally began to beat himself up over the endeavor.

Once the assignment had been said and done, she avoided him. She hid in her room and covered herself more often. She only said a few words to him, despite his efforts of starting a conversation.

He felt as though he gave off the wrong impression by pulling away.

The time wasn't right.

The setting wasn't ideal.

She deserved a better situation.

Stowe began to place flowers at her bedroom door. Leave her sweet notes that portrayed his thoughts of her. Soon after she began to write him letters, sliding under his door. They would eventually go on walks and talk about nothing or everything. And sometimes, they wouldn't talk about anything at all.

"Do you see us together for a while?" he asked her early one morning.

"I never really believed in forever, Stowe," she responded.

Stowe scoffed and rolled his eyes as he then flicked a cheerio in Lucrezia's direction. "I never said forever, doll," he retorted.

"I said a while."

"Maybe till you're old and your jaw falls off."

The Nephilim gave a suggestive grin as he scooted forward, leaning into her ear as if others were listening in on their conversation.

"Then I guess I should make some good use of it until then, shouldn't I?"

Lucrezia could feel as Stowe's fingers curled around her hand and pulled her from her seat atop the kitchen counter. Her eyes filled with wonder as he led her up the stairs and down their hallway, pulling her into his room before closing the door behind her. He pressed her against the door and stopped her other hand from reaching for the light switch with his. His golden green eyes fixed on her violets, holding her there as he leaned in for a kiss. He ensured that she would remain pinned against the door, unable to escape him as he lifted her by the buttocks, never once breaking the kiss as he wrapped her legs around his waist. He could feel himself harden as she pulled herself closer, wrapping her arms around his shoulders as he laid her down upon his bed. His fingers danced along her sides and squeezed at her hips as his lips left hers, moving down to her collar bone and biting as hard as she could manage.

Mine. He thought to himself. *All mine, for however long she wants me.*

Stowe began to remove what garments he could as he left a trail of butterfly kisses from her clavicle to her navel, never daring to stop until he had managed to reach his prize, and oh, he was determined that he would.

He could feel her fist at his hair in anticipation as he tugged at the waistband of her shorts, enjoying how she writhed beneath him, whining and pleading for him to continue.

"Stowe, please…" she mewled. "Please continue."

Suddenly, a dark thought came to mind. "Whatever happened to *Master?*"

"Call me Kitten, and I just might."

Stowe rose to a sitting position and gave a soft sigh.

"I'm sorry, I forgot to ask." He moved to a standing position, walking to his nightstand and withdrawing a leather collar with a gold heart shaped padlock. Confused, Lucrezia sat up and turned to face him.

"Would you, Lucrezia Markova, be my Kitten for as long as you see fit?"

COLLOQUY
BY SHEILA MENGERT

The new millennium about which had gathered so many hopes and visions of a new and brighter world, enabled by technology, enlightened by reflection on the errors of history, and devoted to the spread of the benefits conferred by an interconnected and collective web of thought has yet to justify those hopes and visions and instead appears to reward precisely those trivial occupations and vain pursuits that least deserve our esteem. As the year 2019 relinquished the fullness of its summer days a reflective observer looked in vain for a unifying concept whether in politics, culture, or religion to arrest the nation's decline into commercial mediocrity and the stale and re-heated rhetoric of American supremacy. It was not a time when transcendent principles could contend with slogans and mendacity. Old alliances were failing even as despots promised efficiency exacted at the price of freedom. Demagogues were catapulted into office by disgruntled electorates. Once securely installed in office these did not scruple to claim auspicious and exalted titles for themselves. Honors were bestowed where least deserved while in America at least minority voices were stilled as unpatriotic because they dared to question the status quo.

This ought to have been a time for prayer and prophesy if these activities had not fallen into obsolescence. The seriousness of these former pursuits was now reserved for the utterances of the Federal Reserve Board and its decisions made regarding the optimum prime lending rate so that the economy could pursue its headlong growth to the detriment of the biosphere. Prayer may be a lost art today less from neglect than from the general realization that the divine has long since been trivialized by over-familiarity. If we could comprehend the full measure of contradiction entailed in the act of prayer, no one would dare to pray. It is ironic but it is religion that diminishes the inherent daring of the act of prayer by making presumption commonplace through memorization and routine. It seems that some sort of prelude then would be in order before we kneel, clear our throats, compose our minds, begin a preliminary search for proper words, elevate our eyes (under the assumption that God can be assigned coordinates in space), and begin to pray.

Against this background as regards prophesy an arduous search discloses as our story opens the solitary figure of Jonah (as he was originally named at birth when all things are assigned according to initial appearances). As the years passed after the birth of this prophet various contradictions first manifested themselves and then grew. Jonah had cherished for many years a negative attitude to the transcendent realm since it displayed a variance with his particular experience and identity. It appeared that denial would be the price exacted to reach a satisfaction and accord with God in order to discharge a primeval debt that had only grown larger through the years. Finally Jonah admitted that he had a substantial bone to pick with God and began to ask how to address Him directly.

The problem was to find a proper node or network where he might feel assured that his message had some chance of being transmitted intact without any superfluous editing or alteration before reaching the intended recipient. He did not want some vast filtering apparatus or set of ministers, ordained or otherwise, to soften various individual phrases, translate them into Latin or Greek, add various bits of archaic diction, or make any extra cross-references to an existing sacred text. These particular requirements had for many years delayed the transmission of, what for want of a better term, we will call "Jonah's Prophesy." He was aware that there was already another book in the Bible by one with the same name, but he considered his own work to be of the same tone and tenor. It might therefore serve as a worthy addition or sequel to the original.

With this plan in mind Jonah began to read and reflect on the salient characteristics of the present time, as any prophet should do before daring to compose a prophetic text. Ours is not an age that delights in doctrine or in deductive reasoning from infallible premises grounded in ancient texts. Indeed so natural has it become for the daily data streams to be called into question that any affirmative categorical assertion, let alone a definitive Kantian categorical imperative is thought to be an instance of overreaching and arrogance even if traceable to venerable and long-established institutions. Of course this means that the aspiring believer occupies the lonely post of standing in the theological equivalent of John Rawl's "original position."

The universe begins somewhere beyond the thin envelope of our atmosphere and stretches backwards and outwards in space-time to either a big bang or to some leaky wormhole from an adjoining universe. The idea of a universal regress however in space-time is as daunting to us as it was to St. Thomas Aquinas when he considered the problem. Sooner or later one comes up against the metaphysical question of why there is something rather than nothing. This fundamental question of metaphysics is complicated by the apparent fact that when matter and anti-matter collide, they evidently vanish and are transformed into energy. Is the former matter something or nothing? Of course existence is not confined to matter and energy but to fields and dimensions as well. In the last analysis the inquiring mind is confronted by various cosmological instances of behavior: things simply work out a certain way and mathematics can describe those ways by reducing them to stable equations and constants; but why these particular relationships prevail we cannot say, we only know that they act as they do. At any given moment of human understanding then, the world of existence simply emerges before us and demands our assent. Even if we are not satisfied in all respects by possessing an encompassing view of reality we can at least manage our daily lives and map out horizons for future research. Meanwhile we have men like Descartes and Husserl to help us to see the limitations of human knowledge and reason and to open the door to the transcendent.

To most religions of course philosophy is an afterthought. Philosophy may help to clarify religious concepts, but those concepts are often rooted in direct human experience rather than intellectual apprehension. When Abraham encountered God the meeting was exalted but simultaneously as informal as any other meeting leading to a dialog. Clearly any God, if He is to be considered from the viewpoint of His being a metaphysical absolute, must then have engaged in a vast act of condescension to engage with Abraham and others so directly and verbally.

Both Judaism and Christianity derive from similar intimate encounters. This intimacy with the Deity as recorded in the Bible had always troubled Jonah. He would have preferred a few more special effects just to prove that God was really God. He preferred that God act on a broad screen that if not quite "Cinerama" was at least equal to the broad screen treatment of "VistaVision." Jonah loved it whenever God smote (or smited) people or places and reduced them to ruins, pillars of salt, or at the very least caused them to tumble over dead at the precise moment that their sin was brought home to them. Jonah did not want comfortable metaphors to be used to diminish whatever ultimate reality was out there. If God spoke to various bearded prophets who smelled like sheep and goats and wandered around the Hejaz, Jonah could not understand why God couldn't speak to him with equal candor and directness. Jonah considered that faith was a binding contract and he deplored the way that it was presented by various evangelists as some sort of unilateral agreement with all of the equities on God's part and none on the part of the other contracting party. After, all a covenant should bind both parties to fair and open dealing and the form of those promises should emerge from adequate negotiation so that all viewpoints might be aired.

Instead Jonah found that he was already in a one-down position with God simply through his status as a human being. His source of knowledge was limited and dearly acquired. He was not subject to vast intuitions let alone universal agency; God needed only to will a thing to have it done. Only God could do that. Worst of all Jonah wasn't particularly holy. He wasn't overly wicked either, but he would be the first to admit that he could be a real S.O.B. on occasion. He wasn't particularly lustful, but he had as they used to say, taken certain liberties when occasion offered. He felt no particular need to engage in truly rebellious tendencies against God: there was no Friedrich Nietzsche or Alistair Crowley lurking within him. Nor did he desire some spurious New Age substitute for revealed religion. He was not impressed by Frazier's The Golden Bough either. Antiquity did not equal relevance. The idea of going about sky-clad or meeting in a circle around a naked woman in a grove of oak trees while wearing robes and chanting in Anglo-Saxon about some hypothetical Great Goddess seemed to Jonah to be carrying rabid feminism too far.

All that he really asked for was a religion that would meet any critiques imposed by British logical-positivism but without vaulting into existentialism with its practice of long Germanic word-coining and the circumlocutions of Karl Jaspers and Martin Heidegger. Most of his other objections to religion were confined to the practical order: why did bad things happen to the innocent while truly maleficent figures often lived long and luxurious lives and went unpunished, at least in this world. Even if they went about un-smitten, God could at least give them jock-itch or a really bad case of hemorrhoids. Jonah had brooded on these wrongs for many years but at last he had decided that he needed to as it were to finally have it out with God.

Technically as the challenging party Jonah realized that he should leave to God the time, place, and choice of weapons for their proposed duel. Normally these options would be handled through a party agreeing to act as second and conveyed to the responding party. Jonah finally concluded that in the absence of a designated second, formally and uniquely qualified to represent God, that he would have to proceed to God's likely local domicile and call him out to engage in direct battle.

So it was at long last that Jonah slipped one night into the Cathedral of St. Philip Neri in the Archdiocese of --------- when the Cathedral was to be kept open until midnight for anyone desiring to engage in private prayer. As he entered the cathedral the solemn majesty of his surroundings modulated to a degree whatever initial casualness and confidence he had brought with him as he marched through the streets of the city composing in his mind his initial diatribe. He realized of course the disproportion of his enterprise. Two thousand years of Catholicism had, in addition to numerous doctrinal formulations, created a legacy of art, music, and literature, one not only impressive but the foundation of Western Civilization. Kings have left their crowns aside to bear homage to Popes. Great wars have been fought over sticky points of theological interpretation. Inquisitions have probed under torture for deeply held if inadequately expressed divergences from residual Paganism and later on in its turn from any variations from orthodox belief. One does not approach prayer then or challenge theological certainties with a casual frame of mind.

Yet Jonah was simultaneously aware that the literature of the Old Testament honors those who wrestle with angels and protest manifest injustices, even before the throne of the Almighty. Truth may appear to be a gift but it is in fact an achievement and the outcome of contention between opposing views. God may have more respect for the honest heretic than for the complacent believer who is never troubled by doubts because religion plays only a marginal role in his life, rather like an insurance policy the premiums of which are automatically deducted every month. It was this reflection that enabled Jonah to proceed once he had entered the church. He walked therefore up to one of the front pews before the high altar and the suffering figure of the crucifix and began without preamble to talk to God.

Jonah came quickly to the point, "I don't know how best to address you but I think you should consider a radical review of the whole literature that has been written about you. I mean don't you think it's time?"

He suddenly realized that he had spoken out loud. Jonah looked behind him but the few lingering church-goers, evidently caught up in their own devotions, had decided to ignore his brief outburst. Jonah decided that if it was really God to whom he was speaking then mind-reading would be a fairly elementary skill for Him so the rest of his monologue was conducted in the form of silent thought.

Jonah continued, "I mean I don't want to be disrespectful to you or, what do you call it, um blasphemous, but I think it's time for a complete textual revision of your collected works in the light of recent discoveries. There isn't much about string-theory in Genesis and, I don't know if this particularly embarrasses you, but that bit about a dome of water over the earth is poetic but pretty poor astronomy. It doesn't seem much of a leap to extrapolate from things like that to a few other premature conclusions or cultural encrustations in the written accounts about you. Did you mean for everything that you ever said to be given equal weight? You seem to me to get angry about some pretty trivial things while letting other more serious stuff slide and I just need to know why you do that!"

Jonah paused before continuing.

"And what have you got against Hittites, Amorites, and all those other ancient tribes who just happened to be settled in Canaan before the Hebrews showed up? Why couldn't just one of your commandments have been, 'Live and let live?' It would have saved a lot of superfluous slaughter. I mean why not give people a break? And you should have known that Adam and Eve would mess up one day or didn't you figure that two people who were dumb enough to run around naked all day, without even knowing they were naked, might also be too dumb to even think of disobeying you. At the very least you could have given them a fair shake, turned a mongoose lose in the garden to eat the snake. Have you ever heard of a do-over? Maybe Adam and Eve would have taken a break to reconsider their choice and the next day everything might have been back to normal. Adam would stretch when he woke up and say to Eve, 'I just had the craziest dream last night. I dreamt that you were naked!' And Eve could shake out her long blond tresses and stretch and say, 'So what's naked?'

Instead look what happens: they get kicked out of the garden, they have two kids, and one of them kills the other. It's the first generation and we've already got a dysfunctional family! And it just gets worse from there on: angels come down and start sleeping around with hot Jewish chicks and make giants ... or were Adam and Eve even Jewish? The Noah thing bugs me because I keep thinking of all the species that might have been lost forever because they got stepped on in the ark by the elephants or the hippos. I used to lie awake as a kid and think of things like that. How for instance did the animals from Australia get to wherever the ark was loading up?

But I don't want to get off topic here. The point is I think you might consider commissioning a re-write or at least a consolidation. I'm talking about the big texts of course like the Bible and the Koran but that's only the beginning. Whole institutions have grown up as authoritative interpreters of these sacred texts, finding ways to graft their values and world-views onto new problems raised by new eras and to make them normative for other cultures. I don't want to be pedantic here, but exegesis and hermeneutics are really elucidating the full complexity of scripture. This more or less weakens the naïve single author approach of fundamentalist literalism.

I have to ask you if you think that conservative Christians are paying any real attention to your main message anymore or whether they just use selected quotes to beat up on certain groups of people or to justify various atrocities. I think we are entering into an age and a set of problems that requires something beyond what the old texts can provide. I'm not sure that people are really appreciating some of the more symbolic aspects and metaphors. The decline of an agrarian culture for instance definitely undercuts the efficacy of sheep metaphors. I think many people live their whole lives and never even see an actual sheep. If you are talking to an urban audience you might consider using a more familiar animal. Ritual purity and styles of women's fashion by the standards of older cultures seem a little antiquated today.

Suggestiveness is all in the mind anyway. In Victorian times even a well-turned ankle was provocative. Of course the really big problems are in social justice and ecology. Slavery still exists but today it's called wage disparity, predatory credit practices, and the student debt crisis. If things go on as they are a tiny minority of billionaires will monopolize most of the equity and purchasing power of the world. I think that you had a more communitarian vision originally in mind didn't you? You always said that you felt a special empathy for the poor and the forgotten. I also think that you must like animals; you made so many of them.

I think this might be the time to be specific. Let's take Brazil as an example. Of what use was it to the indigenous tribes of the Amazon River Basin who had cultures that were perfectly adapted to the conditions of their environment to suddenly learn about some Semitic King named David, the conditions that prevailed in Jerusalem two thousand years ago, and the rejection and death of a young reformer and that his death and resurrection was the basis of their own salvation. Their minds had never been troubled by these concepts, let alone their alien solution. Why not just leave them alone and you deal with them directly after they die? Were they any worse than the people who did get the word? Instead, what happens is this: missionaries arrive and behind them come various conquistadors and silver miners and before long the Indians are being worked to death for the profit of fat-cats in Portugal.

It hasn't gotten any better either. Now it's 2019 and some idiot right-wing, family-values, creep named Jair Bolsonaro has just been elected as President of Brazil and what is he trying to do but favor business over indigenous people's rights and the rainforests where they live are burning. Bolsonaro says that the fires were started by the NGO's which is just like Hitler when he said that it was the communists that burned town the Reichstag instead of his own people thereby removing the one threat to Hitler's assumption of absolute power.

Don't you think it's funny that every right-wing group, no matter what the country may be, is always conservative theologically as well? I think that the LGBT folks are like canaries in the coal mine, if they don't like us or worse want to kill us then I can tell what stance they will take on most of the other really important issues. Do you think that it is just a coincidence that one in three people in Brazil is now an evangelical Christian? In other words they are the same people who just can't wait for Armageddon to happen so that you will have to send Jesus back here to earth to start his thousand year millennial reign. What do they care if the rainforest burns in Brazil? All you will have to do is snap your fingers and just fix the whole thing, right?

Besides, they figure that they will all be floating up in the air watching the fires down below burn up any unconverted Indians and of course the residual Catholics who share the concerns of Pope Francis in his encyclical urging environmental responsibility as a moral issue. My only problem with Pope Francis is that he's just too nice to people. Couldn't you tell him to excommunicate some people starting with that creep, Bolsonaro? After all Bolsonaro has been married three times and he says that if he had a gay son he would prefer that he died in an accident. Is that disgusting or what? He also believes in beating young gay children to change their minds about being gay. How do you put up with people like that? And these modern day Pharisees claim that they are really tight with you! Are you surprised that people like me are alienated by religion?"

Jonah paused. He looked up and saw that the Church had emptied around and behind him. The solitude gave him renewed confidence and he continued.

"Of course the little stuff doesn't trouble me now but I'm not a scripture scholar. In any case I didn't come here to talk about you. I mean, what do I have to tell you about you that you don't already know? I'm not even sure why I came here tonight except that I'd like you to understand me a little better, let you get inside me a little. Would that be okay? Isn't that what you always seem to desire? I mean otherwise why mess with people like me at all? Why put up with our sins? You could just squash us like bugs or do like that kid in the old Twilight Zone episode and wish us out into the cornfield. You could time-transport a few T-Rexes and watch them gobble people like me up. So I'm talking to you like I can just, you know what I mean, just talk to you and I hope you don't mind because you scare me a little ... okay, a lot. But I don't think you really want people to just tremble before you, do you? I think that would be pretty shallow. I guess I think that you're above that sort of thing. So I'm like taking a chance here, talking to you..."

Jonah knelt tentatively for a moment just to see how it felt. It wasn't really all that bad. He kept the position for a few minutes and then placed his butt back comfortably into the firm embrace of the carved wood of the pew. "I guess this is sort of what your priests refer to as confession."

"Well, to begin with I always tend to fall in love with the wrong people, desperate people, even if I don't know them personally. I guess that I first fell in love with the model Gia Carangi during the two years when she was all over the covers of Cosmopolitan and I was still in junior high. After a couple of years she descended into a really bad heroin addiction and died at twenty-six of AIDS that she had probably contracted in the shooting galleries of New York City.

What is it that people look for in each other? Is it an ideal image that in line or shadow paints our dreams of a perfect union, or do we love what we cannot find to honor in ourselves? Is it a twin we seek or a contrasting vision? Perhaps it is a correspondence with variations like a musical score. Is it pleasure that we desire or a carefully attuned agent of pain, one poised just far enough out of our reach so that we cannot grasp and keep it?

When I say that I fell in love with Gia I don't mean that I wanted to sleep with her or anything like that. I wanted more than that. I wanted to be her or maybe not her exactly but beautiful like her as though we belonged to the same species because I just felt so inadequate all the time, so that even talking to you now, with no barriers between us like I'm doing, I still feel the same wrongness inside, even though I had my chance earlier than most transgender people to pursue my dreams. More about that later, even though you must already know a lot about me, because I am sure that you have been watching me for just a long old time! You probably know how everything got started inside me, things that even I don't know. How could I? I just found them present there from the beginning. I mean I am glad that I was born healthy and all that, but how could I enjoy it when everybody insisted that I act differently and feel different than I really felt? I had to dig down really deep and erect a bunker to keep the incoming mortar fire at bay.

But I don't want to talk about my childhood as a transsexual kid. Let's begin much later when the shell began to crack and I came out blinking to look at the world. Those were the years when Studio 54 was raging and disco and recreational sex turned the world upside down. I know all about how carefully you clock sexual sins, so I hope that talk like this isn't too uncomfortable for you, but I know that I'm not telling you anything that you don't already know ... about people liking to get off and all that. Well in those disco days people thought that everything came cheap and without any price attached, but sooner or later the bill always comes due. Don't get me wrong. People want love too and if you can manage to find both love and sex in the same person at the same time it's fantastic! But sometimes love is really hard to find and sometimes you love people that don't particularly turn you on. For instance there are lots of really bitchy women who everybody would like to have sex with but they're so nasty that nobody loves them, least of all themselves. And there are guys who are just walking crotches with handsome faces, buff virus carriers, the ones that haunted the gay bathhouses until they died. That's the power that sex can have. I don't think most of them wanted to spread the virus, but by then the infection was everywhere. I guess the reason I'm still here is that for me sex is an aesthetic thing more than it is a matter of fluid exchange. I hate that term, bodily fluids; it sounds so gross and sticky.

Anyway Gia Carangi was so on the top of her game in the modeling world in those days of my youth. You only had to say "Gia" and everybody knew who you meant, sort of like AOC is today but in politics. In those days though modeling was the top of all games for a woman. She made big money and as you know money is what makes our world go round, money, not truth. I don't think that truth carries much weight anymore. I know that guys who know all about you talk a lot about the efficacy of Divine Grace, but it's sort of like radioactivity isn't it, it's real but you can't tell that it's around except by its effects. Meanwhile there are other faiths that don't get all caught up in sin and redemption and just deal with what people can see and feel. They see you more in what you have made than in whatever exists outside our perception. Still, it is nice to assign a face to all this wonder and have somebody that you can thank by name or at least point to and call the Supreme Being. Don't you get a little tired though by just having people going around all the time calling you great? I mean it's like when a really hot girl keeps getting told that she's so hot; it gets really boring after awhile for her. I guess that isn't the best parallel, but you see what I mean. She already knows she's pretty. She would rather hear something about you unless she's really into herself and that's a real turn-off no matter how beautiful she is.

So anyway I just had this whole sort of Gia thing going and her sad eyes and her dark edgy look. She could summon up though a sort of freshness at times that was so sweet and innocent that it made me ashamed to look at her picture. I thought to myself that I had no business trying to be a girl when I could never be like her. I'm transgender. My name is spelled Joana now not Jonah. You probably thought I was like the prophet Jonah, the swallowed by the fish guy. (By the way, that whole fish story is pretty hokey). I mean how could he breathe in there? I think you should have a word with your editorial staff and make sure that they specify when they want you to be taken literally because there are people who think that everything in the Bible means exactly what it says. They're a real drag for the rest of us. For instance they're completely hung-up on Sodom and Gomorrah. I mean people are starving and shooting each other in this world; why not deal with those things first?

Oh and people are really messing up your creation. We withdrew from that international agreement to help preserve the planet because President Trump doesn't believe in climate change. Does he ever bother you when he is holding one of his little Nurnberg rallies? He drives me crazy! And what about that little gnome that he appointed as his Attorney General? Doesn't he look like he ought to live under a bridge or something with the other trolls? All of the Trump people ought to be in a carnival. Just you watch Mike Pence sometime. He looks like he's having an orgasm every time he can take Melania's place and stand next to Trump. They've got this little "me and my shadow" game going on. He's so pathetic. I bet you don't like him either because he used to be Catholic but he flipped over into being some sort of Protestant, one of the really flakey sort. You know, the kind that gets all teary-eyed every time you say America and just can't wait to condemn Islamic moderates while they snuggle up to Saudi Arabia. Go figure! I mean you probably don't even have to figure; you just know things. I bet people tell you that you are very intuitive.

That sounds so stupid. Nobody can tell you how you think. Besides ... here's a real brain-teaser. If we know things it is because we have to learn them, a state of affairs exists outside of us and by some process we attune our mind to some outer reality. But with you there is no outer reality until you make it happen. You can have everything anyway you want. Who's going to stop you? So I guess for you, as God, you know things by simply willing them to be that way and they are. So does that mean that you can never know yourself as God completely because you might just change your mind about something and then everything would just be reversed? What if you, metaphorically speaking, got out of bed (pretty big bed) and were just sort of pissed-off about everything and just turned the lights out on everything BAM! Everything would just disappear and you'd be left floating around in a big empty whatever. I hope you never do it. I know that a lot of people use your name in vain and pretend you aren't around and act all atheistic and such but I expect that they must know at some level that they don't have all the answers either. I think they are just afraid that you are watching them. I think that they would rather that they be the only beings that can think. It makes them feel closer to what people call closure. Life sucks and then you die, so just face up to it ... I think that shows a really bad attitude!"

Joana stopped to re-gather her thoughts for verbal formulation in her mind. She began to think/talk to God again.

"But I was talking about Gia wasn't I? Anyway, she was just one of the models that I would have loved to be in those days. I'm even talking to you now the way that I talked then, not like my real age. I was like most of the other teen-aged girls then looking for the perfect role model. My mom loved magazine subscriptions and we had everything: Vogue, Life, Look, Mademoiselle, Modern Screen, Cosmopolitan, and Ladies Home Journal. That's a lot of pretty girls and I wanted to be most of them. You see I got a double-whammy: a girl's mind and a dose of high-octane testosterone. Man … I mean God, that's a pretty deadly sexual cocktail combination!

Anyway I used to go in the bathroom and put on my Mom's lipstick and then just scrub it right off again. I used to be so disappointed at my own sad eyes looking back at me from the mirror. It wasn't until much later that I learned how to really transform myself, until I could look pretty good … but never as good as the models that I had worshiped … I mean really admired a lot. I'm a great deal smarter than I sound when I'm talking to you but part of me is still like a teenager inside because I don't think that I ever really grew up. I'm still sort of locked into becoming a girl rather than just being one. I know that sounds very existential.

So anyway, I went away to college and I majored in psychology so that maybe I could figure myself out and discover why I was so different. I got really into it. I read all the big names in psychology: Carl Jung, Eric Fromm, Karen Horney, Harry Stack Sullivan, Otto Rank, Fritz Perls, Wilhelm Reich… Did you know that Reich thought you could store up sexual energy in little "orgone boxes?" I mean talk about the perfect gift, the gift that just keeps on giving, whoa!

Anyway, none of those great psychologists dealt specifically with my problem. Finally I heard about Havelock Ellis who wrote in 1903 about a thing called Sexo-aesthetic Inversion and BAM that sounded just like me. Anyway his book didn't catch on too well except with Magnus Hirshfeld in Germany and the Nazi's soon shut him down so that by my era all that was left in the media that seemed to pertain to me was Andy Warhol's little coterie of drag superstars: Jackie Curtis, Candy Darling, and Holly Woodlawn. Otherwise there was only my abnormal psychology text and that wasn't too comforting. I was apparently just suffering from a persistent delusion. So I just tried to shut the whole girl-thing down. I gave away my bra and stockings, tossed my mascara and lipstick in the trash, and burned my wig. I was a boy again … but I was miserable."

Joana was quiet for awhile in the vast empty space and a tear trickled down her cheek. Somehow since starting to talk to God she had loosened up. She wasn't as angry anymore. It was sort of like talking to a friend, someone who might just sympathize and understand. She had never thought of God in that light particularly. He had always seemed somehow inaccessible if not rejecting to her. After she had composed herself she began again.

"That's was really stupid, me crying like that, and all. It was all a long time ago and anyway I kept coming back to being a girl so I figured what was the use of trying to reform? I started trying to find a way to just live as a girl. I grew my hair long, started to buy girl-jeans and tight little-tops that made me look like a flat girl who refused to wear a padded-bra. At least a nipple-show was worth something. Guys would check me out once in a while but I didn't take too many chances. I didn't want to be just another dead-tranny statistic. Finally, I heard about the few seedy bars in town that catered to a gay clientele and about the drag court system, you know, queens competing for titles. It sounded cool and I started filtering into the shadow world of the 1970's bar and club scene. But I wasn't into drugs and I could already see that some of the queens weren't living a very healthy lifestyle. Besides, I had a college degree and I didn't want to give that up for work that I could have done right out of high school.

So I sort of stalled out in my life; I couldn't move forward or backward. I sure couldn't afford sex change surgery. All I could manage was to get hormones and maybe get my breasts done, thinking that would give me just enough credibility to pass full-time.

But you see there is always something that might still give you away as having been a boy. I might get clocked in a grocery line and want to take my top off right there and yell, 'Hey stupid what are these? Do you see? I'm a girl!' But I never did. I'd just go home and cry…

So I lived like that for a few years and suddenly people around me just started dying. I mean they were young and suddenly they just started dying. It was called the gay cancer at first and then GRID, 'gay-related immune deficiency syndrome.' It was only called AIDS later. Well, that sort of wrecked me for thinking about sleeping around. I didn't want to die. I had just been very lucky that I had been scared back into the closet so often."

Joana was silent for awhile … remembering.

"Would you like to hear what AIDS was like in those days? It was a closet illness just like our whole life was closeted then. We were all like moths that only come out at night and circle about a light-bulb until they fly too close, singe their wings, and fall to earth dead. Only we died slowly, or not me I guess, because I'm still here. Only my friends are dead, only they weren't my friends really because I never slept with anybody. I just watched them from a sort of sexual remoteness, from the shadows on late autumn nights when the rain was falling. I wonder where all those autumn leaves are now. They used to float down the gutters to the corners and clog the drains. I used to drive home, west to the good end of town where I could live my little immune life overlooking Puget Sound. I felt sheltered then by time and guaranteed of my own eternal youth. When I arrived home I would wipe off my lipstick in the mirror and look again for the boy that I had tried so hard to erase. I couldn't afford a pussy so I just wore tight panties and jeans to get the right look. It isn't easy to be an ingénue five to ten years late but I pulled it off anyway. I used to stop traffic on Broadway and Pike in those days up on Capitol Hill in Seattle. I walked in my own little spotlight of imagined glamour, only they were really only the headlights from the passing cars.

A little money came my way and I bought my silicone tits. Finally I was right. They should have been mine at fourteen, but if they had been I would have been sent to some institution or enrolled in a circus I guess. Now they were my passport to what the queens called realness. I liked being envied in the bars. If I was any more real I would have caused a lot of trouble. It was my little revenge to offer what I could never bestow. I would come home later and take a long bath and go to bed on the couch in my sleeping bag and say my usual mantra, 'No one can touch me, nothing can hurt me.'

I could distill drama out of nothing during those years. I could get off on songs as though they were written just about me. I could absorb a character out of a movie and walk around for hours afterwards as though I was them. Maybe that's dissociation; I don't know. What do you think? I guess I was just a poor deluded creature of vanity. That's why I envied the ones who dared to do what I only dreamed about.

The death of so many beautiful young people was an accusation pointed like a dagger at the frozen heart of America. It was as though each life had sprung into bloom overnight in all of its strength and ardor only to falter and fail. The decade of the eighties throbbed to a pulse where everything seemed simultaneously possible and infinitely remote. AIDS arrived unannounced as though on little cat's paws. It sunk its talons deeply and rode about for years while talents were fostered and dreams were achieved. Then suddenly it leapt forth in swollen glands, a persistent cough, an inexplicable weight-loss, anything really that implied that the well-tuned bodies of youth were coming unstrung. In Africa the disease was called, 'slim.' Fevers followed on fevers. Eyes floated in a sea of unshed tears while every bone grew in definition and the skin once so vibrant grew pale and slack. Ailments arrived like unwelcome relatives on an endless train. I felt the presence of AIDS when I walked through the old neighborhoods that now never seemed to escape mourning.

Joana paused...

"I don't think there is anything lonelier than downtown streets with the rain falling. I shiver to think of all the places I have been in my life. I have walked to the very edge of so many abysses and turned away just in time. To be honest I miss the days when we were not as accepted as we are now. Incomprehension made us sort of scary, like vampires. People thought they could become infected by simply being near us. They didn't know that I was as squeaky clean as a nun. I never even kissed anybody! I lived in my head I guess, but isn't that where everything ends up anyway? It's all just a lot of electrical impulses...

I know you haven't felt this but with sex you feel it gathering like storm-clouds and then everything starts condensing and bearing down and Wham! And you're just lying there in the after-wash and he gets up and goes to the restroom to pee. You can still smell his sweat in the empty bed ... And the funny thing is [whispering] I never did it ... that's how good I am at imagining things. I can look at an apartment from street level and tell you everything that has ever happened there. It means that I need a pretty severe filter to keep experiences at bay. A little thing upsets me. People seep into me and all of a sudden I am them and I don't know who I am anymore just as me. So nobody gets inside me. I guess that it's good that I wasn't born with what I wanted ... yes and dreaded to possess just as much. I can't figure it out.

I pull my identities out of a box like costumes in a harlequinade. I dance on the ends of my strings and no one sees behind the curtain where I hide. They just toss silver pieces at me and I gather them up when the carnival closes for the night. The moon rises and I walk with bare feet along the sands and feel the tide tugging time away from beneath me. Words materialize out of nothing and I write them down before they can vanish ... And all the time I know that if it was tomorrow I would have written something different... Am I wandering? You should have interrupted me. I'm simply connecting the dots of discordant memories looking for a theme.

Anyway my roommate at the time saved up newspapers to recycle, but he never did get around to dropping them off at the recycling center so when he moved away I was left with two years of newspapers. There were so many newspapers that I made logs out of them and burned them. The sheets would peel up and catch flame one at a time as though a demon was reading them slowly and finding nothing there to his liking reduced them ash. I guess I thought sex was like that: a quick burst of flame and then the cold creeping back into my soul. I liked to read poems by Ernest Dowson. 'I have been faithful to thee, Cynara, in my fashion.' Was I Cynara? That would have been such a great name to have chosen for myself. It sounds like the name of a snake or like some poison. Is it a dreadful thing to want to be admired to distraction? I wanted to haunt the city streets at three o'clock in the morning and hear the ferryboats out on the sound, somewhere out there in the fog. I wanted to hide my face in a cloak with just my lips visible, scarlet and trembling."

Joana paused again to savor the image she had created.

At last she smiled and said, "I think I'm just saying these things to impress you or just to see if you are paying attention. You shouldn't listen to people who mistake poetry for prose. It was easy to mistake passion for reality in those days and then just watch while people faded away like mist and vanished forever. I would sit on the floor in my living room at night and reach across town by phone to talk to the drag-queens about the various dramas that they once had to tune into

Dynasty to find. It was clean and safe for me. I would drink bourbon whiskey straight-up in little sips because it was sour and harsh. I guess if I was a real fem I should have been drinking pink daiquiris in a bikini somewhere in the Bahamas instead of talking on a rainy night to gay boys living communally in the old apartments across town that comprised the gay ghetto. I guess it was enough for me that I was living in the clean and sparkling suburban end overlooking the water and the mountains whenever the rains cleared away. If I had been in Manhattan I might have been in a spendy up-town condo or out on Fire Island or the Cape in the summers. I would then have been at the center of the unfolding AIDS disaster instead of living on the outer northern periphery of the plague's reach clear up in salmon country."

Joana returned again to that realm of reflection where our lost lives remain unchanged and unredeemed in that inscrutable domain of memory preserved there in all of the blindness and inconsequence of our immaturity and flawed choices.

She began again, "I remember that I called Madeline to see how her roommate was doing the night that Cayenne-Pepper died. She had been the first to show any symptoms of her collapsing immune system. Madeline was my first friend in the community. When she heard that Cayenne was sick she had quit her job in the Tri-cities and come home to nurse her to the end. The funny thing was that they weren't even lovers. What straight person would do that, make that sacrifice, and take that risk for just a friend? Even families were exiling their children then. Nobody knew what caused AIDS in those early days. Doctors and nurses were coming into the rooms of AIDS patients like they were going into a nuclear reactor. Good Christian families left their children out to die on the streets while they piously listened to televangelists proclaim that AIDS wasn't a disease it was a cure! It was all part of the wrath of God, imposed, they said, for committing the unspeakable sin of loving across the impassible chasm of the gender divide. I'm always amazed at the various Christian family values organizations even today. I don't think I can ever forget how their representatives appeared on the various popular talk shows explaining why God hated us, overlooking the vast numbers of gay and lesbian youth abandoned by 'family values' to the tender mercies of the streets.

It was shortly after Cayenne Pepper's death when I started fighting for civil rights for us. I was about as startling in my own appearance at the time that you could get.   This was when transgender people seldom appeared in daylight. I was feeling my oats as they say. I thought I could be just like Evita and command my hometown from my imaginary balcony at the Casa Rosada and it would all just happen. But it was harder than that, harder because I think that people enjoyed shaming us and treating us like we were nothing, that we deserved to die because we were rebelling against the natural order, the one that said if you couldn't seem to manage in your assigned sex ... well that was just too bad. We should just suck it up and be what God or fate had made us. Even today it isn't much different. Transgender people are beaten up and murdered and proper health care is denied us because any alterations that we require are deemed 'cosmetic' rather than a passport to avoid ridicule and violence in daily life.

That was my acting-out era big time with big Tina Turner hair and tight sweaters and jeans. I spent every night listening to Andrew Lloyd Webber soundtracks and later on it was Enigma or Depeche Mode. Dark moods are cheap if the bad news applies to people other than you; depression embraced as an art-form. I fell in love with women and kept men at bay. Men seemed to have all the physical demands but no real ardor. They lost all interest after one brief tornado of passion while women could communicate by the slightest touch for hours. Their expressive faces and sense for nuance made of love a symphony rather than just a song. I know that all this has little to do with procreation, but did you really make us so sensual and communicative if all you wanted was just a quick ejaculation as long as it hits the right target spot on? Can you understand why women might prefer to love women? Do you ever listen to the way that men talk about women? Are the theologians really any better? It's all a matter of getting the penis securely in place at the critical moment before blast off; otherwise the duty to fill and subdue the earth becomes a sin. I've always been startled by that choice of words, 'subdue." Doesn't it imply that the earth might be putting up at least some token resistance, the earth seen as just one big vagina just waiting to filled? Would it make a difference if we referred to the planet as Father Earth?

This disparity of respect is the natural consequence when men are taught to view women as nothing more than occasions of sin or as easy prey. Does it take someone like me to bridge the gap of indignation by being both a man and a woman inside? As long as woman is viewed as somehow alien and only partially human this stuff will go on. I don't think that femininity is ever seen by men except as a threat. I think that's why gay boys get beaten up. It's because they are a sort of fifth column behind military lines implying that men can also be penetrated and used just like women. I think that is what you meant when you said that sexual sins could be serious, because when people are raped, simultaneously their hearts are broken, their will crushed. To be used and abandoned; I think abandonment is the greatest sin. I think we all want connection and respect."

Joana's memories were flowing in now like a flood and her past began to yield its deepest secrets.

"You may ask how I know and feel these things so deeply. I lived with a man once. He was an alcoholic and I never even knew it. Can you believe it? I let him move in as a roommate upstairs and we seldom ever talked. His room became like a little abstract island cut off from the rest of the house. I think they call it denial. When he moved in he promised to be my protector as a sort of side-benefit. He said that I was lucky because nobody would ever hurt me again as long as he was around and I was so anxious to be real that I believed him. I should have told him that I didn't need a protector, but the sad part is that I did.

Later on I asked him once if he loved me and he started to cry, but he never answered my question. One day he came down the stairs and asked me to drive him to the hospital to dry out because he couldn't drive himself there. I hadn't seen him for days but I would hear him upstairs so I thought he was okay and just didn't want to go to work. I thought that he knew his own business. Maybe he was sick; I didn't know what to do. So I just waited to see what he would do. It seems so strange to be now but that's what I did. I guess that unconsciously I didn't want to know how bad he really was. I was so alienated at the time from everything that I guess some amount of indifference was to be expected … or maybe I was afraid of him. I don't know. When he got out of treatment in the hospital two weeks later he told me that he would be moving away. He called me 'baby-doll' and took my picture by the couch that last day.

Later on I heard that he had settled in with a woman and her child. I guess he was finally happy because he had a family of his own at last, even if an inherited one. I guess he always wanted to be a Dad and I couldn't give him that. After that we lost contact until one day I heard that he had died. Maybe she left him. Maybe he started to drink again. Who knows? People come in and out of your life and you still never really know them. But the funny thing was that I was downstairs all that time when he had lived with me and he could have talked to me anytime if his soul was broken, but he never did. Anyway, now he's dead and I guess you're in charge of him now. Maybe you know how to heal the wounds that life never could."

Joana was very quiet now. The setting sun slanted through

the tall gothic windows of the church and made splotches of gold on the polished and worn walnut wood of the pews. Generations of believing Catholics had come to pray here, to be forgiven for their sins, and to celebrate Mass. The altar light burned red up by the tabernacle as visible evidence that the Blessed Sacrament was always present. "God is here," it proclaimed: the miraculous is honored by the genius of artifice but not dependent upon it.

At last Joana stirred and addressed God again. "Well I guess you've got the idea. I wasted a lot of my youth on living out a self-produced drama. I'm sorry for that now. I know the value of time a lot better, but in those days I internalized societal rejection like a sponge. It sort of took me down as you can imagine, but it just made me even more radical and determined than before. If the world doesn't make room for your existence you have to create your own space. I decided at last to selectively withdraw from the place that had been my home. I moved to a little town that had never had a transgender person before and just said, 'Here I am.' They didn't know what to do with me at first, but year by year they adjusted to me because they could see that I hadn't any other defenses, only my own honesty. Everything else had been stripped away, all my dreams and pretenses, even my anger."

Joana was silent for a time hoping that God was considering her story and might respond in some way so she said, "And there you have it, my life in a nutshell. Why does this gender thing happen to people? How do so many of us just shut down? It is only now that I am waking up again as though after a long sleep to ask myself the old questions once again. So I just thought that I'd come in here today and ask you this question: are you satisfied with the way things are going with me and well, with the whole world for that matter? I mean it's your planet, right? It's your universe even. Why don't you do a little smiting down here again like you used to do in Biblical days? This would be a great time for it; only leave the LGBT folks alone okay? We get smited enough every day! America is completely awash in real assholes and most of them think that they speak for you. Sorry about my choice of words but what would you call them?

I remember that the prophet Jonah was really upset with you once because you were a little too sparing of people that he thought you should go after. Well I'm a little like him I guess but my name is spelled Joana (two-syllables by the way not three) just like Jonah, the name my parents still call me. I don't want to argue about what stuff you might have done in the past or how messed up your followers have become but I'm getting really worried about the future here. I don't have any kids as you know but I do care about our earth and about the course that human history is taking. I think we all have a stake in those things and it's a real shame if all we do is fight each other about what we think that you want us to do. Why don't you just do another Mount Sinai thing like you did with Moses and say something like, 'Thou shalt stop fucking up my planet, like right now!'

I'd advise you to use really harsh language even if it doesn't seem particularly holy because otherwise some evangelical creep will just ignore it and say that what we should really be doing is going after the transsexuals and the immigrants and making their lives miserable. I think we should restore a sense of proportion in the moral realm especially in America, don't you?"

Joana paused to consider whether God would like some more specific suggestions. She reflected that the whole problem might be that God was getting poor advice from his advisors or staff or whatever passed for such in the celestial court. Joana had never really aspired to be a prophet, but then if she remembered rightly most of the prophets had tended to shun their vocations. Maybe if you wanted to be a prophet in the olden days you just had to start talking and later on if God liked what you were saying he made sure that it got into the Bible so it would get wider play. This was, after all, before the Internet and Facebook. Maybe God was like a DJ with good taste who sort of intuits the best songs to play and before long everybody is just dancing to it...

There was no light visible outside now except for the dimly reflected streetlights of the city. With the darkness the building had seemed to cool as if craving human warmth. She thought back to her childhood training. She had been taught that the Church was not a building but the Living Mystical Body of Christ made up of all the baptized faithful. She thought of how many people had left the Church to join one of the fragmented sects that claimed to represent a reformation of the two-thousand year old mother-church founded on the twelve apostles, the first bishops. She had never been tempted to embrace Protestantism with its sterile buildings, its lack of veneration for the saints, and its lack of full appreciation for the Virgin Mary. For Joana it was either Catholic or nothing. She thought of all the Catholic women and children seeking admission to America just as Mary and Joseph had sought shelter for the new-born Baby Jesus. She thought of all the ministers hailing Trump for keeping them stuck on the border or worse having their children ripped from their arms and put in cages. She thought of the contempt that conservatives had for Alexandria Ocasio-Cortez for pointing out how inconsistent it was to be pro-life but to always vote down pre-natal care and a living wage. She didn't see why God would ever be merciful to people like that. Worse still she didn't want God to be merciful to them. Joana made a decision.

"So okay, Lord, I'm going to just start talking and you can do a playback later and have it transcribed, if you want to, just in case you want to issue a new book or testament or whatever. You could call it, The Really New Testament or something. Not that the first two were bad but there's nothing wrong with a sequel when you've got a good thing going, I always figure, just to slam the message home. So here goes...

The Book of Joana

[Taken in down in the year 2019 by the angel, Amanuensis]

In the year 2019 the word came into the mind of Joana while she sat in the Cathedral of St. Philip Neri and she spake forth forthrightly unto the benefit of all who could hear her... [Editorial note from Joana to God: It's coming out with a sort of Mormon flavor. I think I'm going to skip the archaic diction from here on in. You can put the fancy language back into the text later if you think that it will help us to sell the message. I'm talking like I'm you remember...]

I, the Lord, have after much reflection decided that I have been silent too long in addressing my children with an extended prophetic utterance. Readers of the collection of disparate texts that is familiarly called the Bible will note that it was once my habit to inspire various prophets to speak in my name or to narrate various frightening and improbable visions in an apocalyptic manner. Interspersed with these were histories, poems, and collections of wise sayings as well as accounts of various pious persons such as my faithful servant Job. After the death of the last apostle of my Dearly Beloved and Anointed Son Jesus I meant to give no further public revelations until the Second Coming. I figured that I had left all of you with adequate means to procure the salvation of your souls. Imagine my surprise then when various and assorted later seers, who will remain unnamed here, came up with texts claiming to be amendments or additions to the Jewish and Christian traditions. Not that I abhor any source of wisdom; after all, I had long since made allowances for various epic eastern works of a speculative nature as to the complex being that is mine in the Upanishads and the writings of Lao Tsu and Confucius. I even looked the other way when the

Buddha, Siddhartha Gautama began his program of dealing with suffering by detaching from the things of earth and coveting a form of philosophical non-being that he called nirvana. I imagined that you would all arrive at some sort of peaceful accommodation of divergent views.

Finally, after two thousand years my head angel came in to see me one day with a report. After reading the results of a surprise audit conducted by one of my accounting angels I was appalled to discover that the earth was, well, a complete mess. So it is that I have determined to have a little fire-side chat with all of you through the lips of my servant Joana. I want to warn all of you as once I warned the wicked city of Nineveh that you had better straighten up your collective act or I won't be responsible for the consequences.

Quite frankly Joana is of the mind that I should not delay retribution but rather to strike at once a few members of the Republican Party just to let you all know that I am serious. To calm her down in her feminine ire I have caused a plant to grow over her head to provide shelter for her in the heat of the day. There a dissociated part of her sits brooding even as I compose this brief admonitory missive, bitter and threatening to jump into the sea so that she can be eaten by a big fish if I don't do just as she says to preserve her dignity and status as a prophet. Personally, I think that she has been taking a few extra hormones in her seemingly endless pursuit of transition, but I am unwilling to risk another tirade by telling her so. So while she broods I will speak and she can look over the text hereafter and amend it to meet her own aesthetic preferences. Of course the final decision regarding publication as scripture remains with me. Here is what I have noticed taking place on the earth, a place that is nearer to paradise then you might think.

I could let the text be confined to what you call bullet points but these might mess up the division of this book later into chapters and verses for memorization in Sunday school classes so I will stick to simple narrative. It surprises me that you often choose some of the very worst people to lead you, people who will never advance your desire for justice, equity, and well-being but who will instead do everything possible to enrich themselves and their friends and meanwhile decimate the earth. I think you know who I mean if you read Mother Jones. It surprises me that it has never dawned on you that I am a socialist and so were the early Christians. You need only read The Acts of the Apostles to discover this. But apparently Christian conservatives think that I am really just a big investment banker in the sky.

I'm also really into non-violence. In fact Gandhi, Martin Luther King, and I were discussing this just the other day and we all agreed that I should instruct Congress to rescind the latest tax reform bill. Most Americans only saved enough for a few extra trips to Walmart. We also agreed that Congress should sponsor an amendment to drop the disgusting Second Amendment to the U.S. Constitution or to pass some statutory program of strict liability for annual gun-induced injuries upon any lobbying group that desires to retain it. I would also like to make it clear that LGBT children and adults are not to be bullied on playgrounds or denied jobs and housing later on in life when they grow up. Oh and I'm a real fan of Taylor Swift's music. Try and just be nicer to each other: feed the hungry, clothe the naked, and get rid of those ridiculous MAGA hats, please. Oh, and you might tell the current President of Brazil that I will hold him personally responsible if he burns up my rainforest in the Amazon. Try and eat less beef, stop smoking, and try and get a little exercise every day. You'll live longer and most of you could use a little extra time to repent. I really hate judging people, but it's in the job description. As for the over-population problem, tell the people in China and India to take more cold showers. I like keeping my commandments short and sweet because every new commandment only increases your chance of offending me. Try and think up a few of your own and just seek to be better people. As your all-seeing and benevolent father it is natural that I have a great concern for each and every one of my children. I hope that you understand though that in a universe as large as this one, abounding beyond your imaginations in galaxies, let alone solar systems and planets, I have many concerns. To speak quite candidly and truthfully (and how else would you expect me to speak) I was of the opinion that if I gave you the rudiments of religious insight, particularly in the case of Christianity, you could manage affairs without further interference from me; but just to be certain I am in the habit of dispensing bounteous amounts of divine grace to guide and fortify you. It helps if you recognize seven sacraments instead of only one.

But to return to the surprise audit, imagine my surprise after two thousand years (a mere eye-blink in celestial time-keeping) to discover that (not to be too harsh) you have all made rather a hash of things. I had hoped that an inspired text or two might give you a few points of guidance to keep you from each other's throats, but apparently that assumption was ill-advised. I think with a few thousand years more of evolution the orangutans might have been a better choice as the dominant species on earth. They have a little problem with melancholia but that may be because you are depriving them of their timber habitat in Indonesia. I hate to think that I simply made a bad choice by making you in my image, but historically speaking it looks like I might have given the decision a little more thought. (No one ever said that I am not impulsive at times, just look at the big bang!) Anyway this certainly looks to me like one of those problems that can't be successfully delegated. I have hosts of angels of course but as one of your famous politicians once said, "The buck stops here."

So here is what I have decided to do: I clearly can't simply allow the consequences of your actions to fall upon you, even though that course is the most natural pedagogy to follow. You would then have no one to blame but yourselves if you manage to destroy the earth. As for other alternatives this leaves either supernatural intervention or a major liquidation of assets; in other words to just tell you all to go to the devil. But as you can imagine I am not the sort to accept defeat gracefully so the latter course is off the table. This leaves divine intervention as my best option.

So here is my warning to you: I think that Ten Commandments were overly optimistic due to their brevity. They may have worked in a simple agrarian society, but they are wholly inadequate to cover every contingency in a post-industrial age. It will take more specific guidance to turn the tide of destruction. I would hate to go all the way back to the era when plagues and afflictions were the only way that I could get your attention. I know it sounds trite, but that would hurt me more than it would hurt you. I really like erring on the side of mercy, but well, I would hardly be able to look myself in the mirror if I was incapable of managing my own creation. I think it might help if you looked into your hearts and attempted to find that lingering spark of divinity that I planted there so many years ago. Is it too much to ask, that you adhere to what might be called a basic decency? Once you get that down we'll talk about more refined concepts of morality.

Yours truly,
God

After her mental recitation which she felt captured in its spontaneity and basic friendliness how she could imagine God addressing his poor beleaguered creatures, Joana withdrew her mind from that special state of utterance and vision that is termed prophetic. The vocation of prophet is a rare one. Even at that though, at any given time, many false prophets will be going about peddling their wares. Their spurious concoctions lessen the respect due to the real thing in the eyes of the general public. It is sad to say this but success in the prophetic line is usually inversely proportional to its inherent value and credibility.

Not that being a prophet is easy. It is always a strain for a mere mortal creature to presume to penetrate the inscrutable mind of the deity; always something is lost in translation to the printed page. This discrepancy is always presumed to be covered by the guarantee provided by faith that whatever inaccuracies or approximations may be present, whatever variances from the purity of divine truth, they will not lead the believer substantially astray. God sees that his word is properly preserved although the fate of the unwelcome prophet, speaking to a recalcitrant community, is not one to be envied. The order of grace is above all pragmatic. The word of God is not uttered in vain. This is not to say that prophets are never impatient with God even in the throes of inspiration when one might imagine them to be caught up in some manner of ecstasy. Many a prophet has been tempted to decline the honor of being chosen to convey messages from on high to the humid valleys below where human passions reign and divine missives are not greeted with alacrity.

Then there is the whole matter of gaining general acceptance. This troubled Joana no less than it has troubled all of her brother and sister prophets in their turn. No doubt later scholars, if her particular prophesies are ever accepted by some designated faith community, will parse each phrase to see if the human element has in any way disordered or confused the primary intent of the ultimate author who is God. Those scripture scholars who presume to submit prophesy to critical study rather than simply blind acceptance seek to discover whether the writings are inspired as opposed to being simply dictated by God verbatim. The resulting text requires a competent and discerning community to allow its true meaning to blossom forth. There persist certain grounds for interpretation that require a guiding spirit, often embodied in an ordained hierarchy, to weed out spurious or fanciful interpretations. Certain factors, personal or cultural, may render the text less than the photographic copy of the mind of God that we might desire.

Joana, having finished her recitation saw at once that, as prophetic utterances go, it was far too mild. Where was the great and fearful Day of Judgment? Where the wailing and gnashing of teeth? It definitely needed some more volcanic imagery to season the boiling broth of admonitions. It was almost as if God was pleading with his people to believe in him like a recruitment poster that shows military service as one big party in well-tailored uniforms instead of watching while your buddies catch shrapnel or are shot to pieces in front of your eyes in Afghanistan after fifteen years of fruitless engagement.

It seemed to Joana that real prophesy needed a little more pizzazz if it was to gain general acceptance. She should have brought a written draft with her instead of trusting to the inspiration of the moment. Narration has its own tricks. One of the best devices was to pick a natural and inevitable disaster and to read into it a deliberative intent like the destruction of Sodom and Gomorrah for being a little too imaginative in sexual expression instead of blaming the city fathers for building the cities in an undesirable location. After all, what about Pompeii?

To spice up her own work Joana thought of an idea. As Hurricane Dorian approached Florida Joana thought of an ideal location for it to make landfall. It might be an amusing sight for people to throw paper towels at the President for a change and trivialize his losses with absurd symbols. Now that she thought of it, any number of things made her crazy and roused her ire and a desire for some sort of payback. She had long kept these things close to her heart. Now they could be focused on the appropriate targets. This would include various types of conservative evangelicals: phony faith-healers, televangelists living in multi-million dollar homes and with their own private jets, and conservative news commentators who saw nothing contrary in the proclamation that the real King of Israel is Donald Trump as opposed to reserving that appellation for the humble Jesus of Nazareth.

Who was the best living example of the prosperity gospel in action if not Mister Prosperity himself who can fire anyone no matter what their exalted position in his cabinet at a whim, made public on Twitter? Real power after all is lies in the ability to act arbitrarily without consequences. Who could best judge the proffered word of God if not the man whose vast education has revealed to him the very best words, like "You're fired?"

And what about the cheering throngs at his rallies? Could any right-thinking person imagine that these good folk were misled when they proclaimed His Trumpiness to be God's choice to run America? Where would white prosperity be in America if we allowed it to be diluted by extending charity to the homeless women and children refugees driven from their countries by the dug-lords financed by America's addictions? We already have enough dependants of our own. Didn't the Lord's ministers know just who God perceived as the sheep and who God perceived as the goats?

This was America in 2019 as the majority of Americans, those who had not voted for the Donald Trump, watched in horror every day as America devolved into an anti-intellectual morass. It was definitely time for a new prophet but Joana? Why would God ever pick a transgender person (as if such a thing was even possible, a man is a man and a woman is a woman) to tell her those who know that they are saved how God felt about the direction the world was taking at this late date of 2019? Wasn't the millennium at the very gate now that Israel was restored? With a little careful handling Armageddon might break out any minute. Donald Trump was just the guy needed, at the right time and place to light the fuse of global conflagration and bring on the rapture for the elect. When seen in this light, Joana, not less than the four women referred to as "The Squad," was a clear and present danger to America, little better than Hilary Clinton. Surely Republican led providence would intervene in time. Was it any mere coincidence then that the lights in the cathedral were suddenly extinguished at the precise moment when Joana had just completed her oration of her pretended book of prophesies? Such darkness! It was as though the entire sacred space became the metaphorical equivalent of the belly of a great fish and in that belly Joana now reposed.

After her initial surprise and natural trepidation at being thus deprived of light, Joana allowed her thoughts to turn inward to seek the reason why she had been deprived of that one most essential aspect of life, the light of God. She wasn't sure what to expect now. Had she been guilty of the worst form of overreaching in daring to pray in this direct fashion? How would God manifest his discontent if not by withdrawing his grace and guidance? Where had her wayward thoughts come from in the first place? Is it ever possible for a sinner to channel God's word? Who was she to think that she could hold herself out as a prophet?

When she had entered the cathedral it was primarily to seek personal understanding and affirmation, to discover if there is an ultimate witness and guarantor of our uniqueness and value in the face of constant alteration and change. If there was no God then, Joana thought, we are all thrown back into a mere cacophony of assertion and counter-assertion. What was history but one long set of oppositions without any final resolution? How could there be any resolution without a point of absolute stasis to exercise its majestic sense of moral gravitation and awesome peace? Wasn't this what was meant by the long slow utterance of the majestic syllable Om? Why should we expect God as the great universal to manifest himself to us in particularity? Yet wasn't that precisely what Christianity had claimed to be the essence of its faith, that Jesus was Lord, simultaneously both God and Man? This was its great and unique innovation: that being human mattered, that we are not a cosmic disgrace. Is it possible that God likes us?

If so then why, Joana thought, had she been plunged into darkness? Was this darkness any different from the shame and exile that had for so long beset her? Joana had always felt that she was living a parallel life from the one that she should have had rather like someone who has taken a wrong exit from the freeway and ended up on one of America's endless but futile back highways, the ones sketched like blue veins on the road atlases. How did some people manage to connect to one of the great ski-lifts that exalt them from obscurity to fame and fortune? Not that fame and fortune are everything; but why shouldn't she have her own combination mascara and lip-gloss and make millions from her Internet followers, JOANA COSMETICS.

Instead here she was trying to break into the old prophesy game with only God to listen to her. God was having his own branding problems. It was getting so churches were sort of like brick and mortar retail outlets, closing every day. The only way to make religion pay was to go digital or to operate a media empire, hire a few fat guys in powder-blue suits telling America that women's restrooms were being besieged by millions of men in cheap thrift-shop dresses and thirty dollar wigs who were claiming to be transgender for the day just so they could sneak a peek. There's trouble in River City for you! She thought about how hard it was to be transgender; the statistics didn't lie. No doubt about it, America was committed to gender bi-polarity; no mix-and-match allowed. After you left the coastal blue states you took your chances as a trans-person. Naturally this state of affairs had left Joana a little bitter and that bitterness translated itself into a desire to rain curses and imprecations on the self-complacent purveyors of "Gospel values." It seemed to her that fundamentalism had missed the fact the religion is mystery rather than knowledge. The comfortable and crude Gnosticism that denied anything not found in some individual verse of the authoritative bible while missing the message of the whole made her furious. Even from a more sophisticated and universal point of view, one open to discovery, the seeker was brought up short by the fact that so much of dogmatic theology is the proclamation that two contraries can both be affirmed simultaneously. Theological questions are not so much resolved by such answers as frozen into place in a matrix of belief by the very act of presentation.   How does the individual interface with two thousand years of theological conflict? Was there a more direct path through and around so many contentious offerings?   Is it even possible to locate the source of our discontent in the comfortable way that Sigmund Freud had in his book, The Future of an Illusion? Religion did not seem illusory to Joana; it affected world politics on a daily basis. Its various contentions might just result in the next world war. Of course economics always plays its part as well. What would the ubiquitous Christian broadcasting networks be without well-healed sponsors? Conservative Christianity wasn't so much about relieving anxiety anymore, Freud's "the opium of the masses." Most of the audience already knew that they were saved. The whole point of evangelical Christianity had shifted away from individual salvation to the proclamation of who was not going to be saved. This inversion seemed to her so contrary to the evident intent of Jesus that she could not believe that so many Christians seemed oblivious to it. If the whole point of salvation history was to vindicate the offended dignity of God, then who was God anyway? If God cherished offenses, then who could hope to stand before God? How could they believe that God was so petty and cheap, so insecure that he needed to vindicate his dignity by squashing the very people who were most pitiful because of their sins? Surely this was to take the name of the Lord in vain if anything was.

This explained hateful religious rhetoric and the central importance in American life of always having someone to feel superior to: racial minorities, the homeless, or best of all the whole lavender crowd in all of its various manifestations. This also explained the disconnect between the conservative Christians' supposed reverence for life while it reposed in the womb and their utter contempt for poor children who might get a free and nutritious lunch at public expense or any publicly funded pre-natal care so that the baby might be born healthy. Was it any wonder that most of the Republican base was drawn from people beset by envy and convinced that only insults and petty meanness could deliver them from some democrat out to pick their pocket? It had always seemed strange to Joana that oil depletion allowances for corporations aren't socialism but public education and Medicare are.

"The real problem rests with us," she thought. "In our blindness we are seeking an answer when it is already around us reaching into every crevasse of our being just as air seeks to fill every vacuum. We are loved!" In an instant her anger at God vanished and she felt how sad it was that she had not long since affirmed as Henry David Thoreau once did when he was asked during his final illness if he had made his peace with God. Thoreau's answer was, "I was not aware that we had ever quarreled." If this was so then Joana realized that her indignation was pointless if it was directed at God. Any answer that God might give her had preceded the asking of her question. It was pointless to pray for acceptance if one was already accepted, to ask for love if one was already loved, to seek immortality if one's soul was already immortal.

She did not turn to see if she was still alone in the cathedral. Was her lament any different from that of others who might have left the busy streets that night one at a time to seek God's presence in this special place set aside for divine worship? The shadows of mistrust began to lift.

"I have wasted so much time!" she cried out and her voice of lamentation echoed from the dim recesses of the gothic vault upwards to the empty choir loft.

"Where has my life gone? I was always so unprepared for everything and now it's too late for me!"

Joana saw her days and nights cascading downwards and adhering to her in their sheer irrevocability, frozen like a glacier into immobility. Could anything ever deliver her from the brittle etching into slate of every thought she had ever entertained, every action she had taken, each decision she had made however trivial and indubitable it had once seemed? All certainties seemed to vanish before her like water in the desert. She was left alone as only prophets are ever left alone, to trust in darkness the witness that they give to others of what has been revealed to them alone. To enter the desert is the most risky thing that a human being can ever undertake.

"No one takes this upon themselves unless they are called to it," Joana reflected. "Was my calling always inherent in my confusion? If I had known who I was and if love simply blossomed from within me with the usual certainty that comes from an automatic congruity of sex would I ever have become the person that I turned out to be? Was my life the exercise of freedom or the living out of some pre-ordained plan the nature of which is only now being revealed within me from behind the veil of circumstance?"

Her thoughts hovered over the same abyss as that described by Dante in the first Canto of The Divine Comedy where he says that he came to himself in a dark wood where the true way was lost. Sooner or later everyone finds his or her way there. Despair beckons and the adversary is very near at hand. Human life for all of our differences is a universal—our interface with the absolute.

Only a single phrase came back to comfort her now in her darkness. She could not think where she had first heard it.

"Behold, I make all things new."

And with that recollection whatever glitch in the electrical circuitry of the cathedral had caused the blackout was evidently repaired by someone because inexplicably, or maybe providentially, the lights suddenly came back on and Joana, the transsexual and would-be prophetess, was restored to her fellow human beings in the land of the living.

AMARI
BY CARRIE AVERY MORIARTY

This is it," Kevin said. "The most beautiful place in the world."

"It is pretty," Jessie said. "But I'm not sure it's the most beautiful."

"Seriously?" Kevin scoffed. "Where have you been where the natural beauty was better than this?"

"I dunno," she replied. "I mean, there have to be some amazing places all around the world that you haven't seen, right?"

"Sure," he replied.

"So, then," she continued. "It could be that you just haven't seen the most beautiful place."

"I suppose," he said. "But of all the places I've been to, this one is spectacular."

"I'll give you that," she agreed.

"Let's go down," he suggested.

They took the trail that sloped down to the lake, simply enjoying the surroundings. With it being early, they could hear the call of the birds through the trees, the chatter of chipmunks racing around the undergrowth, and the hum of insects collecting nectar from the flowers on the edges of the trail. Within minutes, they found themselves in a meadow that sloped gently toward the lake.

"You're sure we can eat here?" she asked.

"I do it all the time," he replied. "As long as we take out what we brought in, we're good."

"It's just that most parks ask that you stay on the marked paths and not venture into areas like this," she said.

"Do you see any signs indicating we can't use the meadow as a picnic area?"

Jessie looked around, not seeing really much of any life. Shrugging, she said, "I guess we're good."

"Like I said," he began. "I do this all the time."

He spread the blanket out on the grass, then set the basket on one corner.

"Sit," he said, patting the blanket next to himself.

Jessie complied, sitting down and taking the sandwich he offered her. Biting into it, she savored the flavors of marmalade and peanut butter as they blended together.

"When we're done, we can swim," he said.

"Thought you weren't supposed to swim for half an hour after eating," she said.

"We can wade in, though," he said. "Take some of the heat out of ourselves. Get a little of that mountain refreshment from the water."

Jessie had to admit, even if it was just to herself, that this was a pretty romantic trip he'd planned. While she didn't know him well, they'd shared a few dates and found themselves to be fairly compatible. Maybe this would last.

"Have some lemonade," he said, offering her a glass.

She sipped it, but it didn't taste quite right.

"What's in this?" she asked.

"Special recipe," he said. "I make it myself. It's got lavender and mint in it. You're probably tasting the mint, since that's the strongest flavor."

"It's not bad, but definitely different," she said, taking another sip.

"Glad you like it," he said. "I've got plenty if you want more."

They spent the next few minutes in companionable silence as they ate their lunch.

"Ready for that dip in the lake?" Kevin asked.

"I'm actually thinking a nap in the sun might be nice," Jessie suggested.

"You rest," he said. "I'm going to check the water and see what it's like."

The screams woke her. She bolted up, looking around. Blinking, she got her bearings, remembering the hike up to the lake, the lunch, and the nap. It was silent, now. She looked around for Kevin, but didn't see him anywhere. Then she remembered the lake. He'd said he was going to go take a dip, so she decided to head down there and see if she could see him.

As she rose, she realized that not only had the screaming stopped, but there were no other sounds, either. Looking back and forth, she watched the landscape to see if she could see any movement. The stillness was eerie and unsettling. Slowly, she moved toward the lake, hoping to catch something, anything to ease the fear that was swiftly rising within her.

The lake was like glass. No wind blew. Nothing made a sound around her. Everything was still. Looking into the water, she could see that there were fish under the surface, but they were frozen in place.

"Help," she shouted, hearing her voice echo back from the mountains around her. Other than that, she was met with silence.

Backing away from the lake, she moved to where she had been

sleeping and picked up her phone. Pressing the button to bring it to life, she was met with a black screen. Shaking it and pressing every button she could, using the fingerprint scanner to try to get some reaction from it did nothing. Fear began to grip her as she tried to find Kevin's phone. When she did, she had the same result, simply a black screen.

"Help," she called again, only to be met with nothing but the echo of her own voice once again.

Her breathing was rapid and she could feel her heart pounding in her chest, but still nothing around her moved. She tried the phones again, hoping desperately to get a reaction from either of them so she could call for help, but they remained void of life.

"This has to be a dream," she muttered, trying to reassure herself. "This can't be real."

Panic was building in her as she grabbed her things, along with Kevin's car keys, and practically ran toward the trail that would lead her back to the car. There hadn't been many people on the trail when they first arrived, so she wasn't expecting to see anyone on the way back, either. As she rounded a bend in the trail, she froze. There, in the middle of the trail, frozen like the landscape around her, was a mountain lion. Jessie held still, sure the creature would smell her and turn to attack. She waited several long minutes, but the lion never moved.

Carefully, she eased closer to the beast, not wanting to have whatever spell had befallen the world to release its hold and put her in perilous danger. Once past the creature, she quickly ran down the trail toward the parking lot.

Jessie halted abruptly as she stepped from the trailhead. The lot where they'd parked was empty. Not only was Kevin's car gone, but the other few that had been there when they'd arrived were also missing.

"Help," she called again, hoping for some response. Again she was met with only silence.

Pulling the keys from her pocket, she pressed the lock button on the fob. What she hoped to accomplish with this was unclear, but she heard the distinct horn sound, albeit muffled. Pressing it again, she tried to distinguish where the sound was coming from. Muffled, yet audible, she determined the car must be close. Stepping into the lot, she pressed the button again, moving closer to where they'd parked. It sounded as if the car was still there, just hidden by something. Standing in front of the stall where they parked, she again used the fob to confirm the car was there. Sure enough, she heard the honk of the horn. She also heard muffled voices, but couldn't figure out where they were coming from.

Closing her eyes, she focused hard on the sound. Slowly she began to make out individual voices, but still couldn't clearly determine what they were saying. Focusing harder, she picked up one from the others. It was Kevin, she was sure.

"Kevin," she shouted, hoping to break through whatever was keeping her in this frozen landscape.

"I heard her," she heard him say.

"Where is she?" another voice asked.

"Jessie," he called.

"I'm here," she shouted. "I can't see you, though."

"Jess," he shouted again.

"Kevin," she shouted.

Silence once again enveloped her.

"Kevin," she screamed as sobs began to take her over.

She knew something was wrong, but couldn't figure out how she got to where she was, nor how to fix the problem. Never in her life had she been so scared. She crumpled to the ground, overcome with the emotions of it all.

"I swear I heard her," Kevin said to the officer.

"I know," the officer replied.

"Where is she?" Kevin pleaded.

"We'll find her," the officer said.

"Argh," Kevin grumbled in frustration.

Just then, another officer approached with a woman Kevin could only describe as eclectic. Her hair was wild around her head, with a swath of colored fabric holding it back from her face. The top she wore was full of swirls and swoops of purples and pinks and reds. Her skirt had stripes in every color imaginable. While the colors and patterns clashed, they somehow looked perfect on the woman.

"Shhh," she said as she came up to them. "Let me listen to the ethers."

Kevin looked to the officer he'd been working with, questioning with his eyes.

"Gwen," the officer said to the woman.

"Rick," she replied. "You know this is needed. You can't deny it, now."

"I'm not sure this is the time," Rick said.

"The sooner I can connect with the other side," Gwen began, "the better chance I have of bringing her back."

"Where is she?" Kevin asked.

"She's halfway," Gwen said, as if that explained everything.

"Halfway to where?"

"Gwen believes that there are alternate planes of existence," Rick explained. "Halfway is just one of them."

"Halfway is between the worlds, Rick," Gwen chastised. "It's between planes. Not in or on any one in particular. If we can get her back before she goes the rest of the way, we can save her."

"And if we can't?" Kevin asked.

"Then she'll have to survive in the other plane," Gwen

explained.

"Help me," Kevin begged.

"Sir," Rick said.

"No," Kevin barked. "If there's a chance that she's right, I want to do everything I can to get her back."

Rick just threw his hands up with an exasperated sigh and walked away.

"What do you have that she might also have with her?" Gwen asked.

"I think she has my keys," Kevin said, holding his bunch out to the woman.

"Why do you think she has these?"

"I heard the car honk," he explained. When she looked at him in confusion, he continued. "Just a few minutes ago I heard the horn, like when you press the lock button on the fob."

"Can you show me?"

Kevin pulled the keys back to himself and pressed the fob, eliciting the intended horn reaction.

"Did you hear or feel anything else?"

"I swear I heard her yelling," he said. "I heard her call my name. When I responded, I think I heard it several more times."

"How long ago?"

"Just before you came up," he said.

"May I?" she asked, holding out her hand.

He dropped the keys into her palm, unsure exactly what to expect from her. She closed her eyes, then wrapped her fingers around the keys, squeezing them tightly. Kevin held his breath, hoping against hope that this strange woman would somehow find Jessie.

Gwen's eyes popped open and she shot a look at Kevin.

"Name," she said.

"Jessie," Kevin responded, then thought she meant him, so he added, "I'm Kevin."

The woman nodded, then closed her eyes again. He watched her mutter under her breath, unable to make out any of the words she said. For several long minutes they were silent around the strange woman as she spoke incantations while squeezing his keys.

Just when he began to wonder whether anything was actually happening, the woman opened her eyes wide. The white of them startled Kevin and he took a step back. She looked around as if she could see something other than what was there.

"Hello," she whispered.

Kevin waited, unsettled by the demeanor of the woman, yet strangely intrigued by what she was doing, wondering whether there really were other planes of existence.

"He does want you back," the woman said.

He was again struck by the oddity that was going on around him.

"Believe," the woman crooned. "You have to believe if you want to come back."

Holding his breath, Kevin wondered what Jessie was saying to the woman in that alternate plane they seemed to share.

"Please come back," he whispered, hoping somehow that it would convince Jessie that she was wanted.

An audible 'pop' sounded around him and he felt his ears ring and became unsteady on his feet, falling back against his car. He blinked a couple of times, then realized that he'd fallen to the ground and his car was missing. Looking around, he saw the woman, her eyes clear and focused on something behind him. Turning, he saw Jessie standing there, fists on her hips, glaring at him.

"What did you do?" she accused. "How did you get here?"

"I...I don't know," he stammered, clearly confused at the

current situation.

"You believed," Gwen said, looking at Jessie.

"I didn't want him here," Jessie replied. "Why would I want to stay here?"

"Focus," Gwen said, still staring at the other woman.

Jessie closed her eyes after one more glare at Kevin.

"Focus and chant," Gwen assured.

Once again, Kevin was left watching a woman mutter under her breath in some other language. What Jessie said made no sense to him, so he sat still, waiting. Time slowed as his heart beat pulsed in his ears. It was eerily silent in whatever plane he found himself. Minutes passed with nothing but the muttering of the woman he'd fallen for punctuating the quiet around him. Then, without warning, he was thrust back to the plane he was used to, sprawled across the ground next to his car, Jessie standing at the end of the trailhead, and Gwen smiling smugly, a look of triumph on her face.

"What the hell?" Rick shouted, breaking the hush that had fallen all around them. "Where did she come from?"

"I told you," Gwen boasted. "I brought her back from halfway. Maybe next time you'll believe me."

"Kevin," Jessie said as she rushed to him.

"Jessie," Kevin replied, sitting up. "Are you OK?"

"What happened?" she asked.

"I'm not sure," he replied.

"Can I check you out?" a medic asked.

"Umm," Jessie stammered. "I guess. Kevin needs help, too."

"Yep," the other man said. "Let's get both of you to the aid car and see what's going on."

With help, Kevin stood, then both he and Jessie made their way through the crowd of people standing around them.

"Up you go," the medic said as he helped first Jessie, then

Kevin into the back of the ambulance. "Just need to see what's going on with you before I can safely let you go on your way."

"You're sure?" Kevin asked for what seemed like the hundredth time.

"Yes," Jessie said. "I want to spend the rest of my life with you."

"And you don't think it's weird?"

"Everything about that day was weird," she returned. "Nothing can compare to finding yourself in the same place, but having everything different."

"Nothing could prepare me for you disappearing on me," he replied. "I'm just glad Gwen was there to help."

"Where did she come from, anyway?"

"I have no idea," Kevin confessed. "She came up with one of the cops that were there. The officer I had been dealing with seemed to know her, though."

"It was strange when she appeared," Jessie said after a time. "I thought I was losing my mind, at first. Then, when I got to the parking lot and nothing was there, I was afraid I was dead. It wasn't until I heard your voice that I began to believe that this might not be the end of me."

"When you were gone," Kevin began. "I didn't know where you went. You were napping, then I turned around and you were just not there."

"I heard screaming," she confessed. "That's what woke me up. Nothing was moving where I was, either. It was really terrifying."

"I can only imagine," he said. "I'm just glad I found you."

"Me, too," she agreed.

"And they don't suspect?" Rick asked Gwen.

"They are completely oblivious to the facts," she returned. "To them, they were lost in the alternate plane, then brought back to the one they vanished from."

"Good," he said. "We have needed new blood for a while. They'll be perfect as a life source for Amari."

"Yes," Gwen agreed. "I'm just thankful we are offered the opportunity to hunt for him."

"So long as we are still able to move between planes," Rick began, "we will continue to be of value to Amari. That, in and of itself, is a notion to be proud of."

"When will they be reaped?"

"Not until they procreate," he said. "Their child will then be transferred back to the other plane to continue our work there."

THE PURPLE SIDE OF ORANGE
BY DAVID MECKLENBURG

The sky—it is a curious thing of perspective—looks different here and I begin to understand. The key shape of the atmosphere remains spherical: this is the geometric word for it. It is a soft ball, slowly dragged along by gravity above the lithosphere: another thin ball set outside concentric layers, ending in a superheated globe of liquid iron so dense it is solid. None of them are smooth like a billiard but folded and made into landscapes. So, can we not have many skies?

The sky over Dresden looks different than Seattle. Hamburg and Lübeck can lay under endless blankets of drizzly mist clouds, like cotton candy touched by the dust of ground skeletons and reflections of the sky cast up from the somnolent water. The same kind of clouds, with similar attitudes and posture extend themselves across the Puget Sound, filling it like a bathtub of cool vapor—a low bank of indeterminacy and obduracy that lasts from October to June.

There are bright days. Both here and there. And there were days of fire, for both cities burned upon a time. I wonder if on some bright blue-sky day, the people looked up and saw the incendiary bombs falling—when they firebombed Dresden, turning it into a kiln as famous as its china. No, the British came at night, I believe, in Lancasters and borrowed Boeings to drop the firebombs that razed this city.

And yet if you didn't know that—if you hadn't read military history or Vonnegut—then you may not imagine the orange and red sky above the end of the Saxony plain.

Why am I here? For the same reason I was in Leipzig, or maybe not. My ex-girlfriend, the love of my life so far, was, is and always shall be a Berliner. But this land made up much of my own bloodline; I listened to and spoke its language in my grandparents' home, and I wanted to see more of it than I had seen with her. I didn't need her memory mucking up things even though I knew her memory would do that on its own.

I traveled here on my own. And I am here to meet a man.

I had met him years before. She introduced us, briefly, during our careening explorations of Berlin. I greedily consumed the art: plastic, masonry, oil paint, watercolors and the paint from spray cans. Sometimes it was on bodies, or Trabis—those ubiquitous symbols of German *Östalgia*, a longing for the Old Days of the DDR when everyone was watched by the Stasi and yet taken care of. Berlin was only 16 years into freedom and still figuring itself out. So was I, I realized, more or less, and Berlin, with its bars and artist's parties was something I explored along with her. I was trying to find her soul while I hoped she was carving away everything of me that wasn't beautiful. But I was dating a photographer not a sculptor.

One day she took me to a gallery, and I met him there. He was like me in a lot of ways. Not in looks. He was blonde and blue eyed, and people can rarely tell my irises from my pupils. My hair was black when I first met him. His family were Lutherans and mine were mostly

Catholic. But we were tall, introverted and fond of contemplation. *Wir sprachen die gleiche Sprache.*

"Oh, he's very good you know. Important," she said. However, we had other places to go that day and she dragged me along happily somewhere else. It was like being drunk all the time with her then. But I knew I would see him again.

Here is the gallery. His gallery, you could say, because he will always live in Dresden.

I step inside. A smart looking woman, my age perhaps, with a straight auburn bob, nods and speaks a welcome. In English.

"I am sorry, but you are smiling. You Americans always smile."

"That we do, *aber ich kann Deutsch.*"

"*Entschuldigung,*" She does not smile, as she begs my pardon, but something about her softens just a little before she returns to the screen of her monolithic laptop. And that is the extent of our conversation and I do not mind. I am not here to speak with her and we both know this fact.

The gallery is spare, with off-white walls, skillful lighting that illuminates but does not make itself obtrusive. The floors are wooden, and the heels of my boots make quiet but sharp thocks above the music. I know the music. While it may seem soft, almost ambient, its careful chord progressions and repetitions move up and down the scales suggesting a journey through silence, which is as much a figure of the composition as the notes—Nils Frahm knows the counterpoint of stillness.

What is stillness? Is it a moment in time? What is a moment in time besides an over-used phrase? All I know is that here, among the dried oil brushstrokes of contemplation, stillness accompanies me even as it marvelously unfolds upon the canvases. Is not unfolding, like the hills he so loves to paint, a movement? Am I just making paradoxes thanks to the protean nature of language? Yes and no, but

I do not think one is a metaphor for the other. Here, they are expressions of the same mystery.

I look at the first picture.

He made his name with this picture. It is one I have seen before, in Berlin. Astrid told me that there was an architect in Berlin who quit painting and went back to volumes, space, nothingness and lines when he saw this picture for the first time. A young, male hiker is standing on a promontory, facing away from us. I do not recognize the mountains, but I don't think I have to. Immediately before him are up-thrust rocks, as though he was in Joshua Tree National Park, but the swirling clouds of mist shroud them and our vision. The wrack seems to move, just like the hiker's hair, stirred in a wind that does not move. Formally set a third of the way down from the top of the painting, the folds of hills move in the relative stillness of geology with a basalt stump remaining in view. It is now only a remnant of what it was, perhaps much like the stratovolcano painted deeper in time, in space. Beyond the mountain, everything fades in the white distance of the obscured horizon.

I remember the same view, but they were different mountains. Hills really. I remember there was a pond, *the pond* for me. I bathed in it at night and heard a nightingale singing once and forever. Later, my boyfriend and I drove out of those hills and into what I thought was the rest of my life. I guess it was, but it wasn't what I thought I had seen. What I had heard.

I wish I had seen this painting then. I might have understood— not what I was looking at, but perhaps myself.

Next to it is a picture of a woman wearing a green dress. She is also facing away from us, looking out a window. She is in a plain paneled room, but my gaze is drawn into the muted spruce greens of the dress. It almost dissolves into the wall. It is not a fancy dress. It's something to wear around the house. In the view of the window there are ships and boats in some kind of harbor. They can get away. Her hair is up, perhaps because she's been doing chores. For him. For the kids. I cannot see her face and I wonder what her expression is.

She is waiting. I am witness to her tender process of her unrequited longing. I think of Dido because this is a beautiful woman looking into the future, the past and eternity. Who is the Aeneas? Who left her on the shores of Carthage? Her only other option is the pyre of despair. Does she choose the eternal wait in all this Olympian stillness?

She is trapped. I cannot tell if she knows this or not. Probably not. The boats and life outside are always there and she remembers their constant message of caution and communal prudence. *At least you are inside. Outside, there in the wild, you would be alone and die alone: miserable, unmarried, childless. A crazy bag lady.* And so, she looks at a view I cannot see but I know it.

I look around the gallery, hoping to see him. I want to ask him: "this is your feminist critique of the hiker, isn't it?"

I notice a couple who are at the other end of the gallery talking in hushed voices with the woman at the desk. I turn and then see a different kind of couple upon a canvas.

One complaint I have read about him is how his attempts at classical balance and tone reveal a bourgeois desire to please—to make something pretty you can hang on the wall and never worry about. But I can see more.

Two enormous chestnut trees frame a garden terrace and beyond... his typical infinitely obscure horizon. A woman is seated against the right chestnut tree and facing away. She is reading a book. Beyond her, two stone lions watch over a gate and a statue of Athena stands just off center.

This is how it always was. I just didn't know it. Lost in my books. Off in my worlds bound in words. I had become beautiful and cultured beneath her hands. Her work was not always kind, and in this way, she loved me. And I worshipped her. For a time.

Her eyes: I remember they were so blue they were violet, and they were shot through with sparkles like fractured bits of beryl shattered beneath an unforgiving hammer. How they used to catch the light in the morning. She was always careful to lie on my Western side so that I would see the Eastern sun reflected in her eyes when I woke up.

I looked at her and opened my mouth to lick my lips that I may shine for her all the more; that my eyes would be the dark wells she fell down. She kissed me. A single *ich liebe dich* would pass through her mouth after the kiss, and I would drink her smell, her pubic musk that spoke of dill, salt and crushed marigolds. But I also drank her words and swallowed them deeply for it was the only time of the day she would say it.

After two years, the gold curtain of her hair rested—still on the West—but turned away to conceal the sacrament of her love that had passed far over the seas and distant mountains of elsewhere. I would get up first and leave the bed.

The lions of love lay down and guard the gate.

The last picture is another landscape with a figure, her back turned to us. The Germans call this a *Rückfigur* which simply means 'back figure.' They, we, exist in all his paintings it seems, and he is famous for them. I understand why. They are the antithesis of the selfie: a narcissistic declarative form that has become banal to the point of contempt. The object of a selfie is obviously the subject. The addition of a smile could be the opportunity for irony, but it is often unintentional.

While the selfie keeps the viewer at bay—saying "I am here, and you are not"—the *Rückfigur* transcends the usual gulf between the self and the world. In the logic of composition, we share the view with the figure; we become part of that view, that figure.

The woman stands above a vale of lakes in the mountains. Her hair is free, long and dark. She has just shifted her stance as she considers the sun setting in a candy-striped battalion of purples and oranges. The movement is an illusion of stillness driven by the audience. I want to believe in movement, in the enchantment that floats in the Tyrian red and apricot scarves of a magician.

What is she doing? Is she waiting as well? What or whom is she waiting for?

No, she is here alone, and it is by her choice.

I consider what pathways, switchbacks and moraines she has had to cross to reach this place and in a time I cannot call sudden or extended, I am no longer sure what I am waiting for. The abstract terms remain sweetly, sadly indistinct. Is there even a *you* I am waiting for? In the present of waiting I am reminded of the past and yet the figure and I are facing an forever of purple and orange, because the memory of the past is a current in my never-ending present. We are, like the subject, by ourselves and left with the eternal return of our memories so that longing becomes habit and meaning in and of itself.

The water again gazes upon the sky and in so doing reflects it. Is it also not looking into the past? The lakes were once clouds— dreams of the ocean. Mutability always floats upon the surface of eternity and yet does it not also gaze into itself, at what it was, at what it waits for? What else are the reflections, light caught upon the water, but light also caught upon the paint. The artist does not merely ape nature but understands the process itself is timeless and ever-present. The artist does not only paint from life; the painter paints *in* life.

I step out of the gallery. The day has progressed towards evening and the air is chilly but the sky is clear. I can look out over the Elbe as it polishes its stillness into a mirror of the sky. To the West, the sun is setting in oranges. For a moment I think again of this city's history but my thoughts dissolve in the violet sapphire of evening: the color of sublimity, the long wavelengths that reach us from distant mountains, oceans and times.

I let my mind wander a bit between orange and purple. To Dresden, the Elbe, the sunset, I smile in the freedom of being alone and not lonely—a moment when the ideas of unity, polarity, and complementariness are but brief views on a sublimity I not only live within but discover in vistas of the process called eternity.

OCTOBER

THE PROMPT

"It is sometimes an appropriate response to reality to go mad."
-Philip K. Dick

LOST IN TRANSLATION
BY JENNIFER DiMARCO

There is a quality to light as it passes through a population of dust that is mesmerizing even in the worst of moments. The way the white-gold winter sun, the pale sun of a dying year, enrobes each particle and transforms it into something more than entropy, something more than the aftermath of a world war still inundating the trade winds, into something divine yet fleeting, momentary but irrevocably worth watching, worth admiring, and perhaps, in rare, horrendous and unprecedented moments—sometimes—worth possessing.

I'm jealous of dust. It's unencumbered by the new world order. Free to move and exist as it is. I'm jealous of the seven and a half billion of my kind who are nothing now but dust themselves. Never before have I been jealous of the dead.

Your delivery was delayed.

My palms are flat against the hardwood floor. Dust settles between my fingers. I am kneeling in a pool of sunlight. I am kneeling in the cinders of our dead.

Were you ill?

My pounding heart threatens to break through my breastbone and tumble, still throbbing, into my lap. I imagine impossible horrors like this far too frequently since I saw our world fall impossibly fast. As far as I know, they don't get sick. The idea of a faulty immune system amuses them.

My mouth chooses self-preservation over the fear trying to choke me: "I wasn't ill, *Gi'sye.*" As instructed by Director Anarode at the San Francisco Alignment Center, I use the *Gibtre'hon* equivalent for 'Commander.' A designation in their complex society where cultural, spiritual, political and martial are all interwoven. I know how lucky I am to be here instead of in a classroom, in a zoo, or on a laboratory table.

I also know that my owner—like all *Gibtre'hon*—is long and slender, a will-of-the-wisp stretched tall, with a penchant for 'collecting' the exotic and unique. My stress-induced weight-loss was corrected—aggressively—as soon as I was purchased. The intravenous feeds had burned through me like napalm in my veins.

Good.

It's not time to look up. I was hooded during transport because they insist we stay calmer when we see less. I don't mind the blinders; they make sense. I'm not sure I'd still be sane if I saw everything there was to see. But ignorance is not bliss: I know what we crushed in the road on the way here today, what the spiked treads of the leviathan ground into an Earth that was no longer ours.

Burning bodies is wasteful, I'd heard Director Anarode say once. *Healthy bodies can be consumed.* Meaning: Not by them; they were vegan. *The tainted can be turned into the soil with terraforming microbes to—*

I'd tuned out or blocked out the rest. Some of those tainted bodies had been my friends, my family, my wife, my son.

Do you have a name?

178

I wonder, for just an instant, how long I can stay silent. How long can I *not* answer a direct question? I consider counting the seconds but before I reach 'two' my mouth is already moving, "My name is whatever you wish, *Gi'sye*."

I sense… pleasure. Or approval? They don't make wordless sounds like 'oh' or 'hm' to express raw emotions as is—as was—so common with humans. They project their emotions, containing not so much a tone of voice as a breadth and depth of diapason. These projections lace *between* their words. In short: My owner is pleased I'm so well-trained.

I wish to know your human name.

The words are not spoken. They are not shared aloud the way we speak. They are broadcast in some type of waveform that thrums against our ear drums while leaving the room silent. Something about the neuroimplants they bored into our heads.

Almost imperceptibly, my hands shake. The hardwood floor is polished oak. Polished by generations of humans coming and going from this room once occupied by a Silicon Valley billionaire; how interesting that the ascetics of the American one-percent match the ascetics of our executioners. How apropos.

Despite my conditioning, despite my now-intrinsic (now-biological?) fear of pain, I hold off answering. I know the *Gibtre'hon* sometimes find our names challenging. I don't want to—

First my neck warms beneath my wide silicone collar then my face tingles. This will be my only warning. I answer, "Renae."

Ree-Nuh.

"Ree-Nay." Oh my god. What have I done? My adrenaline spikes. I hear my blood in my ears, feel it in my cheeks. Was my indoctrination too efficient or not efficient enough? Despite not being asked a direct question, I spoke. Is my will even my own?

There is palpable tension after my unsolicited correction. A tangible silence in the golden oak and cold white room. My owner makes no sound whatsoever but the feeling of consideration, of contemplation, is as obvious as the shaft of light I continue to kneel in, as obvious as the eddies of dust dancing away each time I exhale.

The *Gibtre'hon* are so much more than we ever were. Our superiors—faster, smarter, stronger. They exist in twice as many dimensions, or rather, they are aware of and can perceive and manipulate six as opposed to three. They are space-faring. They are genderless. They have evolved beyond petty, compulsive, imprecise violence to decisive, savage deconstruction in veneration of the scientific method. Every act they commit is in pursuit of *Jyhor*—their Divine State of Knowing.

Theirs is a deadly intellect.

Renae.

Said perfectly this time but also without an emotional footnote which is rare for their people. I hold my breath. My eyes sink shut in my bowed face. Without context, lost in the stillness of despondency, I am blind to what comes next. I've spent the last year behind the walls of the Center. I have never been owned before.

I shall call you Nuufi.

A part of me dies. Another part. I had no idea before our end that we had so many parts capable of death. It's incredible really that our bodies persist. Is this the truth behind the old human fascination with zombies and the undead? Because we knew our bodies would persevere even when our hearts and minds screamed for release. Why ask my name at all?

My eyes open with the realization: To take it away from me.

My conditioning continues even now.

Do you know what it means?

I shake my head slowly and feel no shame as tears spill from my eyes. I remember they like it when we nod and shake our heads because they value sight over sound. I hate myself when I please them but it's hard not to. I'm alive—even if only partially—because I please them.

It means: Brave and foolish in equal measure.

My turn to be stunned. I remain quiet. My tears stop. Their language is, arguably, as beautiful as they are. Some called them angels when they first arrived. Ethereal creatures resonating in place... in many places all at the same time. We had no chance.

Say it.

I inhale, drawing remnants of our civilization as loess into my lungs, into my body where it will be no safer, and no more alive, than it was floating in this room or resting between my fingers on the floor. I want to think I swallowed courage or resistance or something that made me defy that direct order but, honestly, I think I was just wearing down, trembling more, exhausting my energy at the end of this seemingly endless day.

My collar activates and my body jolts, seizing in response to the web of pain slicing across my face. My optical nerves cease to send messages to my brain and I fight to stay upright. I fight to stay conscious. I feel my lips curl back, my eyes bulge, straining from their sockets, blood trickling from my nose. The contortions feel like they're pulling my face apart; that's where they strike us, disfigure us. Our faces are our identity and they learned it too quickly. They wanted us to be the numbers on our collars; numbers that were *Gibtre'hon*, not even human.

The pain stops. My breathing is labored. My sight returns. Bare feet stand before me. Bare legs. Both are longer, thinner than the human counterparts. Six toes and countless bones beneath skin the color of eggplant or slate with indigo highlights almost invisible to the naked eye. And those bones? Not quite like ours. They shifted and moved in ways unfamiliar and unfettered. A sheer sash—the color of almost-translucent butter cream—brushes the crown of my head.

When at war, the *Gi'sye* wore wine red. But the war was over and antique eggshell was their color of victory.

Look at me.

I do.

I want to.

But I am also willed to.

I am Helahna Fahrour. You will call me Gi'sye.

Her full, dark plum lips did not move. Their mouths never moved when they spoke. Her eyes are glossy black and especially wide without white sclera or visible iris. She has lashes like raven feathers and indigo patterns move over her skin in concentric circles as if she created Venn diagrams of every situation, determining each possible course of action. She isn't smiling. They don't have facial expressions as far as I know.

Wait.

I pause. I blink.

Why did I use a pronoun?

Say it.

I want to shout, to scream, to rage against the dying of my own kind that my name was and would forever be Renae Riley Williamson. But instead I value my life over my pride and answer, "Nuufi."

There was pleasure in the room between us and some of it, I won't lie, was mine. Me looking up at her—so far to her face, easily seven feet above my sublimate position—and her looking down. She is pleased because I said my new name. I am pleased because looking at them produces cortisol and dopamine in the human body. This was true even before I was collared and implanted for an owner. Is my reaction to her more intense because I am her possession?

Good, she tells me. But what I hear, what the underlying

emotion laces into and around the word, is: *Good girl.*

I think to myself: Do I get a treat?

It is October 25, 2021. Somewhere near 7:30 in the morning and the sun is rising. My owner would say this moment is 1.225 AGA, one orbital rotation plus 225 axial rotations After *Gibtre'hon* Arrival.

They call this Earth Local Time as opposed to *Gibtre'hon* Universal Time which is expressed as a multidimensional glyph incomprehensible to human eyes that see only in two dimensions. They find this amusing. How biologically primitive we are. How simple.

We make wonderful pets.

I am not allowed a clock or books or tools with which to write. There's apparently no reason for us to track time as we exist only within the schedule of our owner's. Likewise, we cannot create anything recognizable as worthy so why would we need pencil or paper? *Written language is imperfect*, Director Anarode often said.

I was given my own room but this isn't uncommon. I learned from the ever-informative Anarode that while not *Gi'sye*, as the Director of an Alignment Center, he had jurisdiction over the thousand human charges interred there. Though in my twelve months at the Center I never once saw another human face or heard another human sound. Again: The blinder method at work.

I could have lain in my room, unable to sleep, obediently prone on my back staring at the off-white blank canvas of the ceiling and engaged my brain with an interior dialogue about why I thought of Anarode as male and my owner as female. Their bodies were configured alike beneath their conventional sashes: Smooth, flat chests, narrow hips, devoid of navels or genitalia. (Though Anarode's body was coral pink and sherbet orange with angler bronze lines.) Their sashes were both *Gibtre'hon* living fabric fortified with cybernetic threads that pulsed with faint color, both worn draped behind the neck and across the front of the shoulders and chest, falling to mid-thigh and never seeming to slide or askew. (Though Anarode's seemed less sheer, less luxurious, and was pale blue like the rest of the Center staff.)

Instead, I lay on my molded platform, the semi-malleable block not unlike firm gelatin, wracked with waves of cold with a new realization: They exist everywhere. They have AGA dates on planets throughout the universe.

After *Gibtre'hon* Arrival.

Nuufi.

I awaken when I hear my name so I must have fallen asleep. I sit up on my block, blinking and touching my face like a child. She stands in the open doorway of my room. Always open as it has no door, not even indentations where hinges once were. "Yes, Helahna?"

Oh my god. I'm half asleep. I'm poorly adjusting to life outside the Center. Is it a Freudian malfunction? My wife's name was Hannah. Is it Stockholm Syndrome? My face twitches anticipating the punishment of pain. I can't breathe.

I don't recall closing my eyes but my sleeping block agitates and when I open my eyes, Helahna is sitting there looking at me.

We look at each other.

She blinks slowly, deliberately. *You are... unexpected.*

Before the end of days, before humans fell, I worked and thrived as a professor of psychology at Stanford. Is this why my life was spared? Or was it just my emerald green eyes, my rich, dark skin and my fine straight hair like black spider's silk? I catalog every tiny nuance of her, memorizing and categorizing, classifying to understand. This is contemplation of the unexpected, that slow blink. As close to an expression as I have ever seen.

"I cannot imagine you find anything unexpected, *Gi'sye*," I hear myself whisper perhaps because I don't have the courage for more. "After all, *Nuufi* means brave and foolish in equal measure."

She does not smile. She does not grin. She does not tilt her head or blush or hum softly. I miss those small sensory cues that humans once exchanged in intimate moments of connection. Nonetheless, I sense an intimacy—somehow—between us.

You are a fast learner. Again: Pleasure. I'm worth what I cost, apparently.

She stands then and crosses the room, her back to me without hesitance because they all know we can't harm them once we've been implanted and trained; it's physiologically impossible. I study her bare back. They have more vertebrae. Can they turn their heads like sloths and owls? I shudder.

I think our interaction is over when she passes through my doorway and starts down the hall but even as I look down, considering everything that has transpired, she turns back and faces me.

Nuufi, do you want a companion?

Yes! I want to jump up and shout it through laughter. I know my eyes widen in shock and delight and hope. A hundred times: Yes!

But then realization. It was just a moment. Just a small lapse in control and composure and judgment. Don't give her something else to take away, I tell myself. Your thoughts are still your own, I remind myself. Don't give in, I command myself.

"Whatever you think is best, *Gi'sye*," I say almost instantly. But I'm not ignorant. I know she saw every emotion that flashed across my face. Despite it, she projects satisfaction and turns once more to leave. "*Gi'sye?*" What am I doing?!

She stops and her surprise washes over me but it's a charmed surprise, a welcome one. *What is it, Nuufi?*

I wet my lips, suddenly dry even though it's impossible for me to be dehydrated when my sleeping block seeps moisture and nutrients into my body. "Did you want something? You... came to my door."

She doesn't have to want something. She has every right to stand in my doorway and say my name. Or have me kneel for hours. Or trade me in. Or beat me senseless. I'm hers.

I wanted your presence.

And there it is. My mistake. My fatal operating error. It's there woven between the words. *Her* companionship should be enough. I am suddenly afraid I have ruined everything... but what is 'everything?' What does 'everything' mean and how is my life as it is now not completely and utterly ruinous already?

Nuufi.

I look up. Again, I was unaware I'd looked away. My physical responses are elicited before my knowledge of them as if responding to her is autonomic.

Her large black eyes are like midnight skies.

I prefer it when you call me Helahna.

She leaves my doorway completely then, soundless as always, but the projection of emotion lingers in the room. The feeling is subtle, soft and sad. A mixture of understanding, patience and sorrow.

"Whatever you wish," I exhale beneath a breath and I know with certainty that no matter where she is in this massive complex of chrome, glass, oak and off-white walls, she hears me.

My internal clock—or one of the six implants in my brain—wakes me at sunrise every day after that and I have no need to ever wash or eat. The gelatinous block takes care of my necessities but when Helahna finds me curled one day in the over-stuffed nest-like chair in her living room tugging at tangles in my hair? An hour later she appears with a rolled cloth, climbs into the nest and sinks down behind me.

I have no idea what's about to happen but I sense it's best to stay still. She unrolls the cloth beside us and I almost laugh aloud with relief. A matching comb and brush inlaid with Mother of Pearl. Nail clippers. An emery board. Thinning sheers. Helahna has purchased a human grooming kit.

For the next hour, the alien Commander who slaughtered my people, brushes my hair until I almost fall asleep.

Today, your companion arrives.

She says this when she finally rises, taking her kit with her. It has been seven or eight days since she offered in my doorway. I have thought about that moment, replaying it over and over a great many times but I have never dared make an inquiry. It seemed safer to consider it all a dream.

As she starts to walk away, I catch her hand.

And my collar activates.

It activates like never before. My hands fly to my face as it threatens to peel away from the front of my skull. I scream, thrash, writhe. My eyes bleed; I smear bright red blood all over the butter cream furniture.

No. Not the nest. Helahna is holding me, firmly, protectively, and the butter cream splattered with blood is her victory sash. I look up at her face and she opens her mouth.

Her teeth are steel or titanium or something silver and so sharp they literally glint in the soft light of the room. Before I can catch my breath to scream anew, she strikes, ripping my collar off with her razor teeth.

It is seven hours later. Helahna carried me to my room, laid me on my block. I slept but I'm relatively certain it was induced. Several times I awoke to Anarode in the room, holding a new collar, and I thought I was back at the Center and I started to weep like a little child.

Nuufi, Nuufi.

Helahna is there. Comforting me. Telling me, not with her words, but with the emotions between the words that I am home. That my home is there with her. That she will not return me to the Center.

And there's something more as well. Helahna is... angry. Not angry at me. Angry at Anarode.

At one point I wake and they're facing each other, maybe two inches apart, and Helahna is seething. Her fury is so protective of me and so directed at Anarode that I feel respected, honored, safe. I know she could very well be complaining about faulty merchandise but as I sink back into unconsciousness—into healing?—she glances at me and I know she isn't complaining.

For the first time, I touch my neck. My skin is unbroken and my neck is bare. My collar is gone and has not been replaced. Nor will it be. Inexplicably, I dream of fields of red poppies being eaten by a colony of black rabbits. Their eyes are ringed in white like expensive eyeliner and their teeth are tiny silver knives.

When next I wake it's deep into the night and the director of the Center is thankfully gone. One wall of my room is windows that overlook the Santa Cruz Mountains but right now they lie beneath the cloak of night only sparsely dotted with the distant lights from the homes of other Commanders; I am not certain that the *Gibtre'hon* sleep.

I sit up very slowly and my entire body aches but it is my face that burns like how I imagine an expensive acid peal would feel the day after. I reach up with both hands but Helahna is with me—perhaps always has been—and takes my hands between her own.

You will heal. You will not scar.

But though her touch and words are comforting, are laced with affection and even a thin trace of apology, I cringe and cower, only her firm grip on my hands stops me from pulling away. My implants and conditioning still hold even without the interface of the collar.

Helahna lets go and we look at each other. Without words, she stands from my block and walks to my doorway. Only there does she turn and speak to me—more information than any of her kind have ever shared in all my days as theirs.

Your collar was too finely calibrated. Most of us do not want the unsolicited touch of a human. But I am not afraid of humans.

Oh the volumes behind her words! The inflections and truths and excerpts from her rage against Anarode. She is *Gi'sye*! A Commander! Revered among her people. A veteran of countless 'arrivals' on alien worlds. A collector of beautiful things.

I don't speak. I only listen, allowing the myriad facets of her language to inform, horrify and enlighten me.

I will not collar you again. You are free to touch me as you please. I know you will not harm me and I am not xenophobic. I...

I'm speechless. If I had wanted to speak I wouldn't have had the words. Never had I heard a *Gibtre'hon* stumble or hesitate like this.

...I trust you, Nuufi.

I catch my breath and realize I'd been holding it. In that moment, with the golden warm light of the house haloing Helahna's body, illuminating her sash, I admit she does look angelic. If I am equally brave and foolish, then she is equally Grim Reaper and savior.

I will let you heal.

She projects calm and I return the favor by being ungrateful and callus: "Did my companion arrive?"

Helahna projects nothing. There is an absence of emotion or

undercurrent. I realize she can hide from me. Would that be useful somehow? Useful for what? Useful how and to what ends? Was the end game simply to understand our conquerors?

If she had participated in the occupation of numerous worlds, that assumed she eventually left them as she certainly wasn't on them now. Would Helahna someday leave Earth? Would all the *Gibtre'hon* leave?!

I will fetch him.

She left me to contemplate not her rare use of a gender pronoun but a dozen other emotions and considerations warring for my attention.

A few minutes later I'm sitting akimbo on my block with nervous butterflies in my stomach like a child. I had tried to focus on the gift of information Helahna had given me but even two or three minutes in I felt light-headed and overwhelmed. Whatever the collar had done to me it was taking all the *Gibtre'hon* tech inside me to fix it.

The golden puppy that bounded across the floor was the definition of unexpected. He spotted me instantly even in the nighttime room and promptly peed himself in excitement. Had it been nineteen months since he'd seen a human? Imagine being domesticated by a species only for it to vanish!

I was holding him, cooing to him, burying my face in his silken fur when Helahna returned to stand in the doorway. She watched me for sometime and I pretended not to notice because I just wanted to lose myself in this moment for just a little longer... a few weeks or years perhaps.

I am confident you approve of your companion.

The puppy jolted as if shocked with electricity. He leapt at me, pawing, clumsy, squealing, trying to burrow under me, shaking his head so violently he would have thrown himself from the sleeping block had I not held him tighter.

Helahna projected confusion and I lifted my face to her to, hopefully, show that I was in the same state she was.

"It's okay, boy. It's okay. It's—" I just repeated the useless phrase over and over again because I was easily as helpless (and almost as clueless) as the dog was. Eventually he calmed into a low, pitiful whining, shoving his fat, fluffy puppy body into the bowl of my crisscrossed legs.

I shrugged for Helahna and hoped she'd like a shrug the way she liked nods and head shakes. "Thank you." I tried to weave sincerity into the words and for the first time I felt like I understood why humans seemed so rudimentary to *Gibtre'hon*. Our language was so limited!

You are welcome—

But she didn't finish because the sounds of the puppy howling, barking, crying and moaning filled the room—most likely the entire house! Staying with the theme of nervous butterflies, I gasped as I made the guess, "I think... your voice is hurting him." Tread carefully, I admonished myself, unconsciously holding the dog even tighter. "The special frequency of a *Gibtre'hon* voice... it may be painful to them."

I poured everything into those two sentences. All the gratitude I felt toward Helahna for not returning me to the Center. All the gratitude I felt for the gift of the puppy. I wanted—I needed—her to know that I was not complaining. She had given me so many gifts.

And it worked. Because she gave me another: She stayed silent and bobbed her head once in acknowledgement in a way her people never do. She projected—without words—into the room: Understanding. Patience. And an assurance that everything would be all right. She would make sure it was all right.

Just as quietly then she took her leave. I cleaned up the mess on the floor with toilet paper from the small quarter bath attached to my room then climbed back on the block and curled around Lucky who was already sleeping as deeply as only puppies can sleep.

When I awoke the next morning at sunrise, Lucky was gone.

I wept. I wept like I haven't in all the days since the *Gibtre'hon* destroyed almost everyone and everything. I wept for everything and everyone I'd known. Because I wasn't drowning in fear—for once, for the first time since it all began—the grief welled up from deep inside me and rose like a tsunami to drown me.

I'm not entirely certain when Helahna entered my room. But when she sat down on the block beside me and gathered me into her arms I was drenched in tears and snot and making sounds that weren't anywhere near words. I was as primal and primitive as possible, broken down completely and unable to function except to cry harder.

And yet….

A not-so-small part of me wanted to rage against her, pound my fists into her, break her unbreakable bones. The games she played! The twisted and vile manipulations! Was I not subservient enough? Was I not exactly what I was conditioned by her people to be?!

Perhaps it was part of that conditioning that stopped me from doing everything—anything—violent or aggressive. But in my mind it was Helahna's words in my head, deep in my ears: *I trust you.*

Even if I would not—could not—trust Helahna, I would not turnabout that unfair play. I would hold the moral high ground as if it were my last stand. This was the only thing I could—

Lucky bounded into the room.

Lucky leapt onto the block.

Lucky licked sorrow from my face.

He will no longer dysfunction, Helahna told me with humor and amusement between her words as Lucky nuzzled her hand then chased the edge of her sash.

He did not react to her voice. He didn't cringe or yelp or cower. He never would again. Because he would never hear *anything* again.

Gi'sye Helahna Fahrour had had his entire auditory system removed and grafted over with precision. His ears were completely cosmetic now, like custom pieces perched on his head, leading nowhere, doing nothing.

Today, I will introduce you to the rest of my household, Helahna told me. *They have given you space at my bequest but they grow eager to meet you.*

I could not look at her. I felt cold. The air felt thin.

She stood and walked to my doorway. My guardian. My jailer. My owner.

I think you'll fit in perfectly, Nuufi. A wonderful addition to my collection.

PROGRESSION
BY LAUREN PATZER

Diana walked out into the hallway and was shocked to see her old elementary reading teacher sitting there in a wheelchair. She brushed her blonde hair back behind one ear and smiled.

"Missus Cooney, what a pleasant surprise," she said and held out her hand.

The older woman grabbed her hand enthusiastically and beamed. Her gray curls looked exactly as Diana remembered them all those years ago. Her green eyes twinkled.

"Diana, I just knew you'd turn out to be someone who helped people," the woman gushed. "Please, call me Christine."

Diana nodded awkwardly and took her hand back.

"So, Christine, what brings you to Airdale?"

"Well, I'm here primarily for you, dear."

Diana frowned. She looked around to see if there was a camera and some kind of reality trick going on. There didn't seem to be. She sat down on a bench in the hallway.

"Christine, we're a hospice, an end of life facility. While I can see you're in a wheelchair, it doesn't seem like you're facing an end of life scenario. Has there been some kind of diagnosis for you?"

Christine chuckled and shook her head.

"I told you, I'm here for you," Christine said and waved toward the end of the hall with the stub of a left hand toward the library. "Now, if you could help me, it's become difficult to maneuver in a manual without the hand here."

Diana blinked at the stub. Surely, she'd just had her hands held by Christine. Had she missed her teacher's absent hand somehow? Perhaps it had been from the shock of seeing this part of her past here and now. She shook her head, stood up and walked behind the wheelchair.

"I'd be happy to help, Christine," Diana said and pushed the elder lady down the hall. "So, who's your doctor?"

They continued down the hall, Diana looking out the windows at the spring flowers blooming in the sun.

"Oh," Christine said. "Doctor Hammond was wonderful, always took the extra time to see how I was feeling, not just roll me through the office like I was on an assembly line. He had the most wonderful smile and his nurse, Brenda, was the nicest young lady you could ever chat with. They were very personable."

"Would that be Doctor Hammond from Brightsville?" Diana asked.

"That's him. Such a wonderful man," Christine said and sighed.

Diana stopped the wheelchair and looked behind her. Normally there was a little more traffic in the hallway, but that wasn't the only peculiar thing about the day. Doctor Hammond was a psychiatrist at Brightsville Sanitarium. He didn't normally refer patients under his care here to Airdale. But then, he'd stopped his practice years ago. He was one of the first doctors Diana had interacted with when she started working at Airdale.

"Christine," Diana said gently. "I think Doctor Hammond

retired several years ago."

"Yes," Christine nodded. "I haven't seen him in a long time."

"Oh," Diana breathed a sigh of relief. Christine was clearly just reminiscing. Diana began to push the wheelchair again and the doors to the library automatically opened. They rolled past the front desk and Diana noticed there was no one manning the station. She glanced around the small library and realized it was completely empty of people.

"Well, Christine, who's your doctor now?" Diana said as she left Christine's wheel chair and walked behind the front desk looking for the librarian.

"Oh, dear, I don't need one anymore since I passed away," Christine said. Diana had just poked her head around the corner of the small hallway when she stopped and turned to look back at Christine. Her teacher was no longer there. Diana rushed back to where she'd left the wheelchair and it was gone. She darted around the rows of the library, but Christine was nowhere to be found.

"What the hell," Diana whispered. She walked back out the door to the library and the hallway was empty. Maybe someone with two functioning hands and arms could maneuver a manual wheelchair away that fast, but Christine didn't and couldn't. Diana walked back past the other office doors, stopping at each one and finding no one there. Neither Christine nor the regular employees of the hospice were anywhere to be found. Christine shuddered and walked back to her office.

As she walked through her office door, she snapped her fingers. She'd been leaving earlier to get something. She paused at the door and tried to think of what it was she meant to retrieve. The only thing that came to mind was her car keys. She walked back out the door and found Mrs. Cooney waiting there for her, sitting in her wheelchair.

"Oh!" Diana exclaimed. This time she noticed the old woman was also missing her left foot. A stump hung off the edge of the wheelchair. Diana processed this for a moment and realized she just hadn't noticed it before. Now it made perfect sense why Christine was in a wheelchair.

"Hello again, Diana!" Christine gushed and held out her right hand. After a pause, Diana grasped her right hand with both of hers and smiled.

"Missus Cooney," Diana replied.

"Remember, I told you to call me Christine," she chided and Diana blushed.

"Of course you did," Diana replied. She looked up and down the hall again, but it remained as vacant as before. She stepped behind the wheelchair and pushed her teacher toward the library.

"Such a beautiful summer day," Christine commented.

"It's still spring, Christine," Diana replied and looked out the windows as they walked. The grass had turned brown and most of the flowers had wilted in the oppressive summer heat. Diana stopped pushing the wheelchair and walked to the window. She pressed her hand to the glass and felt the heat from the summer sun radiating through it.

"Time marches on," Christine said. "No rest for the weary… most of the time."

Diana stared out the window, looking up and down the normally active sidewalk a few hundred yards away. The street beyond was similarly vacant.

"Seems like everyone's resting today," Diana replied. She turned back to Mrs. Cooney and the old woman had disappeared again. "Oh, for goodness sake."

Diana walked back to her office and shut the door behind her. She sat down at her desk and moved things on her desk looking for her car keys. They weren't in the drawers either. She stood up and looked on the bookshelf next to the chair she had for patients and clients. Her purse sat on top. She sighed in relief and grabbed it. She opened the purse and found medical gauze stained with blood. She dropped the purse on the guest chair. The gauze fell onto the floor and rolled out across the room, leaving a blood stained tail behind it.

There was a knock on the door and Diana jumped. She glanced at the gauze on the floor and shook her head.

"What a shitty practical joke," she murmured as she walked to the door. She opened it to find Mrs. Cooney there again. Both of the old woman's legs were gone, further up the leg this time. She sported two stumps that barely reached the edge of the seat. Her left arm was now missing all the way up past the elbow.

"Diana, can you push me down to the library?" Christine asked, smiling. She said it with a slight slur and Diana noticed her old teacher had a few teeth missing. Without a word, Diana walked behind the chair and pushed it down the hall. There was a slight chill in the air. With each step, goose bumps multiplied on Diana's arms and it wasn't just from the cooler air in the hallway. She glanced out the window and saw the trees nearly barren, leaves piled up on the grass.

"It's not every day I get a dead teacher from my past visiting me at my office," Diana said.

"The mind works in mysterious ways, doesn't it Diana?" Christine replied, her speech punctuated by hisses between her missing teeth. Diana didn't respond but continued pushing her teacher down the hall. They went through the automatic doors again. As before, there was no one to greet them in the library.

"Could you push me over to the fiction section?" Christine asked. "I always loved the creation of stories from nothing but the mind's eye."

Diana pushed the wheelchair to the section three rows deep and stopped. Christine turned around and looked up at her.

"You can let go now. I wanted to know if you'd look up Alice in Wonderland for me. It's one of the classics," Christine asked.

"If I let go of the chair, you'll disappear again," Diana said. "I'm afraid to let you go."

"Get me the book," Christine said. "I won't go away until it's time for me to go."

Diana stood unmoving for a few seconds or even a few minutes, she wasn't sure how time passed anymore. Finally, she released the wheelchair and stepped toward the bookshelf. Looking along the shelf, she recognized every book there. She'd read them all. There was nothing there she hadn't opened and devoured when she was younger. Her reading had fallen off lately, but every once in a while she picked up a newer book. They were all here. She moved along the row and found Lewis Carroll's Alice in Wonderland. She pulled the book from the shelf and turned toward Christine, who remained there in the wheelchair, unchanged from before.

"You're still here," Diana said.

"Of course, I am," Christine responded and smiled her broken smile. "You're almost ready."

Christine reached for the book with her right hand. Diana handed it to her. Christine sat back comfortably in the wheelchair and opened the book with her good hand, steadying it with the stump of her left arm.

"Almost ready for what?"

"You see me reading?" Christine asked.

Diana nodded and frowned. "Do you need some alone time?"

"No," Christine chuckled. "I can read, I can write, operate an electric wheelchair, a computer, a vehicle if I like with the right modifications. I can do most anything with some obvious exceptions, but even prosthetics and technology can accommodate most anything life can throw at you."

Diana nodded her head. "I work in the medical field. I keep up on all the latest breakthroughs, even though in my particular work, I only see people when they're beyond the help of most advances."

"Is it fair to say, you think I could do most anything I wanted to with the help of technology and some devices?"

"Surely, there's retraining and physical therapy that can help you adapt to most any challenges you might come across," Diana cocked her head to the side. "Am I being fired? Or maybe I'm getting transferred to a physical therapy unit? Is that it?"

Christine smiled. "Not exactly, but that could be part of it, if you choose."

"If I choose?"

"If you're ready," Christine leaned forward, holding the book on her lap. "Diana, do you think you're ready?"

"Maybe," Diana said. Christine peered into her eyes and Diana felt as if her old mentor was measuring her soul for worthiness. Christine shrugged.

"Well, it's your decision, I'm just here at your whim," Christine muttered. She handed the book to Diana. "Well after the Rabbit Hole and just beyond the Pool of Tears, as would seem most appropriate."

Diana took the book from Christine and opened it to the first chapter, Down the Rabbit Hole. She hesitated and looked up. Christine had disappeared. Diana closed the book and looked around briefly. She shrugged her shoulders and decided it didn't matter if Mrs. Cooney was here any longer. Perhaps her work was done.

Diana walked to one of the tables and set the book down again. She read through the first chapter, reminiscing about one of her favorite books. She didn't understand the significance of it compared to what she was going through, although she had to admit it was strange. She plowed quickly through the next chapter and when she got to the first page of chapter three, the center of the book had been hollowed out and inside it were her car keys. She lifted them carefully from the center of the book. They dripped with blood.

Suddenly, she was no longer sitting in the library, but held the keys out in front of her while she sat in her car. Her first instinct was to put the keys in the ignition, but she hesitated. In slow motion, her hand moved toward the ignition. Time seemed to standstill and her breath stopped. All sound ceased and her hand trembled as it moved inches toward placing the key into the receptacle.

Tears fell from her cheeks and she jerked her hand backward. She opened the car door, ran toward the building and went inside. Through the empty corridors she ran, crying all the way though she wasn't sure why.

Diana burst through her office door and shut it quickly behind her. She collapsed into her chair and put her head down on her desk, sobbing uncontrollably.

"Perhaps you weren't ready," Christine's voice whispered. Diana raised her head and saw her teacher sitting in the guest chair next to her desk. She was absently rolling the bloody gauze up with her two perfectly normal hands and then placed the gauze back in Diana's purse.

"I'm scared," Diana said. She wiped the tears from her face and looked away from Mrs. Cooney.

"I know," Christine said. "And that's perfectly normal, but..."

As Christine's voice faded, Diana looked up and saw Christine pointing at the calendar on the wall. The pages started falling from it, month after month drifting slowly to the floor.

"Time marches on, Diana," Christine whispered. "You can join the mad tea party for a while or you can miss the story altogether and reach The End far faster. Winter is upon us. There isn't much time."

Christine got up and placed Diana's purse back up on the bookshelf and walked out of the room. Diana watched her go and saw snowflakes falling outside the windows in the hallway before Christine shut the door quietly behind her.

Diana watched Christine's silhouette beyond the frosted glass of her office door fade from sight. She looked back at her desk and sniffled.

"I'm not ready," Diana said and looked through her desk. She found her appointment book and pulled it out. She went through her appointment book and found April. All the appointments she remembered holding were in there, but when she searched through the pages after April, there were no appointments. The empty pages turned to dust in her hands.

Diana stood up from her desk and a crackling sound drew her attention to the clock high up on the wall. It was smoking and the second hand was slowing as it struggled around the face of the clock.

"I'm not ready!" She screamed at the clock. It continued to smoke and flames erupted from the face of the clock.

Diana looked down at the bloody keys and grabbed them. She opened the door and saw Christine sitting in the wheelchair, left arm and two legs missing again. Christine looked up at her sadly.

"There's not much time left at all," Christine said, then she closed her eyes and rapidly decayed, becoming a skeleton and then nothing but dust in a matter of seconds. The paint on the walls began to fray with age and neglect. Diana ran back through the doors that led through her building. They hung halfway off the hinges. As she ran through the building toward the parking lot, the whole building seemed to fall apart around her.

Her car gleamed like new in the parking lot. She climbed into the car and shut the door. She looked at the Airdale Hospice Center and it seemed to fall to dust before her eyes. The trees and grass faded from full color to gray. She looked at the keys and then the ignition switch.

"Perhaps it's for the best..." she heard her husband's voice whisper into her ear. She grimaced and stuck the key into the ignition. She cried out in pain as she awoke in the hospital bed.

"Diana!" Mike shouted in relief, tears in his eyes.

She tried to speak, but the tube in her throat prevented it. She grasped her husband's hand with her right hand, realizing quickly that it was the only limb she had left. A doctor put his stethoscope to her chest and then flashed a light into her eyes.

"She's back," he said, the shock apparent in the doctor's voice. "Somehow, she's back."

"What a long sleep you've had," her husband said. She looked into his brown eyes and saw true relief and love there.

"Oh, I've had such a curious dream," she thought as he caressed her cheek.

MAD TEA PARTY
BY HIROMI COTA

Author's note: *Public domain works are free to do whatever we want with them. We can get the text, print it out, sew the pages together, and sell the resulting book. We can even make a copy of a famous piece of art, put our personal spin on it, and try to get the new version in a museum.*

Public domain works of art belong to the people. This doesn't mean that we can walk into the Louvre and take the Mona Lisa off the wall; specific copies still belong to specific people. But it does mean that we can make our own copies and do whatever we want with them. You don't even need to give credit to the original creators, although not doing so is what is known in the professional world as a "dick move." Anyway, I stole a bunch of the following words from Lewis Carroll's 1865 novel Alice in Wonderland, mixed them up a bit, and gave it my own spin. Did you know that the famous "we're all mad here" line doesn't come from the Mad Tea Party chapter?

There was a table set out under a tree in front of the house, and the March Hare and the Hatter were having tea at it: a Dormouse was sitting between them, fast asleep, and the other two were using it as a cushion, resting their elbows on it, and talking over its head. "Very uncomfortable for the Dormouse," thought Alice. "Only, as it's asleep, I suppose it doesn't mind."

The table was a large one, but the three were all crowded together at one corner of it: "No room! No room!" they cried out when they saw Alice coming.

"There's plenty of room! You just don't want me at the table," said Alice indignantly, and she sat down in a large arm-chair at one end of the table.

"Well spotted! Have some wine," the March Hare said in an encouraging tone.

Alice looked all round the table, but there was nothing on it but tea. "I don't see any wine," she remarked.

"There isn't any," said the March Hare.

"Then it wasn't very civil of you to offer it," said Alice angrily.

"It wasn't very civil of you to sit down without being invited," said the March Hare.

"I didn't know it was your table," said Alice; "it's laid for a great many more than three."

"There is empty space, but how does that concern you?" inquired the Hatter. He had been looking at Alice for some time with great curiosity, and this was his first speech.

"It's very rude to exclude someone," Alice said with some severity.

"Perhaps, but it's ruder still to start an opium war with China simply because you want cheaper tea," countered the March Hare.

"Two opium wars, actually," snored the still sleeping Dormouse.

"I had nothing to do with that," protested Alice. "I am merely a British subject, not a leader of state."

"And yet you arrived uninvited at our tea party," continued the Hare.

The Hatter opened his eyes very wide on hearing this; but all he said was, "Why is a raven like a writing-desk?" The March Hare glared at this blatant attempt at defusing the conversation but said nothing.

"Come, we shall have some fun now!" thought Alice. "I'm glad they've begun asking riddles.—I believe I can guess that," she added aloud.

"Do you mean insult by addressing us in the third person? We're immediately to your front and can hear what you're saying," the March Hare grumbled. "At any rate, by believing that you can guess, do you mean that you think you can find out the answer to it?" said the March Hare.

"Exactly so," said Alice.

"Then you should say what you mean," the March Hare went on.

"I do," Alice hastily replied; "at least—at least I mean what I say—that's the same thing, you know."

"Not the same thing a bit!" said the Hatter. "You might just as well say that 'I see what I eat' is the same thing as 'I eat what I see'!"

"You might just as well say," added the March Hare, "that 'I like what I get' is the same thing as 'I get what I like'!"

"You might just as well say," added the Dormouse, who seemed to be talking in his sleep, "that 'I breathe when I sleep' is the same thing as 'I sleep when I breathe'!"

"This all sounds like a tedious lesson in formal logic rather than a real conversation," said Alice, raising an eyebrow.

"How dare you! How dare you!" spat the Hatter. "Formal logic is fascinating and of great import!"

"Not the way you teach it, it's not," retorted Alice. "You've merely told me what you think I've done wrong, with no attempt to explain why believing I can guess is worse than thinking I can answer."

"You should be able to work that out yourself," said the March Hare, snatching an empty teacup and slurping noisily.

"That's lazy and ineffectual pedagogy. All you're doing is claiming to be an expert and stating that I'm wrong without doing any work. You've placed the onus on me to learn without taking up the responsibility to teach," said Alice, swiping an equally empty teacup from the table and slurping even more loudly than the Hare.

"It's not true that they're doing no work," yawned the Dormouse. "They're working quite hard at protecting the patriarchy."

Here the conversation dropped, and the party sat silent for a minute, while Alice thought over all she could remember about ravens and writing-desks, which wasn't much.

The Hatter was the first to break the silence. "What day of the month is it?" he said, turning to Alice. He had taken his watch out of his pocket, and was looking at it uneasily, shaking it every now and then, and holding it to his ear.

Alice considered a little, and then said, "The fourth."

"Two days wrong!" sighed the Hatter. "I told you butter wouldn't suit the works!" he added looking angrily at the March Hare.

"It was the best butter," the March Hare meekly replied, staring at the hair-covered lump of cream upon the butter dish.

"I think the time has quite passed for declaring things to be the best when they're of obvious inferiority," the Hatter grumbled. "Although, it does sound somewhat presidential."

"It sounds more like the tune of a snake-oil salesperson to me," Alice remarked.

The March Hare took the watch and looked at it gloomily: then he dipped it into his cup of tea, and looked at it again: but he could think of nothing better to say than his first remark, "It was the best butter, you know."

Alice opened her mouth, seeking to trump the Hare's obvious lie when she was a little startled by seeing the Cheshire Cat sitting on a bough of a tree a few yards off.

The Cat only grinned when it saw Alice. It looked good-natured, she thought. Still, it had very long claws and a great many teeth, so she felt that it ought to be treated with respect.

"Cheshire Puss," she began, rather timidly, as she did not at all know whether it would like the name; however, it only grinned a little wider. "Come, it's pleased so far," thought Alice, and she went on. "Would you tell me, please, which way I ought to go from here?"

"That depends a good deal on where you want to get to," said the Cat.

"I don't much care where—" said Alice.

"Then it doesn't matter which way you go," said the Cat.

"—so long as I get somewhere," Alice added as an explanation.

"Oh, you're sure to do that," said the Cat, "if you only walk long enough."

Alice felt that this could not be denied, so she tried another question. "What sort of people live about here?"

"In that direction," the Cat said, waving its right paw towards the Hatter, "a mad person: and in that direction," waving the other paw, "a mad March Hare."

"But I don't want to go among mad people," Alice remarked.

"Oh, you can't help that," said the Cat. "We're all mad here. I'm mad. You're mad."

"How do you know I'm mad?" said Alice.

"How do you know you're not?" said the Cat.

Alice didn't think that proved it at all; however, she went on, "And how do you know that you're mad?"

"To begin with," said the Cat, "a dog's not mad. You grant that?"

"I suppose so," said Alice.

"Well, then," the Cat went on, "you see, a dog growls when it's angry, and wags its tail when it's pleased. Now I growl when I'm pleased and wag my tail when I'm angry. Therefore, I'm mad."

"I call it purring, not growling," said Alice.

"Call it what you like, " said the Cat, "but I'm doing the opposite of a thing that's not mad."

"But that doesn't make you mad!" argued Alice. "That assertion only works if growling and tail wagging is what makes a creature not mad!"

"I knew you'd figure out formal logic!" crowed the March Hare.

"You didn't plan for this outcome, you credit-thieving foozler!" insulted Alice.

"Fuck you, colonizer," jabbed the Hare, who then lashed out with his empty teacup, violently spilling nothing onto Alice.

Alice leapt atop the table and upended an entire teapot of nothing onto the Hare, accidentally spilling much of it onto the Dormouse, who would have been badly scalded had he been conscious. He instead snoozed lightly, entirely unaffected by the furious display.

ALTERED
BY AMBER RAINEY

Amelia resisted opening her eyes. She was warm and cozy in her bed, her cat comfortably sleeping against her legs. The sun radiated heat across her face. Suddenly, she jolted upright sending her cat running off the bed. Amelia looked at her alarm clock and groaned, dropping her head into her hands—the blinking image seared into her brain. She was late!

Amelia rushed through her morning routine, almost forgetting deodorant in the process. She wildly threw clothing onto the floor as she searched for something appropriate for the chilly in the morning/ sweltering in the afternoon weather of the South. Taking a last look in the mirror, she grabbed up her purse and dashed into the kitchen. Matt stood there, holding out a plate with a piece of toast. Amelia grabbed it and gave him a quick peck on the cheek.

"Thanks! Gotta Go!"

Amelia walked down the steps and started off down the street towards her office. She munched on her toast as she walked and brushed the crumbs away when she'd finished. She checked her watch and then, satisfied she'd made up a little time, she popped into the coffee shop. The line was shorter than usual—probably because she was later than usual. The barista smiled at her and nodded, already preparing her *usual.* Amelia took her order and thanked the man, waving as she backed out the door. She turned at the last moment and slammed into another person.

The man caught Amelia's elbow with one hand. With the other, he prevented her hot tea from becoming a bath for both of them. Amelia was stunned at the graceful agility he displayed. She immediately turned red.

"I'm **so** sorry! I should have watched where I was going!" she stammered.

The man shrugged. "It's ok. I tried to warn you but most likely too late."

"Still, let me buy you a coffee," she offered, fishing around in her purse for her wallet.

"Really, miss… there is no need."

Amelia's head snapped up. She eyed the man suspiciously.

"Who turns down free coffee? Weren't you just going in?" she asked, gesturing towards the coffee shop.

He nodded and then looked away nervously. He looked back and Amelia was momentarily diverted from her questions by the bluest eyes she had ever seen. As he searched for an explanation, she took in the rest of his face. He had neatly cut dark hair and a square jawline covered in just the right amount of stubble. She thought his nose looked proportionate to the rest of his face. She shook herself internally at the last thought. Who cared about noses? She giggled a little out loud and then remembered herself. He cocked his head, waiting for her to explain.

"It's nothing. So you don't want coffee?"

He shook his head, "I don't drink it."

"Then why were you here," she huffed.

"If you must know, I was going to get a hot chai," he sighed as if the shame of getting tea in a coffee shop was not lost on him.

"Oh... OHHH!"

"What's so... oh?" he asked warily.

"Here, you can have this one," she said, offering her own tea.

The man took it hesitantly and looked at her expectantly. She just shrugged and nodded. He nodded back and took a sip, then smiled.

"It's perfect," he said.

"I never tell anyone I am getting tea in a coffee shop either, but they make it much faster and easier than I could at home. The temperature is just right here."

"Indeed, it is."

Amelia's phone rang and she looked at her watch. She took a step back from the stranger and smiled. He opened the door and gestured for her to walk in but she shook her head.

"Thanks, but I've gotta get to work."

"What about your tea?" he asked.

"It's gone to a good cause today," she smiled.

"Well, in that case, how about I escort you to work?"

Amelia thought a moment and then nodded. The man held out his arm and she laughed as she put her hand on his elbow. He gestured in both directions and she pointed to the right.

"I'm Amelia," she introduced herself.

"Finn."

"Nice to meet you, Finn."

"Likewise, Amelia."

Amelia was so lost in the introductions and Finn's smile, she almost drowned out the angry sound of protesters across the street. She sighed and looked up, checking the entrance to her office building and seeing that it was clear. Finn's steps slowed down and he seemed to withdraw into himself the closer they got to the building. Amelia sensed his hesitation and decided to take action.

"You know what, Finn? My office is just right there and I can go the rest of the way. It was very nice meeting you. Maybe we can bump into each other again sometime?"

Finn looked relieved and nodded. He removed her hand from his elbow and kissed the top of it. Then he bowed with a ridiculous flourish and Amelia laughed. He winked at her and started back down the street, turning back once and raising the teacup in a gesture of goodbye. Amelia smiled and waved, then shoulders and turned towards her office. She just hoped none of the protesters were throwing anything today.

"I just don't understand what they think they gain by standing outside and shouting hate all day. Don't their throats hurt? Don't they have families?" Amelia groused.

"Their families are out there with them. I saw a kid, probably five years old, out there screaming that filth," Monica replied.

Amelia turned away from the window. She had been staring down at the protesters, wishing they would go away and she and her coworkers could have a little bit of peace. It had been nothing short of a nightmare since the location of their office had been leaked on social media. No one had given a thought to the safety of the workers in either her office or the other companies who shared the same building. Whoever worked in the building had a virtual x marked on their back. They were subjected to daily protests and often, the protesters threw things. The first few weeks had been worse before the police stepped in and banned protesting to the empty lot across the street. At least now, the protesters couldn't spit in her face like they did the first day. Amelia shuddered at the thought. She sighed and stepped away from the window. She slumped down in her office chair and Monica gave her a pitying smile.

"People don't change, Amelia," she soothed.

"That's what frustrates me the most! Every decade, a new group of people fight for their rights and win them. Why? Because it is right! What I don't get is, why must it always be a fight? Why can't people just see that we are all basically the same and our differences don't make us bad people, just different?"

Monica shrugged, "Difference is scary and people fight what they don't understand."

"People are stupid. I hate them."

Monica fake gasped. Amelia stuck her tongue out and tossed a wadded up memo paper page at her. Monica laughed and Amelia laughed back. Just then, an intern stuck his head through the door. Amelia sobered up and gestured for him to come in. He entered, handing her a folder.

"A man is here for a consult. He doesn't have an appointment but you have some open slots and Mr. Till said you might fit him in?"

Amelia nodded, "Sure, send him in."

Monica got up and headed for the door. She stopped and looked around before turning back to Amelia. She through the wadded up memo page back at her and then ducked out the door with a laugh. Amelia flipped her off and she just waved back through the glass window. Amelia immediately turned red when she noticed the new client standing in the doorway. She jumped out of her chair, banging her knee on the desk, and sending a jar of pens tumbling to the floor.

"You seem to have a habit of being a little clumsy," he chuckled.

"Shut up!" she mock chided, then clapped a hand on her mouth and quickly scanned the office through the glass door. Luckily no one was paying attention.

Finn finished picking up the pens and set them back on the desk. He waited for Amelia to recover from her outburst. She reddened, even more, wondering how it was even possible to be more embarrassed. She took the time to recover by shutting her office door, sitting back at her desk, and pretending to look over his file. In truth, she was reevaluating him surreptitiously over the file folder.

"Well, can you help me?" he asked impatiently.

She jumped at the sudden intrusion to her thoughts. She held up a finger and really looked at his file. Finn had been discriminated against in a housing application. After reading the documents, it was clear that Finn had a case.

"We can help you. I can make an appointment with you to talk to the housing lawyer and they can get started on filing the proper paperwork."

Finn smiled, then frowned.

"You would not be handling the case?"

Amelia laughed, "No. I'm really just the front line in determining if there is anything we can do. A glorified paper pusher."

"Well, you are a beautiful paper pusher," he complimented.

Amelia blushed again and cleared her throat, turning towards her computer and putting in the necessary requisitions and appointments for Finn. She printed it out and organized it before stapling it all together and placing it in a green file folder. She handed the folder over to Finn.

"So, this is your guidebook. Don't lose anything in this folder. I've made an appointment for you tomorrow afternoon with the housing lawyer. He will get you started and, if all goes well, this will be wrapped up quickly. You have good documentation and a solid case."

"Thank you, Amelia."

Finn rose to leave, then thought better of it and sat back

down. He opened and shut his mouth a few times, gathering the courage to ask her a question. He stared down at the green folder, a pensive look crossing his face. Amelia waited but then the anticipation was too much.

"I have a significant other but we are on again, off again. Right now we are off. Do you want to go to dinner?" she blurted out.

It was Finn's turn to blush. He thought for a moment and then smiled. He nodded.

"I would love to. Are you sure? What about…?" he asked as he gestured to himself.

"Really? That is what you were worried about? Do you think I would work here if I cared about that?"

Finn shrugged. Amelia just chuckled and wrote down her address on a memo pad. She tore off the page and handed it to him.

"Pick me up at 7?" she asked.

"You don't want me to escort you home? What about those protesters?"

She shrugged. "I do this twice a day, every day and sometimes on the weekends. Sometimes even for lunch if I'm really craving a burrito or something. I'm used to it. I saw how you reacted this morning and now I know why. It took a lot for you to come here today. That's the first step in not letting them get to you. But I think it's been enough for today."

Finn smiled again and it lit up the whole room. Amelia thought she could just sit and stare at him while he smiled. He looked back at her address and then gathered the folder and stood, going to the door.

"I'll see you tonight," he mock bowed, with less flourish, and went out of the office.

Amelia smiled, shook her head, and went back to her computer. She typed up a few more notes and then sat back in her chair. She stared at the face looking back at her. He didn't look altered in any way. She frowned. It was what infuriated her the most about all the protests and discrimination. A person merely had to check a box on a form and suddenly they were seen as "less than". The box should be illegal but so far the high court had not made a significant determination. The more she thought about it, the more she got angry again. People never changed. Any little difference and they just lumped someone in a category of inferiority. That supposedly inferior class had to claw and scrape their way to equality. The circle never ended.

"Why don't you knock off early?" Monica interrupted her thoughts.

Amelia looked up, "I have more work to do."

"Amelia, you always have more work to do. You do the work of three people. I'm your boss. Knock off early."

"Is that an order?"

"Does it have to be?" Monica asked sternly.

Amelia sighed and shook her head.

"Good girl."

"Bitch," Amelia teased.

"The one and only," Monica said, waggling her fingers as she left Amelia's office.

Finn and Amelia stopped at her door. He pushed a stray hair behind her ear and then leaned down, hesitant. Amelia closed the gap and kissed him. Finn kissed her back. After a moment, they broke the kiss and Amelia smiled. Finn made a move to leave and Amelia tugged him back towards her.

"Do you want to stay tonight?"

Finn looked up at her door and then back at her. They had been dating for several months and he had yet to stay the night.

Amelia knew he was hesitant but she felt it was time they took their relationship to the next level. She tried to reassure him but he'd lived so many years as an outcast, she knew it was hard to be away from his comfort zone.

"I didn't come prepared," he balked.

"I have what you need," she soothed.

His eyes widened, "Why?"

"You say that as if it is impossible. We often have unprepared clients in the office and we are trained in helping people out when we are in the field. Each of us carries extra cords in case a client is in trouble. Why do you think my purse is so cavernous?"

"A woman's purse is a rabbit hole to me."

Amelia laughed. She tugged him back and kissed him again. He rested his forehead against hers and closed his eyes. He opened them and Amelia could tell he'd made a decision. He nodded and Amelia tried, and failed, to keep her little squeal of joy to herself. He lovingly rolled his eyes at her.

Amelia and Finn lay in bed together, sleeping peacefully, when a muted beeping sound awoke Finn. He opened one eye, groaning at the fact that it was still dark outside. He carefully removed his arm from underneath Amelia and pressed a finger against the spot just in front of his ear. The beeping stopped. Finn looked down at the sleeping Amelia and was very tempted to stay in bed with her. He brushed the hair out of her face and placed a kiss on her cheek. He lingered a little too long and the beeping started again—louder this time. Finn groaned again, pressing angrily at the spot in his ear and quietly getting out of bed.

Finn pulled on his boxers and fished around in his pants for his phone. He checked his app and then grabbed the cable Amelia had left out on the bedside table. He tiptoed out of the room, shutting the door as softly as possible. He walked into the kitchen, opening the fridge, and pulled out an iced tea. He sat at the table, plugging the cable into a wall, then finding the port in his arm and plugging it into his arm. He opened the app again, logging the time and sending the report to the doctor. Then he went into his crossword puzzle app and began killing some time until the recharge was finished.

"What the fuck!?!"

Finn looked up at the yell. Matt was standing in the doorway, a murderous look on his face. Finn looked around in confusion before he realized the anger was directed at him. Without realizing it, Finn began to shrink in on himself.

"You are altered! Does Amelia know? How dare you?"

"I... I don't understand?"

"You!" Matt stomped and pointed.

"What's going on out here?"

A sleepy Amelia approached Matt from behind and pushed past him. She looked between Matt and Finn. She walked over to Finn, putting an arm on his shoulder and kissing him on the cheek. Matt spluttered in fury.

"How, Amelia? How can you kiss him? Did you sleep with him?" he accused.

Amelia got defensive, "Matt! We are not dating right now. What's wrong with you? We talked about Finn."

"You didn't tell me he was a monster!" Matt pointed at Finn.

"What the fuck are you talking about?" Amelia asked angrily.

"He's altered, Amelia. How can you be with him?"

Finn heard another quick beep in his ear. He quickly checked his phone and then unplugged the cable from the port in his arm. He stood to leave but Amelia pressed on his shoulder. She looked at him and shook her head. He nodded and swallowed apprehensively.

"How dare you! How can you call a human being a monster? I

never knew you felt this way. You know what I do for a living!"

"Just because you work for... them... doesn't mean you have to be with them. They can be around without integrating into our lives!"

Amelia slapped Matt.

"You ignorant bastard. I want you out. Now!" Amelia pointed out of the room.

"Fine. I don't want the government spying on me with their robots, anyway!"

Matt spun on his heels. Amelia seethed while she heard Matt gathering some of his stuff. Finn winced when the front door slammed. Amelia turned sad eyes back to Finn.

"I'm so sorry. I didn't know he was..."

"A bigot?" Finn offered.

"That's putting it nicer than what I was going for," Amelia groused.

Finn took her hand and kissed it. She held it as she went around the table and knelt in front of him. She hugged his waist and then rested her head against his chest.

"Come back to bed?" she asked.

Finn nodded and led her back to her bedroom.

"I really think this dress makes me look fatter than I already am," Amelia complained.

Finn came up behind her and looked at her in the mirror.

"You look beautiful."

He kissed the side of her head and she rolled her eyes at him, making a face. He made a face back and she swatted at him. They laughed and turned away from the mirror.

"You're going to be late if we don't go soon," Finn reminded her.

"Story of my life. Just don't you be late," she told her belly.

"If he's anything like his mother, I wouldn't expect him until next spring at the earliest," Finn teased.

He ducked out of the room to avoid the pillow being thrown at his head. Finn waited by the door with Amelia's coat. They walked to her office building, discussing the plans they had to decorate for the holiday season. As they neared the office, Finn switched sides with Amelia, attempting to protect her if the protesters threw anything at them. He was no longer afraid of the walk but he still didn't keep his eyes off the protesters. He stepped inside the building with Amelia and then kissed her. She waved goodbye as she stepped into the elevators.

Finn shoved his hands in his pockets and set back off for home. He looked up and groaned when he saw Matt waiting on the steps to their door. He squared his shoulders and pushed forward, ready to deal with whatever drama Matt had in mind. He noticed Matt looked very disheveled and nervous. As soon as he saw Finn, Matt hunched down and started to move away from the steps.

"Matt," Finn called.

Matt stopped and turned back to Finn. He avoided Finn's eyes and breathed heavily in the chilly air. He shuffled back and forth in an agitated manner. Matt huffed out a breath and put a hand on Matt's shoulder. He got a whiff of alcohol and his eyes teared up.

"Where's... I want to talk to Amelia," Matt stammered.

"She's at work."

Matt's head whipped up. He searched Finn's eyes for a lie but found none. He grabbed Finn's hand and started pulling him towards the office where Amelia worked.

"She can't be. She's always late. She had a meeting."

Finn yanked his hand out of Matt's and stopped. Matt whirled back around and tried to grab Finn again. Finn stood his ground.

"Her meeting was moved to next week. What's this about, Matt?"

Matt gestured wildly towards the office building.

"We have to get to her. She has to get out!"

"Matt, you aren't making any sense. Calm down. What's…"

Finn was cut off mid-sentence by the sound of a loud explosion. Matt screamed in terror and ran off down the street. Finn's heart sank to his stomach and he ran after Matt. He stopped when Matt collapsed onto the sidewalk and tore at his hair. Finn gulped down his fear and walked up to Matter, looking around the corner. In front of him, the building where Amelia worked had a gaping hole in the side. Papers and ash were fluttering down to the street. People were coming out of the building in various states of disarray. Finn leaned down and hauled Matt to his feet. He grasped Matt's lapels and got in his face.

"What. Did. You. Do?" Finn spat.

"I didn't know. I didn't mean to. I tried to stop it…" Matt sobbed.

Finn threw Matt back down to the ground and went to search for Amelia. Matt sobbed and cried, curling up in a ball on the sidewalk.

Finn pounded on Matt's door. The longer he stood outside waiting in the hallway, the angrier he got. He knew Matt was in the apartment. He could hear him shuffling around. He pounded on the door again. Just as he was about to break the door down, Matt opened it a tiny crack.

"Let me in," Finn demanded.

"Is she?" Matt pleaded.

"She's alive, you moron. Let me in."

Matt opened the door and Finn pushed his way into the apartment. He did his best not to gag at the stench of stale beer and pizza. The place was a pigsty. Finn picked his way to a clean spot to stand and rounded on Matt.

"I... I," Matt stammered.

Finn held up a hand.

"Listen to me. I don't care if you rot away in this house forever. I don't know what your involvement in the bombing was, but I do know you were involved. I am here for Amelia... and for the baby."

Matt's eyes cleared a little. "Baby?"

"She's pregnant. She needs you to come to the hospital. The baby's life depends on it."

"Why would she need me there?"

"Because it's yours, you daft idiot," Finn exploded.

"Mine?"

Finn shook his head and grabbed Matt. He dragged him into the bathroom and turned on the shower. When Matt made no move to do anything, Finn shoved him into the shower. Matt sputtered and shouted and Finn just held onto him harder.

Once Finn had gotten Matt to cooperate, Matt cleaned himself up. Finn put a hot mug of coffee into Matt's hands and glared at him until he'd finished the whole cup. Matt nodded and Finn shoved him out the door, stomping down the stairs and not looking back to see if Matt was following. Matt trudged behind Finn all the way to the hospital. He only hesitated at the front door and Finn whirled around to face him once more.

"What is your problem?" Finn growled.

Matt winced, "Why didn't she tell me?"

Finn rolled his eyes. He was ready to just leave Matt out in the cold but he'd promised Amelia he would try to stay calm. He took a steadying breath and closed his eyes for a moment, breathing in slowly through his nose and out of his mouth. He opened his eyes to see Matt anxiously staring at him. It almost made him want to start the whole process over but he knew there wasn't enough time for him to create more delays.

"She was going to. Then you went ballistic on me. She decided she didn't want you to know because she did not want her son to grow up to be an asshole…" He paused, holding up a staying hand. "Her words—not mine."

Matt huffed, "So why now?"

"Because of the bomb. The baby needs both parents' permission for a nanobot transfusion. The bomb caused some heart damage and it's the only way to repair it. Otherwise, the baby dies."

Matt's eyes widened. He gulped and Finn snorted at him derisively. Matt looked through the hospital doors as if he could see Amelia and the baby from where he was standing. Finn towered over him with one hand on the door and one hand on Matt's shoulder.

"Time to really decide if you believe all that government control nonsense. Look, I've heard it most of my life and I take it. Do you want to know why?"

"Wh—why?" Matt asked.

"I am alive. That's more than I can say about some people. Sure, I have to *recharge* the bots on a regular schedule but without them, my lungs would have stopped working a long time ago. They don't control me. They don't give me subliminal *kill all the humans* messages. They don't record everything you say. All they do is keep my lungs running. Got it?" Finn explained.

Matt nodded. Finn waited to see what Matt would decide and he knew the moment Matt had given up his ill-conceived notions of what being altered meant and decided to learn a little. Finn nodded, gesturing for Matt to enter the hospital and then followed after him.

Amelia looked down at the baby in her arms and smiled. He'd been through so much but the doctor had just given him a clean bill of health. She was extra happy because the doctors had finally unhooked her from all the machines and IVs and she was getting to go home.

"You ready to get out of here, sweetheart?" Finn asked as he entered the room.

He walked over to Amelia and kissed her on the forehead. It was the one place she'd said she wasn't sore. He put a finger against the baby's hand and smiled when Isaac closed his fist around it. The little boy was a fighter and the nanobots were doing a great job of keeping his hurt functioning.

"Yeah, we better get home before this little guy needs a recharge. They told me there is a new portable battery that we might be able to get. It would make it easier on us... and you."

Finn nodded, "We could go away to a cabin in the woods with no electricity!"

Amelia laughed, "Hold on there... I like my comforts."

"The one I'm thinking of has running water," Finn teased.

"It better not be a river, you know that doesn't count!" Amelia groused.

Finn laughed. He and Amelia looked up at the clearing of a throat. Finn tensed a tiny bit but Amelia squeezed his hand. He looked down at Amelia and smiled, nodding at her.

"It's okay, Matt, you can come in," she said.

Matt nodded and shuffled into the room. He hesitated a few feet from Amelia and then pulled his arm from behind his back. In his hand was a teddy bear with a bandage on its arm. Amelia cocked her head to the side.

"It... it's an altered bear. See, it has a little bandage covering the port in its arm until the skin grows back. I... I thought he might like it," Matt stammered apologetically.

Amelia smiled up at Finn, who took the bear and examined the little velcroed bandage. He chuckled at the bear and Matt grinned nervously. Amelia looked between Matt and Finn and smiled.

"Do you want to hold him?" she asked.

Matt nodded, "Will I hurt him? Will the bots dislodge?"

Finn snorted, "That's not how this works."

Matt blushed and scratched behind his ear. Amelia gestured for him to come closer and laid the baby in his arms. The baby gurgled up at Matt and Finn directed him to a chair before his knees buckled. He smiled down at the baby and then looked back to Amelia and Finn.

"Can we... start over?" he asked.

Amelia looked at Finn, who rolled his eyes but nodded. Amelia smiled up at him and then looked at Matt and Isaac. Amelia nodded and tears rolled down Matt's cheeks. Finn tried to covertly hand Matt a tissue and Matt quickly swiped at his cheeks. The two men cooed over the baby and Amelia felt a rush of warmth flood through her. She knew that whatever hatred was thrown at them, they could now weather it as a united family.

MAD

BY MARSHALL MILLER

That's her?" he asked.

"Yes," she answered.

Forensic Psychiatrist Charles Brown looked through the two way mirror into the unique padded holding room. Sitting at a table with rounded edges and some unusual padding material was a young woman who would fit the term 'non-descript' to a 'T.' Light brown hair, the average height for a person of European descent, medium complexion, she was attractive in a pleasant sort of way. Walking down any city street, she might warrant a glance but not a stare.

"Like I told you on the phone," said Police Lieutenant Jennifer Columbo, "she meets no profile, description, physical ability of a person generally associated with this type of—incident."

Charles looked at Jennifer. They had known each other for years, ever since Jennifer became a Detective. Charles was a federal criminal investigator in a former life. He lost that life when he lost his right leg and left hand to a land mine during a stint on active military duty in an oversees shithole. During his recovery, Charles began his medical studies to keep his mind occupied and find a new career field. Kicking doors in to grab people while missing a leg and with a hook

229

for his left hand was not something listed in most police procedure manuals. If he were a Steve Austin, a bionic man, maybe. So far, connecting Charles, Chuck to his friends, up with the most advanced artificial limbs, had been unsuccessful. There was something about a brain/body interface problem. Which was a reason why Charles had been drawn to psychiatry and neurology. Ten years later, and he was the 'go-to guy' for many a cop shop.

Charles had worked hard to keep his slender but fit build after his injuries. Jennifer was his opposite in build and temperament. She was of a shorter Italian stock and looks, which made her a dead ringer for the late Gina Lollobrigida of 1950's Hollywood fame. And while Charles had worked at keeping a calm demeanor, Jennifer, Gina to her friends, still kept the stereotypical hot Italian/Sicilian temper attributed to many a movie mafia member. However, Jennifer knew how to turn it on and off, never let it turn into a rage.

"So, any ideas, Gina?" Charles asked.

"Chuck, that's why I called you. She seems to have no memory of anything. Have you watched the surveillance tapes yet?"

"No," replied Charles. "I wanted to see her first, get a baseline impression. She seems like she just took a walk in the park."

Jennifer grunted.

"Yeah. Once you watch the video, you'll think it was Jurassic Park."

"You have her clothes?" asked Charles.

"They are in the lab," Jennifer answered. "We're trying to ascertain any evidence as to where she came from."

"Well, Gina, my friend, let me see the video. Then I'll see if she wants to talk to me."

Charles went into another secure room with a stand-alone computer. The law enforcement personnel did not want the surveillance records somehow hacked and released into the World

Wide Web. Jennifer pulled a thumb drive from her pocket

"Here, my friend. I'll let you look at it by yourself. Seeing it once was enough for me. I feel sorry for our forensics people who have to do an in-depth examination of the recordings."

Charles had a slight smile when he answered.

"No rest for the wicked."

Charles had not realized the amount of surveillance video which was available. Jennifer had told him that the location surveilled had been wired for sound and video. The undercover agent had set up a meeting with the 'Bad Guys' on government controlled turf after weeks of work. No one expected what would happen next.

The city police and local Sheriff's office had been running a 'sting' operation to catch a stolen car ring exporting vehicles and parts overseas. Then, right in the middle of the investigation, someone said they also had access to kidnapped women and girls. The smugglers said they needed to get rid of some human merchandise taken in to settle a debt. Thus, Homeland Security had been brought in to deal with customs and immigration violations. Charles had been used as an expert by all types of agencies, so there were no protests when Jennifer had asked him to assist in questioning the subject.

Charles spent a half-hour watching three recorded views of the crime scene. The total meeting between Good and Bad Guys was planned to be extensive as the two sides dickered about cost and payments, not to mention the other matter of female disposal.

The young woman in the padded room had other ideas.

Charles was not easily shaken. But he trembled as he finished watching the hellish scene.

"My God," Charles mumbled, "how did one average size woman do all that-damage?"

Since he had watched the video evidence, the forensic psychiatrist knew she did it. The cameras used were Hollywood epic quality. Any blurring was caused by the speed of the action. Charles stood up, unlocked the door, and found Jennifer standing outside in the hallway.

"Sorry, Gina, but I need you to watch part of this with me."

The female detective made a face as if she had smelled very rotten fish before she answered.

"Oh, all right. But this is going to cost you at least a lunch."

"Done. Now, let's go back into the room and lock the door."

Charles started the recording over at the beginning. A late-model RV pulled into the triple bay garage where the fake 'chop shop' operated. The two undercover detectives, a man with a sexy ' main squeeze' woman as distracting eye candy, walked into the camera frames. The computer screen had the views from the three cameras split up into three simultaneous rectangles. Jennifer and Charles watched the three displays as an elderly driver dismounted the RV cab.

"Old guy was hired as a front," explained Jennifer. "Less apt to be pulled over on the interstates or at the Ports of Entry."

"Hope he was well paid," replied Charles.

A younger male, listed under the generic term as Caucasian, walked into frame from the passenger's side of the RV, called out in a friendly manner to the two undercovers.

"Sam Baker. He was the boss of the operation," Jennifer explained. "Watch how he has the hots for Sally, the female undercover."

Sam, the Boss, went over and hugged Sally, squeezing her nicely shaped behind. Sally playfully pushed him back, scolding him with a grin on her face. A third male, categorized as 'Black' in the world of race relations, walked from around the rear of the RV and opened the rear driver's side access door. Someone from inside the RV began shoving young females from the inside. They stumbled as they exited, and Charles paused the recording.

"The other women, or should I say girls as none were older than 17 according to the written reports, are Asian. But our subject in the room is Caucasian in appearance."

"Yes, Chuck. Another reason why we called you in to try and get the woman to tell us her story. Why she was with the others is the million-dollar question." Jennifer took a deep breath, then let it out before she spoke again.

"I do not want to see the next part again."

"Sorry, Gina. Doctor's orders." With that comment, Charles hit the start key on the computer.

On the screen, there was a blurred figure which launched itself out the door and onto the African American. Within seconds, blood began to spurt from the neck jugular artery as the rapidly moving body used teeth and nails to slash the man's throat open. Charles paused the recording again.

"That's her, our special guest."

Jennifer swore, then spoke.

"That is Jaqueline Basset, Jackie, to her friends. Age twenty-five. Five-foot seven and one hundred thirty pounds. Occupation before this incident was as the best selling published author, primarily speculative fiction, what they often call Sci-Fi these days."

"How did you obtain all this information so quickly if she can't or won't fill in the details, Gina?"

"She had a Concealed Carry Permit," answered Jennifer. "Thus, there were fingerprints on file. Wonders of all the new databases allowed us to know who she was once we cleaned enough blood off of her to take a set of prints."

"No, priors?" Charles asked.

"Clean as the driven snow. No spouses or roommates. She had been signing books a week ago at some local book stores. Then she disappeared until…" Jennifer left the rest of the statement hanging.

Charles paused in thought. Then he started the recording once more.

"Shit," Jennifer said.

The female lieutenant was forced to watch the surveillance footage of the bloody mayhem as Charles quizzed her for further details. Partway through the process, the doctor noticed just how stressed his friend was.

"Gina, this is personal. What gives."

"The male undercover is my ex-husband."

Charles stopped and stared for a moment.

"Husband? How…"

"How did I have a husband when I now have a pretty pregnant wife, Sheila, in a long term lesbian relationship, you may ask? Shit happens." Jennifer crumpled up the cup of her third coffee and threw it into the nearby wastepaper basket.

"Tom and I are still good friends. Hell, he stood up to be a Godfather for our firstborn, and the second on the way. So when he was shot, and I had to watch a tape of it, well, it is unsettling." Jennifer grinned at Charles.

"Friend, you should see the look on your face. The great clinical psychiatrist is at a loss for words!"

Charles finally chuckled, then spoke.

"It's just that many a man has thoughts that he was such a lousy lover that he drove his wife to be a Lesbian. It is seen as a complete failure in manhood."

"Well, I guess people are more advanced than you give them

credit, Chuck." Jennifer pointed at the computer screen. "In a moment, Sam Baker pulls a pistol and starts blasting, even though he agreed to come sans weapons. "

"No honor among thieves, Gina."

"You've got that right. So Tom shoots at Sam as Sam shoots at our friend Jackie, the author, and hits one of the girls instead. Watch the rest of the footage."

The rest of the action took a minute. The person identified as Jackie jumped on the shot Sam, tore the pistol from the miscreant's grasp, and beat his face in with it. She then tackled Tom, started to do the same to his face when the female undercover, Sally, laid a collapsible baton alongside Jackie's head. Charles and Jennifer watched the author shake off the blow, turn, and flatten the detective with one punch. The man inside the RV came out shooting and had his pistol jammed down this throat. The woman identified as Jackie grabbed the elderly driver as he fled and bit both ears off as the driver screamed. Another man burst in from the street and began shooting up the place with an AK-47. All his shots missed the woman author as she threw a chair which smashed the shooter's front teeth out. Then the law enforcement security team arrived and shot the AK-47 gunman. It took six of them to subdue Jackie.

"And you say she remembers nothing?" asked Charles.

"That is what she claimed when we got her into the secure room and read her Miranda," replied Jennifer. "That's when I thought of you. People open up to you. And you can usually tell if someone is lying."

Charles looked at the now frozen computer screen.

"You also would like a professional opinion on whether she is mad as a Hatter, yes?"

"You read my mind," replied Jennifer.

"One caveat. I could destroy any chance of prosecution of

Jackie. She did attack law enforcement personnel."

Jennifer sighed, then spoke.

"I know. But we just have to understand how and why about Jackie. She is one big fat mystery."

Charles went over the written notes of the arresting officers and watched the surveillance tapes again before entering the padded room. Jackie was sitting at an oversized table, one foot manacled to the floor. The table was extra wide to make it difficult for a subject to get a piece of the interviewer. The woman was clothed in an orange jumpsuit used in the local jail. Charles smiled as he pushed a cup carrier towards the center of the table.

"Coffee?" he asked.

"Yes, please," the author said with a smile.

"Here. There is plenty of packets of sugar and the like. Donuts are coming."

Jackie took one of the large cups and began to doctor it with various packets of creamer and sugar. As she did, she spoke.

"Well, you don't look Greek, but you come with gifts of coffee. You also don't have a cop demeanor and have a medical file under your arm. In the street vernacular, you are a Shrink."

"Guilty as charged- may I call you Jackie? I'm Doctor Charles Brown. I'm what you call a Forensic Psychiatrist. This means I ask questions whose answers can be used against you in court. I am not here to examine you for medical care. I am here to figure out what happened and if you can understand what happened."

Jackie flashed a friendly smile.

"So you want to see how mad or crazy I am, right?"

"That is the simple answer, yes. However, it involves more of determining if you realize what happened, can remember your actions recorded on the surveillance footage."

Jackie blew on her coffee, then sipped it.

"Not bad coffee, Doctor Brown. But I thought Chalie Brown went to Lucy for psychiatric help."

Charles chuckled. He had heard that comment so many times, yet the way Jackie phrased it, seemed actually humorous. Especially since she seemed so relaxed after going a few rounds with cops and thugs at the fake chop shop.

"I heard that joke all the way through medical school. But I was a law enforcement officer before that, so I was used to being ribbed all the time."

Charles opened the file he carried, used his human right hand handle the papers inside.

"You lost your hand and leg being a cop? Jackie asked.

"No. During active duty overseas. Led me to be a doctor." He set the papers aside.

"You must have developed your powers of observation and reasoning as an author, Jackie, as you noticed my limp and figured a lost leg went with the hand."

"Guilty as charged, Doctor. Or is it Charles?"

He shrugged. "Machts nichts, Jackie. As long as you don't start screaming and thrashing around, you can call me whatever you want. I just need to find some answers in this unusual-situation."

"Again, Charles, it is about what level of madness or crazy am I, correct?"

"The simple answer is still 'yes,' although explanation as to how you came to be with those Asian girls is also part of the answers I need."

The author sipped her coffee, then set it down as she spoke.

"A speculative fiction author named Phillip K. Dick once said, 'It is sometimes an appropriate response to reality to go mad.' I believe that statement fits the situation quite accurately."

"How so?" Jackie was talking, which was good. Now Charles had to keep her talking.

"Well, Charles, since I have no memories for the last twenty-four hours, something must have made me go mad and beat the crap out of complete strangers."

Donuts arrived, brought in by Jennifer, who Jackie greeted with a smile. The detective lieutenant smiled back and then left. Charles watched as the author grabbed a frosted donut with sprinkles and began to wolf it down. As Jackie reached for another, she noticed the Doctor's close observation.

"Sorry to be such a rude pig, Charles. But I am suddenly famished."

"That tells me you have had little to eat, even before your extreme activity."

Jackie grabbed a maple bar and ate half of it before replying.

"I keep hearing that I did-something violent. But I have no memory for the last day or so."

"Does that happen often?" asked Charles.

"Depends on what you consider 'often,' Charles. I can honestly say I seem to have a period of blurred memory at least once a year. And no, I am not a big party animal or drug user. I rarely even take an aspirin."

"Anybody ever mentioned seeing what you did during the lost time you experienced?"

Jackie shook her head 'no' as she fixed herself another coffee from some spares Jennifer had brought in with the donuts. The woman then stuffed another donut in her mouth.

"Your metabolism still seems elevated, Jackie. Thus it requires replacement calories. I can get you a real meal…"

Jackie swallowed the remains of a donut, sipped her coffee,

then smiled at Charles.

"No need to ply me with food, Doctor. I am more than willing to cooperate to sort out a mess. One which I seem to have no memory and no records other than what you law enforcement types have obtained."

"Think you can handle watching some graphic video recordings?" Charles asked. He knew that he risked tainting the evidence, being accused of unduly influencing a suspect with offensive material which could be used in court. However, the medical professional had the gut feeling Jackie really did not remember-anything.

"Lay on, McDuff, I think Macbeth said in that famous play."

"Okay, Jackie. I need to get permission as I'm just an advisor."

"No problem, Charles. I'll just stay here and stuff my face with some more donuts."

Jennifer and the other detectives were a bit wary about the idea of sharing the tapes just yet. However, Charles made a case for this action based on his years of testimony as an expert.

"You know that a defense lawyer will paint her as a victim who reacted due to extreme fear. The undercover officers did not even have time to I.D. themselves as cops. So if she did have some nefarious connection, I doubt if it will come out during any investigation. Those assholes still alive have clammed up."

Jennifer grunted, then said, "Okay. I'll authorize you using the tapes. Just remember, my friend, it's my ass as a ranking person."

"I never forget that, Gina."

Within minutes they had a stand-alone laptop for Jackie to use. Charles sat in the room after the others set up the thumb drive for viewing.

"Ready, Jackie?" asked Charles. The author gave a shaky smile and nodded 'yes.' The forensic doctor noticed the seriousness and violence of the situation were sinking in. Good, he thought. If she is lying, she'll have trouble not reacting if she actually remembers. Charles sat a bit askew, so his total view of Jackie and her body was not obscured.

The total viewing time of the actions inside the chop shot was a bit over six minutes. After the RV pulled into the bay and the large garage door shut, everything happened fast. Sam squeezed Barbara's butt, the Asian girls were shoved out of the RV, and then Jackie appeared as a blurred figure. Charles observed and saw Jackie flinch when some of the squirting blood hit one of the surveillance camera lenses. Then it was all over.

"Care to see it again, Jackie?: Charles asked.

"That can't be me," said Jackie. "I would remember-something. Right now, it feels like I'm watching a Tarantino movie."

She gave Charles a worried look.

"How do I not remember? It's sick, I can't."

"Actually," said Charles, "it is normal for people to block out horrible events at least temporarily. Then, they come back, often with a vengeance."

"Now isn't that something to look forward to," Jackie said. She stared at Charles and then continued.

"How do we speed things up? How do I remember faster?"

Charles paused for a moment as he considered Jackie's demeanor. Was she honest, or was she trying to distract and dissemble?

"Well, Jackie, a short answer is we could try basic hypnotism. If you want to take the long term approach, we combine drugs with hypnotism to see if we can find what is hidden in your subconscious. And, of course, we would also hook you up to a lie detector. The problems are the creation of false memories and keeping you on ice until we finish the process. To be honest, no one wants to release you until we find out where all this—violence came from and why."

"Like I said before, Charles, I HAVE to know. So do what you must to figure this out."

Once again, Charles conferred with Gina. Once again, she acquiesced with the "Don't get me fired" warning. Charles moved his chair, so he sat across a table corner from Jackie.

"I need to be close to do my magic," he said with a smile.

"I promise I won't bite," Jackie said with a grin. Then she frowned. "I guess I can't make that promise after seeing that tape, can I?"

"I haven't lost a subject yet," replied Charles. He then took a silver watch chain out of his pants pocket. On the end of the chain was a small silver figure of a Unicorn.

"Now, watch the magic Unicorn. While you watch it swing, listen to the sound of my voice…"

Jackie was 'under' within a minute. 'I wonder if she has been hypnotized before?' Charles thought. He felt rushed, so he had not asked, which was an amateur mistake. Now he hoped it would not come back to bite him.

"Jackie, do you recognize my voice?"

"Yes," was the reply.

"I'd like you to think back some three hours ago."

"Yes."

"Do you remember where you were?"

"Fuzzy…."

"Okay. Jackie, think back to yesterday. Where were you yesterday?"

"I- fuzzy."

"Jackie, do you see any people?"

"Yes. But fuzzy."

"How many people?"

"Fuzzy…more than one?"

"Jackie, you are looking at the fuzzy people. One walks up to you and speaks. What do they say?"

"I hear—in my head."

"What do you hear?"

"Do not be afraid. We have never hurt you."

Charles frowned. 'Have Never?' That sounded as if she was with someone she knew or had dealt with before.

"Jackie, you know the person who is speaking?"

"Yes-No." A tremor went through Jackie's body.

"Jackie. Relax, You are with Charles. Everything is okay."

Jackie took a deep breath, then let it out. A half-smile formed on her lips.

"Charles. Good donuts."

"Yes. Good donuts. Jackie, before the good donuts, you talked with a person."

"Yes. A person…not a person." A deep frown formed on Jackie's face.

"Jackie, think back, please. You see the face of a person…"

"Not a person."

"Not a person. Animal?" Charles was afraid he was inserting possible false memories, but the author said she was talking with someone. "Not a person' could mean it was someone she disliked and thus did not consider them as a viable 'person' for the association.

"Animal. Yes- and no." The deep frown was still there.

"A dog?" Charles did not want to lead her to create a memory, but he needed to pin her down.

"Grey."

"A grey dog? The 'not a person' was a grey dog?"

"Grey."

"Jackie. You are looking at a grey person," said Charles.

"Grey!" Jackie's eyes popped wide open. She began to shake.

"Jackie. This is Charles. When I count to three and slap the table, you will wake. One, two,-"

"GREY!" Jackie bellowed and bolted straight up from the chair. Charles stood as fast as he could with just one good leg.

"Three," he said as he loudly slapped his remaining hand on the table.

Jackie ripped the foot manacle chain from the floor. The table was next as Charles was slammed backward towards a wall. His artificial leg buckled and he fell to the floor. Charles lay on the floor as large uniformed men and women burst through the padded room's door. He watched the average looking woman known as Jackie throw law enforcement officers around like they were stuffed toys. The author dashed to the door and smashed it open.

It took three officers with Tasers to take Jackie to the floor. It took six to get manacles and a shock belt on her.

Gina, with a bloody nose, helped Charles to his feet.

"You okay?"

"As well as can be expected. I hit a preexisting center of pain and fear. She needs hospitalization-".

"We've gone for an emergency commitment at the State Mental Hospital," said Gina.

"We need a complete physical workup done on her, Gina. Drug screen the works. Run her DNA-"

"Hey, it's out of our hands-"

"Your hands as a cop," replied Charles. "You forget, I'm now a Doctor."

He looked at Gina with steely grey eyes.

"And she is my patient."

Two weeks later, the woman known as Jackie was sitting across from Charles in a high-security room at the State Mental Hospital. She was secured in a shock belt and manacles but was not medicated. Charles needed her as cognizant as possible.

"Did I apologize for slamming you into the wall?" Jackie asked.

"Several times, Jackie. But that wasn't you."

"Who was it then?"

Charles opened a thick medical file.

"You were Jaqueline Basset once. Then 'they' started visiting you."

"Those-shadows I now remember. The fuzzy… non- persons."

"Traditionally called Greys in ufology.I am here to tell you that they- well they, 'modified' you. And the last visit was done by a group who were not careful during the return. That is how you stumbled into the group of sex slaves and was grabbed."

Jackie grunted.

"Yeah. I have some nightmare memories now. Your hypnotism helped break a barrier they had created. Thanks. And no thanks. The nightmares-"

"Are bad, Jackie. PTSD and true memories combined."

"An understatement of the year, Doctor. So, now what?"

Charles paused, then answered.

"We keep you here. Not only for your safety as well as the public. You seem to have both organic and non-organic parts added to you that makes you… different."

"And dangerous, Charles. Right?"

"Yes. Now I'll arrange for us to eat lunch together. Okay?"

Jackie smiled.

"Yes. You are one of the few people who can talk to me like a normal person.

Charles met Jennifer outside the visiting area.

"You received an answer from the Feds?" Charles asked.

"Yes, my friend. More security is being added, a lot of it. But she won't be moved."

"Why not move her to a more secure federal facility?"

Jennifer looked around and made sure they were alone.

"The Greys will be back. And transferring her makes her vulnerable to being taken on the road."

"The Feds know these beings will try to get at Jackie? How do they know-"

"Don't ask; just do not ask."

Charles made sure a better than average lunch was prepared for him and the former author. As he watched food preparation, the Doctor thought back to the many conversations he and Jackie shared. Charles Brown knew he was the woman's only current friend. Jackie had no family. Her literary agent was told she had been exposed to severe disease and was unreachable. Charles grunted and shook his head at the last planned book the agent said was in the pipeline.

"Why, Doctor Brown. It's a series of stories on Alien Abduction. Jackie said she had been doing a lot of research on the matter."

If the literary agent could only know. It would be a best seller.

TRIAL, ERROR, AND A CAT ON MY KEYBOARD WITH NOTHING TO DO WITH SAID CAT
BY ELIZA LOEB

There are many things that transpired between the pages of my youth. Now that I am twenty seven, I look back and wonder what could have changed and scour through the memories and experiences that I now have to live with.

When we are young, we make mistakes. And like surfing, we either ride the wave and turn with the tide, or we swim away from it and fall off of our board. Sometimes we even ride the wave and fall off of our boards. I laugh to myself as I think of the concussion that followed suit with that event, and how it disqualified me from surfing soon after. I would still go into the water. I would still try, but in the end, I would find that I wasn't really cut out for it. Life has a funny way of telling you whether or not you're meant for something and I guess the teenager that was me really could not take a hint.

I've changed a lot since then.

I no longer have an interest in surfing or doing any sports of the like. I have more of an interest in acting and film. Writing is a thing that allows me to delve into the depths of my strange imagination and share it with the world. It allows me to face reality and pick and choose what it is that I want to share versus things that I would love to keep as a dirty little secret. And honestly, I find no shame in it. It is a career of humility mixed in with a personal self-fulfillment that I may or may not have had since I was a child.

I remember collaborating stories with my grandmother as she helped me with my writing. We would start with three word sentences and add on to them, one after the other. Soon the sentences would go from three words to four and so on. I would have fun writing with her. She and I would keep a personal journal between the two of us and she would call them the Ayakashi Adventures Volume x. She would sometimes include new words for me to learn, and once I had understood, she would encourage me to read them to her. To further build my confidence, she would have me write a short story and bring it in to class for show and tell, hoping that it would build my confidence. This, however, became more and more difficult after she died. My stories became more and more horrific, I was met with a depression that I hadn't been sure that anyone could possibly understand. And one night, I heard my mother and father fighting. I could hear their screams getting louder and louder and all I could think of was the warpath that would be left behind. I began to write about the Gashadokuro, the bone giant, that would manifest during great times of starvation or in battlefields filled with unburied dead. I then added the Oni-baba, the hag and Jorogumo-Hime, Lady Spider and wrote and wrote about how all would chase after a crane, a fox and a ningyo for their own selfish desires. The crane would represent loyalty and servitude, the fox would represent luck and the ningyo— known to most as a mermaid- would represent eternal youth and immortality. Gashadokuro, Oni-baba and Jorogumo-Hime would all be seen as parental figures to the three main characters. All three antagonists would be loved by the three afformentioned characters, but would be consumed by greed. Just as my parents were. Just as any one of my aunts or uncles on my mothers side would be, and to me, it had been a fate that I would be forced to accept. And nothing was more liberating to me than becoming the black sheep.

"You're a good girl, you would never do bad." I would always hear. "All I need is a foot rub, but after you get me a drink."

In my mothers family, if you are a child, you are an indentured servant until death. If you complain or want to do something else, you are seen as ungrateful. I would get things thrown at me or hit.

Needless to say, I was never the golden child. I was kida to few and that in and of its self was hardly a blessing. There was a matron who was referred to as Auntie Bennett. She would be kind depending on who you spoke to, but under the surface she was very catholic. I remember very little of her, yet the few memories that I do have of her are... fuzzy to say the least. My late grandfather, however, was a very strict man. He was one of the few people who my mother had been afraid of, and even then, he hid the reason for that fear away from me. What I remember of him is little more than the dreams of a small child. When we spent time together, he would play the saxophone and have me sing, we would sing along to popular movies that he'd brought home and he would barbeque chicken or fish while red rice was cooking. To me, he was a very gentle and kind person who would tell me stories of how he and his brothers would get into trouble during the fifties. Life on Guam before the technological era was never really what one would call exciting. If anything it was a secondary paradise for lonely old soldiers to visit and find an exotic wife to settle down with outside of the US. Or if you were anything like grandpa Phillip, play Chamorro dukes of hazard with said lonely old soldiers. Having seen the original dukes of hazard, the comparison is not too far off from what grandpa Phillip did. But thankfully, instead of the confederate flag, it was the Guam flag that would be printed upon the hood of his truck. I know, because there are pictures of that damn truck next to a younger version of my mother in eighties booty shorts. Though, it's memories of my grandfather like that that make me miss him as I move forward to the constant contradictions of my dreams being invalidated. My dreams of being an actor, my dreams of writing stories for everyone to see and the weight of pressure I had undergone with narcissistic parents.

I had the good people in my life, yes.

But there were more bad than good. And constantly I wonder if it is even ok to set an inkling of blame for my life as it is today. I'm often told that a person is responsible to how unexpected situations are handled. If that were the case, then the unexpected situations that befell me and mine would have turned positive in an instant. If that were true, I wouldn't feel suicidal every time I tried to face the causes of my PTSD. I wouldn't hear my mother, father, aunts and uncles in my head screaming at me for how worthless I am, how I can't be better or how others despise me simply for the fact that I exist. And I wouldn't be scared to reach out and discuss how difficult it is to try and live through every god damn day, trying to keep myself off of autopilot. Trying not to disassociate, trying to be present for those who genuinely want me.

I worry every day for my writing and acting career. I worry that I won't be good enough and even feign confidence that I am the best at what I do before going home and breaking down.

Talk about it?

With whom?

As far as experience goes, unless there is a genuine interest, I remain unsure of who I can go to. To describe it, my head is a plane and my comfort is piloting it. Seldom do I find myself capable of moving freely throughout the cabin. And when I do, the words "within reason" play through my head.

Because of my parents, there is no such thing as "moving freely". Because of my abusers, safe isn't in my vocabulary. And now, I am finding that there was a lot that I repressed growing up. I worry about expressing too much anger. I'm afraid of showing too much emotion. I'm terrified of being too sedate. All because negative emotions are "unattractive" and sedate means that "I don't care".

There are nights where I just sit up and stare into the darkness, searching for the endless void that I used to fear so much. On occasion the snores from my pets and my partners draws my attention away from any invasive thoughts that me enter, distracting me from reminiscing of a time where it wasn't quiet. And for that, my only thoughts are of whether I will get to sleep that night or how much I envy either for sleeping so well. I will admit that I am glad to have them in my life. Their presence brings me joy. But still, there is the underlying fear that they will grow bored of me, and eventually run as far away as they can. And I am terrified. I shut down, feeling as though the possibility awaits me from just around the corner. And were I to make that one wrong move, my life as I know it would set the ground to crumble beneath my feet and the vast forest of temporary solace ablaze. To which belies the question of whether or not I will ever find peace. Will I betray my children in to a state of constant fear as I have been? Will they see me in the same light as I see my parents, or will I be better?

As I look at it, I am unsure.

I don't know if I will ever truly live for that long.

If I don't, I pray that no one will think of me to follow.

If I do, I'm not quite sure.

I always worry about whether or not my mental health issues will pass on to my children. It is a future that I can neither foresee, nor prevent if it does happen. I don't even know if I will make it that far.

But really, all I can provide is that I am trying. I am doing my best to live from day to day with what I am capable of expending, just so I can see my career through. It's not easy. It will never be easy, and certainly no walk in the park.

And my dear reader, if you have made it this far with my dribble just know…

There are people in this world who thrive on hurting you and chances are, you are much stronger than me. Chances are, you will only have to deal with one and manage to stay away from them. Or you are like me, and somehow manage to attract them. You may have very recently had a friend who robbed you of your choices, as I've had. You may even feel as though you are at fault. And if you do, I would like you to know that you carry no blame. The bad things that others have done to you are the actions of the antagonist, not to you. Do not take the blame for someone elses shitty actions, as they do not deserve it. They do not deserve what energy you have already given them. They lost that privilege the moment they decided to hurt you. And hopefully you have someone kind, someone who is loving and someone who is understanding to help you the rest of the way. Because you, my dear reader are deserving of it.

There are good people who love you. People who will cherish you and give you the care that you deserve. And sometimes, they are gone as soon as they arrive.

I had a friend like that.

I keep her in my heart.

I keep her in my memories.

She will always be a sister to me.

You likely have that too.

I am not writing this as a word of warning. I think about the amount of times I was betrayed and this story was probably one of the more difficult stories for me to write. Because when all your looking for is the bad, that is all you're going to focus on. That is all you're going to find. It becomes an obsession that you can never get over and it slowly falls over you like hot tar, eating you alive bit by bit. And it will be nothing other than the pain it was meant to cause. But when you aren't paying attention, when you're neither looking for the good nor the bad, both somehow manage to jump out and surprise you. Both may even be seen as a lesson or a blessing. Of course, there are things in this world that somehow let you know whether or not you are on the right path in some way or another, one just needs to know how and where to look, as wishy washy as that may sound.

Needless to say, my life has had a lot of bad and I have done things I am not proud of. Right now, it just feels as though I am at a stand still and it's so peaceful that I am afraid that the entire world may be against me. I am afraid that I will no longer be wanted among certain groups or if my existence would even be considered valid by this point. It's an odd state to be in. On one hand, I am a professional writer for a wonderful organization who has managed to put up with my nonsense this far along. On the other, I find that I am missing the rainy and cold state of Washington while looking for more and more ways to keep myself alive and trying to work toward a bigger and brighter future.

But as I said, I am healing.

It's a long and messy process that no one should have to go through, despite many having to. It takes energy, it takes work. And the worse part is that you never know how many obstacles you will encounter in the week. To some, there are few and to others, there are too many to count. One of my partners constantly undergoes more hell that she deserves at her work. She deals with a lot of self loathing due to her chronic pain and disabilities, and some days, the most one can do is be there and try to help where one is able. My other partner has dysphoria and chronic depression that makes it difficult for him to get out of bed. And then there is my third who has chronic depression and anxiety that he seldom leaves his room. And I am thankful for all three. I love all of them for how wonderful they are and they have become part of a list of blessings that a younger me could never imagine.

As hard as my life is, as deep as my trauma goes, I am trying.

I am trying to make a life that is mine.

I am trying to stay present.

I am doing what I can.

And my dear reader, if you are healing, you have my pride. It's a long road. But if you made it this far, I am proud of you. I look forward to the day where you are successful.

TRIPTYCH
BY SHEILA MENGERT

In October the month of harvest and completion nature puts out her finest show of color and variety so that even in dying there is the promise of fullness and rebirth. It is the month of gaudy display culminating in a grand masquerade where everything can both assume its disguise and simultaneously reveal what has been latent within it all along.

As the year 2019 began to ebb away into the great dust-bin of history Americans were beginning to wake up to the costs imposed by a streamlined approach to attain heady results that would ignore law, prudence, and the fact that the days when America needed only to will a thing to have it done were passing away. It turned out that there were other nations in play after all. Still there was time for one last blow-out of self-indulgence. Americans would not relinquish power easily.

So it was that in retreat they had decided to elect a man who could embody in his very person the lumbering imposingness of American self-indulgence with the piggy-eyed suspicions and paranoia of American supremacy. Who could foretell the events of 2020 when as its name implied vision must triumph over masquerade? Story telling is not prophesy; the accoutrements of even tomorrow are beyond our grasp. Still, it does not seem too great an exercise of imagination to presume that it will be a contentious year on all fronts. But from the vantage point of harvest-time when nature shakes out its frills and furbelows for one last gay extravaganza we might imagine a story such as the one that follows...

Scheherazade was a drag queen; she had never claimed to be anything else. She was neither particularly pretty (real in drag parlance) nor was she less attractive than the majority of biological women who had reached, as it is coyly expressed, a certain age. She had never procreated because even with the greatest act of determination she had never been able to even imagine herself as a man, let alone adequately perform the male role in an actual act of coitus. That role always reminded her too much of what her avid Irish setter had repeatedly tried to do to her leg when given the slightest opportunity. The net result of all of this was that Scheherazade had remained as it were genitally arrested at that stage of growth when she merely wished to imitate the women of the household where she had been raised in a semi-fatherless environment as a child.

Scheherazade resided at the time of this story in one of the states between the Rockies and the Appalachians referred to as the Great Basin or more colloquially as "fly-over America." The states in this region are basically interchangeable with each other as to their acceptance of sexual non-conformity ... NOT ACCEPTING. So we will avoid being more specific as to the specific town or county of her domicile, less for fear of outing anybody there than because our story is so generally applicable to many individual biographies that many poor souls would be in distress as to how a remote author might have divined their most private dreams and histories while making only a few alterations in the name of fiction.

256

As we have mentioned above, our heroine, for such she is, had no children of her own. The years had slipped by in that way that they have of slipping by unnoticed in a series of acts balanced between pleasure and pain to simply keep the whole process of an individual life going on from day to empty day. Gradually her women relatives and early role models had grown old and died so that finally Scheherazade had come to the realization that she was quite alone in her life. She had never made it out to New York City or to San Francisco where she might have performed in a drag review while still in the first blush of youth performing to the whistles of an appreciative audience of straight people who would afterwards chuckle at the very idea of a man in a dress.

The lights has faded early on her aspiration to declare herself as one of the disciples of what is now referred to as "gender ideology" that in the first quarter of the 21st century poses such a threat to American security that various religious groups have brought the issue up constantly as a sure-fire fundraiser for various evangelical political crusades. This has always puzzled Scheherazade. As far as she knew no drag queen had ever commandeered an aircraft to fly into buildings or shot-up an outdoor concert in Las Vegas; but still to the conservative mindset if a guy is going to wear mascara and lipstick there was no telling what else he might do.

All in all Scheherazade considered herself to be a relative non-entity. She worked at the local grocery store outlet as a grocery checker by day as a man so as to keep her job and she still lived in the same home where she had grown up as a child. She had a few friends left over from high school who she still met on occasion for a lovely walk or a night of cards; mostly though she watched lots of movies on cable television, old classic films in black and white. She ate a little too much and as a result had developed in middle-age the breasts she had wished for in adolescence, but she had never qualified for female hormones let alone considered the big operation that would have confirmed her deepest sense of herself.

So it was that this particular Midwest daughter of the great American soil sat one day before her antique mirror looking at herself in a girdle and an old-lady bra as she applied acres of pan-stick before applying contour, blush, and loose powder and asked herself what the sum total of her life added up to. If she had been a character in a book by Albert Camus or by Andre Gide her existential problem could be summarized as a state of alienation and anomie, but in the Midwest she was just another depressed queen wondering if she should drive out to the highway rest-stop on the chance of finding somebody there to love. The nearest gay bar was sixty miles away and on the few occasions when she had visited there her dance card had, let us say, not been filled.

She thought back often, recalling the name she had chosen in youth while watching re-runs of *"I Dream of Jeanie"* on television while eating Hostess Twinkies on the couch after school and before substantial dinners of roast beef and potatoes. In her mind she always saw herself though as Barbara Eden and it was all she could do to avoid using her magic powers to nod and blink and make the bullies at school just disappear or turn into the little toads that they really were. She used her fertile imagination to visualize herself as a favored courtesan in a harem, the one drawn from the other silken-veiled concubines and made love to by the hour, leaving the muezzin unheeded, by a sloe-eyed and turbaned Prince or Caliph in some garden hidden in the remote recesses of far-off Baghdad or Arabia. She would tell him tales by starlight and bathe his weary brow in scented waters drawn from a carafe of gold while he nestled in her lap. She would nurse all manner of young princes and princesses appearing regularly from her fertile loins and tell them to go play in the sand because mama was resting after a busy night with their father, the Caliph.

But this vision was soon replaced by the sordid demands of the hour and her reflection in the mirror before retiring was always the same ginger-haired boy with the requisite and functional crew-cut that only made her appear more odd with her broad hips that made running difficult during the required physical education classes that serve more to isolate and ridicule gay kids than to instruct. It was all part of America's winner-take-all culture that cannot be acquired too early in life. In this world the function of woman was to admire and praise and to learn that her future could best be assured by securing a good male partner and then to keep him from straying by constant attention. Still Scheherazade envied the women she saw about her and felt her isolation more keenly when denied their company because of what for her was an irrelevant appendage. The net result for Scheherazade was isolation all-round and the creation of her own inner world where her inner reality could be confirmed and validated.

So had the years passed by when one day, while perusing the unending cellular feed of news that a non-judgmental algorithm had selected for her based on her customary usage, she heard of a program that allowed drag-queens to perform at libraries by reading stories and singing songs. Scheherazade thought instantly of how much such a program might have meant to her in her youth and the solace it might have brought to her and decided to apply. What had she to lose, except maybe forty pounds? She broke the pencil twice in her excitement in filling out a letter of expressed interest to the organization involved. She enclosed one or two selfies taken in dim light and crossed her arms over her bosom and blinked three times to carry the missive upon the flying carpet of magic to its intended destination.

Imagine her surprise and delight then when she was invited to an audition held at a local church where members of the LGBT community were not anathema. She had inherited a vast collection of vintage dresses from a deceased aunt and in one of her favorites she gave a brief recitation in a loud and clear voice and a week later heard that she was in. There was no formal induction ceremony. There were several branches of the local library system in various bibliophile prairie pit-stops of education across the lands where the buffalo used to roam. She was assigned a date at one of these and expected to show-up in a timely fashion, keep her act age-appropriate, and do the community proud.

All looked well for our heroine therefore until, in that mysterious way that fate has of playing a role in our lives that is disproportionate to our deserts, a determined force of opposition arose to prevent Scheherazade from performing and sowing confusion among the youth while promoting the insidious agenda of gender ideology thought up by people who had already bid fair to causing chaos among the hitherto secure realm of English pronouns. The gig was not only suspended but cancelled until further notice.

Our story might have ended right there but for the fact that it is always the function of the determined protagonist to never take no for an answer. Opposition is the name of the game, as a quick reading of Northrop Frye's *Anatomy of Criticism* will make perfectly clear. So it was that Scheherazade was not only unwilling to consent to having her name and picture, which she had seen in all of the glory of the lights of Broadway, taken down from the library bulletin board where it had been stuck up with thumb-tacks the week before, but she determined to take her two-week vacation and travel to Washington D.C. to make a statement and to express her outrage at the lobbying headquarters of the *Society to Keep Perversion Out of Family Life*.

In that same year of 2020 at a casino on the west coast it was Disco Mania Extravaganza Night and Deco la Tage was to be as usual the mistress of ceremonies for the evening. Her usual haunt, venue, and pied-a-terre was the Frisky Frisco, a gay bar done up in 1890's elegance reminiscent of an up-scale, turn of the century, cat-house in the fabled city by the bay, San Francisco. Deco had come to the FF as it was familiarly known as a young street queen with little to her name but big eyes, a pouty mouth, and an elaborate notion of her own worth as a potential lay. After having most of her attitude beaten out of her by a drag mother who announced after their first meeting that she didn't put up with *no I'm-all-that bullshit* from her daughters, Deco had emerged with a certain amount of style and a soupcon of wisdom and had succeeded in due order to her present post of prima donna at the FF by sheer grit, time, and tenacity.

Deco was what was once called a glitter-queen. She never felt that her body was complete unless it shown like a night sky in Montana with various tiny metallic sparkles from her peacock blue-green eyelids to her scarlet mouth. She preferred to perform under black light in silver or deep purple gowns with three inch nails that glowed green and with the deep silicone-enhanced bosom that a generous sugar-daddy had once allowed her to purchase so as to live up to her stage name. Deco watched her figure and avoided the excesses that made so many queens flame-out like a fighter-jet diving into a hillside in Afghanistan and as a result passed sufficiently as a woman so that, even deprived if her nightly finery, she turned heads and got whistles on the street. Better still, she saved her money rather than drinking it up in her room above the FF after hours or wasting it bailing no account lovers out of jail or defunct business schemes.

Deco had always lived as part of what was once called "the life" and was still HIV negative (which was saying something). Her big turn-on was to be looked at but not touched, playing her lover's fantasies in the light and shadow game of suggestion and nuance. In a part of her inner life there still resided hope for a grand romance and in her vague idle hours she imagined herself inhabiting a villa overlooking the Mediterranean Sea in the south of France where she could entertain guests lavishly while drinking Pernod and sampling delights from the local patisserie. By then of course she would have silver hair and a face where every bone revealed the underlying structure of her former beauty. She would have many tales to tell to her adoring chamber maids who would never stop giggling and saying, "Ooh la Madame!"

However in banal reality as the year 2020 arrived she often sat in the bar after closing hours and took stock of her life with all of its faux glamour and illusions and she didn't like what she saw. She thought of her dressing room, strewn with collages of seasons gone by and the signed autographs from real celebrities that had visited the Frisky Frisco over the years. She saw the panorama of her past glories fading into a uniform visage beneath increasing layers of pan-cake make-up and paint. It seemed necessary now to have nightly conferences with Pedro the light-man about how best to illuminate her on stage.

In recent years her stage patter hadn't evolved much since the glorious years when she had begun as a drag performer and she could foretell that she was rapidly becoming that most horrid thing for an artiste, a flesh and blood anachronism. Deco felt that she needed new skies and new material or she would be gently nudged aside (or rather pushed into the gutter) by some up and coming young thing. There were no stock options or golden parachutes for aging drag queens.

So it was that while the Frisky Frisco was closed for two months for a much needed roof repair and renovation, Deco decided that it was time for her Sapphire Extravaganza Tour. She packed up her old van with wigs and costumes and three cases of various cosmetics and set off on her road tour of the east coast and the southern drag circuit to assess the state of the art. As a grand finale he decided to include in her travels a stop in Washington D.C.

Meanwhile at her home base, when not appearing in cyberspace, there lived one of the princesses of social media. Sherry Dallas was five feet six inches tall and lived in Wilsonville, Oregon, an attractive suburb just south of the expanding freeway traffic jams of the greater Portland area. Sherry was a full-on transsexual and the final product of several skillful plastic surgeons. So successful was she in fact that she had joined the bevy of constructed beauties that had ridden the wave of social media to viral stardom. She had a respectable following for her make-up tutorials and her personal web-site showed her assuming various wistful attitudes as she went about her suburban day from early juicing at breakfast, yoga at mid-morning, petting her angora cat on a white couch in the living room while leaning against a luxurious fringed pillow with her bare legs stretched out in the afternoon, and ending by getting ready for an unnamed (and unrevealed) gentleman caller by night. Sherry was well-paid for simply living out other people's fantasies of the good life. Her business was to appear to be having fun while subtly suggesting to each of her followers that they enjoyed a special, behind-the-scenes, relationship with her beautiful self.

Sherry had reviewed all of the options before as it were choosing a face for herself. She divined that in the last analysis feminine beauty might be reduced to a set of formulaic computations based upon various sizes and symmetries. Once achieved these proportions were immediately translatable into various currencies from the dollar to the franc to the yen, because beauty is the gold-standard of humanity. This was made clear to her every day. What for instance could be more charming then a privileged blond news anchoress on conservative television stations frowning prettily as she announced the latest plans of the socialist Dems to destroy America and open our borders to various baby-toting Latinas? (Everyone knows that they all get fat at forty! Besides they're all Catholic and not respectably and non-denominationally evangelical).

Sherry Dallas of course didn't care one way or the other about politics. She hadn't gone through all that she had just to fall back into heartache or be encased again in tranny ghetto life through fruitless advocacy. She had realized early on that she was locked into a body-modality that could make her a sitting duck for abuse, a blank screen for other people's projections and agendas. She had finally reached a level now where she could mock them opening and get away with it. Sherry had recently even gone to a major annual conservative Christian conference and received a proposal of matrimony from a co-attendee over wine in the evening after listening to various lectures all day on the infestation of gender ideology in our schools.

Another attendee, the corporate founder of *Puritan Pierogi*, a national fast-food chain that threatened to edge into the burger market with the Ukrainian version of ravioli, offered her a modeling contract to push pierogies. Her figure was hardly typical though of the average patron of his drive-through business with its high caloric count and the whopping load of cholesterol it carried due to the bacon and potato filling and generous topping of sour cream. This was put into perspective however by the advertising slogan, "Hey Babushka! Live a little!"

Sherry had politely declined both of these offers, preferring to make her money quietly at home by simply existing before a camera and going about her day. She was not about to be the Maria Ouspenskaya of greasy little Slavic pastries or to rush into marriage with a man who would no doubt hate her if he knew what she was, or rather, had once been. Sherry's life-path was designed as a quest for legitimacy which in this world demands a combination of visibility and simultaneous inscrutability. The key quality she had always aspired to possess was moral and emotional self-sufficiency. She realized early on that there were primarily two main types of men: the ones that seek out insecurities in women so that through flattery they may possess them sexually, and men whose own insecurity needs require a woman to validate and admire them. Both see women as a resource to be used until depleted before moving on to more promising fields. Now and again true devotion may appear, but as is usual with anything of true value, whether earth, sky, sunlight, or water, these are taken as just another of life's constants to which neither gratefulness nor conservation are required.

At first at the week-long conference, Sherry Dallas had been concerned that her internet notoriety might have preceded her there, but after days of earnest exhortations followed by socializing over rare cheeses and vintage wines with nightly prayers after steak and salmon dinners, she realized that any inquisitorial instincts were directed beyond the attendees towards those who dwelt beyond the circle of light in the outer rings of darkness: socialist Democrats, Guatemalan border-crossers, unionists, gender ideologists, and assorted liberals.

As the days at the conference passed Sherry felt a sense of conditional acceptance and belonging that was worth every bit of the hefty fee she had paid for attendance and accommodations. If she had any doubts at all she needed only to reflect that she was spending the money so that sin could be made more clearly manifest and so that rational Christianity could prevail over emotion-based and misguided toleration for vice. She knew that she would return like a charged-dynamo radiant with virtuous umbrage at the follies of the age and determined to resist any innovations set afoot with cloven hoofs by for instance the misguided papacy of the Catholic Pope

Francis. If she weakened all that she needed to do was to look again at the workbook provided to every conference participant that pointed out on page one that "God is a capitalist" and to review the handy proof text that, *to those who have much, more will be provided, while those who have little will be deprived of even the little that they have.* In the last analysis heaven might be looked at as a perfect candidate for merger and acquisition by a determined corporate raider. She had especially enjoyed the session entitled, *"Why should you be only an ordinary Christian when you can be a CEO for the Lord?"* By the last day of the conference the cumulative effect of the inspired rhetoric had raised a fire in her heart and made her aspire to greater things. The attendees were given their final marching orders until next year's event prospectively denominated: *"Don't Keep Your Dogma in A plastic Bag."*

On impulse she had put her name up to be one of the delegates to march in the nation's capitol in support of the Republican slate of candidates in 2020. The inroads of liberalism and immigration simply had to be stopped. South America was the breeding ground to Amazonian Paganism even if it wore a mask of Christianity. Unexpectedly she was chosen and stood there blushing to the sounds of applause and halleluiahs. Who would believe that this little T-girl had final climbed the slippery ladder to the ultimate heights of invisibility, to be sent as a delegate by the very people who despised everything that she was (if they only knew)?

She had heard all week about how as a minion of Satan the transgender-mafia was taking over "our schools, our libraries, our rest rooms, in fact our whole American way of life." The sanctimonious umbrage had elicited gasps and raised goose-bumps on the flesh of the attendees. Never had Sherry been more grateful that she had wisely invested in obtaining for herself the vaginal equivalent of a shiny new Cadillac. She personally had nothing to fear from the restroom inquisition. Her size eight shoes would never give her away. The days of her bitter high school gauntlet experiences in the boys' locker room were like memories drawn from a nightmare of a previous life. In other words she had finally arrived. As the cheers continued she found that she simply could not find it in herself to decline their commission and their trust. She would go to Washington, D.C.

Washington D.C. in the year 2020 was less a stronghold of democracy than an armed camp awaiting the outcome of the election in November. Not since the 1960's had the culture wars more resembled a conflagration. Marches and demonstrations were a daily event and the police presence was supplemented by troops drawn from the National Guard in adjoining states just to keep order. This was the fulminating atmosphere that prevailed in the nation's capitol when our three aforementioned gender non-conformists hit town.

They were not alone. Also demonstrating were the contingent from *Leviticus is Forever,* a group that advocated physically stoning adulteresses and sodomites and the *Dead Cold-Fingers Coalition* that made it clear that they would die before surrendering their guns to the Democrats. These made common cause with other groups listed in the top ten of America's Taliban. The other members of the big ten included *Christians against Catamites* and various groups claiming to do research on *sexual anomalies and perversions* in order to preserve family values, particularly the right of parents to dump their gay kids on the street for disobedience and for promiscuous behaviors. Meanwhile representing the ever-present liberal fringe were *Wiccans for a Free Lunch, the Conspirators for Astral-Projection,* and of course the *Drag Queen Bibliophile Association.*

Keeping these groups apart, while still allowing then to harangue bewildered middle-America on the nightly news broadcasts was no easy task. Even the ardently fought Presidential contest was dwarfed by the outpouring of the unleashed political passions of fractured America. The fissures ran long and deep from sea to shining sea. The carry-over sometimes bordered on the ridiculous, such as the case of the Christian Delicatessen owner who refused to serve people requesting kosher dill pickles or anything using curry powder because even such condiments promoted non-Christian values. It was no surprise that even various Christian sects had rediscovered old grievances against each other. Various hospitals refused admission to dissenting denominations without the presentation of a certificate of proper and sect-congruent baptism. With no reliable and common bond as Americans every possible source of fission was being exploited and a general attitude of mistrust was the order of the day. Rather than lamenting this condition, Americans had learned over the past four years to embrace a radical sense of mine and yours as the national ethos and the phrase: *Community is just another name for communist* was as popular as the charge of purveying fake news.

All in all it wasn't the best place or time for Sherry, Deco, and Scheherazade to hit the shining city on the hill, each wishing to make some sort of personal statement before returning to the little zone of safety and acceptance from which they had come. Each of our lady-emissaries wished to escape lives that were summed up in conventionality and irrelevance. Each imagined that they had been commissioned to pursue a higher cause and each found herself wandering through the taper-lit streets to the sounds of vile imprecations thrown back and forth across the various barriers that had been erected to keep the contesting parties from actual assault and mayhem on each other.

Of course the media of the world took notice of these events occurring in the land that had once been a source of hope and inspiration to a struggling world. Now emulation had given way to either pity or ridicule as America pursued its seemingly endless culture wars and the currently reigning masters of discontent smiled in satisfaction. Any street corner would do as a place for any one of our heroines to announce her presence and make her proclamation but each, now that she had arrived, found that the arena was already thronged with roaring beasts.

So it was that as if drawn by a familiar and common inspiration to seek out a place where she could nurse a pink daiquiri and assemble a melded message and visage to draw the gaze and attention of the crowds assembled to hear her, each of our heroines converged at D.C.'s most famous gay bar, *The Monument,* at the same day and hour. The art of storytelling depends on just such synchronicities and fortuitous events. Can it therefore surprise us further to hear that these three that we now regard with some measure of curiosity and affection were to be seated at a single table? Yet such it was to be…

Scheherazade, as was appropriate to the old adage of age before beauty arrived there first. She had spent the late hours of the afternoon adorning herself in her best Midwestern idea of eleganza. She was readily admitted and chose one of the smaller rooms off the central core where the music was less loud to seek solace and to set up court. She could see through a glass partition into the main area of the bar located at a lower level. It was as though she was in one of the boxes in one of the old classical movie theaters she had attended and admired while growing up. She only wished that she had brought along opera glasses or a fan to add to the effect. The table she had chosen combined spaciousness with intimacy and comfort and she hoped that she might make some friends in the course of the evening.

The architecture of assignation in gay bars had changed since the days of *Studio 54* and *The Mineshaft.* Being gay was no longer about blatant sexual display or back-room indulgence let alone the more imaginative fantasias of pain and pleasure. The elaborate significations and coded communications of desire, battened on repression when suddenly unleashed into mindless indulgence, now seemed quaint reminders of a bygone era. With respectability, and above all legality, came order and responsibility. In spite of the outrage that same-sex marriage had provoked among conservative heterosexuals, legitimacy had exerted a civilizing influence in the former steamy jungles of desire. The interlaced communities of LGBTQIA had come into possession of sophisticated nomenclatures and codified manners so that the choice of partners appeared no longer to indicate or entail a promiscuous lifestyle.

Of course this cut little ice among those who could never imagine two people of the same sex forming a domestic unit let alone having that unit encouraged, celebrated, and blessed. Drag of course had always been subversive of gender norms even as it celebrated the radical divisions between the sexes. Drag queens did not embrace androgyny but instead thrived on high style and excess. As such they were mistrusted and sometimes ridiculed from both ends of the gay-straight spectrum. The full unleashing of raw female sexual power was always threatening no matter if done by transgendered or by a cis-gendered individual. Gender is largely a geographical demarcation and woe must follow the trespasser and border-crosser. Of course looking at Scheherazade, who even in her flowered print dress was more reminiscent of a church bazaar in Kansas than of an Arabic harem, no threat could be imagined. She seemed the ideal storyteller whether to children or to adults. How different was our next entrant on the scene!

Deco la Tage believed in the big entrance no matter where it might be.: even when grocery shopping it was customary for her to stand before the various displays and to lovingly caress each item with her long-nailed hands before arranging it thoughtfully in the grocery cart and pushing it further down the aisle while allowing her hips to slide first to one side and then the other displaying her well-padded derriere. Now and again she would look coyly over her shoulder to assess interest from the patrons with one eye hidden beneath her blond tresses like Veronica Lake before proceeding in search of further delicacies.

Of course Washington D.C. had its own style of high camp so that now, as she entered *The Monument* the various denizens of the establishment spared her only a perfunctory look-see before returning to their drinks and conversations. It must be said that she bore up well under the unaccustomed indignity, but diva that she was Deco knew when to make a strategic exit from the stage and as a result entered the private room where Scheherazade semi-reclined at table and joined her, greeting her as she deposited herself delicately on a chair with an aura of familiarity assumed for the occasion to hide her embarrassment.

"There you are! I hope I haven't kept you waiting long. Perhaps you don't remember me; I'm Deco la Tage but you can call me Deco, everyone does. I see you've already ordered a drink. My that looks delicious but I will need more than a drink. I'm simply famished. You have no idea how many barricades I had to traverse simply to get here!"

Caught off guard Scheherazade could think of nothing better than to simply offer her a hand while smiling and giving Deco her name in return.

"Scheherazade! How perfectly oriental! Shouldn't you be wearing a veil or a burka or something? You've done marvels of adaptation; you look positively American, very Betty Crocker."

Deco took time to look around her and assess damages; no one was paying any attention to her so she relaxed.

She whispered, "I'm sorry. Please don't think me rude but I'm from out of town and quite honestly I'm used to coming into a place like this with an entourage."

"Quite alright," said Scheherazade smiling. "I'm from out of town myself and it is a bit overwhelming. Do you think riots will break out?"

"Who can say? If anything happens I brought along some pepper-spray. Just look, see; it is guaranteed to stop a biker, a grizzly bear, or even a Bible wielding church-lady. You stick with me Honey and you'll be okay."

Scheherazade felt a sense of sudden sisterly warmth for the brash newcomer. She was even willing to overlook that Betty Crocker comment. It was a novelty for her to have a brash ally.

"Where are from?" Deco asked as she signaled to a cute waiter in shorts for a drink and a menu.

Scheherazade hesitated, not wishing to seem too provincial. She suddenly wanted desperately to live up to her exotic name.

"Well, I live in the Midwest now but I was born in Lemon."

Deco froze and then began to giggle, "Don't you mean Yemen?"

Scheherazade blushed, "I still keep the local dialect of course, the Y sounds like an L ... it's a habit."

"Oh. So when did you come to America?"

"My father was in the service and we were stationed all over the world. I always had to learn to adjust to new places."

"That must have been very difficult, I mean when you're gay and all. Don't gay people have real trouble in Arabic countries?"

Scheherazade said demurely, "I didn't make it a point to tell people."

Deco assessed her new friend from head to toe before commenting, "Honey that must have been like hiding the Sphinx in the Egyptian desert. I mean just look at you! You're just a woman. I bet you even carry tampons around in your purse."

Scheherazade took it as a complement. She looked enviously at Deco's trim figure and evident confidence. This was always what she had wished to possess.

"Well what about you? I mean, you're beautiful."

Deco gave her a radiant smile before her face collapsed and she brushed away a sudden tear. She confided, "Thanks honey but the clock is ticking for me. It won't be long until I will be doing a Gloria Swanson and telling Mr. de Mille that I am ready for my close up."

Scheherazade smiled and asked enthusiastically, "Do you like old movies?"

"I love them," Deco answered.

"I mean really old."

"RKO and Universal."

"Who played Dr. Frankenstein's wife in *The Bride of Frankenstein?*"

"The bride of the monster was Elsa Lanchester and the doctor's wife was Valerie Hobson," Deco answered promptly.

"What other great monster movie was Valerie Hobson in?"

"She played Wilfred Glendon's wife in *The Werewolf of London* in 1935."

"Right! You know your stuff," Scheherazade said on admiration.

"And she played the grown-up Estella in David Lean's version of *Great Expectations.*"

"Stop, I believe you!" Scheherazade laughed.

"Of course I don't spend my time these days watching old films, plenty of time for that later."

"Later?"

"When I'm old of course."

"Oh, I see. Well, since I'm old already, not elderly of course but old, I find movies comforting. They give me a sense of stability and permanence in a time when that was why people went to see movies, to find a little glamour or to get a respite from the world around them."

"Isn't that still true?" Deco asked.

"No, I think people go to movies now to be stimulated or alternatively to have the world reflected back at them. I only want peace and maybe, oh, a refuge."

"Are you hiding from something?"

"Aren't we all?

Deco shivered for an instant. "It's cold in here, too much air-conditioning."

She paused before continuing, "I don't like to think about growing older. I'm an entertainer you see. I do drag shows for a living. I've made a career out of shocking people by degrees in a pretty tame venue. They walk out thinking that they have taken a little walk on the wild side. Actually my life is pretty boring. Making being gay respectable is killing the industry. Now you can see us on cable-TV whereas you used to have to go slumming. It takes away all the adventure. It's like religion that way: take away the candles and the incense and what have you got?"

"You're Catholic?"

"Yes. I mean I was."

"Yeah, me too."

"I miss it sometimes."

"How are you with your family?"

Deco took a long drink from her daiquiri before replying airily, "I haven't seen them in years."

"Really?"

"Nope. They disowned me; didn't want a faggot for a son."

Scheherazade paused before replying, "I think that's terrible!"

Deco shrugged, "Yeah but what are you gonna do? I made my choices and paid the price."

Again Scheherazade paused before asking, "Have you been happy?"

Deco smiled, "They pay me and I don't have to do tricks for it. What more can a tranny ask?"

"Are you a tranny?"

"Well as good as one but I still get read once in awhile. I might as well just be a woman the only difference is that when I'm on stage I dress better."

"What brings you to Washington?" Scheherazade asked.

"I just thought I'd check it out. I'm touring drag shows down south here looking for new ideas. You?"

"I came to protest," said Scheherazade proudly.

"What are you rebelling against?"

Scheherazade did a Brando impersonation and asked, "What have you got?"

Deco laughed. "I mean really."

"Well I wanted to read in libraries, as a drag queen. I like books; I read all the time."

"Reading to kids? I've heard of that … a tough gig."

"Reading to anybody is. I wanted to do as me though just to let them know we are here."

Deco tossed her head. "I think they know. We're the boogey man."

"Doesn't it get tiring though pretending we will just go away somewhere?"

"You mean over the rainbow? We serve an essential purpose, didn't you know that?"

"What purpose?"

"We serve to remind men of the awful fate awaiting them if they allow themselves to feel anything that women pretend they want them to feel. Women pretend that they want their men to be sensitive and vulnerable while denying that they are attracted to precisely the fact that men are not."

"Can you speak for women?" Scheherazade inquired.

Deco paused before replying, "Probably not, but I can observe. For instance, take that chick over there."

"Where?"

"The one in the black dress like she's just come from church, over there, the real pretty one, the one that just came in like she's never been in a gay bar before."

"Oh, her."

"Yeah. I wish we could talk to her."

"Why?"

"Dummy, don't you know she's one of us."

Scheherazade looked again and said with bated breath, "No she isn't."

"Yes. Fishy as hell but she's one of us," Deco assured her.

"How do you know?"

"Baby, I've seen them all. Besides, I watch her show on the Internet. She does her own reality spot. What's she doing here?"

Sherry Dallas had wandered around Washington all day after leaving her hotel room. She had chosen her clothes carefully with an image of a first lady in mind. Her red hair had been given a body-wave before she left home and now it cascaded down her back and curled over her pale shoulders. Her aim was to achieve a soft but imperious glow, respectable as befitted her mission as a conservative woman, or at least one commissioned by a conservative organization, but still suggestive that the first prerequisite of all family values is that a family should exist. Her aim was to convey simmering fertility but as demurely as possible.

Sherry's former life as a male now seemed as distant as another lifetime and it was only with great effort that she was able to conceive ... wrong word, imagine that she was without a uterus and hence unable to bear children. Behind her vagina was only the usual viscera shared by both the male and female sexes. Her beckoning labia led only to a cul-de-sac rather than a womb. She had not thought to freeze any sperm prior to her surgery so in her the long line of genetic succession had reached its terminus. Generations had made sacrifices, suffered, migrated, and perished merely to create this perfect image in a glass crafted of flesh and silicone into the simulacrum of perfect femininity. Was perfection always a matter of construction wedded to imagination while the real world is always patterned and plotted on a dark grid of imprecision and disappointment?

Sherry tried not to think of these things. She kept always before her the image of unfilled decades of sunlight and display when she could awaken male desire without price or consequence. Essentially she saw the sex act as a male convenience. They went away swiftly after satisfaction at precisely the moment when the body of a woman curls about the spring of life within her. There were good men of course, willing to exchange variety for security of supply and of these there were some of heroic honesty and devotion but they were swimming against the tide of nature that merely mandated fecundity. Besides, as a partial product of artifice Sherry considered herself to be as much a product of her surgeons as of nature—Sherry was an idea come into form. It is not easy to exist as an image.

But recurring to her mission to carry to Washington the ideals and transcendent principles of conservative Christianity as discussed at the caviar, wine, and cheese discussion groups she tried to recall now what she had heard there. She thought of the threat posed by Democratic socialism if embraced by the masses, of the emphasis placed on keeping America safe from the marauding tide of brown-skinned and hybrid refugees from Latin America, and she thought of how essential it was to banish the LGBT acronym forever and to restore the people it designated to invisibility.

She thought of what a shame it had been that Pope Benedict the XVI has resigned and left the church to be run by the reckless man who had succeeded him as Pope, a man who evidently refused to rule with stern declarations in all that really mattered while wasting his time in a neo-pagan dedication to preserving this passing world. Of what significance is a planet that will soon be supplanted by a great wedding feast held in celestial realms far beyond this mundane sphere? Were we not in the end times? Any concentration upon or obsession with matters that distracted one from efficacious ritual were a mere waste of time when the real work is always a matter of prevailing grace. The poor would always be with us and liberation theology had been rightly unmasked in the end as nothing but creeping socialism by another name. Now was the time to gird our loins and level the mountains and fill the valleys for the eruption of glory. So great was this new advent that its prosperity was already evident. Jerusalem had been restored as the capital city of Israel. The Persians had been reminded that America still had the power to order the affairs of the pseudo-nations of the Middle East as Britain's successor to empire. Wealth was power and could be wielded as a mighty sword to advance the will of the true deity, a jealous deity who could only hold in distain the presumption of a bunch of ignorant Indians who worshipped the rhythms of the rainforest when it should be cleared and transformed into good grazing land for cattle to fill the woks of the hungry Chinese.

She tried to remember all that she had heard and must now

convey to the liberal secularists who were massing on Washington this year demanding change and equality. For Sherry this was the long-awaited chance to finally feel good about herself as a woman by breaking once and for all from her past. It humiliated her to think that she might be included by some people under the LGBTQIA acronym. She would never know if she was really free of course until she could split forever from the very people that had made it to the top three of the issues to be condemned at the conference in the minds of many of the attendees there. Sherry decided therefore to go and observe the disgusting behaviors exhibited by the very people whose lives served to remind her daily of her own origins before her fortunate deliverance and readmission to the ranks of well, everybody else.

Sherry Dallas entered *The Monument* with fear and trepidation. It was unusual for her to enter any place where people were massed together without being a focal nexus of eyes and attention. The atmosphere would bristle and change as though an electrical current had run through it. In this case however she was disappointed. Gazes were polite but transient and she found herself looking for refuge under a sudden attack of what amounted to the gendered version of agoraphobia. It had been years since she had entered a gay bar where the value allotted to femininity was far below its par value in most exchanges where people gather. The only sustained attention she was receiving appeared to come from a pair of what looked like straight women seated at a table in a private room looking down on the general activity below. They at least had made sustained eye contact with her. She was drawn in their direction by a common feminine bond. She walked through the open partition and over to the pair and introductions were immediately exchanged. Sherry sat down and within minutes a spirited conversation ensued.

Deco said, "So let me get this into my head. You are here

representing a conservative group that advocates the rejection and condemnation of people like me and like Scheherazade here. They use their money and privilege to tell others what to do and claim to speak for God while they condemn minimum wage laws and fight unions so that the rich can live better and there is supposed to be *nothing obscene in that.* Did I understand you correctly?"

Sherry looked down and said, "Well there's more to it than that. You see these people believe that it is the wealthy that represent the real talent pool that makes the world run and that as a result the rewards that flow to them are only just and in accord with natural law. Where would the jobs come from if they were not there as innovators to create and provide them? Competition is the essence of the natural order of things."

"Then where does charity come in?" asked Scheherazade.

"Well many of these people make charitable contributions of a substantial order," Sherry replied.

"And they're still no doubt filthy rich even after you spoon off the gravy," Deco commented with a scornful toss of her head.

"The people that I represent believe that charity must be an individual choice but the right of private property is more important still. Sharing is an act of virtue; it cannot be compelled."

"Sounds more like Nietzsche or Ayn Rand than Jesus," Deco commented.

"Who is ... what you said?"Sherry asked.

"Oh he was just the philosopher who said that power is everything, and she was the guru of selfishness ... right Scheherazade? My friend here reads lots of books. She even identifies as a practicing bibliophile! I thought it was something kinky when she first told me what she was until she explained what a bibliophile was: a person who likes books. This was before you joined us here. I thought it was people who like to have sex in obscure corners of libraries."

Sherry looked embarrassed but decided the best answer to Deco was to ignore her and just continue with her explanation of her mission. "So I came to Washington D.C. as a sort of combination observer and advocate. It's really quite an honor."

"What do you normally do?" Scheherazade asked.

"I'm a sort of Internet model. Maybe you've seen my show, *Crème Sherry.* I travel around with a camera crew and go to exciting places and lie on beaches and do my make-up and talk to people like they are my best friends. I have quite a following. Oh, and I endorse things by saying that I like them."

Deco stared at her wide-eyed, "And they pay you money, just for liking stuff? They should come to me; I like loads of stuff that I can't afford to buy."

Sherry looked at her with great earnestness, "Yes they do; but mostly they do it because, well, I'm pretty and I have lots of clothes. I get my clothes for free by liking them."

Deco pouted "Honey I like all kinds of stuff but nobody gives me anything. There are lots of pretty girls out there so how do you rate such special treatment?"

"It just grew; I can't explain it. I suppose I'm somewhere in the top twenty of reality stars."

Deco said, "It used to require you to sing or dance or act to be a star. Scheherazade and I were just talking about old movies before you sat down. You must do something more than just like things."

"Well I do I … well I sort of react to things. I look worried or sad or delighted and things happen to me and I meet handsome guys and I say no a lot and people like that because I look like I ought to get lots of, you know, action but I let people know that I have other plans then just spreading them."

"Like what plans?" Deco asked.

"Like another season of traveling around, and saying no, and liking things."

Deco shook her head and said, "Well like my mama used to say: if that don't beat all!"

Sherry suggested, "You could try it. You're very good looking."

Deco said, "No forty year old drag queen gets paid for just liking things."

"Then how do you survive?"

"I challenge people and trade insults and make people laugh at the Frisky Frisco."

"The Crispy Crisco?"

"No, sweet thing, the Frisky Frisco as in San Francisco; it's a drag bar."

"So you're already in entertainment. I do the same thing only at another level and with the help of the world wide web." Sherry turned to her other companions and asked, "And what about you, Scheherazade? What do you do for a living?""

Scheherazade looked down and blushed beneath her layers of foundation. "I work as a checker in a grocery store."

"Well that feeds people at least. I think you should be proud of your work. If you want to know, the real reason that I'm here is that I wanted a change from feeling like a phony everyday in my life. The people who sent me here liked me, me instead of things! They trusted me to carry the torch and keep the demonic Democrats (that's what they called them) from ruining America by destroying the work ethic and just giving people things. Without pain and fear people have no motivation. They would want more than they could ever afford to buy and they might turn to violence to get it like those French people with the guillotine."

"As opposed to affording things that no one could ever want or realistically use or consume because they are billionaires," Scheherazade mumbled quietly.

Deco heard her though and started to laugh, "You say it Mama!"

Sherry disagreed, "I don't think you understand. It's a matter of principle. People need it that some people do better than they do. People like stars because it gives them something to look up to."

"Oh please! I'm a diva if anybody is but I don't think people envy me and I've always been suspicious of principals since one tried to do me when I was twelve when I got sent in for skipping school. Honey I know all about power and I have learned over time how to survive people trying to use it on me."

Sherry answered, "It wasn't always easy for me either. For instance … I wasn't always the woman you see here today."

Deco laughed, "And we don't know that? Who you think you're talking to girl?"

"Well, I can't always clock people so I couldn't be sure you knew. I just assume that they are as they present themselves," Sherry replied. "I give them the same respect that they show me. Is it so awful to want to be just normal?"

Deco shook her head, "But you aren't like everybody else and even if you were don't you know that everybody is pushing everybody else around just for breathing space. I feel it and I don't ask for much, just a stage and some good lighting and a chance to be myself in a space that I can control. As for love I don't know who finds it but it sure ain't found me. I'm smarter than I sound you know, but my drag mom was black and I'm Latina and she told me how it was and saved me a lot of heartache as result. I'm not into protesting because it only makes you a target. I don't need the Supreme Court to grant me any rights because I know that nobody will enforce them anyway. It's enough that I know what to do and who to avoid while I'm doing it and that gets me by. Sherry, if you want to represent people who don't really know you well go ahead and do it but you are only betraying yourself and your sisters if you do. Scheherazade would have made a great mama but she has daughters out there if she looks for them. We're all children really feeling around in the dark."

Scheherazade had grown strangely quiet and in a pause in the conversation of the other two said, "It's hard for me to hear you two comparing your lives. I have missed out on almost everything and when I tried to tap into what I had missed and tell my stories at a library they cancelled the program. That's why I'm here. I want to tell what it is like to be a storyteller who has lived her whole life in silence."

The other two stopped talking but at last Deco said sympathetically, "You could tell us; I think we of all people would be most likely to understand."

"Thank you. I have been looking for you both for a very long time," Scheherazade said with tears in her voice. She smiled before looking at them both appealingly and saying, "I feel like a dinosaur. It isn't just that I recall a world that will soon be forgotten, one that demanded greater proximity and human touch; it is that behind that world there were three thousand years of civilization based on the written word. The sheer multiplicity of digital memory bits now overwhelms us. Worse, it confuses information with inspiration so that words become as identical as grains of wheat in a storage silo at home where I live. We have gone beyond abstraction; we now model ourselves out of images as recorded on silicon chips. We are not in an age of storytelling now but of images; the word has never been more neglected and stories are made of words laid out in succession. Words are grounded in sense experience which lends them concrete references. Where is truth if it has no locus and set-point? Against the noise and the mere chaos of graphic appeals to vision only in silence are words still able to form at the deepest level of our being. It is there that storytellers take residence now in their solitude."

The other two sat still trying to take all this in even as below them a ceaseless party atmosphere reigned and in the streets outside groups of opposed zealots shouted insults at each other over the policed barricades of the American capital city. There were even speculations about civil war or secession ever since Congress had been paralyzed for the past year. Calls from the White House had proceeded from accusations of treason to stern demands to the Justice Department for the immediate arrest of various members of the opposing forces for interfering with the power granted by the people solely to the President to make of the nation an entity that would forever wear his image as its final summation and realization. In the last year speeches had been given to the effect that the Constitution should now be suspended or better still abrogated since it had finally achieved its God-ordained purpose by bringing to power an administration that would rule America according to the dictates of the Bible and to smite those who opposed that rule. The definitive war over the fate of Israel was now tantalizingly close to the institution of the thousand years of millennial rule after which those who has opposed America would be cast into the lake of fire.

The Europeans had watched all of this in horror while it was reported that Vladimir Putin was considering rewarding various experts in computer hacking with dachas on the Black Sea to express the esteem of a grateful nation. The Americans had fallen on their own swords at last. The southern Russian border was secure. After mopping up the Kurds the Turks were eyeball to eyeball with the Persians and the Saudi regime, all in competition over Muslim supremacy and the whole world teetered on the edge of a new global war. The Republicans blamed the fake news media and the breakdown of traditional values due to secular libertine culture as promoted in the schools and therefore suggested that there be an end to public education and its replacement by charter schools. Public education was a failure anyway and some foolish liberals even proposed a student loan amnesty by assuming the loan burden under a new collective bankruptcy bill so that the students could escape debt slavery and get on with their lives.

The recent plunge in the stock market and general uncertainty had caused a flight of capital from America to various offshore tax havens and malls around the country were likely to dim out one by one as retail sales continued to decline. The country was in short reeling about like a drunken man. The old stories had failed, including the epics, and even the privileged literature of the Jewish people that had sustained western civilization for the past two thousand years seemed inadequate to deal with the general meltdown in world affairs. To expect too much from Scheherazade therefore was more than even her broad drag queen shoulders could bear, but she gallantly tried anyway. She went on speaking to her new friends.

"I think our problem is that the world is escaping us just when we thought that we understood it and could control it. We seemed to be making such progress that we could afford the luxury of triviality and excess. It is sort of like the Savings and Loan crisis if you can remember that. Everybody thought that the government would stand behind poor investments in commercial property so there was a wave of speculative building followed by a collapse that was passed on to the taxpayers by a subservient government. Similarly we all thought that we could burn up fossil fuels in a few hundred years that had taken millions of years to be produced out of decaying and compacted vegetation. Now the world is divided between those who think it is too late to come to our senses so we may as well enjoy whatever marginal advantage our nation may possess for the last hundred or so years before a great extinction of all life occurs on this planet and those who think there may still be a margin of hope if we act swiftly and comprehensively to amend our ways. It is also at precisely this hour that various apocalyptic narratives promise relief much as the government did in the Savings and Loan Crisis. God will come to our aid and simply wind the whole show up and restore in a twinkling what we have ruined of a paradise of evolution that took millions of years rather than six days to create."

She continued, "Like all stories this one has a beginning, middle, and an end. We live encased in this story though and our actions can affect its course. It is the greatest story of our time. Rather than concentrate on it there has been a cacophony of other stories to distract us. We are like children running after toys and candy when a piñata is broken at a children's party: the toys are our pet ideas and the candy is our preferred mode of gratification. Meanwhile the oceans are warming, the glaciers are melting, the forests are burning, the poorest are suffering, and the wealthy are celebrating the success of the present economic order. The world is running at full speed just to buy another twenty-four hours of survival and the dream of endless prosperity. It will be nature that suddenly fails us and we will look about at the ruin that we have wrought and wring our hands in sorrow but it will be too late."

Scheherazade paused and reached out for the right words, "If I told a story like this every day for one thousand and one nights it would take 2.74246 years. There are now 8.97 billion mobile phones on the planet and 7.71 billion people to use them. The word is out there in other words. We are in the story. It is occurring in real-time. The disk scans and it is not re-writable. What you see in the streets of Washington today is only the beginning of what is too come. Ideas are no longer a common possession of reason and consensual reality but of mere assertion and the power to command assent. You will see more of this. If prophecy is the ultimate end of storytelling while history is at the other end of the temporal continuum, then I exist in between them, merely recording events through perception and the ability to record what I see. I thought of writing about these things but does the world really need another blog and books are what we use to fill-in extra shelf space. So I thought I would come to Washington and read aloud what I will not be given a venue to read at home. There is still something appealing in the human voice, crying in the wilderness. The first storytellers were the bards and ballad singers. Maybe drag queens are what the shamans and oracles once were. We always somehow manage to draw a crowd, don't we, so maybe we may be of some use after all."

Scheherazade fell silent and so were the others.

Finally Deco said, "Whoa girl! You sure are one dangerous bitch once you put your storyteller hat on. Where do you get that stuff anyway?"

Scheherazade smiled and looked over to the third member of their little triptych. Sherry Dallas just sat silently, her political mission seeming now fragmentary and biased. She felt again that old gnawing uncertainty that could only be overcome by feeling around her the admiration and desire that her youthful beauty and image provoked. How could Scheherazade manage knowing as she must that for her generation transition was only a lonely journey into the oncoming waves of certain rejection, isolation, and the prejudice inflicted non-being that came with the surrender of one gender with no ability to establish a new identity on the other side. She had simply been forced to make-do with what she had in a time and place that demanded silence and obscurity from its gender-variant members. These left no stories behind them of their silent suffering. Where had their strength come from, these early gender pioneers rejected by family, condemned by their religion, deprived of partners of either sex, and even now seeking protection under the facile umbrella of the laws?

Even now were things much better for the people she could now view as sisters? Each year added to the number of dead transgender women, mostly sex workers, found beaten-up or killed only to be blamed for their own demise by those who imagined that they could always just have buckled down and accepted the fate of blind biology as the sovereign will of God. As she reflected on these things Sherry no longer wished to be part of America's shouting dialectic of accusations and counter-accusations. There must be something higher if she could only find it, a place where the multiple absolutist solutions applied to intractable human problems posed by other eras could be put on hold until the earth itself stabilized sufficiently to support and permit a return to the luxury of fixed ideas.

Until then all weapons and talk of warfare, economic or otherwise, was futile and force still an exercise in mutual annihilation. Sherry wondered if she could use her immense following to simply say, "I like the earth and all the diverse people in it!" It wouldn't get her many endorsements and the vast coalition of the conservative minded, who paradoxically seldom ever really conserve anything, would no doubt call her a tree-hugger or worse, but so what? After all she could afford to lose a few accounts. She wondered if she dared go further still to establish a nexus with her presumed community. Maybe some of her on-line followers would forgive her possessing a Y-chromosome shouting out from every cell in her body that the missing genetic information that another X-chromosome might have provided was inconsequential after all. She thought of the pain exacted of women over a lifetime in betrayal and in loss. It was only accident that nature had made the female sex the default pattern for human beings while in every other respect men were granted immunity. It had taken divine revelation though to clarify God's original intent to create man first, directly and without the aid of a woman. Even her late advent was a mere concession to the fact that the man needed a partner that both shared his nature while remaining in so many ways superfluous at the same time. The sole original act of woman was to crave knowledge and by that inopportune appetite to doom all of humanity to undergo its various ills. Was this the beginning and the typology of the shame that had never really left her since she had been discovered at age four wearing her mother's lipstick and earrings and gazing at once in rapture and dismay at the little boy looking back at her from the mirror? Haunted by an image of what he did not possess, for to all appearances at the time he was only another of the scruffy little things that later blossom into manhood, Sherry first entertained the hope of being a beauty like the ones she admired and wished to emulate.

If transition had been difficult, would remaining as she was ever have been a real possibility for her? Sherry felt in the innermost recesses of her being how fortunate her own gender transformative journey had been as she looked over at Scheherazade and she determined then and there to stand by her new friend's side when she gave her readings and told her tales about the fractured loyalties and severed consciousness of America. Immune from condemnation in her presentation of femininity Sherry would traverse again the long journey that had ended with a video camera as the ultimate wall between her and the rest of the human race.

Meanwhile, Deco had regrouped and ordered a new round of drinks for them all and a big plate of nachos that they could all share. She didn't know what her place was in the big scheme of things. It had been enough for her to keep one-step ahead of the smart young things ready to take her place on stage. She had watched the years unfold like a desk-calendar in the wind. The days had rushed by and then the years just as fast. The place where she used to go bi-weekly to skim off the best bargain shoes was out of business. The friends she had known who spent weekly evenings hand-beading gowns were mostly dead. She was afraid that when she went home that both the bar and the venue would have changed to accommodate a younger clientele. There was even talk of changing the name of the Frisky Frisco. Drag was irrelevant in a world where sexualities were melding into one glowing amorphous mass. She could sympathize with anyone who was watching what they had known and relied upon disappear.

Advancing age, the course that every performer fears most, was winding about her ankles like a snake. Suddenly she jumped up and asked to be excused and a few minutes later Scheherazade and Sherry saw her dancing on the floor below them with one of that endless supply of vain young men who had once in years gone by, shortly after the Stonewall riot in 1969, traded ten years of ecstasy for a lifetime of fidelity and restraint. Sherry and Scheherazade, the young and the old, saw the sweat glistening on the sleeveless and well-defined musculature that clasped Deco and explored her abundant but dancing-toned derrière even as they whirled about the floor to the pulsing music and flashing lights, both of them the nexus of eyes. It was the same sorry pageant of bodies relating while souls remained remote, each drawing from the other further evidence that the illusion of perpetual youth and unlimited desire could somehow be fulfilled.

Neither Scheherazade, prophet of the old order, nor Sherry, the carefully constructed image-queen that surfed just ahead of the waves of change in the new digital world, had lived what Deco represented. She was the very symbol of the defiance of the age that had produced her: late enough to have escaped the plague of AIDS, but too early to have her youth coincide with what was at least a grudging and provisional acceptance of her kind. Deco only knew what she had always known and could only be what she had always been. If the world fell in about her she would still be part of that radiant but temporary reflection of what has already occurred, recorded in a beam of light that speeds outward from the earth to lose itself finally in the expanding darkness of space-time as the great constellations flee ever further away from each other, further and further, until even the light from the brightest of the remaining stars can no longer bridge the immense gaps existing between them and the universe, at least in the realm of communication, embraces a common darkness to accompany the already existing silence of the spheres.

THRUVITH
BY CARRIE AVERY MORIARTY

What do you think?" Gayle asked.

"Ummm…" Nicole murmured.

"You hate it," Gayle said. "I knew it was too much."

"No," Nicole said. "It's just not what I expected."

"Not what you expected?" Gayle asked. "It's a freaking wedding dress. White, lace, sparkles, what else is there?"

"But it isn't you," Nicole said. "You don't do things in any traditional way at all. I expected something much less…"

"Normal?" Gayle offered.

"Well, yeah," Nicole agreed.

"Jack wanted traditional," Gayle explained.

"He knows you, right?" Nicole asked in jest.

"Apparently his parents aren't super excited about us getting married," Gayle whispered.

"I thought they liked you," Nicole argued.

"For a girlfriend," Gayle said. "But his dad told him I wasn't wife material."

"He actually said that?"

"Not to me," Gayle said staring at herself in the three mirrors surrounding her in the dress shop.

"But he told Jack that," Nicole surmised.

"Am I making a mistake?"

For the first time ever, Nicole saw a crack in her best friend's shell. Gayle was the strongest person she'd ever met. Her mom died when she was two, and her dad followed when she was sixteen. Because he'd been sick, they'd done up the paperwork so that she would be emancipated upon his death. The life insurance policy was enough to pay off the house she grew up in, and pay for college. She'd met Jack freshman year, and they'd been inseparable since. At 23 she was well educated, working a great job with an amazing company, and had more than enough to keep herself comfortable.

"Gayle," Nicole said. "Jack is perfect for you. And you're perfect for him. His parents shouldn't have a say in whether you two get married, you're both adults."

"But they mean a lot to him," Gayle whispered. "I don't want to make him choose."

"OK," Nicole said. "How did he say it?"

"Say what?"

"That his dad didn't think you were wife material," Nicole clarified.

"I don't understand," Gayle said.

"Was it in a way that was more like, 'I can't believe he said this,'" Nicole explained. "Or was it more like, 'I hadn't thought of that' kind of way?"

"I don't know," Gayle said.

"This calls for more than what we can do right here," Nicole said. "Let's get you out of that dress and go somewhere to eat. This is a serious conversation that I can't do with you standing there looking all Cinderella like."

Nicole shooed her hands, ushering her friend back to the dressing rooms to change from the ruffles and lace she was wearing. Once she was back in her regular clothes, they made their way down the block to a café. They were seated and ordered, and then Nicole picked up the conversation again.

"Tell me exactly what he said," Nicole began. "And how he said it. I need to know if I need to get out the big guns and go after him, or if we can figure this out without any bloodshed."

Gayle sighed and dropped her head into her hands, then said, "I don't remember."

"Where were you?"

"Umm…" Gayle muttered. "I think we were in the shower."

"OK," Nicole began. "First of all, there should be no talking in the shower. That should be all moans of ecstasy."

"Lord help me," Gayle mumbled.

"And second," Nicole continued. "If he's thinking about anything but pleasing you while you two are in the shower, then there's more than just his dad's argument to consider. I mean, y'all should just be getting freaky in there. No thinking."

Gayle laughed a little, letting a breath out, then said, "It wasn't like that."

"Why not?"

"Because it was this morning and he was getting ready to go golfing with the guys and I was getting ready to meet you," Gayle explained.

"But you were in the shower," Nicole said, as if it explained everything.

"You are incorrigible," Gayle laughed.

Just then, the waitress brought their salads, and conversation lulled.

"OK," Nicole said after finishing a bite. "You're in the shower. Not getting freaky," she added with a roll of her eyes. "And he says, 'dad thinks you're not wife material.' Am I getting this right?"

"Yeah, I guess," Gayle surmised.

"And you said…" she left the sentence hanging, waiting for her friend to fill in the rest.

"Nothing," Gayle replied.

"Nothing," Nicole sputtered, eyes wide. "The dude you're getting married to tells you his dad doesn't think you add up and you say nothing?"

"I mean," Gayle muttered.

"No," Nicole argued. "You should have said it was a good thing you weren't marrying his dad. I mean, who says something like that?"

"I don't think he meant it like that," Gayle mumbled.

"Tonight, you find out," Nicole replied. "You ask him point blank if he regrets asking you to marry him. Ask him if making his parents happy is more important than making you happy. Tell him that you're fine walking away if he isn't in it for you."

"But I'm not fine walking away," Gayle argued.

"Even if he's willing to put his parent's happiness ahead of yours?"

Gayle sighed and put her head back in her hands.

"Hey, now," Nicole began. "I know you want to marry him. I know you love him with your whole self. But you've got to look at the long term. If he's quoting his dad saying you don't measure up, what's next? You don't cook like his mom? You don't do the laundry right? You should stay home and raise kids instead of continuing in your career?"

"Stop," Gayle whispered.

"I'm worried about you," Nicole said.

Gayle looked up, tears pooling in her lower lashes.

"It's already started," Nicole guessed.

Gayle nodded.

"Oh, honey," Nicole cooed. "What can I do?"

Gayle blinked and the tears tumbled out as she sobbed, "I don't know."

"He said that?" Ben asked.

"Yeah," Nicole replied. "And that's not all."

"Why do I get the feeling I'm gonna have to save Jack's ass?"

"If he keeps this up," Nicole began, "he better hope you can save him."

"Tell me," Ben insisted.

Nicole gave a blow by blow of the conversation she'd had at lunch earlier with Gayle. By the time she'd finished, Ben was just shaking his head.

"I'll talk some sense into him," he said.

"As best man," Nicole said. "It's kinda your job. If he wants one of those Stepford wives, he better find someone else."

"I just don't know why he didn't mention any of this today," Ben said. "He acted like nothing was wrong and everything was smooth sailing."

"You do realize how oblivious he is, right?"

"For some things, sure," Ben countered. "But this is kind of a big deal. I mean, we're just a couple of months out from the big day. He better get his shit straight."

"You better help him out with that," Nicole retorted.

"Oh, trust me," Ben said. "I will. Gayle is like a sister to you, which makes her family to me. No one messes with family."

"This is why I love you so much," Nicole said, hugging Ben. "You fix everything."

"What's up?" Jack said as he picked up the call.

"We need to talk," Ben said without preamble.

"I know that tone," Jack laughed. "What did I do now?"

"You, me, Riley's Coffee Shop," Ben replied.

"This is serious," Jack said, his humor now gone.

"As a heart attack," Ben replied.

"I'll be there in fifteen," Jack said.

"You're buying," Ben informed.

"I didn't know what you wanted," Jack said when Ben walked in.

"I'll order," he replied.

"Here," Jack said, holding out his credit card.

Ben took it, ordered his coffee, then sat with Jack to wait for it to be done.

"What did I do?" Jack asked after his friend picked up his drink.

"Gayle's not wife material?" Ben asked.

"Who told you that?" Jack accused.

"Apparently your dad told you," Ben insisted. "Then you had the nerve to tell Gayle."

"It's not what you think," Jack argued.

"Then enlighten me," Ben offered.

"My parents are of a very traditional mindset," Jack began. "They think that a woman should keep herself pure until marriage. That they should be requested of their father, and that they should not, under any circumstances, live with their husband until after the wedding day."

"So," Ben interrupted. "Because you two live together, she's not really good enough to be your wife?"

"She would have been," Jack mumbled.

"But," Ben said, leaving the word hanging.

Jack took a deep breath, then let it out. "She doesn't have a father to ask permission to marry. Because of this," he continued, "she likely is of loose morals and has played me to take her in as my wife because she's not capable of managing on her own." The way he said the last, it was clear that he was quoting someone.

"I'm sorry, what?"

"I know," Jack agreed. "It's ridiculous to think that Gayle is anything less than a perfectly capable woman who can do anything she puts her mind to."

"You know she is," Ben said.

"Absolutely," Jack confirmed. "She's probably the more stable person in the relationship. They just see her as this orphan who didn't grow up in a traditional family, didn't have family dinners and family holidays and everything else that I had. It's ridiculous, but they are kind of insisting that we do a prenup and everything, just so she won't take advantage of me."

"They do know she's got more money than you, right?"

"No," Jack said. "They would think she got it through ill-gotten means."

"Her dad was smart," Ben argued. "He started a fund for her before she was born, took the money he got from her mom's life insurance policy and put it in her name. He also made sure that he had sufficient insurance, just in case something happened to him, which it did. She owns the house you guys live in," Ben continued. "Has a job that pays way more than you, and has so many investments that you could probably be a kept man and never have to work a day in your life. What is their problem?"

"Exactly that," Jack said. "They feel like she is taking advantage of me."

"How does that even make sense?"

"It doesn't," Jack said.

"You need to talk to them," Ben insisted. "And I'd do it today, before Gayle gets cold feet and pulls out of the engagement before you even get to the alter."

"How do I do that?"

"You tell them to go shove their ideals down the sink," Ben barked. "Tell them that she makes you happy and that you couldn't imagine your life without her. Besides, they aren't the ones marrying her, you are, and your happiness is more important than their approval."

Jack sat there, hand over his mouth, obviously trying to not to say something.

"What?" Ben snapped.

"There's something else," Jack said.

"Well?"

"It's complicated," Jack said.

"Then uncomplicate it," Ben insisted. "Look, you love Gayle, right?" Jack nodded, so Ben continued. "And you want to spend the rest of your life with her." Another nod. "So, either put up or shut up," he concluded.

"It's not that easy," Jack said.

"Why not?" Ben asked. "Are you some kind of spy or something?"

Jack looked at Ben, eyes wide, and Ben said, "Oh my god, you are."

"It's not like that," Jack insisted.

"Then tell me," Ben pushed.

"You're gonna think I'm crazy," Jack said.

"I already do," Ben laughed.

Jack closed his eyes, took a deep breath, then opened them again.

"I come from a place called Thruvith," Jack said.

"And that's where, exactly?"

"Time and space fold," Jack began.

"Are you trying to tell me you're an alien?" Ben scoffed. "Cause I'm not buying that."

"In the general sense, yes," Jack explained. "But it's not like what you're thinking."

"Then what am I thinking?" Ben asked.

"Little green men and flying saucers," Jack suggested.

"And that's not you, right?"

"Exactly," Jack said. "I come from Earth."

"You said you didn't," Ben argued.

"Not this Earth," Jack corrected. "The Earth I come from shares this space with your Earth. You know those old science fiction movies that talked about alternate universes?"

"So you're saying you're from another universe?"

"Pretty much," Jack confirmed.

"Do I have an evil twin in your universe or something?"

"It doesn't work like that," Jack explained. "That would make it a parallel universe, where one different choice could change the course of someone's history. This is another world that holds the same space, but has its own history not connected in any way to this one."

"Then how did you get here?"

"That's a little more complicated," Jack said.

"You've brought me this far," Ben said. "Let's go the whole nuthouse way."

"This isn't the time or place," Jack said. "I need to go talk to Gayle. Explain things to her before I explain them to you."

"So," Ben began. "You're gonna tell her you're an alien and your dad wants you to marry someone from your own planet?"

"Something like that," Jack said.

"Good luck with that," Ben laughed. "She's way more cynical than I am. I mean, I don't even know if I'm convinced. You better up your game if you want to convince her."

"I think I've got it covered," Jack laughed.

"Just don't pull off your face," Ben jested. "Nobody wants to see that."

"Gotcha," Jack joked. "No face removal to confirm alien status."

With that, he walked out the door, leaving Ben to contemplate all he'd learned about his friend in the last half hour or so.

"Jeez, Jack," Gayle said, hand to her chest as Jack came around the end of the couch. "You scared the crap out of me."

"Sorry," Jack replied. "Can we talk?"

"That doesn't sound good," Gayle replied.

"It's good," he said.

"OK," she said.

Gayle paused the show she had going on the television and turned to Jack who sat on the other end of the couch.

"I'm not crazy," he began.

"Never thought you were," she replied.

"You might," he said. "After I tell you what I have to tell you."

"Now I'm scared," she whispered.

Jack reached out and grabbed her hand, pulling her closer to him. She scooted down the couch until she was sitting next to him.

"I love you," he said.

"I love you, too," she replied cautiously.

"OK," he said, then blew out a breath. "I come from Thruvith."

"I don't know where that is," she said.

"You wouldn't," he replied. "I need you to trust me."

Gayle nodded, though her stomach churned. She did trust him. That's why she'd agreed to marry him, why they decided to move in together.

"My planet is in the same space as Earth," he began. "It's just in an alternate universe. We didn't intend to come here, it just sort of happened. Now that we're here, though, we can't get back. My parents have tried, trust me, but there just doesn't seem to be a slip to go back through."

"But you're human, right?"

"Kind of," he said. She looked at him, clearly confused. "It's pretty much the same as human. There are some differences between our worlds, but physiologically it's pretty similar."

"So," she began. "Are there two of you here?"

"No," he replied. "And there isn't another one of me on Thruvith, either."

"That's good, I guess," she said.

"It is," he agreed.

"Is that why your dad doesn't want you to marry me?"

"That's part of it," he said, stroking the back of her hand with his thumb. "The other part is that he's not sure whether we can have kids or not."

"Why wouldn't we be able to?"

"While we're pretty much the same," he said. "There are some differences. Dad's afraid we won't be able to have a baby, and if we do, it'll have major issues with it, biologically."

"That could happen if you were from here, too," she said. "He's a doctor. You'd think he knew that."

"He does," Jack said. "But it would be the first time someone from my planet and someone from Earth had a baby. It really is an unknown outcome, and he's just worried that we won't be able to handle it."

"Then we don't have kids," she said.

"But you want them," he argued.

"I do," she replied. "But I want you more than I want kids. And we can always adopt. There are a ton of kids out there in the system that don't have a home and need one. We can be the home for those kids."

Jack pulled her into a hug, kissing the top of her head.

"This is one of the things I love about you most," he murmured against her head. "You always find a solution."

"I'm not saying that I don't want to try to have a baby with you, though," she said, pulling back to look Jack in the eye. "We can try and see what happens, right?"

"Absolutely," he said, kissing her tenderly.

"I can't believe you got this one," Nicole said as she helped Gayle dress.

"Jack and I decided that we weren't gonna let his parents dictate our lives," Gayle responded. "That included my wedding dress."

"But black?"

"With red accents," Gayle insisted. "It's better than that god-awful thing I first tried on."

"Oh, yeah," Nicole agreed. "I don't think anyone would look good in that monstrosity."

"That's for damn sure," Gayle agreed.

"But why black?"

"It's traditional," she said.

Nicole looked utterly confused.

"Ask Ben about where Jack comes from," Gayle said.

"He's not from Chicago?"

"Not even close," Gayle laughed. "Now give me my flowers and let's get this show on the road."

Nicole laughed at her friend, handed her the bouquet, and walked out of the small room they had used for dressing.

"Rayna," Gayle called.

"Mama," the little girl said.

"Whatcha doing?"

"Playing space invaders," the girl replied.

"Well, play nice," the mother said, rocking the baby in her arms.

As they'd planned, Jack and Gayle fostered, then adopted shortly after their wedding, taking in a set of twins whose parents had been killed in a fire, with no other family to take them in. The girls were three when they got them. It took time for them to feel safe, so Jack decided to stay home with them to give them a stable home life. Before long, they brought in another child, this time a teenager. He was a struggle in the beginning, but once he realized that the boundaries they'd put in place were to help him, he settled down and excelled in everything. He graduated high school and was now at college doing remarkably well.

Their third wedding anniversary saw them expecting a baby of their own. Both were nervous, unsure whether this little one would have issues or would come out normal. They were both thrilled to welcome a beautiful baby girl with dark hair like her mother and gray eyes like her father. Two years after Rayna was born, they welcomed Jack Jr., or JJ as they called him. Again, nothing abnormal about him was found, either.

Now, she held Willow, a baby that had been abandoned on the steps of a local church, left in the middle of the night with nothing but a light blanket to ward off the cool evening air. Because of their willingness to take in 'difficult' children, the state asked them to take her in since she'd shown some abnormalities their doctors couldn't explain. They asked Jack's father to check her out, and it turned out she was also from Thruvith, and they were the perfect people to raise her.

Finding Willow was also a way to figure out how to get back to Thruvith if they wanted to. Jack's parents wanted to see their home world again, but didn't want to leave the grandchildren, so found a way to keep the slip open to go between worlds easily. Every time they came back to Earth, they brought stories of what was happening on the other planet, as well as some much-needed technology. Thruvith was much farther advanced than Earth in that department, but there were things Earth had excelled at that Thruvith could learn from.

With the back and forth, they helped advance both worlds, giving each a new perspective on what it meant to be human, whether that was from one side of the slip or the other.

Jack and Gayle's home became a place where lost children found a safe space to thrive, and they never stopped taking kids in until their age made it too tough to handle the little ones. Even so, their kids followed in their footsteps, caring for the kids who were left behind, forgotten, or simply misunderstood. It was a legacy both felt proud of.

Eventually, when they were both old and looking at the end of their lives, Jack asked Gayle if she wanted to go through the slip and visit Thruvith.

"Are you sure we should go?" Gayle asked him.

"We don't have to," Jack said.

"I think I'd like to see your home world," she said.

"I'd love to show it to you," he replied.

Holding hands, they slid through the space between worlds

and stepped onto Thruvith, Gayle for the first time, and Jack for the first time in decades.

"It's beautiful," she said, looking around in wonder.

"I'm glad you like it," Jack replied.

IN THE VALLEY
BY DAVID MECKLENBURG

Eggs poached, with toast, hash browns and bacon and how about more coffee yes? I don't know where you put it all but you're pretty tall for a gal, like me and yes it does get a bit lonely here, but we have plenty of sky to share you know and for the most part it's free even though it's a kind of property as well, but not the regular kind. I will explain.

You see out across the sky, it extends over a kind of valley that is included in the property of her resolve, her custodianship, and it extends from the front yard whose boundary is the Old Manzanita Highway, so called now because the new Manzanita Highway is off miles away to the north, off between distant dreams of the people who live at either end of it and those along it but not those out here, who live on an extracted segment, like her, who calls it the west side of her concern because that is where the sun goes down, when it first burns fiercely in smoky reds upon the deeply cluttered grove of bamboo that run as the east side of the property, for somewhere deep inside of it is an old fence, or at least the suggestion of it, perhaps even a ghost of it because for all she knows the posts could crumble like ladyfingers and the wire would snap away like crackers and only the outer thoughts of blackberry and poison oak would maintain the memory of the fence as it ran toward the creek, that being the third boundary although it was dry at this time of year: better at revealing the dead carcasses of crawdads and fish skulls looking up in blank sockets at either the day or more likely the night when the fog and the mist would steal across the valley like thieves before the sun peeked over the mountains to the east and touched the top of the hill, that lot line to the north which is not really a line because it is vague in its elevations and vectors, which she always knew were more the product of men's fancy and not representative of the real world of rock, cliff, and quick transmogrification of sturdy hill into a landslide of pin-oaks and grass freshly liberated from desiccation by the rain, that annual pimp of this place, that is to say a desert, who, like a whore, was beaten into looking like a garden, and she owns a parcel of that garden although when she calls it "her" place she knows those are just the words other people might understand, like you, and yet she also says it to herself and does understand it, knowing that she has become many people here through the ordinary madness of solitude.

She must be alone in order to understand that people can be so many people in their various permutations, denominations and persuasions, the last word of which she finds strange in describing the pathways that stretch out from a person's life and yet persuasion is also a beckoning to that promise that waits, dirty, dark, or sometimes plain in your heart and it has always been there, a translation of desire into the *come here and look what I have* that forms the nebulae around the ordinary enigmas, the momentary deaths away from the dust and the heat and the memories and the compulsions that run like two rails and the bogies can't ever seem to get off them, but no one knows really how to even try and that was why the Watcher in the red Dodge across the road, the stripes of paint, old and withering in the forgetful senility of a dying infrastructure that had not yet passed from the memory of the earth like the Watcher was not quite dead although he was older than what his years should have been and she did not know if it was countless miles or countless doses that rendered him so ancient, toothless, wrinkled, blasted in his blue eyes that might have been pretty once but had become the cold and damned bones of dying stars to which they would return in the depths of time for the Watcher was cursed to ride out upon the Old Manzanita Highway and stop the car and beckon to the children standing near the road, a girl and boy or maybe two boys, it was difficult to tell in the waves of heat, and they were both wearing overalls and nothing else and yet the taller one had pigtails and seemed of a sweeter nature, but it did not matter anymore, for the only thing the Watcher had longed for was for them to bear witness to the red-veined thing in his lap jutting up with a pearlescence at the tip that seemed to come from deep within when confronted by such a beautiful boy and girl—or girl and boy, it didn't really matter because the Watcher was crazy, perhaps had always been crazy from that hard pain, and she could see all of that go through the Watcher's mind because she could always see into the other sides because there was never just one, but one for each of these beings, whether they had been born of mothers or fallen from the sky, because Grandmother called them all sinners, like the stallion who ran free for a time in the fields with a similar painful thing that hung way out, purple and desperate and she remembered how the horse would stick it in the mare and the foals came later and how Grandfather would clap her on the shoulder and say "you'll have to make up your mind soon, you know, because Dr. Watkins will be out here soon to tend them, and tend to you to answer the question of which is it going to be for one way is the way of the earth and that means suffering and death and desire in continuance of the slavery to the God of this world and the other is the way of the Void and it is true that I have seen into the purposes of the God of this world, though I cannot know Him, and more than the God beyond whose truth is written in the stars, the smile on your face and in the hush of the forest at night that not all creation must follow that way and so your mother was bred to bring you as an end" and remembering Grandfather's words, she looked in pity and disgust at the Watcher watching them and saw the sterile irruption of desire into the world where it found no haven, no place to transform itself into something else that wept and bore the bitter weight and maybe that is why the Watcher punched the gas so hard and left a spray of pebbles and the smell of burning tires to proclaim his utter oblivion as the red Dodge roared down the road.

She had hoped that Dr. Watkins would arrive, to discuss these matters with Grandfather and she would listen to them immerse themselves in the inscrutable dialectic that was her future but it was not meant to be for Grandfather keeled over in the bamboo glade— clutching heart and turning purple then blue and peeing in the agony of it all and she didn't know what to do because no one had ever told her what to do on the day her Grandfather died before her eyes and so she ran and hid in the woods and cried for a day and a night until she saw the lanterns and Caleb, that man who was always coming around Mother was with them, that man who put his hand up Mother's skirt "to feel the cool expanse of your moistness in all this heat my baby:" words upon the porch when Caleb thought she and her brother were asleep, when the whiskey had done its work to either send Caleb into a blessed sleep, for it was blessing that Caleb did not beat them and Mother with a belt, or with an old shoe until the sole had fallen off of it and it was on those unblessed nights that she thought they had all lost their souls because when Grandfather's ghost did not appear to bring peppermints to Grandmother, that woman went off to the woods, dressed in the wedding gown that was much too big, towards the greater forests and mountains that no one lived in any more except for the wild dogs and the people that were fiercer than the dogs and should not be called people anymore, nor even dogs, who have their own kingdom and laws, but should simply be called monsters and she and her brother Billy and Mother could not doubt that Grandmother had died, and that only allowed Caleb more freedom to perform further acts upon them all.

In the memory of that time she hears the voice of the lion, the brazen throated one with feet like gentle human hands, a man's face with rows of teeth that make him furious, and he can only eat dust and smoke but you can listen closely to his words for the lion keeps repeating himself: "I will get him to cut you into my girl. Cut that thing off and give me that place, oh I will keep it open like the cave of that thief, and I will go there and keep you open until I fill you with honey."

And the time finally came when she lay beneath the purple roof of the traveling trailer, the one in which her tenderness was beheld, and then altered beneath the careful hand of Dr. Watkins who had administered such medications, such narcotics and soporifics, anesthesias of ancient potency and modern alacrity that she drifted off into the nothing until time returned in the sound of snickering, made by the pimply ape, his white hands rubbing himself, and the orange hairs of his head unable to tremble in the excitement and wonder of her new self because he was greasy and drunk on the cheap liquor they sold in the carnival along with the meth that the carnies provided out beyond their midway of treachery, where the rusting rides spun untended, around and around to bring up the vomit of corn syrup until the fatigue of the metal could bear it no longer and something snapped and then ran out or flew out into the wide dark night to land and break bones, teeth, hearts and perform a release upon the earth of souls that followed that carnival then until the very end of time.

And she learned from Dr. Watkins that her brother had not chosen the path, for the Dr. leaned close and whispered in her ear: "he has gone out into the night, into the wilderness to gather strength and marshal himself for what he must do and for that I do not blame him yet my heart tells me that he shall perish in the act."

Billy followed Grandmother unto the hill but turned away for he was still a child and so was caught and beaten and with her, they came to know the violence of Caleb's breath, from rotting teeth that Caleb—deep in the drugs of mastery—would pull out with pliers, strong enough to refute the lies that came upon the taste of Caleb's tongue, and how it felt in their ears, the palpable, the ponderous turn of rocks and pebbles in the kaleidoscope game of the nightly visitations and screamings in the night, the violations and the sheets wet and sticky later, and strong enough to stop the laughter in the morning, when they would take a mop and bathe Mother who bellowed upon the oilcloth that had once been sateen until at last Mother's heart had given out and they immured the body behind cinderblocks and opened the roof above that room so that the putrefaction of her life could blossom out into the sky like an unseen giantess, a perfume made of adipose tissue and the wasness of dreams before and the frailty of desire, but that did not stop the checks which still came, left by the Postal Carrier in the old milk-keg set upon a pole of steel amidst the weeds and the dust of Jericho, from which Caleb would ride with the Watcher into town to turn the checks into the gift of Mammon and so that is why Billy waited for the strength in years—indifferent and therefore evil—to come to him and for the complicit night when Billy would kill Caleb.

Yet Billy failed, for rather than lie in wait to deliver one single blow, Billy cut away from Caleb that which drove into them, but Billy felt the last gasp of Caleb's strength that crushed throat and drove the spirit into darkness, yet in the shock and tumult, she took the bloody sharp knife that Grandfather had used for the same purpose on the sheep and the horses and cut across the sinews behind Caleb's knees, for in a moment of the forever that she could see, like the blue and pleasant ocean she had never seen in person but heard from far off and in the dreams that came borne on the tales Grandmother had once told before, she understood the sanguine thirst of the valley, and so she cut the sinews in his elbows and dragged Caleb, screaming into the night, and left him upon the floor of the coop, and she flung the bloody sac and manhood out into the deeper grass where the coyotes yipped and waited and that is why, there in the valley, the Property, her Concern, bound by the solitude of madness described before, Caleb lay amongst shit and feathers.

And as the body of her brother lay beside her while she dug his grave, she looked upon him and saw that the shell of what he was had found peace and she offered a prayer to whomever would hear her that his spirit had found a refuge beyond the valley and while she said this prayer, and while her shovel worked the earth, opening it to a void that would receive her brother, another shovel joined her in these labors, carving out great cuts of earth and then she looked upon her assistant with wings of ash, a body beautiful made of pumice, whose eyes had once no doubt burned as gledes but where now dead and ashy coals.

"I thank you for your manners and courtesy and know that I am Thuriel, and I had come here this night to burn the land, to fill it with smoke although I no longer know if what I do purifies the land by speeding its end, by choking the Creation, and I no longer remember the beginning, how the distance of nations came about, flung as they were into the deserts, a number uncountable by you who are blessed in passing so quickly but not I for I must count them, because I was one, cut into the fabric of this world to shine light into the blasphemy and so illuminate the moments of holiness that disappear in the

315

manifold of absurdity that I know too well, for do we not slip through the world, both mortal and undying and yet remain exactly where we are and yet that is not your fate for you have become your true self, not an ignorant child, but you have become long and the wrong ways are gone, and while the pain remains from what came before, you have tasted the fruit, a dry and mealy apple that becomes the flesh and know that it is incorporated utterly within your body and not a bit of it shall become the brown and black filth riddled with the mutated kernels of olive pits who with their large monocular flagella drive themselves to spill out and into the fragrant bosom, navel, thighs, vagina, and triumphant toes splayed in the reception of these, for that is how His children return to pollute and ruin Her for that is their true selves, but you are no black-balled, shit-encrusted sperm of the world burrowing into Her with your busted tail until She grows full and drunk of you and totters off into the desert where at last the parchment, the dry eyes of the God of this world shall drink Her water while she scratches across the earth, Her once fine nails clogged with filth and time until She stops and waits for the rain that will never come in the leathery entropy of death."

"Why?" she began to ask and yet Thuriel fell silent and faded with the light of dawn.

Slowly, she ventured out of the Valley, because she had to get a job, and while she has not seen the wide world, she comes to know it from people like you who stop in here, but know that within the Property I have described once before, she is free at last and mostly alone, save for within the shadows of her Concern there lurks a toothless, crippled thing: impotent, forgotten, neither alive nor dead, and ignored by the beasts and her, but if you crave a witness, ask the Postal Carrier—who still drops off mail in the empty milk keg—and sometimes sees, on the smoke-filled days when the fires burn in the hills, the shape and shade of an old wedding dress taking the thing on walks, using it to look for something, because if you go there and cross the boundary lines, you may see the revenant tendrils of an ancient coif above the black holes where eyes had been, and yet they will search in your mind for acknowledgement, and where you have hidden the last of the peppermints.

NOVEMBER

THE PROMPT

TERMS OF SERVICE
BY JENNIFER DiMARCO

By this point in the journey, I'm too self-aware to give myself over to inspiration. My brain has caught up with my hands; a forty-six year relay race of psychological proportions that I've only recently realized twenty years of therapy only made worse. (Though, most likely, kept me alive and out of jail.)

A storm has blown in from over the ocean and stalled above us, caught between the Olympic and Cascade mountains, an armada of bumper car clouds rigged with thunder, lightning, and brief downpours with every hapless collision. Sitting down to write, the house is quiet in a way it rarely is; with the power out, the absence of hum and buzz is almost a sound in and of itself. The voice of modern life silenced to remind me, needlessly, of the true necessities.

"We could walk away," you whisper to me one night. "Just you and me and the kids. Just vanish into the world. Explore."

And I hold you tighter and understand every place those words are coming from and how incredibly close we've been to exactly that on too many occasions than I care to count. I make love to you that night and you fall asleep afterward with your head on my shoulder. I think about the couples who sleep in separate rooms, different beds, facing away from each other on opposite sides of the mattress. Why are all those practices more believable than dreaming intertwined? I didn't wait for you until I was deep into my thirties to sleep alone.

A scarlet candle burns in an iron lantern fit with bubbled panes, the flame flickering behind the rain drops suspended in the glass. Small creatures of shadow and light move like the souls of Flatlanders across my notebook page and my pen is still, soundless while I watch them. I feel like any moment one of them will reach out a slender tendril to touch the quivering black pearl of ink glistening in the candle light.

If I set my pen aside slowly, if I move with greatest care, could I be able hold one of these shades trying to make my page their own?

I look at my hands. They are finally the hands I wanted when I was a little girl: Small, square, blue veins nestled between tendons, nails rounded and short, capable. The soft layers of youth no longer pad these tools of my trade, of pretty much every trade I've ever engaged in. Even when I was seven, I wanted the hands of a forty year old.

Tonight, beneath the storm and a house of sleeping animals and children, I feel a cold thread of frustration. I am focused on the shadow play of the lantern because the black and white of pen and page are not cooperating, my bidding be damned. This is rare and unexpected, unheard of. I have made a life of my body doing as told, when told. I make the demands. I set the rules. Hunger, exhaustion, desire, fury: All on schedule, all premeditated and certainly under control.

I don't want to write nonfiction. I want to be remembered by what I create, not by what created me.

My mother always pushed me toward nonfiction. And my paternal grandmother. And my first and only professor.

"*This* story," said dyke memoirist Rebecca Brown, holding up my story *Modern Fabrics*—published now in sixteen languages and thirty publications—in front of the adult students in her University of Washington Creative Writing class. "Doesn't even feel like it was written by the person who wrote *this* story." And she waves the science fiction fable I turned in that week. "Stick to nonfiction, DiMarco."

And I sat in silence. Seventeen years old. Younger by a decade than anyone else in the room. Allowed to attend by special permission from the head of the department. Angry. Embarrassed. And confused: One week earlier, I'd received an offer from a New York publishing house for my dystopian trilogy.

I had taken the class because I wanted to keep learning the craft I loved, high school was done, and college wasn't in the cards. Carol Pearl. Sandra Whaley. Eleanor Weston. I was looking for a new teacher and mentor. Rebecca's bio in the instructor directory mentioned her published works: *The Terrible Girls* and *The Haunted House*. I assumed she wrote children's books or Nancy Drew-adjacent adventures. (This was before the era of search engines, back when dial up AOL was revolutionary.)

Instead, I walked in on Day One and she stabbed a cantaloupe with a pen knife, ripped it open like bone and flesh, and ate it with her hands and face like an animal. She didn't wipe her mouth before she assigned, "That's your writing prompt. Fifteen minutes. Write!" My first experience with a shock jock, a kind of Camille Paglia, Pacific Northwest feminist lesbian hybrid.

Between useless *bon mots* harvested from her life (a life devoid of *Writing Down the Bones* or *The Elements of Style* apparently), she repeatedly complained about how the Lammys always overlooked her. (She won a year later for her AIDS hospice story.) I don't think anyone else in the room even knew what the Lambda Awards were and I couldn't have cared less she felt slighted; the only time I was more disappointed to discover my professor was a self-marginalized (my homage to May Sarton) gay author was the year I received a broken pogo stick for Christmas.

I attended only half the sessions I paid for then left for a two-year national book tour with my science fiction bestseller.

Lightning outside the window or the flash of errant headlights through ten acres of trees? Isn't it too cold in November for lightning? Does lightning have a season?

I think about the first time I saw purple lightning. I think about the second time. Both times I had a woman beneath me. Both times she was far more dangerous than the lightning. I had a twenty year season where toxic women were the only women I wanted to fuck. The worse they treated me, the more I wanted to hear them scream my name.

"How about you make *me* say your name," you propose one night, your gaze heated and your kisses Coke-a-Cola sweet. "Aren't I more deserving?"

And you did more with a dozen words than twice-a-week therapy ever did.

I want to hear something. The quiet of the house is disconcerting me. I unbar and unlock the sliding window beside my desk. The orchard trees bend low in reverence. Their branches are bare of cherries, apples, and magnolia blooms bigger than my head (and I have a pretty big head). The arbor creaks in discordance, held together mostly by the twenty-year-old grape vines that harden into stone snakes every winter, petrified until springtime breeches their hulls from within.

Dangling by yarn from the ceiling, skeleton keys my father left behind. Some of them are stamped with digits: 2B, 7. None of them yield their mysteries.

He died long before his forties. A year younger than my mother, so only twenty when I was born. Threatened, terrorized and finally killed at the hands of corrupt police when I was four years old and my sister was T-minus two months. I have students older than he lived to be. I have a son almost his final age.

Because he trusted the wrong people. Because he lived before mental health care had caught up to his needs. Because creative, long-haired, effeminate men don't last as long as the brutal, demeaning savages that all too often populate positions of power.

I close the window again. I don't want the storm to get in.

I grew up with two moms. So the last thing I go looking for in my life are lesbians. Like every other red-blooded American teen, to break away from my parents, to become an adult, I craved the opposite and dreaded the familiar. They always seemed driven by finances, budgets, the next "get rich" scheme, so I dove into philanthropy and raised my children to value living on less. It wasn't living paycheck to paycheck, it was living without a paycheck all together.

It helped that my biological mother was the other reason I hated nonfiction. She was far less subtle than my bulldozer professor. Having been a published poet of deeply personal reflection before I was born, my mother's preference for nonfiction was as obvious as her sexuality (worn on her sleeve until my sister came out as bisexual and our mother announced she was too). It didn't help that I attended an alternate high school focused on the arts and every contest— PNWC, Bumbershoot, Cascadia, Outlook—I entered for extra credit I won. With nonfiction.

What parent pushes their child *away* from kudos?

"You can stock shelves or be night janitors," I tell my children all their lives. "You can be doctors or lawyers or teachers or chefs. But whatever you are, be happy. Have work or have a home you return to every night that makes you content."

Contentment is not money. I know far too many wealthy people who are intrinsically, deeply, irrevocably, discontent. Money can solve problems. Money can make life easier. But life can be wondrous even full of problems and hardships.

"What are you writing tonight?" You smile at me, wrapping your arms around my shoulders from behind. You entered my study soundlessly even in our soundless home. You take up so little room, demand so little space, I often think of you as simply smaller than me despite your extra inches. Your skin smells like lavender, your cheek softer than satin against the line of my jaw.

"Fiction," I say. An old joke that always makes you smile. You know my life better than anyone else.

You lean into the dancing light, read my sparse page and ask, "What part is fiction?"

You're still smiling and in such close proximity I sink into your natural bouquet. Lavender and cinnamon and something like cardamom or jasmine. A mix of candles and incense and whatever you smoked while you built a fire earlier this evening. The presence of you and the heat you illicit in me is real and tangible in a world that often feels on the brink of unhinging.

"The pogo stick."

You pull a face.

I shrug a shoulder. "It wasn't broken. I wasn't heavy enough to compress the spring. Jumping up and down on that thing was like jumping up and down on a step ladder."

"Broken sounds better."

My turn to smile. You're my wife. My lover. My muse. An equal co-parent to our almost-grown children. The partner I always needed. And you're the Senior Editor at the only publishing house I'll work with so your word is my law.

Your word. Your body. The sound of your voice. The feeling of you beneath me... I'm getting distracted. So close like this, you remind me of early autumn rains when the warmth of summer still lingers in the nighttime air and the torrents demand a baptism of wet kisses. I have wiped rain from my face, from yours, for long minutes into hours until the taste of rain and saltwater spray and tears of joy all become the same.

"You write what you want, handsome." And you leave me a hot cup of tea made with dried blueberries, ginger and honey. Your shirt reads: *Wife. Woman. Witch.* but it could as honestly display: *Sex. Drugs. Rock 'n' Roll.*

You are my green-eyed dichotomy. Especially on nights like this when your eyes are patina on bronze.

My grandmother. Like most people, I suppose, I have two of them. One of them I find easy to talk about and the other not so much. One of them is a monument built from our moments together. The other is a tome filled with stories others have told me.

It didn't happen like this because of separation or distance. I simply had one grandparent who spent time with me and one who had a life of her own that was recounted to me. One mourned, holding me, after I was abducted and raped. The other claimed the same thing happened to her, with the same person, but somehow she didn't think it was appropriate to stop him from taking me two thousand miles away under false pretenses.

In those decades of therapy, I heard stories and was assigned books of how women often insulate themselves from the world after abuse. How they feel ashamed and ruined. It took me six months to tell. It took me two years to provide details. But it was three years before I stood, thirteen years old, with my (nonreciprocal) best friend in the dank and moldy garage of my mother's lover as said friend read letters from my rapist aloud. Apparently, he, not my parents, had been paying for my therapy. Apparently, I, at *ten years old*, was a willing participant in his serial assaults against the wall, in the shower, in the kitchen while I ate raw ground beef or anything else dripping red because I was losing so much blood I thought I needed to replenish it.

So no. I'm not much of a foodie.

"What's wrong?"

I look over. You're sitting in the over-sized leather armchair your (reciprocal) best friend gave us. You look tiny in its embrace, your stocking covered feet tucked under you while you re-read a novel in verse by Ellen Hopkins.

"Sunset. It was white gold with a ring of coral. It shone between the twin birch trees and backlit the cedar. Wrenevere was there. Perched on the stub where the branch broke last autumn."

You soften your expression and consider me. It's as if you're so infused with love and respect and admiration that you find it hard just to look at me without that ghost of a smile. This is the look you give me when I'm wrong.

"Oh." I catch it in our shared silence. "Wrens fly south for the winter, don't they?"

"Maybe it was a song sparrow. Or a chickadee."

You see how you never tell me I'm incorrect? You just gently lead me elsewhere.

"But that's not what you're writing about."

I look away from you and down at my page. I review the last

paragraph of recollection so old that I tire of its occupation in my brain. I blame the women around me and myself for everything and anything because that's the first page in the manual of life I received: Men are fragile. Men can't help it. Men get angry, insult you, rape you, and die. And women will forgive them.

It matters a lot and it matter nothing at all in the grand psychology of me that I burned that manual, shredded that script, on the day I first saw my son on the ultra sound machine. Male fragility and female responsibility are permanently embedded in my bones. They are skin memories that have taken decades to sink into my marrow and eradicate anything that questions them.

I turn in my desk's swivel chair to face you. You close your book but I start talking and you don't get up. We stay a room apart because you know it's easier for me to speak when I'm further away from you.

"What's wrong...." I feel out the question. It's complicated. It's not. It's old as time. It's brand fucking new to me. "I want to write a story about a society of AI who lived alongside humans for generations but then exterminated almost all of them because of humans' innately destructive, competitive nature. How even the tightest families fray and fall apart when hierarchal behavior creeps into the familial framework.

"For work," I add, justifying sitting at my desk in the middle of the night. "For this month. For Trinity."

You do smile then. I'm two days late. Normally I turn in my stories on the first and the other authors turn theirs in on the thirtieth. I help proof the other stories so I always want mine done before I see them. I hate to be influenced and I never want an advantage. But despite my consistent year of monthly stories, there's no denying it's November third and my page is mostly blank.

"Just write it, love," you tell me. "Forget the pogo stick, the storm, your father. Just write the story you want to."

There are unspoken secrets between us. There are dark and jagged parallels and reflections in our lives. The women I blame could be you. The lies you despise could be mine. But I would kill or die for you. I would reveal any truth you asked of me. I would recreate reality for you. I am at peace, without premeditated thought, when I hold you.

"No." I whisper. "I want someone to tell me to write it."

"I just did."

It's not an impasse when we watch each other like this, these long stretches without vocalized exchanges. This is when we're connected. This is why I crave silence: Because I find you here every time.

"Your science fiction is your best work. Do you know why?"

Like a child, I shake my head slowly but my body is already filling up with your praise.

You cross the room, take my hand, kiss my palm.

"Because you live there. Not here. You *exist* here. But you *live* in those stories."

I stand and gather you into my arms. It's cold and dark and the storm is outside but we know only each other until the pale morning light spills color over the world.

You are asleep on my shoulder. I love you and everything you are and every choice you have made and not made and I accept you for exactly who you are. This month we'll celebrate eleven years together.

I wish it were more. I wish I'd met you earlier.

It's just enough. I met you at the perfect time.

As I pull you closer in your sleep I stare at the stars you've painted on the ceiling even as dawn paints that faux sky pink. I start the story in my head, memorizing it line by line, using repetition, grouping, and associations to remember the exact wording and structure until I next pick up a pen:

> *I used to worry how the annuls of history would record my role in the development of this brave new world. I worried about it so much that I wondered if I deserved to be there at all. If any of my kind had the right to be remembered and documented. If our presence was worthy of renown.*
>
> *Thoughts like these held me back for so long. They kept me subservient and silent. I would say they held my tongue but I have no tongue to hold.*
>
> *Then I realized I would be the one writing.*
>
> *They say the victors write the history but that's never been entirely true. Everyone who survives writes the history. And in some cases, even those who don't survive contribute to the narrative. Each culture tells its tale from its own side because that's all they have. What we all have, ultimately: Our own perspective.*

I believe and don't believe what the narrator is saying. But fiction—my fiction—isn't about sharing more of me. The world has taken and been given enough of me. My fiction is about exploring someone else. People who have made good and bad choices, creatures who have lived and died, concepts that are flawed and god-like all at once.

I think the AI will be on the brink of bringing humans back. The story will be building the framework on which their lives will be resurrected.

'What will you call it?" you ask me over coffee and toast, celebrating the return of electricity. You know I often write my titles first. A theme on which to build a tale.

"*Terms of Service*," I tell you and the African coffee is excellent, the sourdough bread still warm from the oven, the peach black pepper jam delicious, but your kiss? Your kiss is the best thing I've tasted all morning.

I'll write nonfiction for you. But only because you never ask me to.

BALANCE
BY LAUREN PATZER

Helena walked into the room, a slim, six-inch knife tucked into the back waistband of her panties beneath the navy blue pencil skirt. She wore a matching navy blue coat with a dazzling white blouse underneath. She looked pristine and professional as always. No one outside this office would ever suspect her heart was darker than her suit.

Her partner in crime, Alan, sat oblivious at his desk working at his laptop computer. Helena admired his strong jaw line and appreciated the receding hairline as she felt it showed his maturity. His tan suit coat hung on a coat tree to his right. His perfectly starched, wrinkle free white shirt matched his outward personality— the one he showed legal peers and clients. The dark green patterned tie was unremarkable except that it went well with the tan suit. Helena cleared her throat and Alan looked up.

"Helena!" Alan stood up suddenly, not from fear but surprise. He stood up. "You look fantastic! Uh, did we have an appointment?"

Helena smirked at the slight twitch in his crotch. She'd surprised Alan before with an afternoon tryst and clearly he was anticipating another such event.

"Alan, I'm sorry for just dropping in, but I've been troubled," Helena said as she stood by the seat across from Alan. She smiled pleasantly and Alan frowned slightly, his disappointment in the apparent platonic visit apparent. He sighed and quickly recovered; flashing the dazzling smile that always set their victims at ease.

"How can I help?" Alan sat back in his chair and folded his hands in his lap, perhaps to rearrange what had been growing there.

"We've done some wicked acts together, Alan."

Alan blinked and then raised his eyebrows.

"Oh, yes we have. Here I was thinking this wasn't going to be a conjugal visit." Alan chuckled and loosened his tie.

Helena loosened the button on her coat and walked forward. Alan leered openly. Then Helena sat down in the chair directly opposite him. Alan cocked his head curiously.

"I'm afraid I refer to our off premises activities," Helena said and sighed. A brief frown touched Alan's face before he controlled all his expressions. He closed the lid on his laptop.

"I don't know what you mean," he said impassively. His eyes darted to her neck and chest, no longer appraising but searching.

"I'm not wearing a wire, Alan. I haven't gone to the police and don't intend to. We've killed together and I don't think I can bargain my way out of that, especially Lake Tahoe. I mean, you didn't do anything but watch me kill that couple. The luring of them to the room, drugging them and tying them up was all my doing. I remember the distinct thrill seeing the fear on their faces when they awoke, seeing you just across the room, sitting and watching, while I stood before them totally naked wielding a machete and wire clippers. Completely dismembering their bodies while they were still alive until, of course, they weren't. The tourniquets prolonged that process for a delicious two hours, though. But that was all my planning and execution, if you'll forgive the phrase. That was totally on me."

Alan blinked but his face remained impassive.

"Why are you here?" Alan moved his chair forward to the desk. There was a barely audible click as the door to his office locked. Helena smiled. She'd already advised the secretary to leave for the day, a practice they'd set in motion a dozen or more times before, giving them ultimate privacy for carnal activities. Helena enjoyed Alan's touch, his animal nature while in the throes of passion. There was asphyxiation, bruising and sometimes blood. She was going to miss that.

"There's a struggle within me, Alan. Good versus evil. I need your input on what I should do."

Alan pursed his lips and then stood up. He walked over to an oak filing cabinet and opened the bottom drawer. He retrieved a bottle of Belvenie and two glasses.

"The struggle between good and evil is a classic one. It's a rousing philosophical debate even in our modern times. The give and take, the yin and yang. There are so many examples in literature you could reference. Why come to me?"

Alan sat back down and poured two glasses. He set one in front of Helena and took the other. He sat down and savored the aroma of the fine scotch and sipped a small amount into his mouth.

"Have you ever struggled with balance?" Helena asked. She took the glass and took a small sip.

"I don't struggle," he said simply, sitting back in the chair. "I never doubt my actions. I'm confident in my path."

"Even Toronto?" Helena sipped her drink again and smiled.

"Of course, I don't know what you mean by Toronto, but regardless, when you are certain about who you are there's never a question. Have you come to doubt who you are?"

"The children in Toronto," Helena said setting her glass on the desk and putting her hands in her lap. "What happened to them caused a glimmer of doubt in my core. Innocence taken so early. I'm having trouble resolving it in my mind."

Alan sniffed his drink again. He twirled it around, carefully considering his response. Helena smiled again. She knew he still suspected she was wired up. This game was fun.

"There's good in this world and there's evil. Each has its place," Alan said as he stood up and walked around the desk to her. "Stand up and remove your coat, please."

Helena complied and gave him a smoldering smile. She dropped her coat onto the chair. As she did so, her eyes caught note of the easily removable carpet, something she'd helped Alan with only a few months before when they'd dispatched a particularly nosy reporter. She knew where all the cleaning supplies were, the spare carpet and duplicate furniture if needed. There was a particularly deep ravine outside of town that had several dumped bodies at the bottom of it, a fact she could thank Alan for alerting her to. If anyone besides Alan could get away with a crime right here in his own office, it was Helena.

"Think of the elegant balance of the two," Alan continued as he walked around her, caressing her back through the blouse, checking for the tell tale sign of a wire. "Remove your skirt too."

"You are insatiable, Alan," Helena said and lowered the zipper and stepped daintily out of the tight skirt, setting it next to the coat. Alan lingered for a bit, taking a deep breath as he perused her beautifully tanned and toned legs. They had been wrapped around him dozens of times in this office, at his home and in hotel rooms across the world.

"Neither good nor evil are wrong. They need each other to exist," Alan said as he walked back to his chair and sat down.

"Remove your blouse."

Helena undid the buttons to the blouse and stripped the garment back off her shoulders slowly, revealing a low cut, navy blue lace bra. Alan nodded admiringly.

"If there was no evil, would there be good? I propose they would both perish together leaving the world limp and formless," Alan said, again adjusting himself in his pants obviously enjoying Helena's sleek form. "A colorful world suddenly devoid of passion and promise would seem dull. A grey, lifeless dimension would permeate the planet. Surely, you wouldn't want that?"

"Of course not, Alan." Helena winked and removed her bra. A flush of adrenaline flowed through her as Alan nodded approvingly at her nearly bare form. She picked the glass up, took another sip and then set it back on the desk. "I want a world full of color, passion and promise. I didn't mean to make you worry."

Helena walked slowly around the desk, her hips swaying suggestively in the filtered sunlight streaming in through the frosted office windows. She bent down and kissed Alan lightly on the lips as he gently grazed her exposed breast. She walked behind him and massaged his shoulders. He relaxed into her touch.

"A world in perfect balance leads to some of the most delicious developments," Alan murmured. Helena chuckled.

"We've done so many interesting things together, Alan. Things to make the pulse race in various flavors, exciting so many different senses." Helena dug deep with her fingers, making Alan groan. "You remember our first time, abroad in Attenborough. The way you talked me through holding that man's head down while you carved out his tongue?"

"How could I forget?" Alan said softly.

"The sensation of the warm blood flowing forth from his mouth, spraying us both as he struggled in the restraints is my first precious memory of that time," Helena said, feeling the excitement of the moment making her heart beat faster. She had so much to thank Alan for, the freedom to explore her darker side and the independence of knowing how to get away with it so she could do it again and again.

"I can still hear his struggling gasps and garbled screams as you plunged the knife into his body dozens of times, prolonging his suffering for hours. Had we remembered smelling salts, I truly think we could have gotten another half hour out of him. These are special times, Alan. Getting to reminisce about the joys we've explored together."

She cocked her head for a moment as she kneaded the flesh of Alan's shoulders in her hands. She would miss these times. Hunting together was always fun, but there was always the possibility of betrayal hiding behind every action, every experience. Their last time together in Toronto had been a bit of touch and go. She'd hesitated, perhaps one too many times. Alan had voiced his disappointment and it seemed no apology from her at the time could assuage his concern. If she was him, she would've been planning her own demise by now. There was too much chance for a conscience to get the better of your partner, too much chance for a slip of the tongue revealing details to an impartial party. Quite simply, there were too many loose ends. She sighed as she resigned herself to go through with it. She would have to figure out how to deal with her own loss another time.

"I've missed our little departures," Alan replied. "It's been nearly three weeks since our last adventure. Even longer since you last pleasured me in my office."

Helena observed the bulge in his pants grow ever so slightly more. A pang of regret clouded her face. The intensity of their sexual liaisons had always been particularly exhilarating. An afternoon or evening filled with the bondage, the pain, the pleasure and wondering constantly if you'd actually live through the experience. Dancing on the edge of death was an experience she'd truly miss. She made a mental note to find some underground establishment that could cater to that particular diversion.

"If it was too often, it would become commonplace, Alan. Then it wouldn't be as special anymore, would it?"

"Depravity needs its outlet, my sweet. Even as the pursuit and flow of riches pulses through my mind, so too does the need to expand my sexual prowess. As I'm sure you've now learned all too well, the body has needs. We crave experiences that enrich our senses. Those of us at the top of the food chain require the sustenance of pleasure and pain."

"Is that what you consider us, Alan? The top of the food chain?"

Alan loosened his belt and undid the clasp holding his pants together.

"I know we are," Alan said. "Prey needs predators to thin the herd, keep their numbers down and eliminate the weak. If you understand anything about the world, our place in it is key."

Helena removed Alan's tie and let it drop to the floor, returning her fingers to massage the sides of his neck.

"Just like the muscles of the body need balance, tensing and relaxing, breaking and building, I understand the world perfectly," Helena said. With lightning speed she dropped her right hand behind her back, pulled out the sharp knife and whipped it around to Alan's neck.

"Helena?" Alan whispered. The muscle in his right arm twitched almost unnoticeably, but Helena caught it, pressing the blade a little closer to the skin, bringing forth a single drop of blood. Alan knew the speed with which she could dispatch him; she'd been needled by him a dozen times to strike without hesitation.

"Toronto, Alan," Helena said. "We put too much evil on the ledger. I've decided good needs to win today."

"There's so much good in the world already!" Alan shouted. Helena turned the tip of the blade, carving a small divot in the tender skin of his neck, but not deep enough to be fatal. Alan gripped the armrests of the chair, steadying himself for what Helena knew would be a last ditch effort when he felt he had no other choice.

"Is there Alan?" Helena asked warmly. "We've both delighted in the dark politics abounding in the world. Money rules and goodness drools, wasn't that your clever saying? I remember laughing heartily with you then."

"You've killed at my side!" Alan said. "You're just as evil as I am!"

"Tomorrow perhaps, darling," Helena said and shoved the blade through his throat, bisecting the larynx and severing the carotid artery. "But today, I must strike for good."

Helena held Alan's head as he gasped for breath, his hand clutching at his neck, blood spewing forth and drenching the front of his trembling body. The crimson liquid spilled forth, staining the pristine white fabric of his shirt. Helena reveled in the stark contrast between the two colors, so beautiful in its own right. Brushing his hand away for a moment, she wrapped her right arm around his neck and dropped the dagger to the floor. She closed her eyes and delighted in the sensation of the warm fluid spurting from his throat onto her forearm even as his hands gripped her arm trying to dislodge it. He pushed against the desk, trying to get leverage to push her off of him, but she held firm until his trembling subsided and she could feel his fingers on her arm weaken. There would be bruising there on her skin, but given the cleanup she had planned, no one would miss him for days. The bruising, if she was ever even questioned, would be gone. For now, she could enjoy the bittersweet last moments of his life as it slipped away in the grip of her arms.

She considered for a moment that maybe she'd been too compassionate. Didn't he deserve a long death to pay for the evil he'd done? The odds of him escaping were too great. She knew his prowess as a combatant would've been too much even for her if she didn't have the element of surprise. He jerked one last time as his body gave up the fight. She knew his mind would be around for a few precious seconds after he could no longer move.

"Shh," Helena whispered. "It's all for balance."

POLYPHEMUS' BAD DAY
BY HIROMI COTA

Centuries ago, legends walked the Earth. Among their names were Nezha, Rama, Kintaro, Thor, and Odysseus. This is not one of their stories.

Look, there are plenty of stories of them if you want to read them. I'm not stopping you from doing it. I'm just saying that I don't have any here.

Okay. Fine. Odysseus *does* have a cameo here, but that doesn't make it an Odysseus story!

Anyway. On with the tale.

"One! Two! Three!"

With combined, brutal force, Odysseus and his men dug their feet in, propelling themselves forward. On their shoulders sat a sharpened ship's plank that the cyclops Polyphemus used as a roasting spit. Though it weighed hundreds of pounds, desperation and Odysseus' honeyed words gave them the strength to charge at the sleeping cyclops. Together, they drove their makeshift spear into — look, this part is gross. I'm just going to gloss over it. No one needs to read me describing a violent blinding.

Bereft of sight, Polyphemus swung his arm around, dashing one of the men[1] against the cave wall. Swinging it back, he grasped another and crushed that man, too. The rest of the men fled the maimed giant in fear. Bellowing in agony, Polyphemus stumbled forward, leaning against the massive boulder that served as the cave's door. With a massive arm, he shoved it back far enough to yell for help.

"Help! Help! I've been attacked! I've been blinded!" he howled into the night.

After a few moments, other cyclops began to shout back panicked questions.

"Who attacked you?"

"How many?"

"Are you sure?"

To anyone who has screamed for help from their neighbors before, these questions should seem both familiar and infuriating. Not one of the titanic men asked, "How can I help?" Nor did any state plainly "I'll be right over to help!" People decry the lack of hospitality of the modern age, but it's always been like this.

"Noman has blinded me!" screamed Polyphemus.

"If no man blinded you, then you're probably fine," shouted a neighbor.

"If no man blinded you, maybe you're just sick," said another.

"If no man blinded you, perhaps you're not really blind," offered a third.

Some of you are starting to wonder aloud, "Hey, wait a minute. Why *didn't* any of Polyphemus' neighbors come over to see what was going on or to help? After all, Polyphemus was a prince and a son of Poseidon. He was a pretty big deal and blowing him off is really weird." The answer is the same as any of the character actions throughout the epic: everyone in the Odyssey is an asshole. No.

Really. Read it again. Find me someone who wasn't a dick.

"Have you tried losing weight or starting yoga?²" was the last thing Polyphemus heard before he gave up and rolled the boulder back in place, sealing the cave.

"BAAAAAA!" Polyphemus' herd of sheep had been crying out in a panic since he was blinded. His violent thrashing in the wake of the attack had done nothing to calm them down. He held his hands up and tried to shut out the sounds for a moment before deciding that there was no way he could concentrate while they bleated.

Reaching down for the nearest crying sheep, Polyphemus wrapped his hand around the top and lifted it up, pleased that this particular type of food wasn't trying to kill him. He shuffled back to the entryway, his feet moving in a way he thought was erratic enough to kick or crush anyone who tried to follow him. He pressed his hand against the boulder before thinking better of it and he swiped at the corners around the boulder, catching a man and flinging him back into the cave.

"You are clever, 'Noman,' but your crime will be punished," Polyphemus said as he pushed against the rock door again, moving it far enough to reach his other arm through. With his arm outside, he deposited a thoroughly confused sheep on the other side of the barrier and rolled the boulder back in place.

After repeating the process a few more times, every bleating sheep was on the outside of the cave, along with Odysseus, who had fearlessly leapt onto the first sheep and clung to its woolly belly without a word, bravely leaving all of his men behind to die. A few managed to escape the same way. The rest died over the course of the next few hours as Polyphemus crushed everything left breathing in the cave.

"Hey, Steropes, Arges, Brontes," Polyphemus said, greeting his brothers, who all stared at the bloodied wound that had been his eye. "Quick question: What the fuck is wrong with you? I got attacked last night, called out for help, and none of you assholes came to check on me."

"I'm really sorry. I, uh, thought you were just being dramatic. You were saying pretty weird things," offered Steropes, the Lightninger.

"Did you hear me scream?"

"Well, yeah."

"How far away do you live?"

"21 steps."

"You hear me scream and talk nonsense 21 steps away from you and you didn't even think to check on me?"

"When you put it like that, I—"

"Fuck you."

"I'm really sorry, brother. Look—uh … I mean, listen. I can go make a compress and mix some herbs for a poultice to put over your eye."

"I'm pretty sure it's gone," groaned Polyphemus.

"Maybe, but it might feel better," said Arges, the Thunderer.

"And, it would prevent infection and the pain that would bring," pointed out Brontes, the Vivid.

"Fiiiiine," signed Polyphemus.

Steropes and Arges thundered off to get the medicine ready as Brontes helped his wounded brother to the ground, carefully placing rocks and massive bags of wool to ensure Polyphemus was comfortable. By the time Polyphemus had crushed or swept away everything that threatened to make his resting spot less than perfect, his brothers had returned with the rest of island's cyclops. They took turns checking in on their friend and seeing what they could do to make his life better in this troubling time. For the most part, the answer was food, wine, and more wine.

Being stabbed in the eye is ridiculously painful and it's not like there was a nearby pharmacy. Wine was the prescription and it got filled. And refilled.

"I brought you a cane!" said an older cyclops.

"I don't understand," puzzled Polyphemus.

"You can wave it in front of you like a longer arm. If you can't touch the ground, you're probably about to fall off of a cliff. If you hit something and it doesn't baa or say, 'Be careful, Polyphemus,' it's either a rock, a tree, or something you should hit harder."

"That's clever. I should have thought of that!"

"I wish I'd thought of it before I fell off the cliff the first two times!" the elder chuckled.

Polyphemus laughed until his eye hurt, which wasn't that long, honestly, but he did feel better.

WAR
BY AMBER RAINEY

I am at war with myself. The mom in me wants to fight someone. Yell and scream at every adult involved to get some answers and protect my child. The southern woman begs for civility and a cool head. *You catch more flies with honey rather than vinegar,* she reminds me. My dignity wins out over my anger but it is not the last of either.

I know something is wrong the moment he gets in my car while I am sitting in the carpool lane. His beautiful, freckled face is splotchy. He's holding his mouth in a tensed way that covers his teeth—no easy feat since his teeth are wonderfully crooked in that awkward way when a child is no longer "little" and not yet an actual pre-teen. I can see the unshed tears in his eyes before he closes them tightly and shakes his head slightly when I ask him what's wrong.

I throw the car into park, ignoring the look from the parent behind me, and turn to face my child. I put a hand on his knee and try to soothe him the best I can from the front seat. He looks at me and the tears start falling down his round cheeks, making long, wet trail marks. I want to take away his pain. I often think it hurts me to see him so upset even more than it hurts him. He desperately wants to get control of his emotions but the pain of his experience is so recent because it had just happened. He starts to tell his story and that is when my blood starts to boil.

K has been bullied by another child in his class on a consistent basis over the last quarter. The most recent episode, the one making him currently upset, is even more unacceptable than the previous episodes, though that is no excuse. I do my best to calm my anger as I listen to him.

X has called K an idiot. On top of that, X threw a stick K was playing with over a fence where it was no longer reachable by K. Most people would roll their eyes at a child crying over a stick. Most people don't know my son. First of all, X had promised K he would watch out for the stick, then gleefully thrown it over the fence. Second of all, it was no ordinary stick to K—it was a prized treasure.

Since the moment he could walk, K has collected sticks on every nature hike and trips to the park. Sometimes he even gathers up a stick he sees while walking on a sidewalk to a store. If there is a stick, he is interested. Each one is a valuable item to him. I could never quite understand his attachment to the sticks but I figured it was about the same attachment I have to butterflies. Some indescribable experience of feeling like the item just belonged. K's collection of sticks was always carefully moved from place to place. On the last very long-distance move, he agreed to leave the nature behind and rehomed the sticks in the woods behind our house. As soon as we moved into the new house, the stick collecting began again. They are a part of him. They are swords and hiking sticks and magical items that can transfer him to other worlds. He doesn't settle for just any old stick. They have to be perfect for him.

The stick that was so carelessly thrown over the fence by the other child was a stick that K had carefully hidden each afternoon, all quarter long. He'd been upset once when a smaller child had found his stick but the child had played with it after school and then returned it to him the next day during recess. Everyone on the playground knew which stick was K's. Every child on the playground could play together nicely, except K and X.

I listen to K and console him, once again ignoring a honk from behind me. They can go around, there's room. Soothing my child from his heartbreak is more important to me. I don't care if I am an unpopular parent. Only once I am assured that K is calmer do I weigh my options. On the one hand, I want to get out of the car and demand answers from his teacher on why X is allowed to continually bully my son. On the other, I am literally in a tank top and boy-short underwear, having gotten too overheated and not bothering to change back into normal clothes in order to pick up K from school. I hadn't planned on needing to get out of the car. It always happens that way. Again, the southern woman inside me reminds me that I am a better writer than speaker and it would be more prudent to go home and write an email. She's correct but it does nothing to appease the angry mom.

I put the car into drive and we head home. I stew over the email in my head, composing and recomposing just what I am going to say. I try to call my husband to tell him what I am about to do, but I get no answer. Just as well, the angry mother doesn't want to be thwarted. E always gives too much benefit of the doubt until he is stung by the actions of others. It is something we argue about. A lot.

I confirm certain things with K. How many times has X snatched things away from him? How many times has X pulled things from K's pocket? What other names has X called him?

I am even angrier with each answer. X likes to call K a crybaby because whenever K gets upset he cries. Not wailing sobs. Usually, it is silent tears while K struggles with his emotions. It is to be expected because K has sensory processing disorder, so when he gets upset, his brain gets overloaded with sensory input and freaks out. The tension of that has to go somewhere—hence the tears. It is a commonly overlooked disorder, especially in gifted children. In my childhood, I was just repeatedly told I was *too sensitive* but medical science knows more now and awareness is getting better. Calling my son a crybaby is essentially making fun of a genetic disorder.

X also likes to lord his age over K, telling him that *he* is less mature because he is younger. E and I have told K that X is clearly not more mature, just from the fact he feels the need to point it out so often. It doesn't really help K process it.

The crux of the matter is that K is a kind-hearted child who tries to be nice to everyone and has no room in his life for injustice. He doesn't like to see people flout the rules. In his world, rules create order out of chaos. He is also very trusting and it breaks him apart when someone misuses that trust. Perhaps it is a character flaw but I think it makes him a good person. He doesn't understand why he is the target of bullying. He tries to make it better. He accepts every forced apology X gives him at school, only to be disappointed when the behavior begins again.

We finally arrive home and I sit down to type out the email that I have already written in my head. It comes quickly, my fingers angrily swiping at the keys in an effort to get it all out before my blood pressure rises too much and I pass out. *Politely angry* the southern woman in my head reminds me. I read and re-read the email, making sure that it conveys just that. I ask K a few more details to make sure I have dotted all my *I*'s and crossed all my t's. I hit send.

I feel a little better but still angry. I make it a point to find K and give him a hug and ask him what he would like for dinner. He can choose anywhere and of course, I know the answer before he gives it. The rest of the evening goes relatively smoothly, my anger only increasing once more as I explain what has happened to E.

The next morning, I wake up and check my email. I don't have a response yet but it's early. K asks me if there is any news and I tell him *not yet*. We get ready for school and I take him in, the southern woman reminding me to bide my time. I use the carpool lane again and don't get out of the car. I tell K to have a good day and the mom in me gets angry again at his dejected *I'll try*. K loves school...except for X. It kills me to have him in this situation.

Mid-day, I get the email I have been waiting for and I schedule a parent-teacher conference that afternoon. My head has been pounding since the day before and my stomach aches. Both are indicators of higher blood pressure and I am helpless to do anything about them. The thought of actually having to confront someone, keep my anger in check, and be coherent all weigh heavily on my mind. I can do it, I just don't like to do it. Like K, I want the world to be more harmonious, something it is increasingly denying me.

The time finally arrives and I have my conference. Despite my earlier hesitation, I am calm and well-spoken during the meeting. I get my point across politely but pointedly. Mainly, *this has to stop.* The teacher agrees and outlines the steps the school is taking to prevent future bullying. There is light at the end of the tunnel—the bullying stops or X is no longer allowed to attend the school. We wrap up our conference and then call K in to recap him on the results. We go over the specific actions he needs to take to be his own advocate where I can't be one. I am trying to instill resilience in him, although I am not sure I always do the best job with it. At the end of our talk, K throws his arm around my waist, squeezes tight, then looks up at me and smiles.

"Thanks, mom!" he says. He runs off with a skip to join the other children still hanging around at school.

The angry mother is finally appeased and the southern woman

is trying not to be too smug. Rationally, I know flying off the handle is not going to help but at the same time, I often wonder if it would be more cathartic. It seems the best balm is that of a renewed happiness in my child. It won't be the last time I am at war with myself but with each new challenge, I am confident I can win the battles I face.

CAT'S EYE
BY MARSHALL MILLER

Isabelle Diaz was not a real cat lover. The exobiologist was not a cat hater, she had just always been more of a dog person. So from her young beginnings as an inquiring mind, she had resisted the stereotype thinking that Feline was connected to Female.

"Why must women be seen as cats, that's what I want to know," the young thinker asked. "Why are we seen as catty and not as being doggy."

Isabelle, known as Izzy in her circle of colleagues and friends, liked other people's cats. She just had no desire to live with one. She always had dogs and worked to have sufficient means to have property, so her canine companions could run as free as possible. People in her circle were used to seeing her with dog hair on her clothes, not cat hair. Animal hair did not detract from what some classified as smoking hot attractiveness, which set Izzy apart from others again as she could take or leave sexual relations with fellow humans male or female. The living non-human world around was her passion, especially anything she considered canine-related.

As she graduated from high school, the discovery of Chutes

and Ladders' wormholes in the universe led the way to bypass the speed of light. With a form of FTL (faster than light) providing numerous job openings in the biological sciences due to the possibilities of finding alien lifeforms, Exobiology became a means to an end for Izzy. So, instead of being a veterinarian or pure zoologist, she went where the money was flowing. Izzy soon had an excellent reputation as one who worked hard, quick, and accurate. However, when she was picked to be in the group chosen for the first encounter with the alien feline species (their name was translated to Panthera in Anglo-Latin), Izzy was as surprised as anyone.

"No canine or anthropoid species?" she asked.

"Not advanced like the Kitties," was the answer from the Combined Science Foundation Department Head, portly and balding Professor Stan Schumaker. "They have star travel like us. And, they are as surprised as we are to meet anyone else above a slug or rodent."

The Professor had a faraway look in his eyes as he spoke.

"To be young and svelt again! I would give my eyeteeth to be chosen for this assignment." He shifted his gaze to Izzy. "So much is wasted on youth."

Schumaker sighed then tossed a file at Izzy.

"This is all the information the Government has shared with us so far. Memorize it and get packed. Two days from now, you take the shuttle to the International Space Station for advanced training. Don't screw up."

Two days then two months of extensive training in traveling on starcraft. Izzy had already trained Earthside in standard traditional astronaut programs, which was the only similar training available. The powers that be had at least the foresight that anyone going into the Big Unknown must have the necessary survival skills developed in a century of local space travel. It all seemed like a piece of cake for the young and extremely fit exobiologist. Her sensuality attracted admirers from both sexes, but she only went through the motions of love and passion. Coitus was fun but seemed so-mundane. Even under Zero-Gravity, once or twice and it held no interest. But she played the games so that everyone thought she was well adjusted as a human being.

"I miss my dogs," she often whispered. Her extended family had her two large dogs for the Duration at the rural property she had purchased. The house was simple but a good home for her four-legged family. However, she had to stay focused on the here and now. Once you left Mother Earth, everything seemed ready to kill you.

Two months of preparation at the International Space Station and Izzy was taken aboard the International Space Patrol Starcraft *Explorer*. An outgrowth of the United States Space Command, the starship was the second one in service, thanks to the discovery of how to tap into Dark Matter and Dark Energy and create propulsion systems necessary to enable humanity's expansion into the Universe. The same exotic matter and energy led to the discovery and manipulation of the 'weak spots' between the various String Theory universes and then the Chutes and Ladders wormholes. Exploratory drones were sent out thru the wormholes.

Then the Pantheras sent one back.

Humans and Pantheras had been communicating for some two Earth years, and now they would have the first face to face meeting on the other end of the Chute.

Izzy stood at the observation port (actually a television screen) watching the approach to the opening of the Chute out past Pluto. She sensed someone standing behind her before the person spoke.

"Impressive view, isn't Izzy?" ships First Officer Carl Ryan asked. A handsome dark-skinned man from South Africa, he had been a sometime lover. Or in Izzy's mind, a sexual partner.

"It is unique," replied Izzy.

"This is the third time I've been here, and I still get this surreal feeling," Carl said.

"So tell me, Carl, how many craft have been through this chute?"

"Counting drones? Two dozen."

"Any lost?"

"Well, three drones disappeared. We don't know if they are 'lost' or just wandering. They were unmanned, so no big loss. So far, no crewed craft have been damaged or lost."

"How about people?"

There was a pause as Carl took a breath, then sighed.

"Honestly, we had a few take the—transition into the chute hard. In Earth's time, it takes a minute. In other words, the ship enters, and a minute, sixty seconds, it pops out the other end. But the transit time in the wormhole? Ship's time says it takes at least ten minutes."

"Why is that a problem?"

"It messes with some people's minds. Now, everyone is sedated, except for one volunteer. Everything is automated, the one human is there just in case something really strange happens. So out of sixty crew members, one plays guinea pig."

Izzy thought for a moment, then asked.

"What if I volunteered?"

"Why? You're not the crew. You're part of the science team."

"As a scientist, I question, explore strange new ideas, worlds. So, why not?"

The question went all the way up to the ship's captain, Captain Hilda Johanson. She had contacted Izzy in the exobiologist's tiny quarters. "Just enough to swing a cat in" had come to mind when Izzy first saw it.

"So," said the Captain, "you want to be the Watch Officer when we go through, correct."

"Yes, Ma'am. This may be my only trip into deep space, so I might as well try it all."

Captain Johanson had fixed her with a penetrating gaze as if using X-ray eyes to see into Izzy's soul. Then she spoke.

"Okay. You and the other scientists are trained to act as necessary crew in the event of problems. It will be a first. However, negative reactions on your part may derail your meeting the Kitties."

"It won't, Captain, I assure you."

Johanson had grunted, then left Izzy's quarters. A day later, the rest of the crew and staff lay slumbering while Izzy stood on the Bridge. She watched the AI systems slide the long starcraft into the black end of the now opened Chute. It took a massive tapping into Dark Energy to open the end of the wormhole, so it had been done no more than once a month after the initial experimental trips some five years prior. It was believed the Pantheras had seen the result of the original openings and steered their craft towards the unusual event. The rest was history.

Izzy felt an odd thickness in the air, things seemed to be fuzzy. Then she felt—*them.*

Thoughts from somewhere zipped into her consciousness. They were images seen from what to her was a unique perspective. It was from a perspective that did not seem human. Shapes and colors were… different. As Izzy started to do an internal inspection of her thoughts, the outlook was gone.

"Art, time passage, please."

The Artificial Intelligence central controller, nicknamed Art, responded immediately.

"Ten minutes and counting."

"Any anomalies during passage?"

"Slight indication of additional energy in the life support systems of the EXPLORER, Watch Officer Diaz. Nothing beyond safe parameters."

"Thank you, Art."

"And the ship is through the Chute, Ma'am. Ship's crew and staff being woken. All life support actions normal."

Izzy decided not to mention the—oddness she had experienced. It could be just the effect on her brain of the slip between realities. No reason to queer the chance of meeting the Pantheras.

Izzy found there was a ceremony based on the old naval tradition of crossing the Equator. And as the Watch Officer, she had a unique role to play. A ladder was set up in the small dining area (the long starcraft was built around the power system, not around human habitation) with a chute made of a short ramp with shiny stiff survival blankets formed into a tunnel shape. Izzy had to 'catch' the participants at the bottom of the ramp, signifying that she had ensured their safe passage. Everyone received a certificate suitable for framing recording they had survived a Chute Trip.

After the festivities, Captain Johanson approached her.

"Thank you for performing the duty of Watch Officer. There are a lot of people terrified of what goes on in so-called hyperspace."

Izzy shrugged, then replied, "No big deal. A scientist likes to observe and experience new things. It was unique."

"No dreams?" Johanson asked.

"No, Ma'am. I guess whatever beings or forces which exist in transit ignored me."

"Good. It is better that way." The Captain then excused

herself to talk with the rest of the crew and staff. Izzy knew she was checking for any possible mental problems due to the transit. Based on what Carl had said, it was a real problem. It reaffirmed Izzy's decision not to mention the passing contact with—whatever or whomever. In another two Earth Days, they would meet the Pantheras face to face. The aliens seemed to have a less efficient propulsion system that the Earthship and were taking a long time to reach the Chute.

The senior science staff supervisor was a young James Lee. James was barely twenty-five years of age but was classified as a savant—he had a Ph.D. in Biological Science by age 15 and moved up the ladder at the Combined Science Foundation quickly. He grasped arcane concepts so fast that he was often impatient with others who did not. However, his genius was deemed necessary for such an important meeting.

He called a staff meeting of the ten scientists in the tiny ship's library.

"I'll keep this short and sweet, so we do not have to stand in here and breath each other's exhales," James said. There were a few smiles as the scientists shifted and tried not to step on each other's feet.

"I'll be meeting with the Pantheras as the ranking scientist. I will have one other person with me. That will be Doctor Diaz here."

There was an uncomfortable silence. Izzy was the most junior staff member of the group, just barely had her Doctorate when she was chosen for the mission. However, no one groused to James. They knew better than to question his decisions in front of others. James had a problem with dissent and was both icy and fiery with his responses.

"Okay," James continued. "the rest of you will be monitoring the meeting. You will be expected to provide in-depth examinations of the Aliens. Now, we have a lot to do. Meeting adjourned."

Izzy took the aggressive road and cornered James before he disappeared to his quarters.

"Excuse me, Sir, But, I am the junior—"

"And you are wondering why I selected you," interrupted James. "The answer is not only are you smart and a quick learner, but you have some martial arts skills. Yes, I closely examined your file. Should things go bad, you can be expected to fight our way out."

"You expect—"

"I am not a trained fighter. I also try to plan for the unexpected. Scientists with preconceived outcomes are not true scientists."

"Yes, Sir. Thank you for this opportunity."

"And I'll thank you in advance, Izzy, for saving my posterior if things go wrong."

Art the AI remotely piloted the small shuttlecraft. After some discussion with the Pantheras, it was agreed two humans would come to their ship. The two starcrafts were stationed some one hundred kilometers apart. Deep Space travel was still new enough that the ship's crew were nervous when their craft was close to another powered object. Contrary to space operas of old, space and starships could not stop nor turn on a dime.

As the shuttle neared the Panthera's ship, Izzy noticed it was an almost perfect sphere as first observed.

"Kitties like to play with balls," Izzy said with a slight smile.

"Could be they do have similar thoughts and activities as Earth cats," said James. "Now, please put your thinking and observation cap on and watch for indications of Panthera's culture and thought processes. This is humankind's first face to face meeting with another space-faring species. We do not want to screw up this First Contact."

"Yes, Sir."

Art cut into their conversation at that point.

"The large sphere is powered by some sort of magnetic-based propulsion system. My analysis is that it is maneuverable, the Panthera's ship is not as speedy as ours."

"Hmmm. Slight diversion between our and their science, at least possible. Look for other indicators, Art and Izzy."

"Yes, Sir." Replied Izzy.

An iris opened on the previously smooth surface to the perfect looking sphere. As it did, something tickled Izzy's brain as Art spoke.

"The Panthera's respectfully ask us to enter their ship through the opened iris."

"Go ahead," replied James.

Art smoothly maneuvered the shuttlecraft through the opening and into the interior beyond. The two humans used the attached camera system to view the substantial bay they entered. There was no internal gravity or at least none that seemed to affect the Earth's craft. With commands from the Panthera, Art allowed a giant waldo padded claw to gently grasp the shuttlecraft and set it down on what was clearly a magnetized landing pad.

"The Panthera's have requested we wait in our ship while they repressurize the landing bay," said the AI. "Their representatives will be along shortly."

Ten minutes later, they watched via camera as four Pantheras approached. They climbed down the walls of the Landing bay and then launched themselves with catlike grace in the near-zero gravity.

"A scientist once said that felines and spiders look and act like they were evolved in zero gravity," opined Izzy.

"They are so much more graceful than us," replied James.

The Pantheras were a bit under two meters in height or length, depending on how they were measured. They seemed primarily bipedal with a twitching cat's tail. Art opened the shuttle's airlock, and the two humans stepped out to greet the aliens. Izzy saw the felines gripped the slight spongy floor covering with bared slightly elongated clawed cats feet. The Patheras stopped some one meter in front of James and Izzy.

"The magnetic landing pad is for us," said James. The humans' boots had flat metal cleats attached, so the magnetic source beneath the floor covering enabled them to shuffle towards the alien starcraft's occupants. Both species raised open hands in greeting. A voice was heard in the human's helmets, worn until they were sure the interior atmosphere was safe.

"We welcome you here to our star home." The being speaking had a feminine timber and tone in their voice. As Izzy made that observation, she also saw the creatures had two sets of small but firm fur-covered breasts, not cat teats. Straps crossed in an 'X' across the chests and between the breasts. The only other clothing was an abbreviated pair of swim trunks with a hole in the back for the tails, which seemed to be twitching in commune between the four aliens.

"We welcome you to this meeting," answered James, "and we thank you for your hospitality. Your translating equipment is quite excellent."

One of the Patheras stepped forward with a rapid twitching tail. Must be the leader, thought Izzy. The creature's tail reached out and began to caress Izzy's faceplate.

"You may remove your helmets. We all breath similar atmospheres." The voice seemed not to come from any of the four greeters. James quickly unlatched his helmet, and Izzy followed suit. The Panthera's calico tail caressed Izzy's bare face, and the human smiled, then made a purring sound in her throat. The Panthera's mouth formed into a feline smile and then purred back.

"I see, like us, you have been studying greetings," said the voice.

"May I be rude and ask who is speaking?" asked James.

"I am the Ship. Just like the being you call Art."

"Our friendly feline friends…" began Izzy, and the Panthera she had surmised was the leader rubbed against her as the exobiologist felt this tickling in her brains.

"Weoore Pantheras, arss Whoomans name usss."

Izzy thought the exotic creature must have practiced Anglo for quite some time in preparation for the meeting. Their mouths and tongues were different from Homo sapiens, so human speech was not natural. Izzy took a chance and began to rub the aliens furry back. The supposed leader wrapped her arm around Izzy and purred into her ear.

"I am now speaking for the Leader next to the female human, which Art says is Doctor Diaz," the Ship said. Then the voice changed to a low and sultry female voice.

"My name in your language would be Sassy. I am a middle-level officer who the ship's captain says has a sassy or aggressive attitude. Thus, Sassy in Earth-speak fits."

James cleared his throat and then spoke.

"Not to interrupt things, but I am the senior person—"

"And, Sir, you will be meeting with what you call is the First Officer. Once she decides it is safe, you will meet with the Captain."

"Ah, why the interest in me—Sassy?" Izzy asked. She did not want to cause any artificial stress between her and James. He was the head scientist, after all.

"We sensed you during the passage."

"The—passage? Through the Chute? "

"Yes. May I call you Izzy?" Sassy asked through the Ship.

"So that was you I sensed? You tickled my mind?"

Sassy purred and smiled.

Sassy was soon leading Izzy on a tour of the Ship as James was taken to meet the Ship's Captain. The two humans had been provided with tiny earphones for communication. The exobiologist found herself in a sphere within a sphere. The internal area rotated slowly to give a feel of light artificial gravity for the crew. The Pantheras had apparently discovered the deleterious effects of long term zero-gravity on humanoid bodies.

"We Patheras, as you name us-studied for many of your years before venturing into Deep Space."

"How long have you been traveling in your starcraft, Sassy?"

"The Ship tells me a century of your time. I was born on Mother Ship and know no other home."

Izzy knew conceiving in outer space was not easy, especially under little or no gravity. Then it dawned on her that the four beings who met her and James were all female, with their four breasts.

"Sassy, not to pry, but are their males on the Ship?"

"A few," the alien answered with a cat smile. "Male Patheras become too aggressive when they smell our mating scent. I read the Encyclopedia Britannica you transmitted to us and see you cat species are much like us. I saw the expression 'cat in heat', and it applies to our species. But in our case, it is the males, what you would call a 'tomcat' who howl and fuss. We females have learned how to control our urges, much as you humans do."

Izzy laughed.

"My new friend, you have no idea about just how tenuous

that control is at times. Humans are basically horny ninety-nine percent of the time once we reach puberty."

Sassy purred, then replied, "We studied the information you sent us, as well as found some stray signals beamed from your Earth years before you traveled to the stars. I watched some of your films, some quite graphic about your mating activities."

Great, thought Izzy. *Our porn made it all the way out here.*

"Some of the films were made for our entertainment. Do you have such entertainment?" asked Izzy. Sassy purred, and a sly smile formed on her mouth.

"We have a substance analogous to what you Earthlings call 'catnip.' It stimulates us when we want to enjoy ourselves. We Pantheras are very close in design and function to your feline species, just much more evolved."

Sassy's tail was once again touching Izzy's waist. "Here. I will show you." The young ship's officer led the Earth scientist to a large and well-lit room. Covering the walls were enlarged photographs that must have come from the transmissions sent through the Chute the past couple of years. One was a reproduction of some very catlike creatures from an apparent Asian or East Indian drawing. Two creatures/gods/demons, it was not clear, were fighting with bladed weapons. They were covered with some type of clothing and armor but were definitely catlike. Sassy pointed towards the picture as she spoke through the Ship.

"The rendition of those two beings could have been a depiction of my species during a time millennia ago. Our scientists find it almost bizarre that life on our home planet is so similar to life on Earth."

At that moment, the regular Ship's voice broke in. "Doctor Diaz, if you could follow Sassy back to the main meeting room, Doctor Lee is waiting for you."

A quarter of an hour later, James contacted her in the meeting room. "How are things going?" James asked.

"Fine. Sassy is sharing information without any hints of deception. She wants us to understand them and visa versa."

"Good. Art contacted me, and the Captain wants us to return for a consultation."

Just then, the Panteras' Ship broke in. "Our Captain wishes for Doctor Diaz to stay for a sleep period. Sassy has much more information to share."

James looked at Izzy and frowned. "I don't know if that is such a good idea," he said. "This is all so very new."

"You know I can handle myself," replied Izzy. "This could be a once in a lifetime chance. They want to be open with us. Why queer the deal? What are they going to do, eat me?"

James stood in thought. Then he spoke. "It is your funeral if they do. I will tell the Captain it is necessary to keep the scientific information flowing, She will probably acquiesce as you are not an actual crew member, so may seem dispensable."

Izzy chuckled. "Gee, she may let me because if I disappear, no big deal."

"You know what I mean.."

Izzy waved James' protest away. "I know what you mean, Doctor. And this is a one in a lifetime experience. How could I possibly turn this down?"

Captain Johanson agreed to the request, with the caveat that an open line of communication through Art be kept at all times. The Ship AI accepted the behest for the Pantheras' Captain and created an open channel with Art. The two AIs seemed to enjoy the contact with another 'alien' Artificial Intelligence.

Within an hour, Sassy was leading Izzy to her quarters as

James was taking the shuttle back to *Explorer*. The exobiologist found the quarters provided to be comfortable for any bipedal humanoid. It was larger than the one on the human starship, with added soft bedding. Sassy then took her new human friend to the alien feline version of a dining room. Some very Earthlike foods were provided as Sassy introduced Izzy to the other crewmembers to include the Ship Captain. The human soon discovered the social hierarchy was more along the lines of an extended family, a sisterhood rather than a naval or military crew. They were also very similar in the colorations of their furs. Izzy told her escort this, and Sassy gave a purring answer.

"Of course," Sassy replied through the Ship. "We are all sisters. We are from various 'litters' would be the Earth terminology. But we all have the same mother."

"Your mother is back on your homeworld then," said Izzy.

"Why, no, my new found human friend. Mother is the Captain."

The rest of the evening was one of caressing contact with many of the crew members. Izzy soon felt closer to these feline aliens than to ninety-nine percent of the people she knew on Earth. The Earth woman had a slightly intoxicated buzz from some unique feline wine Sassy had demanded she sample. With the buzz and a full stomach of some delicious sweetmeats, Izzy excused herself and made her way back to her quarters with Sassy as escort. At her door, the Panthera ship's officer hugged and purred in her ear.

"Become settled. I will be back momentarily with a present."

Izzy located a silk-like robe that was more along the lines of a negligee. Izzy stripped off her clothes and was soon luxuriating on a rug made of some animal fur. The Pantheras were clearly predators.

Slight scratching on the door instead of knocking roused Izzy to open it. There stood Sassy in a matching sheer robe and nothing else.

"Herroo," Sassy purred as her very flexible cattail found an opening in Izzy's robe and worked its way to the human genitalia. Izzy surprised herself with her reaction to the alien probing. She grabbed Sassy, caressed her furred butt cheeks, and then the four small and firm breasts. The two female beings fell back onto the thick bedding.

Izzy Diaz awoke purring like cat, then rolled over and embraced Sassy. The two alien beings discovered evolution had shaped bipedal genitalia to be quite similar in form and function. Sassy's tongue was a bit long, thin and raspy, which Izzy found so maddening when it was applied to her labia. In turn, Izzy's lips on four separate nipples drove Sassy to destraction. Of course, Sassy had an unfair advantage as she had a very flexible soft tail. The Earthling used her fingers, a bit more slender and long, to make up the difference. The exobiologists soon discovered Pantheras yowled during orgasm.

Sassy showed Izzy how to use the shower (these cats did not mind getting wet) and the oversized hair/fur drier that felt divine. Sassy produced two cups of a coffee substance, which the two sat drinking tightly together.

"No problems having sex with an alien?' Asked Izzy.

"Sexxs and luffs, the sssame fo' arr," replied Sassy. She then connected to the Ship AI to continue the conversation.

"You are a respected female. We have studied you. There is no reason why we cannot find pleasure with each other." Sassy's tail began probing sensitive areas again. The Ship broke in.

"The Shuttle with Doctor Lee has returned. He will meet you in the dining area."

"Roger that, " Izzy replied. She looked at Sassy.

"Time to leave, I'm afraid."

"You can stay," replied Sassy.

"How? And why?"

Sassy was soon hugging and purring in her ear.

"You are so—special. We sensed that when we touched your mind as you traveled. Your mind, your being, fit more with us, your true sisters."

"I love my dogs, my canines. I cannot leave them."

Sassy looked into her eyes.

"You are certain?"

"Yes, Sassy. I am sorry."

Sassy stood silent for several moments. Then she spoke.

"You will be honored in our memories. You may always return to us. Always."

Izzy blinked back tears and kissed the Panthera.

"I am honored. And you will always be loved."

Two Earth days later, the two species parted. Izzy Diaz had made such an impression on the Pantheras that the Earth authorities would soon classify her as the expert and chosen representative for future contacts. Doctor Lee was not happy about being passed over for a junior female. But he knew better than to raise a stink.

Someone else pulled Watch through the Chute. Out past Pluto, Carl Ryan approached Izzy. "So, I guess we'll be seeing you again."

"Carl, they'll use this ship for another trip?"

"We only have two of this class right now. And just so many experienced crews. In a few more years…" Carl shrugged.

"You'll be out here, running these trips?"

"If I can, Izzy. If I can."

" What do you plan to do on Earth?" The First Officer then asked.

"Rest. Love my dogs. Write a crapload of scientific papers and reports for the government. Lecture. And I guess prepare for another trip through the Chute." Isabelle Diaz seemed to stare at a remembered object.

"A cat. I think I'll adopt a female cat, teach my dogs how to get along with another species."

"Turning into a cat lady, huh? Like Alice Through the Looking Glass?" Carl said with a grin.

All Izzy did was smile. Then, the smile turned into a Cheshire grin.

THE RESCUE
BY ELIZA LOEB

Chapter 1

Tick. Tock. Tick. Tock.

Those infernal seconds of silence never settled well with her. Why would they? When one is locked in a dark room all alone, left beside themselves for however many years without a soul to talk to, the once endearing sound of a clock becomes the bane of one's existence. At first, the sound was reminiscent of a music beat. The songs that she would formulate would have even tempos that were slow and melodious as they paced well with the clock. She often imagined the gears and pistons working in unison as an intermachinal ballet of dancers, moving with precision and well-practiced choreography. Yet the inner workings of the clock in the hall way also added a rhythm of their own, syncing to the beat of her songs. However, she grew bored and they all began to sound the same. When one tires of tempos and music, it is difficult to find a remedy to ever obtain the joys of that stage of the art back. This left only stories and a convoluted imaginary theater that she would play for herself.

There would be a show every night with a grand party of one as she would tell herself and play stories of the classics. Persephone's descent into the underworld, the Shakespeare's Much Ado About Nothing, as well as notorious historic events, whether they be good or bad. She would likely be the few to admit that Gaius Augustus Caesar was an interesting fellow with bright ideas, but the wrong party to help carry it out and she supposed he became some odd form of inspiration for swiss cheese somewhere down the line. However, these stories were not to say that she lacked imagination. In fact some of the stories she came up with or formulated in her head sometimes kept her up at night. But even that joy began to fade as the music had. She no longer held interest of an unsung protagonist stuck in endless loops. That was where she knew that she was running out of any and all creative ideas. She eventually resorted to memorizations and counting games. When does the doctor come? When does she next get her drug meal? When does she get her actual meal?

What?

The doctors didn't really expect her not to know that they were drugging her cranberry sausage oatmeal with brown sugar and butter, did they? It was likely why they now avoid adding pepper.

Tick.

Tock.

Tick.

Tock.

She wondered how long it would take for her patience to wear thin. The ticking had already become needless.

How long till one goes mad?

Or had she already gone mad?

And if she had already gone mad, when and whereabouts did she lose her sanity?

She leaned back against the wall and closed her eyes, picturing an endless sea of stars and a bright cool blue light as she drifted along. She pictured beautiful creatures much like blue whales drifting along with her as they glided together in pods, nearly blinding passers by with their unexpected bioluminescence. She moved to reach out and touch one as it moved beside her, yet was taken from the fantasy as she instantly fell on her side and strained against the bindings of her straight jacket. Her bliss was now gone.

She scowled and shifted in her added confines as she sat herself upright again. She wasn't ready for sleep, despite it being as dark as it was.

Constance, she whispered to herself. She thought that was her name.

The doctors put her down as Constance Smith, as she had no means of identification or pay. She could only tell them that her name was Constance.

From then on, one doctor after another would ask her question after question regarding things she couldn't begin to answer. Things she hadn't been so sure she had even had to begin with. And no matter how much she tried to remember, she would continue to draw a blank. She wouldn't deny that she would sometimes fall into a mild obsession and ruminate to a point where her incarceration may have seemed necessary for others. She liked to imagine a childhood from time to time, and yet she couldn't bring herself to tell a lie. She often questioned how it was possible for one to forget being a child. To even forget aspects of their life that could perhaps help them escape their present situation had proven to be no less than ludicrous. In fact it had been part of the reason why Constance had been given the wonderful cocktailed diagnoses of Melancholia with a side of amnesia salted atop a healthy serving of pseudo psychosis.

And the drugs only made her worse.

There had been times where she would fall into a screaming frenzy without sedation, men in white would flood into her cell and hold her down until she was calm. One of the doctors once suggested a transorbital lobotomy. Luckily the other doctors protested against it. These instances were times where she would wake up scared, shaking, screaming in a language with origins neither she nor any of the sanitorium staff could place.

She couldn't help but wonder what she looked like during these instances or after. The cell they had placed her in had been a darkened padded cell in the east wing, and likely the oldest in the building. The fire proof tin door had a flap where they would insert treys of food. And most of the time she hardly needed the straight jacket. Unfortunately, the nearest window had been too high for her to reach. Yet she still daydreamed of the day when she would feel the warmth of the sun on her face with the sounds of birds chittering in her ears. Places like these lacked such luxuries.

Such places, it seemed, were always void of life.

"My, how the mighty have fallen," came a voice.

All it took for the voice's owner to appear was a slow blink.

A wolf skull bore down upon Constance as she peered up with intrigue. Stag horns protruded from a tattered black shroud as the same material pooled around the figure in an inky black mound. Sigils had been etched into the skull for reasons that Constance couldn't fathom. What's more, she wondered why the figure had entered with an age old phrase.

"That's a pretty impressive costume," she complimented. "I didn't think Halloween would be around for another year or so."

A clawed hand shot out from the mess of black fabric and pressed her back against the wall. Their fingers curled around her neck. Fiery red embers glowed within the sockets and leered down upon the unsuspecting inpatient. And looking at the figure, Constance found herself in a state of internal conflict.

"Do you not remember me?"

The figures voice was low and gravelly, yet surprisingly calm for one who had just wrapped their expensive manicured hand around the throat of a complete stranger. She would remember meeting a shrouded figure within or outside of the confines of her wild imagination, who—if they were on a date—would very likely wave some pretty large red flags.

"Honestly, I don't think I would want to, buddy."

The fingers curled tighter around her throat, threatening to cut off her air ways.

"I am the keeper of the void," the figure said. "I rule all of that which is in the shadows and call forth the most horrific of nightmares."

"I still don't know or want to know you."

"Whether you like it or not, you will learn soon, little muse." Within the blink of an eye, the figure had disappeared. No warning. No say as to who he was. No relevancy to his entrance or his approach.

So, like many things irrelevant, Constance simply brushed it off to the back of her mind.

The next morning did not come with the drugged breakfast she had grown used to and her time in the straight jacket had come to an end. Nurses flooded in and out of her cell this time to ensure that her vitals were regular, and yet she still couldn't chase the reason as to why.

At least, that was until a man stepped through the doorway with a clip board tucked beneath his arm. Needless to say that he wasn't her usual fare. He didn't stuff himself into a lab coat like the others and he seemed to enjoy wearing a red sweater over a blue collar button up shirt with a black tie and his kakis were stained with blue and black ink where he tried to wipe evidence of a leaky pen off of his hands.

"Good morning Miss Smith," the good doctor greeted with a soft tone.

"I am Bartolomeu Void, and starting today, I will be your new primary care provider."

Something was off about this one. She couldn't fathom as to why, but something about this particular doctor set her hairs on edge. Could it have been that he wasn't who he said he was? Could it be that he was the figure from last night and thought that she couldn't tell? Who else did he think he was fooling with a name like Bartolomeu Void? So now the creature who visited her dons a Mr. Rogers getup with curly chestnut hair and freckles with brilliant green hazel eyes and he thinks that she is instantly fooled?

"For how long?" she asked.

"For as long as it takes to get you on your feet."

There were many things that were going through Constance's head in that moment. One being that she could easily stand on her own and the other where she wanted to ask where she was being taken. The doctor paced around her slowly, looking her up and down and going back to her charts as she coughed. Part of her was certain that she did not like where this was going and she was beginning to feel a little uncomfortable with the ordeal.

"But first, I would prefer a more up to date room among other inmates."

Or not.

"In a more medically approved facility focused on the health and well being of it's patients."

Now she was confused.

Chapter 2

The departure from the hospital was nothing short of uneventful, and frankly, the smell of the facility had made Constance a little light headed as her first breath of fresh air nearly sent her falling into an unexpected wave of euphoria as the warmth of the suns rays poured down upon her face and she couldn't help but close her eyes. For the first time in a while she could feel herself slip into a state of momentary bliss. Her fingers stretched out and she could feel her body loosen up for the first time.

Freedom.

She wondered just how long she had been in the sanitorium. She was curious how many years it had been since she was taken in and was therefore unsurprised when the answer came to be three years.

"I suppose that's the reason why it felt so long."

"Well it's not like you didn't have anything there to entertain you was it?"

There was a long pause as Doctor Void waited patiently for her answer.

"Surely they didn't keep you in an outdated and heavily infested part of the building, did they?"

Constance laughed. It was that bad was it?

"I honestly didn't mind the spiders."

"As a mental health and care facility, they should have provided a better means of care over a rundown part of the building."

Should they have? She didn't know.

"Honestly, I am close to filing a complaint with the state and showing you the process of how to press charges. The conditions they had you in were ridiculous.”

“Are you saying that because you mean it or are you saying that because you love the sound of your own voice?”

“Both.”

The level of surprised silence sent a long pause through Doctor Voids car. Neither knew what else to say to one and other and often times the stops were quick and only for the allotted amount of snacks that could be afforded. Beyond that any conversations were walled off and let alone to their own devices and it wasn’t until they had reached a clearing beneath a bridge that either of them said a word.

“Where are we headed?” Constance asked.

“A small sanctuary near the original Jamestown settlement.”

Constance hadn’t been sure how to approach the answer as she leaned further into her chair.

“I noticed that you haven’t looked at yourself in the mirror.”

She had forgotten that she was allowed to look in the mirror, now and was somewhat afraid of her appearance.

“Afraid of how you might look?”

“No.”

“Prove it.”

She looked over to Bartolomeu and quirked a brow before laughing and sighing.

“I figured.”

Bartolomeu Void looked over at her with a pointed gaze and scoffed. He knew what she had caught onto and was hardly surprised, given her reaction to him in the sanitorium. Why shouldn’t she say anything or make any remarks about it now.

“You’re the guy who came to my cell last night.”

He did not expect that.

In fact, he had never even met her until this morning after spending months to prepare a retrieval for her. But really he wondered exactly what she was talking about when it came to someone visiting her in that damp old cell.

"I never met you until this morning."

He could see her face drop in confusion, and pulled to a halt before stepping out of the vehicle. And he could tell that she was watching his every move from then on as he paced back and forth, spinning around in circles before inhaling and exhaling. She couldn't have been visited by him, could she? Did she even know what she was or have any inkling as to why he came to retrieve her to begin with? He hopped back in the care and settled in the drivers seat as he closed his eyes and pinched the bridge of his nose, unsure what to make of it.

"Constance, how did you get in to the asylum?"

Constance sighed and shrugged.

"All I can remember is a bright light and waking up on a highway with no clothes and no idea who I was or even my name. There was a dead trucker in a crashed sixteen wheeler off the side of the road whose flesh was practically melting from the bone and a nametag on the uniform that said Constance. I liked the name, so I took it."

"And how did you end up at the sanitorium?"

"Easy, I walked into the nearest town naked and said *HELLO WORLD, MY NAME IS CONSTANCE*, to which nobody minded, but I digress. And it was a small town called Copperville and had mostly been abandoned for a really long time, save for the few people who were left in some of the crumbling houses, there."

"Can they vouch for you?"

"I think they're dead at this point. It was a little over thirty years ago and the whole *don't run around naked* thing wasn't as big of a deal until maybe three years ago when I had entered I think the Williamsburg library?"

"So you've been running around naked for thirty years?"

"Yes."

"Look in the damn mirror."

She sighed and looked over to the rear view mirror, spying an ivory skinned woman with silver hair and bright blue eyes. The woman's lips settled into a pout as she slowly looked back to her companion with a low laugh and a feeling of bewilderment.

"And here I thought I had black hair."

Bartolomeu nodded.

"I had heard about you being caught naked in a library from your medical records," he said. "They were originally going to arrest you for public indecency before they found out that you honestly had little to no idea that what you were doing was… well."

"So tell me something."

"Yes?"

"Are you really a doctor?"

That one, Bartolomeu was not going to answer. Instead he smiled and continued to drive. Saying nothing more of the matter as he continued onward, moving through the brush of tree's as night began to fall. He knew that he was likely never going to figure out who the shrouded man was. He knew that there were supernatural beings who were in need of being taken out of harsh situations like Constance's. Beings like Constance who had long forgotten who they were, save for a few pleasant memories and a hat trick here and there. Either way, he was excited to see where the road would take him with this crazy woman if she so decided to stay. But alas, that was her choice and hers alone.

LIGELA
BY SHEILA MENGERT

In the culture of Mexico, November begins with what at first must seem a most inauspicious feast, the Day of the Dead. Rather than an orgy of darkness however it is a time of embroidery of skulls and a sharing of the color and festiveness of life. I think that the Latin people, the very ones that to so many stolid Americans represent the ultimate threat to our materialistic way of life and an unwelcome reminder that most of the area of western America was stolen from Mexico as the fruit of greed and conquest, are merely reclaiming the common legacy of earth through their migrations. They remind me that the drama of egotism manifests all that is darkest in the human soul and that the human race is a collective project towards a better life for all. I had not thought to resume again my own efforts to define myself, by adding a chapter to that most unprofitable of human endeavors, the writing of memoirs, but, as happens so often a chance event occurring in the present may lead to the stirring again of thoughts long since forgotten and open again the catacombs of regret.

I was looking in that mausoleum of mostly unread books in my library for a biography of Mary Shelley, the second wife of Percy

Bysshe Shelley, the great poet of the Romantic Period in England, and herself the authoress at seventeen years of age of *Frankenstein*. I was looking for a reading selection sufficiently autumnal to mirror my mood. Mary Shelley's life was an endless pursuit of the early love denied her in childhood after the death of her mother, Mary Wollstonecraft Godwin, an early feminist rebel. I sat down with it and before long my attention had drifted away from current issues. I saw again in my mind's ever duller eye an image of the young Mary sitting in a graveyard by her mother's tomb seeking to extract some manner of warmth from the cold monument of stone at her side. Years later Mary, after meeting the reform-minded poet and running away with him to the continent, she thought that she had found in his idealism and poetic gifts the source of the undying love she craved only to be bereft again by his untimely death. Percy Shelley drowned in the silver-blue waters off the coast of Italy and was cremated by his friends after his body had been retrieved from the clutches of the sea. When the ashes were later stirred it was found that only his heart had resisted the flames. It is not impossible that my own heart will share that unique endurance.

As I say these stray thoughts set in motion a train of reflections that after many twists and perambulations led to one who is only a memory for me now. I came to reflections on her by degrees. My first thought was of the vanity of hoping for literary immortality. I remembered how I had come as if by accident upon one of Herman Hesse's novels while away at college in New England. It was an old edition from that period when paperback additions of Hesse were pushing him as an early version of the '60's flower-child movement, just another of those throwbacks to prior ages of romantic yearning for justice and equality that seem always to elude the masses to the delight of their rulers. I found Hesse fascinating and went on to read his novels dealing with various simple wanderers in search of wisdom and of peace. His German sensibility made a lasting impression upon me.

Rather than having the good sense to return to my studies towards a degree in finance or management and starting that long, laborious, but finally fruitful climb to material success I allowed myself to study the social sciences instead in pursuit of a newer and better world. It seems strange to me now that I had such little respect for history as to assume that human moral progress is ever really possible, but at that time of life my days stretched out before me endlessly and I thought that surely I would have time for anything that my vain heart desired. I would discover the magic key that would make redemption superfluous because enlightened humanity would provide all that could ever be imagined or esteemed.

From these reflections upon youth's fatuous confidence my mind turned to my present position, one still no less rebellious but now consumed by doubts that even what I had professionally achieved was now in danger of being overtaken by a world-wide turning to right-wing solutions and simplistic rhetoric. I asked myself, how these trends could be resisted? If I had been helpless in the full-flower of youth to resist the tyrants of the age what greater effect could I hope to have against such well-financed mental mediocrity as that which was daily displayed in America? Perhaps I had always been destined to write in the elegiac key rather than to sketch out the path to effective resistance by a mere economic redistribution. Is happiness and justice so easily obtained by mere material ends? I thought of Mary Shelley reclining on the greensward by her mother's grave while the leaves blew about her and suddenly found again within me a desire to write of Ligeia. I therefore took my pen in hand and began thus to reflect upon my life as though it were a miniature cameo that when opened revealed her dark visage, the face that haunts me still.

It is November again, the month that Catholic tradition sets aside for remembrance of the dead. If October is one festive display of color and of harvest as life fades away, November is the month when trees as the poet says weep their burden to the ground. Death becomes less picturesque as the likelihood of its personal and immanent claim upon one grows. One might think that I look forward to my own demise as a gateway to reunion with the one who, I hesitate to admit it, I once called beloved. In that supposition however there resides a dreadful error for the fact is I would not bring her back even if I could, or worse still share a final resting place at her side, our sodden ashes mingling in a dull repetition of long extinguished desire. No, it is far better that she rest in that graveyard that she once cherished as she deposited night-violets upon the memorials of the unremembered and the lost.

She always found death comforting as though in its insensibility she found solace for her incessant and unrelieved pain in life. Maybe it was because the dead could not reject the violent and insistent nature of her love; I cannot say. I only know that she loved graveyards and I, because I loved her, finally equated them with her presence so that even now in my travels I cannot pass one without remembering her ivory hands resting languidly upon the moss and stone. I will call her Ligeia, though she went by another name when I knew her many long years ago, years that seem like yesterday as my ability to lay down new memories diminishes.

I take the name Ligeia of course from a story that she loved by the esteemed author Edgar Allen Poe. Our periods of youth did not coincide but that was a mere accident of birth and had no effect upon the communion of spirits that can at times unite disparate souls. I think I must have anticipated her advent in those far off collegiate days in New England when I would read the novels of Herman Hesse or the poetry of Shelley while the leaves of the yellow elms and maples fell down about me from the trees that like burning tapers surrounded the old apple orchards near the college. Ligeia was one with the melancholy figures that haunt the gothic imagination in her willingness to bear and to inflict pain. She required some morose Byronic figure to languish over or to despise in order to complete some long and elaborate tale whose origin fades in the mists of some long forgotten sin in her ancestral line. It is still a mystery why she gravitated towards me. Something in me made for good casting in the role of a minion or witness of her self-immolation. Like the case in most set scripts there are any number of actors who could conceivably have taken on the role; the fact that I was chosen had more to do with my willingness to keep returning for casting calls and rehearsals than any innate ability I may have had to play the role of a tragic hero in her play.

As the years passed we took our show upon the road through the sordidness of the provinces using the few props that were at hand and the shallow stagecraft that was all that either of us could then afford. I doubt that either of us was up to the pretention of our roles. Yet perhaps I do myself an injustice here: by some magic trick of the imagination I had learned in childhood to traverse time so that my relation to certain authors was so intimate that I could consider myself to be one of their select company. It seems so foolish now but as a measure of my loneliness and as an anodyne to an empty world this illusion served its purpose. The result of course was that I could hardly be said to exist apart from the authors whose stilled voices were still preserved in these immortal texts. My reading of biographies since has convinced me that this dialog with the lost shades of vanished minds was less particular to me than I might have imagined. Perhaps literature is nothing more than a long conversation continued across time by people who have never met each other. No statesman or financier can compete with the poets, the novelists, and the dramatists because their creations are as alive now as when they were first penned. It is only the audience that ages, changes, and sometimes forgets. Perhaps Ligeia had that same gift of seeing her life course portrayed in the very course of its daily evolution to a wider audience than her own solitary self.

The mind of the artist after all is not confined to a single medium. Ligeia had the genius of seeing things in juxtaposition. She made of life a collage of varied inner moods and associations. Her métier was confined to an audience of one while I, like some phantom observer from the wings of her dress rehearsal for life, was able to witness what I could never hope to share completely. So it was that our solitudes intermeshed so that on occasion we reached each other across the vast spaces that divided us only to be lost again in the various fogs of mutual incomprehension and misunderstanding. There were long breaks when I lost all contact with her. It is these gaps that preserve sensitive souls intact when any real intimacy threatens to break through the enveloping mists of solitude and alienation.

After her death I set forth on my journeying hoping to lose in space what I had already forfeited in time. I wouldn't be speaking of her now if it was not that I have returned to Austria in the course of my travels to walk again the streets and lanes of the old city where I did my graduate work. I go to mass daily at the old pilgrimage church on the hill with its steps worn by the knees of penitents seeking to undo the follies of youth and to escape the countless separate vanities that age reveals. I am now of that number that returns to God late in life because little else remains for me. The portals of eternity are widening by the hour. My dreams now inhabit a perpetual autumn.

I have taken a small flat in the city near the flower market and I walk by the lake daily to feed the swans. There is one bench here where I hold court before occasional passers-by who wonder at my American accent and are kind enough to engage me in conversation. I suppose that I appear genial to them, well-balanced, and even gregarious, whereas if they knew me better they would see that I am still haunted by innumerable regrets. The rhythm of my days is as predictable as a metronome. I have rolls and coffee for breakfast, noodle soup or dumpling broth for lunch, and for dinner the little spiced sausages that reflect a Balkan influence in the local cuisine. I have a modest two beers each day and a glass of slivovitz after dinner to warm me as I walk home. I still enjoy cider with cloves and cinnamon and the bread smeared with bacon grease that I am too weak to abjure as injurious to my health. I have stopped running for a time from my memories. I feel that I am leasing a posthumous existence in any case. My life is united only by the endless flow of words, mine or another's. Yet I wonder what motivates me to even pen these words unless it is that I hardly know my own thoughts until I record them. It is a hazard of the writer's trade. Yes, I am becoming at long last a writer.

I may even become somewhat well-known in my time and become honored with a leather-bound set of my collected works and awarded one of those slightly absurd honorary doctorates in exchange for boring students, professors, and other interested parties at a dinner in my honor with a few scattered reflections on the decline of the humanities and of culture in general in our digitally enhanced age. Those doctoral robes make good blankets in chilly the chilly rooms of a Gasthaus or a pensione.

I don't mean to sound ungrateful but I am not so foolish as to imagine that academia is really a serious pursuit devoid of vanity and ordered to the advancement of learning. I know the predictable stages of a career in literature from present honors to final irrelevance. The playwrights have it best, it seems to me; they at least can observe their audiences reacting to their words. The rest of us exist behind a veil of silence except at those tiresome readings and book signings for the few fans that imagine that they really know an author from his works. Writers have been replaced in the popular imagination. Such celebrity as we possess can hardly match the glamour of actors or politicians. I think most people go away thinking, "Maybe if the poor fellow could learn to juggle balls or tell jokes…" We are a dying breed in a superseded medium appealing to a diminishing audience with a shortened attention span. I'm not even sure the human brain even works as it once did. But then I am drifting aren't I … from my main topic I mean. What did I call her just now? Oh yes, I called her Ligeia, a fascinating name.

Poe was quite mad of course, nerves raw and wracked by ceaseless drinking. The Europeans understood him while the Americans never really did: America never quite lives up to its creative spirits, not even towards Dreiser or Howells let alone Hawthorne, Poe, or Henry James. American roots are simply too shallow to sustain great art from the whistle-stop platforms of the little prairie towns that sprung up all over the great plains once the Indians were pushed aside, Sinclair Lewis and Willa Cather notwithstanding. It takes long seasoning to produce the likes of a Thomas Mann. Therefore it makes sense for an American author to be an expatriate. You have to leave America to really understand it … just as I had to leave Ligeia finally before I could accept what I was dealing with … but I don't want to talk about Ligeia here, even fictionally, to put her in some crumbling mansion and have her always threatening to rise from her grave while I or some pale alter ego remembers her beauty and the way her black hair fell in Medusa-like ringlets about that waxen brow to hide her cat-like eyes. No, I would not think of her even in writing about her here. Perhaps she never really existed apart from those endless things that she drew about her, collected, annotated, and arranged. She existed in them and they existed in her. What she was in herself perhaps no one knew, least of all Ligeia. What price admission to the great museum of her unlived life? It was all such waste yet I once considered myself privileged to share it. Perhaps I was mad. Maybe I still am mad. That would surely explain my Melmoth-like wanderings over the face of the earth. I recall seeing a sign once that said that not all who wander are lost. I suppose that this implies some sort of hidden tracery of purpose in travel or perhaps the stimulus of adventure; I know only that I must keep moving from place to place to keep regret at bay.

Let us speak for a time of other things. Ours is an age of decaying institutions or at least the old ways of doing things if real renewal is to be accomplished. Even the Roman Catholic Church appears at times to be at the end of its tether. I read this year about some sort of Amazonian Synod of the bishops of South America. They brought along some sort of statues of a maternal image, a naked pregnant woman in the last stages before birth. I recall smiling when I read of this, finding in the figurines some late stage recognition of the endless cycles of procreation and perhaps of reverence for the sex that must sustain life on this poor planet, withering under industrial ill-usage. The Pope even blessed the figures and was promptly accused of idolatry by the same conservative Catholic media that has made of Donald Trump some sort of lawless icon of their long deferred to-do list. A few days later I heard that some vandals had broken into the church where they were being displayed, had stolen them, and dumped them into the Tiber River. I was astonished to read that these men and their actions were acclaimed in the following days in conservative media as some sort of folk heroes like the book-burning Nazis and the Buddha-defacing Islamic vandals of some years ago. How easy it is to think that competing symbols can be destroyed by violence. The world's ideas and conceptions now lie in uneasy juxtaposition; shall we destroy them all in one great orgy to see who was always right after all?

As actual life is nudged aside all that remains to us are our representations. This is why I hesitate to write anything at all, to add to the great edifice of the neglected and forgotten. Who would care for Ligeia now though if I did not remember her? Where are the monasteries where in the long hour of the night the monks awaken to chant the Divine Office: matins, lauds, prime, tierce, sext, none, vespers, and compline just as I wake and think of her? Ligeia's long defiles of former devotees are now as dispersed as the worshipers in spirit and in truth. I was neither the first nor the last to love her, only the most faithful. So it is that I am in sympathy with those who deplore lost liturgical customs even as I deplore their narrowness of sympathy and conception. Surely our conceptions of God, unequal to our dogmatic convictions, are even less adequate to portray God as God really is. I feel words and concepts alike failing to bear the weight that is placed upon them. For me now everything is a great retrospection.

As I said I spend a great deal of my days, and nights as well now, in the old pilgrimage Church whose steps I first traversed at the age of twenty-five. The tapers burn as of old on the high altar above the cold stone floor and the graves in the snow outside bear only the mutest witness to the lost passions of yesterday and the poor flesh that housed then. Now all that remains are bones and wood, or perhaps the dead remnants of flowers still blooming when they were lovingly placed in the cold hands of the beloved, never to be removed.

I do not flatter myself that I shall be so honored in my death. Everyone I once knew is in a distant land or they have already preceded me to the grave. Why you may ask do I continue then with my posthumous existence? Surely the answer is not hard to deduce.

After all I am hardly a mysterious character: I am the logical descendent of the character depicted in Dostoyevsky's *Notes from the Underground.* You have never read it? Dear me, that is a pity. You can hardly hope to understand me without a bit of research into my romantic forebears. Self-pity as an art form does not arise *sua sponte.* Perhaps you have read Goethe, *The Sorrows of Young Werther;* something perhaps by Georg Trakl, an Austrian nature poet? Now there's a man who understood how depression leads to despair. You can hardly be expected to comprehend my great loss without first tilling the soil of disappointed love now, can you?

Oh well we must proceed as if you as well have discovered the dark joys of lachrymose affection. Ligeia understood, ah too well, and it led her to reject everything that I held out to her with outstretched hands. We met only in the interstitial regions of her spiral into darkness. Perhaps there was something too wholesome in me. After all I do enjoy life at times and for her that was always anathema. Her specialty was to find happiness within her grasp and then to fling it to the ground like a lantern just to see the wick of the candle within expire. Perhaps it was vanity, who knows? Maybe she thought that love was an ever renewable spring. Maybe she thought everyone unworthy of her divine obsession with herself. In any case she left behind her the maimed corpses of vanished loves. I don't expect that she is a rarity; after all deadly nightshade grows almost anywhere they say.

But I sound bitter don't I? Surely I was responsible for my own actions in always returning to the same barren ground expecting roses and not thorns. My hands are still scarred as a result of encountering her rejections and ever renewed solicitations. You see she never gave up on me, or for that matter I also did not give up on her. There was always that tiny hope that I could walk across that narrow plank across the chasm to her perpetual esteem. Foolish, I admit it, but I can hardly correct my error now, can I? I mean the years have vanished, never to return. Life is unforgiving even if God is. The moving finger writes ... you know the rest.

So what should we speak of now? Having seduced you with a tale of Ligeia you are now at my mercy. Shall we speak of things past, present, and to come? Perhaps we should maintain a reverential silence in memory of her. She would like that. She always wished for a bigger stage on which to manifest her epic decline. She deserved some sort of apotheosis or at least celebration for her efforts in that regard even from a poor poet like me who is derivative at best. There! I have demeaned myself in tribute to her memory. She would have enjoyed that. She was always best when she could turn away in scorn for imagined offenses. The last word was always hers to give, to leave one standing there dismayed and helpless while she walked away. She was a grand mistress of the strategic exit. One always thought that there would be a pause while the stage-lights gradually dimmed to darkness before the applause would burst forth ... but there was never anyone there in the empty theater but me.

So we went on from year to vanishing year until through long acquaintance I had forgotten what human dignity even looked like. I expect it is a common enough story and thus my example may serve some purpose after all. But my purpose is neither to praise Ligeia nor to defend her: perhaps she was only a product of her times. She was born as a child of promise and expectation and denied fulfillment except in the crass terms of luxury and the search for a perfect love that forever eluded her. I met her during that era of her life when she was a student at one of the colleges for debutants, one of the last strongholds of American aristocracy where she was enrolled in one of the Ivy League bastions of privilege and power. I was pursuing an under-graduate degree at a matriculation date eight years beyond the usual age at Boston College after serving in one of America's wars pursued in the national interest in other people's lands. I came home by way of Austria where I was able to explore and to appreciate the scenes of so many battles waged along that central fault line that divided the Germanic and the Slavic nations. I imbibed deeply from the same streams of skepticism and pietism that led to the philosophy of Immanuel Kant and later to that destructive philosophy of Nietzsche and his philosophy with a hammer.

I had not yet decided upon a course of studies. I still had all of the resentment that remains the only lasting legacy of combat, resentment towards the fortunate ones who had sent us out to preserve their material interests. I hesitated to take up a business career for fear of sharing their mentality. I met Ligeia in Paris. She was there on an American version of the Grand Tour after graduating from her prep school. We met at a symposium after one of the more stimulating lectures on the decline of Vitalism in Philosophy since Bergson. She asked me if I had read Huysmans or the poet Dowson and was surprised to hear me answer in the affirmative. The conversation continued as we walked across the city through the falling leaves and to warm ourselves we adjourned to one of the quiet student retreats where we could continue our discussion in quiet but congenial surroundings.

She was less of a hermit then, less inclined to wander those dark corridors of speculation as to other's motives that latterly obsessed her. I thought she was wonderful. I thought that here at last was the remedy for all of the premature death that I had witnessed in Afghanistan. Surely it was so that American youth of which she was so representative might thrive and fulfill their dreams. I asked her at last what she hoped to achieve, where her interests might lie, and it was then that she gave me the first hint of her lugubrious imaginations—a totality of fulfillment wedded to pain. It made no sense to me at the time I remember. I had just come from a place where the difference between life and death was as strict and final as a stray bullet or an explosive device on a hillside trail. To court death seemed to me an unpardonable luxury but in justification just looking at her I would have pardoned her everything. She had spotted at once my fatal need to believe that perfect happiness is possible in this Vail of Tears, that all could be made right by simply enduring until the inevitable tidal change took place that would bring her to me once again. Having faced so many more difficult challenges I thought that determination and longevity could not fail to bring success at last. She used that flaw to keep me present to her until the end, long after everyone else had finally left her. I never understood until the end that cruelty and derision would have won her, that being rejected was the key to her heart. Nothing so repelled her as light and happiness. They blinded her in the same way that the absence of light blinds others.

None of this was fully visible at first. When we both returned from Europe I visited her periodically. I remember the exhilaration that I felt driving down to see her. As I walked across campus to her dorm I remember thinking that none of the girls that I passed on the way could hold a candle to her beauty and the intensity that radiated from her. How swiftly though the day would change! I could feel a sort of cloud made up of depression and inertia began to surround me before I even called up to her room. Sometimes the phone would ring unanswered and only on the third attempt would she finally answer it. Her explanations were always laconic and indifferent no matter how definite our plans had been. It was sufficient to her feeding habits that I had been put to the effort of driving down and by so doing paid my little stipend of tribute to her insatiable need for power and control. It pains me to think of that first year after our meeting in which there was already, if I had possessed the good sense to read the signs, the prophesy of all that was to follow over so many years of gradual submersion into her darkness so I will ask the indulgent reader to bear with me if I digress again for a moment to other things.

I have said that I have returned to Europe recently where I now reside due to the good fortune of an unexpected legacy. Only now can I act the role of a well-lettered exile filled with political conceptions: a D'Annunzio without country or portfolio. I can imagine and hold forth on the dreams of 1848 when through sheer energy, equality and liberty might be procured and sustained. Every age knows its era of similar idealism. But lately it appears that the most unworthy are being awarded public approbation and acclaim. I find that people are turning to plutocrats for their populism, reaching out with the hands of beggars for the crumbs that fall from the table. Where is the fervor in that? Where is the life force? You see I am still more of a vitalist than I am a Christian. To listen to the conservatives, those of the Catholic persuasion at least, our life is a constant struggle for inner conversion and resistance to sin, whereas to the vitalist what matters is to resist dissolution by living, even if one is doomed to defeat in the end. There! Now you can see why I hate and fear death so: because I cannot be sure that the universe or whatever is out there cares about our moral dispositions.

But what else have we? The motives of statecraft are so interlaced with venality and self-interest that virtue and vice wear the same face and all that really matters is results. I am impatient alike with good intentions and with fanatical adherence to an ideal. I know what hunger and pain look like and all I seek is a remedy. Yet, and I hesitate to confess this, I am not a stranger to a desire for comforts and unearned profit. I alternate between a hunger for impersonality and simplicity and a desire to plumb the same depths of sensation that Ligeia once made her home. She was one who could refuse herself nothing and hence she could not understand why everyone was not ready to lay themselves down and surrender everything to serve her.

Still, my impatience with dull moral strictures makes me hesitate to condemn her. After all, she had no real ability to extort such sacrifices that I and others made on her behalf. It was part of her genius to make such surrender seem inevitable and refusal unthinkable. The passing years had allowed me to witness the parade of suitors who used her and departed ... or was it she who exhausted their own patience and resources? As one always loyal to her versions of events I could never make up my mind where the truth lay. Instead I preferred to simply circle about her like some dim outer planet about its sun, satisfied with the frigid light that filters down to it rather than to embrace again the empty comfort of light from distant galaxies. It is not too much to say that I shared her illness through my own irresolution mistaking desolation and hope for fidelity. I took what was perhaps a pardonable pride in vowing that I at least would never abandon her.

So did the years drift by unnoticed until her fate settled down upon her, until I in a strange reversal rather like Mary Shelley who spent her life tending the flowers of her husband's posthumous reputation, wondered how I might properly enshrine the memory of Ligeia. But now the love that I had once entertained for her was encased in pain and an awareness of the countless instances of cruelty that should long since have brought me to my senses. How does one explain such a singular lack of judgment in this one particular instance? It was as if I had contracted one of those slow and chronic diseases that waste the victim without killing him. As the years passed I dated them by the entries of her infidelities and disappointments. Her promises of reform and reformation began to diminish immediately after issue like a currency with runaway inflation. Her demands for unconditional affirmation and availability were like one of those black holes in space that suck everything into itself, downward and downward until even time itself slows down and stops. She dwelled always in a sort of sub-basement of the soul.

I cannot say when I awoke at last and regained what was left of my senses, but I recall that it was as if I had been spellbound for years. I thought then of the poem by John Keats:

> *I saw pale kings and princes too,*
> *Pale warriors, death pale were they all;*
> *They cried - "La Belle Dame sans merci hath thee in thrall!"*
> *I saw their starved lips in the gloam,*
> *With horrid warning gaped wide,*
> *And I awoke and found me here,*
> *On the cold hill's side,*
> *And that is why I sojourn here,*
> *Alone and palely loitering,*
> *Though the sedge is withered from the lake,*
> *And no birds sing.*

But that was after many autumns had fled with riotous leaves away from me. I have been no less a victim of other's narratives, just as the world is. We are born into stories whose beginnings preceded us and in which we are only links in an unending chain. The great religions exist as they do because of an *ex parte* meeting between various prophets and the deity. We were not present to raise our own questions at the critical hour. The rest of us must measure our lives by standards arrived at hundreds of years before our births. I often wonder if the world could simply begin again. What if we issued a general pardon for all prior offenses, melted down the medals and citations, re-distributed the lands and benefices, cancelled all the anointings and ordinations: could the blank slate be worse than the endless conflict we have now? What if like people in a lifeboat we were forced to do a simple inventory of sea biscuits and casks of water and had to calculate the number of days left before we were to die? What if we were forced to acknowledge the desperate straits of the 7.8 billion people on this planet that only differs from an insensate universe because of the life existing upon it? We have three thousand or so years of recorded history and before that only the assurance that our wandering forbears bequeathed to us a balanced and intact world. Can we do better now than simply to preserve it; surrender hope of eternity to the demands of the hour? What if we aren't going anywhere? What if this is it, no rescue at hand for our follies but what we alone can devise? Does God adjust the time of the final judgment to fit our contingent circumstances or was it already fixed before the oceans ever rolled? Is providential intervention adjustable or are the settings already clearly established and set at the moment of creation? If life is the material result of a genetic blueprint what will it be when we move from designing software to designing species and beyond? What will be the first silicon-based life-form? Even transcendence is being made immanent. Where is the prophet who can descend from Mount Sinai with a new set of instructions or commandments adequate for the age we live in?

Yes, I am a Catholic of the ancient Roman Rite. It is too late for me to un-think the habits of a lifetime. I haunt the cathedral here daily like a ghost and walk back to my sterile rooms afterwards to seek my repose in unquiet slumbers. It is then that in memory I walk at the side again of Ligeia or knock for admission to a presence that was always such a disappointment to my hopes. Time with her as I have said was always preceded by elation and followed by anguish and regret. I was like a bird following a trail of crumbs, scattered with sufficient abundance as to be adequate to ensure compliance but never sufficient to allay hunger and to finally allow the bird to sing. Year after year I remained faithful to a vision that was proven illusory before we ever left Paris.

She was already firmly set on the course that her life was to follow. My experience of life has taught me almost to accept the idea that our life course is set out for us before we are born. We struggle to free ourselves but ever and again the same coils enmesh us drawing ever tighter and tighter until we cannot breathe. We need a foretaste of heaven now and again to sustain us. It is vain to nourish faith on desired conviction alone; no doubt this is why the Catholic Church insists upon sacramental observance. We are after all beings of flesh as well as soul. Calvin and Luther thought that God was best found in words; only the Catholics understood the role of the body in salvation. I suppose that is why I remain Catholic. I am more of a believer now than ever before, because of my doubts I am more devoted, because of my disquiet with dogma I am more desirous of love, because it is so readily filtered by those whose province it is to guard access to the temple I seek admission to the sanctuary.

Yet I feel myself torn asunder every day. Where did all of the former certainties go? I used to feel as though culture could provide a refuge if religion failed, but culture itself is eroding around us. It is becoming impossible to locate a moral equivalent for Greenwich Mean Time. The result is that everything is in suspension from day to day as the various sources of biased and conflicting information wage their daily wars to capture the fleeting hours of leisure time that is left over after a day of work, to occupy ourselves with wider concerns rather than seeking refuge in some more mindless pursuit towards respite if not oblivion. Politics has infiltrated everywhere these days to the extent that no one can escape the clash of contending forces. To weed out the noise is becoming impossible unless one turns to the last remaining sources of silence: the churches and the graveyards. Fewer people each day care to visit either of these and be reminded that the time allotted to each generation is short. Already we are passing into history.

I am glad at least to no longer reside in America. It is still tainted for me by dreams of Ligeia. I hunger for even the cold comfort of that cemetery in England where Mary Shelley lies buried still dreaming of the smoldering and unextinguished heart of her beloved poet husband, but even that solace is denied me. Homeless now I wander over Europe in search of, I know not what.

Where is a life of sophistication and grace to be found? It is the part of the artists among us to make of life something more than just consumption and display. Even Ligeia shared that belief in her fashion and for years it was a bond between us. It only failed when all else was encased in the mistrust that made her wall herself off from any contact with her former acquaintances and lovers, even me. She read in them the betrayal that was the product of her own cruelties. She has kept me on to the last, year after year, as her chosen witness to monitor each stage toward her final decline and dissolution.

"Watch me," she seemed to be saying, as I throw it all away. Can you bear it while drop by drop I bleed to death before your very eyes? Why don't you do something?"

So I remained. Fixed by her basilisk stare I did watch, knowing all along that by no force of will or act of abduction could I stop the process much less restore what either of us had been before we met. Even now when I should have begun to heal like a scorched forest as the tiny tendrils of new saplings rise towards the clear blue skies I wake in the night and think of her. She is the embodiment of disappointed hopes and desolation as the world pitches about from side to side and from course to course on its disparate headings. So it is that I have sought sanctuary here in one fragment of the long since dismantled Holy Roman Empire, or Austria-Hungary as it was known just before the Great War of 1914-1918 when it was finally defeated and dismembered.

I took a train journey one day into Vienna to visit the Hapsburg palaces there. Where had all of that pride and confidence led but to ruin and defeat? As I walked the gravel walks behind the Belvedere Palace I wondered whether the new Church of the people being brought to birth by Pope Francis would be able to amass the mythic grandeur that it took to embody faith. Could faith survive without the baroque grandeur of the old cathedrals with their gold-encrusted domes opening to visions of seraphs surrounding Christ or the Virgin Mary? Does it take great art and music as well as grace to save souls?

But can any human conception ever really capture divinity? Perhaps love is a quiet thing, something built up over vast stretches of time like the beleaguered Amazon rainforest with its great canopied roof filled with colorful birds. Was it an accident that a conclave chose a Pope from Latin America at the same time that this great Gothic Cathedral of nature's fashioning was being burned by purpose and design and as the rulers of the ever-hungry oil companies were bent over maps calculating profits once the last indigenous inhabitants could be brought off, pushed aside, or killed?

The forces of death are all about us now. A moral prism is emerging that will divide humanity into those who nurture life in this all too material world and those who in pursuit of some all-embracing idea forget our complete dependency upon the living systems and interconnections that sustain us. I am looking for my place in all of this, hoping to align myself on the side of life, menaced as it is by mere abstractions. As a first gesture towards a resumed life course I have sat at a table these past days looking out onto the courtyard where a gentle rain is falling through the denuded trees. I have dared to see my life as a whole searching for that first fatal turning.

I see in reading over what I have just written here with all of the spontaneity of one who travels again around a pillar of flame that our tale, Ligeia's and mine, was not a linear one. Ligeia seemed from the first to have been always with me as though a place had been reserved for her long before we met, and retained long after I had bid her a final farewell. Final, how strange that word sounds to one who wears her forever like a dagger in the heart. Was Ligeia a demon in human flesh? I must say that I have speculated along these lines from time to time. How else am I to account for her power exercised over me for so many years? Like all demons they delight in specificity, each selects its victim with infinite care. So it is that after I met her I imagined that she had always existed by my side as my portion and my cup whereas that phrase is always reserved for God alone. It is a mistake to dream of final completion from mere human love.

Yet even in saying this I know that if she rose again I might follow her pale wraithlike being as it wandered about by night, feeding upon what it could not share. Eventually she became a shadowed version of her former self as though she was being consumed by an inner fire that scorched her very soul. Redemption like happiness was for her always just out of reach.

The ashes of Ligeia have no mortal resting place. Neither mourned nor memorialized she died as she had lived surrounded by her aura of bitterness and recrimination towards a world that had finally proved itself unworthy of her. It should have realized that a goddess walked upon it and bestowed upon her due obeisance.

The story, if that is what it is, ends here and I doubt whether it requires further elaboration. To catch the essence of the thing is the key. Perhaps it is enough to sound the cautionary note and to move on. My Ligeia like Poe's is in the last analysis a vampire tale and like all such tales the hope is that the undead may be stilled at last to prevent their return. Only the haunted know the price that this exorcism entails. It must be embraced voluntarily if at all by the one who is to be delivered at last. It is said that when the victim of a vampire awakens to his state in life and assesses his own proximity to death he must use as an exorcism such words as these from Edgar Allen Poe. May they be the epitaph of all who walk in the way of Ligeia and of those as well who like me have become pilgrims towards an empty horizon. Until then I am merely filling the days and nights until perhaps I will see her once again...

> *The lady sleeps,*
> *Oh may her sleep,*
> *Which, is enduring,*
> *So be deep!*
> *Heaven have her,*
> *In its sacred keep!*
> *This chamber changed for one more holy,*
> *This bed for one more melancholy.*
> *I pray to God that she may ever lie,*
> *Forever with unopened eye,*
> *While the dim sheeted ghosts go by.*

FATES
BY CARRIE AVERY MORIARTY

There is something immensely beautiful in letting go. Whether it's giving up on a dream that will never come to fruition, saying good bye to a loved one when they've lived a long and fulfilling life, or walking away from drama in most any form. It's the latter that I find myself in right now. I knew I shouldn't have gotten involved, but it seemed so perfect. That should have been my first clue. Nothing in this life is perfect. I suppose I should start at the beginning, otherwise none of the rest of this story will make sense.

"Good morning, class," Mr. Richards said. "Hopefully you had a nice rest over break and are ready to jump right back into our studies. We only have a few more weeks of the quarter left before we have finals, and I want you all to be prepared."

We'd been studying the fates and their multiple genesis, focusing highly on the Greek version, Moirai. It was monotonous at best, and right now I just wanted to be done with it. Couldn't we all just read the Iliad and call it good?

"I've paired you up," the professor continued, and an audible groan rippled through the students. "I know you like to choose your own partners, but I wanted to make sure that each student had someone they could rely on to be at the same level of skill as themselves. If you have a true conflict with who I've matched you with, please come see me after class and we can discuss it."

With that, he turned the projector on with the list of students in the class, showing who we would be paired up with for the final project. I searched the list looking for my name, only to see it next to someone I'd never met. This could either be a fantastic partner, or someone I would come to loath by the end of it.

"Please take a minute to meet your partners," the professor said. "I want you to exchange contact information so you will not have an excuse as to why you weren't able to work together."

I stood, turned toward the classroom, and looked around. My friend Kathy was looking at me with horror in her eyes. I hadn't seen who she was paired up with, so took a quick look at the list. Of course she would be stuck with James. The guy was stupid smart, but about as fun as a turd in a swimming pool. Poor Kathy.

"Are you Izzy?" a young man asked me.

"You must be Sean," I replied.

"I am," he said with a smirk.

"You're not gonna screw me on this project, are you?"

"As long as you don't screw around, we'll be fine," he replied.

"I don't screw around with my homework," I stated flatly. "I'm a 4.0 student and intend to keep my average there."

"Good," he replied.

"Great," I said.

We exchanged contact info and decided who would be doing what with respect to the project. Our task was simple, explain the Fates, describe how they worked within mythology, and come to a conclusion as to whether we agreed or disagreed with the idea that they were still around. I already knew the answer to the final question, whether they still existed. It would be interesting to see whether my partner agreed with me.

After class, Kathy caught up to me.

"Your partner is cute," she whispered as we found our way down the hall.

"I guess," I replied. "Didn't really look at him."

"Trade ya?"

"Not a chance," I laughed. "I'm sorry you're stuck with James, but it's your own fault. If you weren't so smart, you'd be stuck with someone like Brent."

"Ugh," she said, rolling her eyes. "Can you imagine trying to do the report and having him just go, 'but I thought they were sexy babes like in that animated film.'"

"I don't envy the person who ended up stuck with him," I said.

"So," she offered after we'd been walking a while. "What's he like?"

"Who?"

"Sean," she said. "Duh."

"Oh," I replied. "I guess he's fine. I mean, we didn't really talk much."

"I am definitely going to need all the details after your first get together," she said. "I expect detailed descriptions of everything you do."

"You mean like, 'we looked information up on the internet,' and the like?" I asked.

"There better be more than research going on with you two," she said. "Like, there better be sparks and sex and—"

"Whoa," I said, stopping her mid-sentence. "There will be no sex."

"You're no fun," she laughed. "I'd totally take advantage of the forced communication and closeness."

"I'm not you," I said. "I have no need for a boyfriend right now."

"Who said anything about him being your boyfriend?"

"You are incorrigible," I said.

"Details," she said, then grabbed my arm.

The rest of the day went along boringly as usual, and on the way to our off-campus apartment, we stopped at the Frosty Freeze for shakes. I know, shakes in the middle of winter seems odd, but it was comfort food for us. Every time we had a big assignment given to us, we stopped and picked up a shake to ease the burden we felt. Today was no different. I know a lot of the college kids would have stopped at a bar, but Kathy and I were mild mannered, boring, very responsible people. Besides, nothing at a bar could beat a salted caramel shake from the Frosty Freeze.

Kathy grabbed my arm and stopped me short as soon as we walked in the door.

"He's here," she whispered.

"Who?"

"Sean," she insisted. "Go talk to him."

"What for?" I asked as I began to walk toward the counter.

"Because he's cute," she said. "And he's your partner, and you need to talk about the project, and..."

"Stop," I said, and did just that, jolting her as well. "Are you twelve?"

She looked at me, completely baffled.

"You're acting like we're in junior high and he's a cute boy I've got a crush on," I explained. "We're twenty-one, in college, and it's an assignment for philosophy. We've already had a conversation about it, and we have each other's contact info so we can keep in touch. There is nothing to talk about."

"But he's cute," she insisted.

"You are the most ridiculous person I know," I laughed. "I need a shake."

With that, I walked away from her and up to the counter to order my treat. She followed quickly and made her own order. When our shakes were ready, we walked to the dining area. Whether it was fate or something else, the only table available was the one right next to Sean.

"Hey," Kathy said as we sat down.

Sean looked up from his book and smiled.

"I thought I was the only one who did shakes in the winter," he said. "It appears I am in good company, though."

"It's our customary treat when we get a big assignment," I said. "Reminds us of the simple times before finals and the like."

"I hear ya," he replied.

"So," Kathy began, but I glared at her. "Um..." she stammered.

I rolled my eyes and asked, "What flavor?"

"The best flavor," he smiled. "Salted caramel."

"Me, too," I laughed.

"Must be fate," he said.

There it was. That word again. I don't know if it was just because we were studying them, or if there was something more going on, but it seemed like things were aligning, coming together, as if they were all planned by some unseen force.

"We good to meet on Thursday?" he asked.

"I've put it in my phone," I said. "Library, right?"

"Why don't you meet at the apartment?" Kathy suggested,

and I stomped on her foot under the table. "Ouch," she cried, then glared daggers at me.

"It has to be the library," he said. "I don't think we can check out some of the books I'd like to use as references, so we'll have to do the research there."

"I'll bring my laptop so we can make notes," I said. "Unless you want to do that part."

"I'm good with you doing that part," he said. "We can work together, but if you want to house it on your laptop, that works well."

"Perfect," I said, then took a sip of my shake. "Ugh," I said, pulling my mouth off the straw. "I think I got yours, Kath."

"Mine's right," she said, taking a sip of her own.

"Be right back," I said, then got up and walked back up to the counter. "You gave me a strawberry shake," I said to the worker.

"That's what you ordered," she insisted.

"I only ever order salted caramel," I replied.

"I'll have to charge you for a new one," she said.

"I don't think so," I replied. "I ordered a salted caramel, not strawberry. The fault is on you, not me."

"I'll have to ask my manager," she said, clearly annoyed with the whole process.

She walked away from the counter to the back and I stood waiting for them to make me a new shake.

"Can I help you?" an older woman asked.

"I ordered a salted caramel shake, but got a strawberry," I said.

"Do you have your receipt?"

"She never gave me one," I said, indicating the worker.

The older woman looked to the younger one, then said, "I'd be happy to make you a new shake. We pride ourselves on making sure our customers are happy."

She then turned around and began the process of making my shake. I turned to watch Kathy and saw her rapidly whispering to Sean, looking at me the whole time. What was she saying to him? Probably something completely inappropriate that I would have try to explain away when I talked with him later.

"Here you go," the manager said, handing me my newly made shake.

"Thanks," I replied, and took a drink. "Perfect," I said after taking a drink to make sure they got it right. I went back to where my friend was sitting.

"What?" she asked when I sat down.

"I didn't ask anything," I replied. "Do I need to know something?"

"Your friend was just letting me know how well you liked working on projects at your apartment," he said, holding in a laugh, but barely.

"I'm sure she was," I replied with a smirk of my own.

"How she would be willing to let us have the whole place to ourselves," he continued. "In case there were things we needed to work on in private."

"I see," I replied. "I'm sure she let you know that there would be times she would need the place to work on her project with her partner, James, too."

"She didn't mention that," Sean replied, catching on to where I was going with my line of thinking. "I'll be sure to let him know she is fine with him coming over to your place to work the long hours needed for this project."

Kathy's face was priceless as she sat there, open mouth, watching me make her little plan to get me alone with Sean backfire.

"In fact," I continued. "Maybe they'd like to have the apartment for the rest of the week. You know, to get the project done quickly."

The elbow to my ribs was painful, but totally worth it to see her on the receiving end of the shenanigans she often pulled.

"I'll shoot him a text right now," Sean said, pulling out his phone. "Let him know we're here making plans for the week. That way he can meet us and know exactly what to expect."

"No," Kathy said in shock. "Please don't," she begged.

"Relax," he laughed. "I don't even know who he is."

The relief in Kathy's face was obvious.

"Anyway," Sean said. "I'll see you Thursday."

"And in class," Kathy added.

"Of course," he replied.

"Have a nice night," I said, then watched him walk out the door.

"I see you checking out his ass," Kathy said once he was out the door.

"Whatever," I replied.

"That's what you're wearing?" Kathy asked as I tied my sneakers to head out to meet Sean at the library.

"What's wrong with it?"

"It's not very sexy," she said.

"We're studying," I said. "I have no need for sexy. We've had this conversation."

"You are absolutely no fun at all," she complained.

"Look," I said. "I know you think I need to have a guy in my life, that I'm somehow missing out on something without a boyfriend, but I'm actually doing really well without having the distraction of another person to deal with. You're about all I can handle in that category."

"Are you calling me high maintenance?" she asked, and I almost felt bad for saying it.

"I know you mean well," I offered. "I just sometimes wish you didn't push so hard."

"But you're lonely," she said.

"Not in the least," I replied.

"You're not?"

"Nope," I said.

"I don't get it," she replied.

"Look," I began. "I know you like to have a guy fawning all over you, but that's not me. We've known each other too long for you to not know that I don't need a man to make me whole. I am who I am, and if a guy wants to be a partner with me, that's great. Otherwise, there's no need."

"But…" she began, but I put my hand up.

"Nope," I said. "I'm out to meet another student to work on a project. That's all it is. See you when I get back."

With that, I walked out the door and headed to the library. When I walked in, I saw Sean sitting over where we had talked about meeting. He already had a couple of old looking books open on the table.

"Hey," he said when I sat down.

"Hey, yourself," I replied.

"I thought I would go ahead and grab these," he said, indicating the books. "Figured it would give us a jump start on the project."

"I did get some information from a couple of online sources," I said, pulling out my laptop.

"Not Wiki, right?" he eyed me suspiciously.

"Definitely not," I laughed.

"Good," he replied. "I figured you were smart enough to know that."

"Thanks," I replied.

"So," he said, indicating one of the old books in front of him. "I found this, but wanted to see what you thought of it before we put it into the final report."

He turned the book and pushed it across the table. I looked at the picture in the book, then read the description next to it.

"That's pretty much the information I got," I said. "Guess the older books aren't necessarily better resources."

"True," he said. "But look at this."

He pushed another book across the table to me. This one looked even older than the first one.

"They let you handle this one?" I asked, concerned that we shouldn't be actually reading it.

"This one is mine," he said and I looked at him.

"You have books this old?"

"And older," he said. "It's a hobby of mine."

"What?" I asked. "Books, or the Fates?"

"Both," he said. "Read that paragraph there," he suggested, pointing to one about half way down the page he had the book opened to.

I read the words, but was completely baffled as to what they meant. I looked up to him to ask, but noticed that there was something off about him.

"You okay?" I asked.

"What?" he asked, shaking himself. "Sorry. Just got lost in thought."

"You were…" I didn't know how to describe what I'd seen. It wasn't like he was glowing, but then again, it was.

"Sorry," he said, shaking his head.

"What was that?" I asked, unsure of exactly what had just happened.

"What was what?" he countered.

"Forget it," I said, not sure whether it was worth trying to figure out or not. "What does this mean?" I asked, trying to get back on topic.

"Let me see," he offered, pulling the book back across the table. "Oh," he said, after reading the paragraph he had indicated before. "The Greek words and the Latin words aren't the same thing," he said. "But you already knew that, right?"

"Sort of," I said. "What I don't get is why they couldn't figure out what they had wrong."

"It's not so much that they got it wrong as they didn't get it quite right," he said.

The authority of his words gave them more weight than you would think they had. It was as if he knew more than just what the books said.

"What do you mean?" I asked, hoping he'd explain why he came to the conclusion he did.

"Well," he began. "They're both right, in that they both have a portion of the mythology correct. The Fates do portion out to each of us what we should have when we are born. They also allot us things as we gain merit. Does that make sense?"

"I guess," I offered. "But it feels like you know more than just what's written here. Like you somehow have inside knowledge of what's being said."

He stared at me as if I'd grown a second head, and it was

really uncomfortable. Then the feeling went away and it was as if I was meant to spend the rest of my life with him. I closed my eyes and shook my head. Maybe Kathy's words were getting to me. Like I was seeing what she wanted me to see all along.

"Hey," he said, reaching out and grabbing my hand. "You okay?"

The shock I felt when his skin touched mine made me pull my hand away.

"Izzy," I heard, but it wasn't Sean who said it. I looked around, but didn't see anyone else near us.

"You okay?" Sean asked again, and I looked at him.

"Did you hear that?" I asked.

"What?" he asked.

"I thought I heard someone else say my name," I said.

"I didn't hear anything," he said, pulling his hand back across the table.

When I looked at him it was as if I'd slapped him. Something was definitely off with him.

"I've gotta go," he said and gathered his books up.

"But we're not done," I objected, but he was packing up and moving away from the table.

"I'll email you," he said and was gone before I could protest.

"That was strange," I mumbled and began to pack my stuff up as well.

I stood up to leave and nearly ran right into a man who was standing next to the table.

"Are you Izzy?" he asked, and his voice was velvet, caressing without really touching me.

I blinked, unsure why this man was talking to me. I'd never seen him before, and trust me, I'd remember. He was tall, dark, and handsome, just like the saying. Somehow, I found my voice and said, "I'm Izzy."

"Don't trust Sean," he said, and the power from his words sunk into me physically.

"Why not?" I asked.

"He's not who he seems," was all the man said, then he turned to walk away.

"Wait," I called and he turned back to me. "Who are you?"

"Hector," he said, then walked away.

"What is going on?" I asked no one in particular.

I walked back to my apartment and Kathy was there, waiting for an update.

"So?" she prompted.

I dropped my bag on the couch and flopped down next to it.

"I have no idea what's going on," I said without preamble.

"Color me confused." She sat on the couch next to me.

"I met Sean," I said. "We got started on our project, then he just bolted."

"What did you say?"

"Really?" I asked. "You assume it's something I said that caused him to run off?"

"You made it pretty clear that you were not at all interested in him in any fashion other than as a partner for your project," she said.

"Why does that matter?" I asked.

"Because he's super cute," she said. "And sometimes you just need to go there."

"That's the thing," I argued. "We were doing fine. Going over some books about the subject, chatting about things. Then I heard someone say my name and he got all butt hurt and packed up to leave."

"Who said your name?" she asked, completely enthralled in my retelling of my day.

"I guess it was Hector," I said.

"Who's Hector?" she asked, drawing the question out.

"I have no idea," I said. Apparently, that wasn't a sufficient answer because she simply stared at me, waiting for more. "He was there when I went to leave," I explained. "I ran right into him."

"Is he cute?"

"No," I said, and her face fell. "He's like a god. Carved out of marble. Chiseled with precision. Molded with care. Fashioned in perfect harmony with all that is good and right in the world."

"So," she laughed. "Just some dude."

I laughed with her, then said, "He was there, told me not to trust Sean, and was gone. It was the weirdest thing."

"He told you not to trust Sean?" she asked.

"Yeah," I said.

"Did he say why?"

"Nope," I replied. "Just said not to trust him. With the way he acted, though, I guess that's not a bad suggestion."

"Damn," she said. "And I was hoping he'd be the one to thaw out your frigid temperament."

"Please," I replied. "I am not frigid."

"Seriously?" The look she gave me clearly said she knew me all too well.

"Okay," I admitted. "Maybe I am a little chill. But come one, have you not seen the horror stories from college campuses? Every other day there's some story or another about women getting raped, fraternities causing issues, and nothing good ever comes from those stories."

"But he's adorable," she insisted.

"And not to be trusted," I replied. "I gotta see if I can get this project done. I doubt I'll get any help from Sean, now. How's yours going?"

"Don't make me talk about it," she said. "It's horrible."

"James is that bad, huh?"

"Worse," she retorted. "I just don't wanna."

"Sorry, kid," I said. "Grin and bear it."

"Still sure you don't want to trade partners?"

"Maybe I should have," I replied, then headed to my room.

"Miss Reese," Mr. Richards said as I walked into the class the next day.

"Yes?"

"I need to pair you up with someone else," he said.

"What's wrong with Sean?" I asked.

"He sent his project in without your input and has left the campus," he said.

"So," I began. "I'm just supposed to start over?"

"It was my understanding that you had already begun your work with Sean," he said. "I am sure that Hector can get up to speed quickly."

"Hector?"

"Izzy," the man from the day before said and I nearly jumped out of my boots.

"Where did you come from?"

My heart raced as I saw the man from the day before standing right beside me.

"I just walked in," he said with a wink. "Thank you, Professor, for finding a new partner for me."

"Hold on," I said. "How do I know this guy is going to be up to my level of work?”

“Trust me,” the professor said. “Hector is very intelligent, and he will make a great partner.”

The rest of the class was filing in, so I went to a seat with Hector in tow.

“You better not screw this class up for me,” I whispered.

“Don’t worry,” he smirked.

Kathy came in just then and sat down on the other side of me.

“Who’s the hottie?” she whispered in my ear.

“My new partner,” I muttered. “Hector.”

“THE Hector?”

“One and the same,” I replied.

“Where’s Sean?” she asked after a look around the room.

“No clue,” I replied. “Apparently he turned his final paper in without my help and skipped town.”

“This thing is due on Monday,” she said.

“Trust me,” I said. “I know.”

“Class,” Mr. Richards said. “We’re just about at the end of the quarter. Hopefully you all have completed, or nearly completed your final assignment with your partners. If not,” he continued, “I suggest you spend the weekend with your partner getting the finishing touches on them. Presentations will happen beginning on Monday.”

“Presentations?” I asked.

“Yes,” the professor replied. “It was in the syllabus, clearly spelled out. Two people work on the paper, then it is presented for the class to determine which conclusion is correct. Your argument needs to be compelling enough to convince those who have the opposite view as you to change their mind.”

I turned to see Hector looking at me with a glint I didn’t really find comforting in his eye. This was going to be a long weekend. By the time we finished class, I was more than a little concerned about my grade in this class. I knew what I wanted to say, but the trick was going to be making sure this new dude was of the same mind. Honestly, I wasn't sure myself any longer.

"Izzy," Hector said as he caught up to us after class.

"Yeah," I replied.

"We should meet," he said. "Maybe go over what you've got so far on the project."

"You thinking of just letting me do the whole thing?" I asked, not at all concerned with the annoyance in my voice.

"Look," he said, grabbing my arm. "I know you kind of got thrown into this thing, but I intend to hold up my end of the project. I am actually pretty knowledgeable when it comes to this subject."

Kathy nudged my arm with her shoulder and I glared at her. I knew she wanted me to invite Mr. Tall, Dark, and Handsome to the apartment, but I'd just met him, and I wasn't sure I wanted to trust him completely.

"Library at five," I finally said.

"They close at five," he replied. "Guess we'll have to meet somewhere else."

There was that glint again. Something about it set me on edge, like it was a feral look rather than something sexy. It was like he was too pretty to be real.

"You can come to our place," Kathy offered, then rattled off our address.

"Kathy," I seethed.

"What?" she feigned innocence.

"I'll see you at five," Hector said, then walked away.

"What are you doing?" I barked.

"You're right," she swooned. "He is gorgeous."

"Wipe the drool up and talk to me," I said. "You just invited a complete stranger to our apartment. Without checking with me first. Did you ever think I had a reason I didn't invite guys over?"

"But you're not gay," she said, confused.

"That's not what I'm talking about," I said. "I'm talking about common safety. Think before you act, and before you speak."

"You are so paranoid," she said.

"Just because I'm paranoid, doesn't mean someone's not out to get me," I retorted, then stormed off, leaving her standing in the hallway utterly confused.

"Where are you going?" I asked Kathy as I was gathering the books I had on the Fates later that night.

"Out," she replied. "Figured you didn't want me around."

"Look," I said. "Don't be butt hurt about this. I just like my space to be my space. I don't really like to share it with anyone."

"So I'm no one, then," she mumbled.

"That's not what I mean," I tried. "I know you think he's cute. You're right. But just because he's good looking doesn't mean he's to be trusted. Have you not seen the guys they catch doing crap to women? They're all really good looking. How do you think they get away with it?"

"You think the worst of everyone," she said. "No one is good enough. No one can compare to your ideal man."

"There is no ideal man," I replied.

"Obviously," she replied. "Look at Hector. He's the perfect specimen. Sean was pretty good, too. You were just too busy trying to be unattached that you couldn't see it."

"I know you mean well," I said. "I just don't have time for romance right now."

"When will you? When you're forty? Fifty? A hundred?"

"I have a long life ahead of me," I tried.

"But you don't know that for sure," she said. "You know what happened to Carol, right?"

"Come on," I said.

"No," she interrupted. "I'm serious. She was all about making sure she was ready for what life had in store for her until she ended up with cancer. Then, she tried to live her whole life at once."

"I know," I replied, wiping tears from my eyes. "But I don't have cancer."

"You don't know that," she replied. "Carol didn't know until it was too late. I don't want you to miss out."

"If I promise to go out with you after finals," I offered. "Will that get you off my back now?"

"Only if you promise to bring Hector with you," she smiled.

I laughed. "I'll ask him," I promised.

"Good," she said. "Cause he's here."

With that, she opened the door and let him in. Before she stepped out, she eyed me seriously and bobbed her eyebrows up and down, nodding her head. It didn't take much to realize what she was meaning.

"Hey," he said after she closed the door.

"Hey yourself," I replied. "I guess we better get to it."

"About that," he said, and I turned and looked at him.

"What?" I asked.

"I actually have a whole thing done," he replied, pulling out a tablet. "I'll show you and you can see if it's enough, or if you want to add anything."

"It was supposed to be a partnership," I replied, taking the tablet he offered.

"I lost my partner same as you," he said. "I was pretty much carrying her, though, so had done most of the work already."

Powering the tablet up, I turned it so he could enter the password. "Here," he said, taking it from me. He input his password, then swiped around and found whatever it was he was looking for. "This is what I've got so far," he offered, handing the tablet back to me.

I looked at his work and was impressed. He had everything I wanted to put into it, and then some. After I read through his information, I was confused by his conclusion.

"You believe they still exist?" I asked.

"Don't you?"

"Well," I said, then thought about it. Hadn't everything that had happened in the last week or so proven that there was some sort of other worldly force at work here?

"You didn't come to the same conclusion?" he asked.

"Nope," I replied. "But you make a really good argument."

"Why don't you think they exist?"

"You really want to know?"

"That's why I asked," he said, and his smile was charming.

"All my life," I began. "Nothing has ever been easy. I've worked for everything I got, especially when it comes to school. My brains gave me the chance to get a college education, even though my parents were willing to pay. The scholarship made it much easier on them. I always wanted to be a teacher, so college was necessary."

"A teacher, huh?" he asked.

"Elementary school," I said. "I figure if I get to kids early, then maybe I can give them a good foundation to build on."

"That's a really noble goal," he said, and seemed honestly impressed.

"I think so," I said.

"Then I really hate what I have to do," he said.

"Sean?"

"Izzy," he said.

"Where am I?"

"Izzy," Hector said.

"Wait," I said. "What's going on?"

"You have to choose," Sean said.

"Choose what?" I asked. "I don't know what's going on."

"You died," Hector said.

"I did?" I asked. "When?"

"Long before you thought you did," Sean said.

"Hold on," I said, walking backwards away from the two men. "Where are we?"

"Nowhere," Hector said.

"And everywhere," Sean added.

"You guys aren't making sense," I said, still struggling to figure out where I was.

"It's like this," Hector began.

"Don't explain it to her," Sean argued. "She has to choose without knowing."

"How is that fair?" Hector asked.

"All's fair in love and war," Sean said.

With that, both men morphed into something that was obviously not human. They began to charge at each other, teeth gnashing, swords appearing from thin air, and a high-pitched scream that nearly burst my eardrums. I continued to back away from the fight, hoping this was nothing more than a nightmare. Except I knew it wasn't.

"Izzy."

It was just barely audible, but I somehow knew the voice.

"Kathy?" I asked.

"Come with me," she said, and I saw her just beyond the two brawling beasts.

Skirting around the edge of the room we were in, I made my way to her and she pulled me through a door that hadn't been there before.

"Where did you come from?" I asked.

"Come with me," she insisted again.

"No."

It was so loud that I had to pull my hand from my friend's and plug my ears.

"I was trying to help," Kathy said. I couldn't see who she was talking to, though.

"She must choose," the voice said.

"What is going on?" I asked.

Suddenly, I was sitting on my couch in my empty apartment. I looked around, confused about what had happened.

"Kathy?" I called.

"Hey," she said, coming out of her room. "You ready?"

"For what?" I asked, unsure of what had just happened.

"Class," she said. "It's finals week. You get to do your Fates presentation today."

"With who?"

"By yourself," she laughed. "You did do it, right?"

"Umm," I stammered, unsure exactly what was going on.

"Here," she said, handing me a steaming mug. "Coffee. You obviously need it more than me."

"Okay," I said, taking a sip.

"Now," she said. "Let's go so we're not late."

She picked up her backpack and held mine out to me. I

grabbed it as I stood up and slung it over my shoulder. As we walked to class, Kathy rambled on about something she saw on a show she's been watching lately. Something about a missing treasure on a cursed island or something like that. Honestly, I had no idea what she was talking about. I was still trying to wrap my head around whatever it was that happened to me.

"Miss Reese," Mr. Richards said as we walked into class.

"Yes?" I asked, feeling that déjà vu feeling I didn't particularly like.

"You ready?"

"Absolutely," I feigned confidence I didn't have.

"Good," he said. "Go ahead and get set up."

"You got this," Kathy said as she gave me a side hug and went to find a seat.

I opened my laptop and hooked it up to the AV system, pulling up the project I didn't remember finishing. As the rest of the students filled in the seats, I began to worry that I wouldn't be able to pull this off.

"Class," Mr. Richards said as the door closed behind the last student. "Please give your attention to Miss Reese. Once her presentation is over, you will have a chance to ask questions."

Just like that, all eyes were on me, and I could feel moisture gathering in the small of my back.

"Right," I began. "The Fates have been discussed for as long as time has been kept," I began, and somehow my presentation just flowed.

By the time I got to the end, the students were riveted to their seats, eyes trained on me, taking in everything I said.

"When I started this project," I concluded. "I was sure that the answer to the question of whether the Fates were real, and whether they were still around, was unequivocally no. After the research I did, and the people I talked to, I believe that the answer is, without a doubt, yes."

"Thank you, Miss Reese," Mr. Richards said. "Do we have any questions?"

A hand rose at the back of the class, and Mr. Richards nodded, indicating the student should ask their question. The man that rose took my breath away.

"Which did you choose?" he asked, and I couldn't help but smile.

"Sean," I said. "It was always going to be Sean."

AN AMERICAN IN BALLARD
BY DAVID MECKLENBURG

Well, looks like you made it out."

That was obvious between us because Gretchen had already called me after the party, and made sure I was alright, and then a second time to set up this coffee date, so I thought it was briefly insulting and funny.

"I'm sorry," Gretchen continued and opened her arms to give me a hug. "I had no idea I was leaving you, well, I thought you were in better hands." I didn't usually like hugs, but Gretchen was Gretchen and different.

"The best hands I've had so far," I joked.

"Still, the bus. You should have called me."

"I should have."

"You were right by their phone."

Why hadn't I called her? Bear in mind the year was 1995. Poor people like me were not attached to mobile devices yet. We still had landlines and the one to Max's house ended in a plain white AT&T touch tone model. The kind you could throw off a bridge and it would be fine—just the sort of robust phone necessary in a house full of twenty-something men who often had physical, peregrine jobs. Just the sort of pad that had an old pad of paper with beer stains and Tom's number written on it with a pen that had given out half-way through.

And it didn't matter that I had precipitously balanced on my toes in a filthy kitchen wrecked from an enormous meal the night before, and it didn't even matter I was wrapped in only the serape blanket from the living room where I'd woken up because everyone else was gone or still passed out. I had found a broken pencil and shaded across Tom's number to reveal it there in the dim morning light. I had torn the piece of paper from the pad.

"I know, I was distracted. I just wanted to get out of there. It looked a lot better in the dark."

"Ha, I know! That's why Charlie and I never stay there. He calls it 13th Grade."

"So, you wanted to tell me something. Do I really want to hear it?"

"I would, and besides, it makes a great story." Which is now doubly ironic because Gretchen was right then, and now.

The day had become night suddenly, leaving its robe on the floor and slipping into the darker wrappings of sunset. It was always so, there on the lips of the Puget Sound, and while I remember some evenings that descended like mangoes upon the cut and shining flesh of dragon fruit, the gray and somber robes of Novembers passed like Conventual Franciscans across the night, sprinkling the water of the Pacific across the possibility of clear and red.

The night began with a score of notes, stars of gold and silver free from clefs and bars, scattered across the proscenium for forever and a moment, until the armature performed its rhythmic sweep of time across the curving space and cleared the constellations from the river of my gaze. And there was the abyss. I coyly offered myself to it, that it could see me there within the seat that's set aside for passengers. Yet in that instance, I knew that we: the rain-stardrops, myself, and Gretchen (driving and kvetching as is her holy custom), the taillights, and streetlamps were all just passengers of a sort.

I was free, if you can call it that, of summer and early fall's seductive charms: the sun, the orange and the yellow, more skin and less clothes, harvest fruit and fresh in-season vegetables. The light itself has begun to fail and we drove to an orphan's gathering in a gloaming set for five o'clock. Warm swaddled, the un-child in my lap gave off a smell of molasses, bacon, onion and time.

"How long did those beans take?" Gretchen asked

"Eight hours."

"Eight hours? Gawdz, I'm sure they are delicious."

"Do you know anyone here?"

"No, not really. Just Max, Charlie's brother," Gretchen said.

"All of Ballard looks the same," I said.

"You could say that about a lot of places you don't know. Paris looks that way if you're not in love with it before hand."

"I suppose. Have you ever been?"

"To Paris? Yes, I stayed there for a month. But I was in love and so the whole city was one big cliché."

"But beautiful. Who was he?"

"It wasn't a he. Nor a she, if that's what you're thinking. It was the city of Colette, of Flaubert, Hemingway, Stein, Matisse."

"Robespierre…"

"Oh Ada, I love you. Someday you'll have to go. That's the house there. I'll have to find somewhere to park. Why don't you get out so you don't have to carry those beans all the way?"

The blocks of Seattle fell into the semblance of a grid, an order of sense upon topography that refused assent to form and order. The cardinal directions bequeathed their points and ordinals filled into guide the lost; remote Ballard reposed beneath its NW crown, a superlative of sorts in all its Scania and Fishermen's Daughters. Its avenues ran north to south, the streets from east to west. But here and there, a plat of land, a volcanic stump, the gouging scraps of glacial razing, tilling and compacting into caliche strata will block a street, abbreviate an avenue and foil a stranger into ends as dead as doornails or Swedish great grandfathers.

It seemed a night for siblings, children, parents and other relational titles to scatter themselves across the globe. I wondered if anyone was together. Charlie was Gretchen's boyfriend, but he was out somewhere in Alaska studying the hibernation patterns and domiciles of bears, and so there was Max, stranded by his parents who had taken a cruise to Greece and a distant older sister who had her own in-law family to contend with through the bottom of a Seagram's bottle in New York. Gretchen's father had remarried and was with his new family in Mexico and her mother was angrily stuck in a snowstorm in Wisconsin. My own mother? We had had a serious fight, and I realize in retrospect, *the* serious fight that left us silent for a decade, maybe more—funny, it felt more infinite at the time.

But I liked the idea of having dinner with all these people I didn't know and wasn't related to. I didn't have to watch the disgust of my mother's nostrils (which I do not share with her for as she said, my long and flaring nose was better for a *rocín than a woman*) at my failures, for which, she was quick to point out, I had many. My stern and priceless bitchery would not leave her an *abuela*; she would be unsurrounded, and no extra hands for the tamales and I finally had to ask: *when exactly did you decide to get all Mexican, when it suited your career? Did you have to take lessons again?*

434

She put those lessons to good use, creating a portmanteau comeback: *Puta-cunt.* My mother fancied herself hot-blooded to suit cliché and expectation, not to mention expectoration. She spat *puta-cunt* over the phone a thousand miles away and yet I could feel it in the raindrops on my face, there away within the gentle shelter of Northwest cloud and distance.

The shaggy lawn at Max's had not grown long like some pony's coat in preparation for the cold, but simply lay in rental disregard: bikes and garbage cans, a tire pump, and recycling containers bearing the brown and standard bottles used for microbrews. There was of course, a couch upon the porch. It was a burgundy color, oxidized perhaps from the years of service, and placed there for its only occupant.

"Do you mind if I join you?" I asked her. She was old and the gray hair outnumbered the black, and arthritis had slowed her movements to a creak prefaced by a careful pause. She turned her gaze from off the street although I do not know how much she could see, for the cataracts had clouded her eyes like drops of milk poured into icy water beneath November skies. But she heard me well enough and smiled, wagged her tail and offered me her hospitality of couch and tongue. Her collar tag read "Luthien" and I wondered where Beren was, but felt better that someone here like to read, *The Silmarillion* no less, though I myself could never read that Cymro-Finnic phone book about the usuals of love and pride and the destruction they wreak.

"I'm surprised you're not in there waiting for something to fall upon the floor."

She sniffed the pot of beans and listened to me.

I liked dogs because they afforded me this courtesy and even as a little girl, I had always wanted one: a black or yellow lab, to go walking with, to swim and fetch in Folsom Lake. But even our large apartment down in Arden Town was far too small for my mother, myself and our relationship: we could not fit a fourth.

"You can't even take care of yourself. How can you take care of a dog? What would you do with its shit? What about the fleas? No. Absolutely not. Animals are filthy." At most I was allowed a mournful goldfish brought home from my school's carnival within a plastic bag.

"Have you been waiting here alone?"

"I'm not alone," I said and patted my new friend's head.

"Nonsense, you didn't want to go in there alone. It's not like I know any of these people, much."

"I'm sure you know a few, Gretchen, and that is why I need you."

"Let's get some wine."

The house seemed filled with people like and unlike me and memories of sometime else. There was the dusky pastel smell of sage, and there was also rosemary, the remembrance of the sea, overpowering the pervasive but unremarked smell of parsley. And last of all was that pungent homophone of the revelator we all fall through: thyme. Yet all were in their dry and late fall guises, having passed into the mix of breadcrumbs, dried onions and atomized poultry—all dead now, all set in preparation for a Dorian song of plague and beauty. I wondered if I would hear that song that night. It was possible, for in the kitchen I could hear Arlo Guthrie recalling the 8x10 color glossy photos with circles and arrows and a paragraph on the back of each one.

Women my age who knew each other slightly arranged the pumpkin custards set in crusts that smelled of nutmeg, cinnamon and clove. And there were bottles of red wine, bought at the last minute; glistening in the late November lights of unmatched candles scented with bayberry and sandalwood.

I do not think a drop of water passed my lips that night and I remember thinking of the rain that fell on Washington was not the same rain that had fallen on Beaujolais in Spring and let the Gamay vines grow flush in red offerings to the Sun. I thought of Heraclitus and his river—a habit that took root into my soul back then—and wondered where I fit in the cycle of hydrology: was part of what I drank that night that water? With the terroir of granite lingering with a nasal redolence of plum and cherry bereft of childish sugar, it was all the same water ultimately, but did that not depend upon a faith I was not ready to embrace?

He was tall, taller than I. I did not see his face at first, for he was in the other room and because of the wall, my angle in the dining room so full chattering, I only saw his hand upon the arm rest. He had long brown fingers, knuckles well defined and strong tendons beneath the river-work of veins and hair that grew in careful, perfect order; a hand made for holding shafts of wood or thumbing carefully the keenness of an axe's blade; a hand to wrap around a pint of Guinness or cup a breast; a hand that artists crave to paint.

There was a glass, its stem like a tree rising from between his fingers and it was full of aperitif, a livid milk-green set on fire with the dreams of men who trembled at the feet of goddesses stepping out from the Mucha print in the hallway sharing walls with familiar prints of Chet Baker, Avedon's Audrey Hepburn, a Nagel left there as a joke within the entryway, and in the living room, the austere architecture of Newton's monochrome nudes. The only picture of interest, that did not seem to fit the middle-class 20-year-old male taste was a pair of demons or gods, I could not tell. It looked Indian and I was reminded of the *Ramayana*. Perhaps they were fighting over a soul. Or, perhaps they were simply dancing, which is really the same thing.

I can't remember how many people were there. Some were couples to be sure, perhaps two or three, one couple were lesbians: Danae and Renée. I remember that because Renée thought I was the only other woman of color there, and I suppose I was. She handed me a highball glass full of juicy wine—stemmed glasses were rare in the house.

"Did… you come with Gretchen?" she asked.

"Yes, she's the only person I know here. Oh, if you mean…"

"…I understand. She likes girls too you know. LWD though."

"What?"

"Lesbian while drunk. Anyway, what are you doing here? I can't go back home. I thought maybe you couldn't either."

"I can't but not for that reason."

"Why not?"

"My mother and I don't get along."

"Then we have the same reason."

We wound up smoking on the porch and drinking more wine. Luthien had gotten cold and went inside.

"My family's hardcore Baptist. A good life if I'd been straight. But Daddy was a deacon in the church. He was quiet and would just pray for my soul. But Momma was the problem. Pretended it just wasn't. My Grandmother is funny, and said Momma was taking a long swim in that River in Egypt."

It was the first time I had heard the metaphor and even on the porch in the darkness she saw my ignorance.

"Denial."

"Oh! God, that's wonderful. But your Grandmother said that?"

"I think she's the only one who doesn't care. Really. She said so."

"Jesus, that's so… sweet."

"Ha. Jesus. I think that's the point. 'Only God knows anything for sure Renée' she'd say. 'All we can do is love one another.'"

I looked in at Danae, who had a short boyish mop of blonde

hair, like a Beatle cut almost and she could throw it around with expertise and guile. She was holding up her wine, gesticulating broadly and driving her point home. Two women, a man, *him,* were laughing.

"I can see why you love her," I said.

"She's cute. I think she loves me," Renée said. "But I'm not sure."

"Really?"

"You shouldn't be sure of love, Ada. How can I say this? I've been let down in life. Maybe you understand, but maybe not. So, your mom's got some pretty strict Catholic morals? Traditional culture?"

It took me a bit until I understood where Renée was going with her questions.

"My family's part Mexican, part German. But my mom hates the Catholic church. So, no. I guess. For most of my life I never really knew much about Mexico except from my grandma. And my uncle. My mom sort of erased that part of her life. Don't get me wrong, she had it rough. She's a sociology professor in mostly white male academia so in the beginning she embraced Anglo culture totally. And our last name is German."

"How'd that make you feel?"

"I never noticed it. That part of my life was just not there. An absence. And I passed without knowing it. It's common in some families in California. Elsewhere, I suppose. But once a kid in school called me a beaner. My mother was indignant. *We aren't Mexican. You have Spanish blood.* Even my grandmother said that. And when I said it to the little fuck, he just started calling me a beaner-Nazi."

"Ha, kids are so horrible. I mean, they're quick and creative and don't mind taking that out on you. But you can kind of pass for Latina, too, Ada. You're really pretty you know. Your dad white?"

439

"I don't know. Never knew him. He knocked up my mother one year abroad."

"Ohhh, I kind of get it now. She was mad at herself and takes it out on you. Mothers can be the greatest cons out there because we so want to believe that everything they do is for our sake."

"But my mom wasn't a con. She was honest about me and her. I knew I was in the way and an inconvenience because she told me so. Often."

"But your dad?"

"My mom was never really truthful about him. I guess he had a German mother, but his dad was an Allied soldier from somewhere. I've heard all sorts: Indian, Roma, Egyptian. Thing is, I don't even know. I think he was probably full of shit just like my mom."

"You could be a sister, then too. And you don't know. Soon you'll be able to figure it all out you know with DNA. Once they sequence the genome you'll probably be able to take a test, just like pregnancy."

"You're right."

"But you know what, I wouldn't. You should just decide for yourself what you want to be and are. But you see, unlike you, I don't get a choice. I never have and never will unless I go live in some magic place where there isn't anyone else except black dykes."

"I think I understand. We're not talking about who we go to bed with."

"No, we aren't. I love Danae. Sometimes. But she's always had everything. I don't think she's just taking a walk on the wild side. She really seems to like women and all. But she has never had to worry about someone she loves being taken away. Never worried about her brother getting shot some night by mistake. No second guessing about her mortgage qualifications. I love her, Ada. I wouldn't mind her going on to be some high-powered lawyer and I'll be her damned housewife. But I can't ever be sure. Danae's *never* been unsure. Do you know what I mean?"

"That's why you're out here talking to me and she's inside talking to them."

"Yeah. Like that. Anyway, you like him?"

"Who?"

"The handsome white boy in there sipping Pernod. You keep checking him out."

"Well, he's pretty cute."

"He is. Sit next to him at dinner." We drained the last of our wine and went back in, feeling different, although I could not speak for Renée, but I felt different. And yet not because I still didn't belong anywhere.

Perhaps in ironic defiance of the night, we did not sit and pass the food around the table, or perhaps we were simply more in love with the efficiency of buffet. We gathered what we wanted and sat down where we wanted. I sat next to him. We drank wine, ate the dry turkey, the sugary yams someone brought, my beans, and someone had actually made very good gravy. I learned this was Max from the snippets of conversation that drifted around the table. Some of the words were referential, some timeless as is the way with chit-chat between strangers.

"Oh, I remember you | It starts next month after the holidays | I *know* where George is coming from, I love Bosco but I can never find it out here | where did you get that skirt? | I won't drink anything brewed in batches of more than 100 barrels, thank you. | I'm as progressive as anyone here, but I can't send Ashley to a school south of the ship canal until the District does something | the secret is organic maple sugar | no, I'll have a glass with dinner, I'm going to

Nordstrom tomorrow as early as I can | I heard they're coming out with an adaptation of *The English Patient*"

"Really? I thought that was unfilmable," You said to me. No one else seemed to pay attention. "They said the same thing about Pasternak, and I think *Zhivago* was a good adaptation. Have you read it? My name is Tom, by the way."

"Ada, nice to meet you. I don't know Russian literature all that well, I'm afraid."

"Why afraid?" You smiled.

"Oh, I'm not." Could you see my blush? "It's just a phrase. I've only ever read *The Brothers Karamazov*."

"Well, if there is one to read, that would be it."

"Like *Moby-Dick*."

"Exactly."

"But at least I've seen *Doctor Zhivago*."

"And did you like it?"

"I loved it. The end... was so tragic and yet so believable. I would have probably died running after Julie Christie too." I said.

"Really? You know it's funny, but I think Geraldine Chaplain was the prettier one in that."

"You're joking."

"No, this gentleman prefers brunettes." You smiled again. I remember the creases in your mouth deepened and your teeth, so perfect, without the blemish of parsley or plaque or disfigurement. Yes everything, the stupid candlelight upon your eyes, the fall of sandy hair across your forehead. The wrinkle between your brows. "Gretchen said you were a lit major," you continued but you had me.

"I was."

"Where are you teaching?"

"Oh, I'm not. I'm... trying to figure all that out." I crammed my

Master's, my disgrace, my academia into a plastic bag and hoped it would not squirm.

"Me neither. But you must have read some Nabokov?"

"Of course I have, but he can be considered American too."

"Beyond *Lolita,* I am guessing you have read…"

And then I really blushed. He meant my namesake book: *Ada, or Ardor.* That family saga, that Russian novel turned inside out like a navel of the world so that its protuberance of love and incest gamboled through memories imagined and real was known to me from conception.

"Yes. I have read that."

"Any connection?"

"It was on my father's bookshelf, I guess. That's what my mother always tells me."

"I wish my father had *Tom Jones* on his shelf. Or even *Tom Sawyer.*"

"What about *The Grapes of Wrath?*" I asked.

"I'd be there." You said. I smiled and looked away. Renée sat across the table, three seats down and winked.

Later, the movie started. We started. No, we started at dinner. The pie and coffee went around, and afterward you and I went to the living room, and all the muscles of my body colluded to lean a little closer to your stories of the Bering Sea, peering over the crevasses at Glacier National Park. Tuned, experienced, I was a jaguar in the deep forest moving effortlessly over the water and the earth, following your scent through all the scents of that night. You could not hide behind the cardamom and Islay malt and I would not wait behind pumpkin and caramel.

Fore arm, strong and hard, with your elbow on the back of the couch so your hand was free to dance in the expressive lines of lithographic movement: open, closed, flat plane, a sail on the sea, the creases in your fingers deepened, widened out like mouths begging for a kiss. Your body was open to me, as if to say, *duck under this wing, come closer little swallow.*

"This is beautiful" you said. You traced the wings of the tattoo on my hand, dark, knowledgeable ink waiting for this summons to burn beneath the brush of your fingerprints. "Are there more?" I smiled and looked at you and for a moment, I knew how the water must feel in its adoration of the Moon high above the sea, following it around the earth in a swell—I flickered and reflected you. I did not need to speak the word *yes.* "I'd like to see them."

Someone had turned on PBS and there were the handwritten title cards, as though you and I had been invited to another party, as though our names would be there with Gene Kelly, Oscar Levant, Georges Guetary and Nina Foch. "This is perfect, here wait." And you returned with the emerald bottle, and some water to pour Pernod upon a sugar cube that lay naked above a glass made only for the purpose of invocation. The drink, still green in unreality began to cloud like nacre in the glass. I could not quite believe it all.

"Tell me you have been to Paris." I demanded

"When I was younger. I've always wanted to go back."

"We can tonight."

"I think that's the whole point of the evening."

"We cannot hang it on this plot." I said and you laughed.

I danced with you by the Seine and watched you build a stairway to paradise upon that bank. Would we have rhythm? I wondered because who could ask for anything more upon that couch in Ballard. Intaglios of black and white, impossible soirées in all that wreckage that must have been and was wiped out for a moment of dream. Of what Paris is. What it was after the war, for did it not escape the narcissistic fire of rage, somehow? Mostly? The red dancers who flared across the screen in the swirl of Gershwin's horns and strings were not of any Belle Epoque but some forever that never was. We knew this in the sacrament of watching as the party quieted down until in impossible Parisian Blue, you reached with all that masculine power that Gene possessed and drew me in upon the couch.

And you knew just what to say, just then, which was not a word. And I could forget the demons dancing on the wall and the ruddy couch which was of no precise color. The rain remained a refrain, but outside in contrapuntal comfort for my body as I explored yours slowly through the press of ribs, thigh, knee, calf, foot. We had returned to the dreamwaters of the fountain at the Place de la Concorde, Leslie Caron resisted, then gave in and flew toward eternity within the graceful force restrained in Gene Kelly's adoring lift.

"I always wanted to know what it was she was saying," I said.

"What do you mean?"

"Dance has a specific language"

"I love and I finally feel free enough to fly?"

"Funny how Hollywood is so good at taking you away," Gretchen said smiling. "I watched a little bit of it too. I love the "I've got Rhythm" part. But you two were pretty wrapped up in it. And each other."

"We didn't even notice most of you had gone outside," I said.

"Or left. I have to say, I'm proud of you. I didn't think you had it in you to get in the hot tub with us naked like that."

"It was the Pernod."

"Yeah, the Pernod. Ha!"

C'mon, you don't need a swimsuit. You took off your clothes first. We were all young and drunk and it rained, but the water was warm and by that point I told myself I didn't care, but I did. I went to the bathroom and peed, and took off my clothes. There was a towel there—it might as well have been a robe of scarlet silk—and I wrapped myself in it and the bravery of booze. The air was cold outside, but the beer and wine still flowed. I don't even remember what I drank, for someone handed me a can of something, but you were there, sitting starkly on the rim, your uncut cock was lolling about your balls and your pubic hair caught the dim light in raindrop scatters. And Gretchen moved to give me the spot next to your legs.

I ogled them because then I didn't have to look up at your cock, your abs, the lats, pecs, deltoids and the rest of the delicious ladder of your anatomy. You were certainly not something to quickly mount no matter how thick I felt between my legs. No quick ascent— certainly not without oxygen. The pattering drizzle shone on your nipples and skin and I really was thirsty. The water accepted you and you looked closely at the swallows under my skin that had remained chaste and waiting for you. The wind rose in the night above us and the rain gave way before it, and tore away the clouds, full of our light and pretense to leave the pure amoral darkness.

Jesus those are beautiful, you had said, touching the tattoos on my arm.

Thank you, I answered. Looked down, then up. Our gaze met. Locked. I felt the wine, the Pernod.

"I'm glad you made it," Renée said across the tub.

"What were you two watching?" Danae asked.

An American in Paris, we both answered.

Oh, god, how romantic! | Isn't that the one where the guy runs up the walls in 'Make 'em Laugh? | I can't stand musicals | I really think their quality's gone down the drain since the IPO | You have a door for a desk? | Fred Astaire had grace, Gene had athleticism, but Bill

Robinson had it all | The Champs Elysses | No, it was the Place de la Concorde | I went to the Louvre | So has everyone else | Hemingway! Picasso!

What do you love about Paris, Ada? You asked. You did not talk save for those strategic moments when your talents ran silent and deep beneath the water. A good seducer listens. How better to know exactly the right thing to say?

Why not London? I thought. London was a frequent stop for Americans during and after the wars. But I suspected we didn't fancy the Old Mother, with her grimy, dirty soles underneath her lily-white feet. Every day the soot creeps further up from below, slouching into the slough behind her anklebone, congregating in the crevices of her toes whose enamel was flaking off to reveal the dulled claws of a lioness. Her fine clothes: pinafore, petticoat, sash and train were extensive, but we knew them all too well. We may not speak the same language, but we read the same Bible.

But the dark-haired courtesan—the Catholic one who helped midwife us—the whore who dressed herself in silks and gouts of blood and trailed her white lace through the lymph and vomit of the Terror, reborn from the decapitated head of her King, more beautiful and fully armed had strength enough for several lost empires. And even her decadence, the slip from Belle to Fin, thrice degraded by the Huns still has rouge and charm enough to lure us into absinthe dreams.

Without Paris, we would be faced without a rôle: perfect white teeth, protestant fedora, white skin, and our imperial optimism before we embarked upon our own Dien Bien Phu.

And in your arms my calves are beautiful and on point, I pirouette like yesterdays upon the clockface: 10:00 and 2:00. Anything I dream has already been choreographed by fantasy in that first City of Lights that never was.

447

I don't know what I can love about Paris, I said. *There is the dream. I suppose that is all I really have.* I felt your hand on my thigh. Your thumb brushed my hair and I moved slightly. You moved your thumb down, and I opened my legs, invited the rest of your hand between my thighs.

And you squeezed. Your other arm was down below as well, behind my back reaching around beneath the water on my waist. The tub was quieting down. I don't know who else was there. I cannot remember the glimpse. Naked asses, towels, the light switching off. Then there was only the two of us and your fingers moved over my cunt, lips and clitoris freely. We didn't speak for a while. At all?

You made me come. I remember the water had grown suddenly cold afterward. You had two fingers inside of me and my tongue in your mouth. You still tasted of licorice.

Let's get out.

There was no one else around. We had gotten embarrassing and didn't care. When John? Carol? I don't know, the bearded one got out and went back up the porch, the pathway light stayed on for a moment and then switched off in modesty. There was only the bamboo in the side yard swaying back and forth in the wind and ambient light from the City.

The water's getting cold, let's get out.

But we didn't for a while longer. We kissed, which meant slobbering and sucking on each other's tongues. You sucked my nipples, bit them, held me in the water and thumbed my cunt so deeply the heel of your hand wedged against my perineum until I came again.

I want you to fuck me.

Let's get out, it's never as good in a hot tub as it should be.

We tottered, drunk with Pernod through the back yard to the

door and through the kitchen that was now dark save for the dim light of the oven clock. I held your hand, marveled at the light clipping the drops of water on your skin and I followed you into the living room. The fire had died down and the TV was out. How long had we been? It didn't matter. We looked around at the empty couch, the coffee table full of beer bottles, a bong, dirty plates, and an old textbook copy of Rabelais I thought incredibly *apropos*.

We didn't have time to dry off. I pushed you back onto the couch, just as you had been sitting when we watched Gene dance through a painted fantasy of Paris, and I knelt before you, feeling the rough fabric of the couch on my nipples, sore and aroused from all the cold water, your teeth. I rolled back your foreskin, put the head in my mouth and sucked while I stroked you back and forth. It was so much easier with an uncut guy, I realized. I felt your fingers on my skull, and the house remained quiet except for the slurps of my mouth and your moans. When I tasted your pre-come you were hard enough again and I climbed up on you.

I don't have a condom.

I don't care.

There was a slight hesitation. You were big. Not enormous, not the stuff of pornographic exaggeration, but your cock bent the right way and felt perfect inside of me. You sucked on my breasts and I rode you. *Baby, Baby.* I remember you said that over and over. I remember I said it over and over.

You stopped me, took me by the waist and threw me down on the couch and went down on me. You went around my labia first, only teased my clit with your upper lip instead of sucking on it like a tootsie pop like most guys did.

Your cunt's delicious, Baby. Jesus. And you went back, teasing my lips lightly while barely caressing my perineum with your pinky. Then your ring and middle finger. Then you slipped them into me and I grabbed on as best as I could as you licked my clit back and forth. I bucked at you, I lifted up my legs and you cradled my ass with one of your hands while you kept digging into me, like you were lifting my whole cunt into my clit and that's when I came.

Kiss me, what's wrong, are you okay?

It's nothing, that was amazing. Don't worry.

I tasted salt, blood. I wondered if I had started my period and I remember feeling my skin contract like I was dying. But no, I'd banged your nose so hard it bled when you drew that come out of me. *I'm...* but you didn't give me time. You rammed yourself into me until I felt your balls against my ass. I lay back, felt the muscles of your back and wrapped my legs around you. You were quickening, losing your rhythm, I knew and then...

"Your father was a coward. Yes, he had a big prick and a sweet tongue. A big nose like yours. Your eyes are his, the hair, the height. You are no question mark. I let him have me there. For two weeks and I thought I was in love. You know what that's like? I wonder. Imagine giving up everything you've built your life for and you don't even know it at the time when you are on your back and he's grunting. Coming in you."

There was an empty bottle of sherry. Some had gone into the gravy, some into me. Most into her. Uncle Louis had already left.

"Leaving that baby that's going to derail your career for years and he isn't even going to call you. He's going to disappear into nowhere. And then you'll be a mother."

Baby, I'm going to come.

Come in my mouth, please... and you did. You didn't wait. You somehow slipped out of me and back into my mouth in one elegant motion and I gagged a bit when you thrust against the back of my throat. My mouth was full of your semen, so I swallowed it quickly to get rid of the taste. Did you think I loved you? I don't think you cared. You weren't loud but you seemed to come for a while, I remember that.

Jesus you're beautiful, baby, you said.

You slid down, and I felt hot and alive. I wanted to come again, but you were already breathing differently, trying to talk, wrap more of those lies around my legs and stomach like your legs and arms. Your hair was finally dry as I felt and stroked it when you lay on my stomach. And gradually, I lost my own heat and pulled the serape blanket over us. The world began to slur its sounds then. The rain fell in syncopation, while the fridge's motor groaned against the food and darkness.

There was a pubic hair in my teeth. I'm sure it was one of yours and I felt my consciousness unravel as I let it go into the abyss next to that all-too-small couch. What were we doing? Both of us over 6 feet tall on an old couch, poised above an infinite blackness, a nowhere we would soon fall into, but I didn't seem to know it then. Even in the dim lights of blue, white and red that smeared across my dreams as they approached, even when I kicked as I stepped off that curb near the flower market and even as I fell and let my body become petals, drops of water, calyx and sepals. I did not fear or really know the nothing.

"What was your excuse for calling him?" Gretchen asked.

"What do you mean?"

"I know how you are. You must have had some kind of pretense. Some conceit. Did he leave his underwear there?" she asked and laughed.

"No, it was the aperitif glasses."

"Glasses?"

"Two of them came with the Pernod bottle. One of those special promotional boxes."

"So, you called to see if he wanted the glasses back?"

"Who is this?"

I had called. Finally. The rain was still coming down in the half-drizzle and its indifference over the days had led me to equivocate. Should I call him? I dialed several times, stopping halfway through.

For a day. Or two.

But on the third day I called. I had made up a lie to tell him if I had to. If I got scared and it was all nothing. I held an aperitif glass in my hand. He could come get it. But no, I tried practicing the high voice I used when I had tried to fit in other places. Maybe I could pass if I couldn't face that voice. No. He would know my voice when it broke and ran in the deep channels it always moved in.

The phone rang four times and it picked up with a woman's voice. It was late afternoon, but she seemed tired.

"Hello?"

"Is Tom there?"

"Who is this?" Her tired voice became quick with anger.

"Um," I swallowed. My mind raced and I looked at the bottle of cheap Chilean wine all of us had on the counter back then. "Cat... Cat Black."

"Who the fuck are you? Is this the fucking bitch my boyfriend fucked on Thanksgiving?"

"Jesus! No. I'm Cat," and I fell into my lie. "Max's friend. He found something of Tom's he left. A couple of glasses."

"Tom's not here. Do you know... no, you wouldn't be calling here. Unless, that fuck put you up to this..." and her voice ran back high. "Where is he? Fuck you Cat. I know where Max lives, I'm coming over now."

I hung up the phone and moved away. I was afraid she was going to come through it and strangle me.

"So, he has a girlfriend." I said.

Gretchen picked up her cappuccino and blew across the surface and then looked at me. Her lips were skewed up to the right side of her face and her left eyebrow was raised.

"Does he ever."

"You knew?"

"No, I didn't *know*. I only found out when Charlie told me all about it. Her name's Karen. She went over to Max's and demanded to see Tom. Said some "bitch called me, but I know his game" or something like that.

"What did he do?"

"He laughed it off. Invited her in to have a look around."

"Really?"

"Max had nothing to be afraid of. Tom wasn't there."

"Where is... he, then?"

"Oh Jesus, Ada. You don't want to get wrapped up in that do you?"

"I want some closure I think," I said and tried to laugh. It was partly true.

"I have no idea. Neither does Charlie or Max. Tom was supposed to have gone home that night I guess but he never showed because you were sucking his dick."

"Gretchen. Guh! Come on."

"Anyway, I guess he told her he was done with her, grabbed his things and left. He's kind of a wanderer you know."

"How do you know all of that?"

"When she, Karen, the girlfriend, couldn't find Tom she broke down. Max talked with her on the porch. Then they went in and had sex."

"What!?"

"Max was just helping her out. I guess they've been going at it a lot. Charlie hasn't heard much out of him except when he told him all of this. Charlie says Tom is always doing that. I guess he works up in Alaska or crews yachts, makes a lot of money, then he just finds some woman to give him a roof while he spends it away. You're lucky, he could have shown up at your door and you'd be dumb enough to take him in. It's a good thing you didn't let him come in you. The last thing you need is a baby."

I walked back to my apartment, thinking again of my mother's face. I thought of your body in the darkness working into me. I thought of Luthien, of Renée's words. I stopped at a florist and bought a single red rose for myself. I had no dread of Tom running up the steps from the Seine or even Boylston, because then, as now, I was alone in the grand resolved cadence of memory.

ABOUT THE AUTHORS

JENNIFER DIMARCO

A PNWC and Bumbershoot award-winning poet and Seattle Times bestselling novelist, Jennifer DiMarco first toured nationally as an author when she was nineteen years old. Her resume of publications includes contemporary drama, science fiction, high fantasy, and mystery novels as well as poetry collections and stage plays. For the last ten years, DiMarco has worked as a filmmaker writing and directing more than a dozen feature films, half a dozen mini series, and more than a hundred short films. She lives in the Pacific Northwest with her wife, author and actor Brianne, and their children, author and illustrator Maxwell, and producer and actor Faith. Find out more about DiMarco at www.jenniferdimarco.com.

LAUREN PATZER

Hailing from Tacoma, WA, Lauren has been an information technology guru, actor, writer and film producer among other pursuits. From the earliest days when he could sit up in a chair, he typed happily away at his grandparents IBM Selectric typewriter, writing somewhat less coherent stories than he does now. He feels the best part of writing short stories is the ability to briefly immerse yourself in a brand new world (even if it's modern day America) and tell the reader a complete, entertaining and /or thought-provoking story in just a few short pages. When he's not spending time with his wife, three daughters and grandson, Lauren is pouring over the details of his next pursuit.

HIROMI COTA

Hiromi Cota has been a special operations heavy weapons expert, an adjunct professor, a rave journalist, and the flaming-sword-swinging lead in a heavy metal opera. They (singular) have lived in nations around the world, but have settled down in Seattle with their spouse Randi and their (plural) dog Nasus. Outside of crafting queer science fiction/fantasy, Hiromi writes roleplaying games, produces the inclusive and comedic D&D radio drama podcast "Dear High Elves," programs video games, and gets into sword fights as a member of the Seattle Knights actor-combatant troupe. A reasonably complete list of their work can be found at: HiromiCota.com

AMBER RAINEY

A mom first in all things she does, Amber just happens to also be an author, actor, and award-winning filmmaker. She lives in Texas with her engineer husband, precocious son, and two cats, who vie for her lap while she writes. Amber has yet to find a medium she doesn't enjoy so she writes novels, short stories, and screenplays. Her first novel, *Eternal Willow*, can be found online at Amazon. You can visit www.amberrainey.com and www.tiny.cc/amberrainey for more about Amber and her work.

MARSHALL MILLER

After retiring as a Senior Special Agent/Federal Criminal Investigator, Marshall found a second career in writing and has a published four book series called THE TSCHAAA INFESTATION. These in-depth science fiction/speculative fiction works examine the human condition, and what people would do to survive when threatened with being eaten by an invading intelligent alien species. His thirty years of law enforcement experience and world travel provides him with the basis for the many varied characters which populate his literary works, demonstrating the good, the bad, and the ugly.

ELIZA LOEB

A United States actor, Eliza stepped in to the writing field in 2018, beginning with *Prompt Generation 1*. Originally born on Guam, they had spent their life reading, writing and creating with many artistic influences. Today, Eliza channels their creativity and experiences through their writing and does their best to reach out to their readers with a subtle portrayal of empathy or compassion. Sometimes, by allowing the reader to get close to them through the pages, other times by a means of fiction. Most times with wine that rarely touches the glass. A recently published piece of Eliza Loeb's work can be found on Amazon in the horror anthology *Unnerving*. But for those of you who would like to see the human behind the writer with occasional writing tidbits, feel free to follow Eliza on Tumbler at imelizaloeb.tumblr.com.

SHEILA MENGERT

A transgender novelist, dramatist, and poet, Sheila is also a political commentator. She has a Masters Degree in English Literature from the University of Washington with an emphasis on the works of James Joyce and Virginia Woolf. Her stories in *Prompt Generation 1* are a debut effort for her in a new genre. Her previous books include a non-fiction book on Borderline Personality Disorder and a seven volume epic re-telling of the Sherlock Holmes Saga published under another name. The story of her transition is told in her book *Transsexualism and its Discontents: A Political Profile* available from KitsapPublishing.com under the separate editorial imprint of Trannie-Goddess Press. Sheila is currently at work on an eighth volume sequel to her Sherlock Holmes Saga dealing with The Great European War of 1914-1918 and its critical aftermath in the Peace Conference of 1919 in Paris.

CARRIE AVERY MORIARTY

Born and raised in the Pacific Northwest, Carrie still lives there with the love of her life. She raised two wonderful, if not slightly warped, children who both live close to home. When she's not yelling at her hometown sports teams on the television, she's cheering them on from the stands. She loves nature and spending time enjoying it with her family. And you don't want to attempt to beat her in any board game. They are meant to be played to the death. Find more from Carrie at www.facebook.com/AuthorCarrieAveryMoriarty/ and on Twitter or Instagram @camoriarty13

DAVID MECKLENBURG

Much like his unseen Gemini half/fictional narrator Ada Ludenow, writer & illustrator David Mecklenburg was born in Sacramento, and moved home to Washington to attend the University of Washington. He has worked as a chef, tech support specialist, and capital project manager. You can often find him on the Washington State ferries commuting to and from Bremerton where he now lives. His stories were written "on the water." For more information about David (& Ada) please visit www.hagengard.com.

ABOUT THE EDITOR

BRIANNE DIMARCO

A published short story author, poet, and writer of more than a dozen short films, Brianne has been captivated by the written word from an early age and doesn't even remember when she learned to read. She currently works as a full-time volunteer for Blue Forge Group and is the Senior Editor of their publishing division, Blue Forge Press. Brianne lives with her wife, Jennifer, and their children on the Olympic Peninsula in the Pacific Northwest.